...nurse, a secretary, a teacher, and has run her own business. Now she's settled on writing. 'I was looking for that elusive something and finally realised it was variety – now I ...ve it in abundance. Every book brings new horizons, ...ew friends, and in between books I juggle! My husband John and I have two beautiful daughters, Sarah and Hannah, umpteen pets, and several acres of Suffolk that nature tries to reclaim every time we turn our backs!'

Laura Iding started writing at a very young age and loved to read, devouring everything in sight. As a teenager, she volunteered as a Candy Striper at a nursing home and fell in love with nursing. She worked several part-time jobs to put herself through nursing school, and one managing job and two degrees later, she found she could embark on an old dream: writing. Now Laura is thrilled to combine her favourite careers into one – writing medical romances for Mills & Boon.

After completing a degree in journalism, then working in advertising and mothering her kids, **Robin Gianna** had what she calls her awakening. She decided she wanted to write the romance novels she'd loved since her teens, and now enjoys pushing her characters toward their own happily-ever-afters. When she's not writing, Robin's life is filled with a happily messy kitchen, a needy garden, a wonderful husband, three great kids, a drooling bulldog and one grouchy Siamese cat.

A&E Docs

A&E Docs:
Her Knight in Shining Armour

CAROLINE ANDERSON

LAURA IDING

ROBIN GIANNA

MILLS & BOON

HarperCollins*Publishers*
1st Floor, Watermarque Building,
Ringsend Road, Dublin 4, Ireland

A&E DOCS: HER KNIGHT IN SHINING ARMOUR
© 2021 Harlequin Books S.A.

The Secret in His Heart © 2013 Caroline Anderson
A Knight for Nurse Hart © 2010 Laura Iding
The Last Temptation of Dr Dalton © 2014 Robin Gianakopoulos

ISBN: 978-0-263-28208-5

THE SECRET IN HIS HEART

CAROLINE ANDERSON

CHAPTER ONE

SILENCE.

No bleeps, no clipped instructions or clattering instruments, no hasty footsteps. Just a blissful, short-lived hush.

James stretched out his shoulders and felt the tension drain away. The relief was incredible. He savoured it for a moment before breaking the silence.

'Great teamwork, guys. Thank you. You did a good job.'

Someone chuckled. 'Would you accept anything less?'

He grinned. Fair cop, but it worked. Their critically injured patient was stabilised and on her way to Theatre, and for what seemed like the first time that day the red phone was quiet. Time to grab a break.

He glanced up at the clock. Ten to four? No wonder he was feeling light-headed. And his phone was jiggling again in his pocket.

'Right, this time I'm *really* going for lunch,' he said drily. 'Anything less than a MAJAX, you're on your own.'

There was a ripple of laughter as he tore off the thin plastic apron, dropped it in the bin with his gloves and walked out of Resus, leaving the rest of the team to clear up the chaos and restock ready for the next emergency. One of the perks of being clinical lead, he thought wryly as the door dropped shut behind him. God knows there were few enough.

He took the shortcut to the coffee shop, bought a coffee

and a soft wholegrain roll stuffed with ham and salad, added a chocolate bar to boost his blood sugar and headed outside, drawing the fresh summer air deep into his lungs.

One of the best things about Yoxburgh Park Hospital was its setting. Behind the elaborate facade of the old Victorian building a modern general hospital had been created, providing the community not only with much needed medical facilities, but also a beautiful recreational area. It was green and quiet and peaceful, and he took his breaks out here whenever he could.

Not nearly often enough.

He found an empty bench under the trees and settled down to eat his lunch, pulling his phone out simultaneously to check for messages. It had jiggled in his pocket more than once in the last hour, but there were no messages, just two missed calls.

From Connie?

He frowned slightly. He hadn't heard from her in ages, and now two missed calls in the space of an hour? He felt his heart rate pick up and he called her back, drumming his fingers impatiently as he waited for the phone to connect.

She answered almost instantly, and to his relief she sounded fine.

'James, hi. Sorry, I didn't mean to disturb you. Are you at work?'

'Yeah—doesn't matter, I'm on a break now. How are you, Connie? You've been very quiet recently.' Well, not even that recently. Apart from the odd email saying nothing significant and a couple of ridiculously brief phone calls, she hadn't really contacted him since she'd got back from Afghanistan after Christmas. It wasn't just her fault. He hadn't contacted her, either, and now he felt a flicker of guilt.

She laughed, the soft musical sound making him ache a

little inside. There'd been a time not so long ago when she'd never laughed...

'What, you mean I've left you in peace, Slater?'

'Something like that,' he said mildly. 'So, how are you?'

'Fine. Good. Great, really. Ready to move on.' The silence stretched out for a heartbeat, and then she said, 'Actually, I need to talk to you about that.'

She sounded oddly hesitant, and his radar started beeping. 'Fire away.'

That troubling silence again. 'I don't think it's something we can do over the phone,' she said eventually. 'I'd thought you might be off today as it's Sunday, and I thought maybe we could get together, it's been a while, but obviously not if you're working. Have you got any days off coming up?'

'Tomorrow? I'm off then for a couple of days. I don't get many weekends at the moment—crazy staffing issues—but I can always come over and see you tomorrow evening after you've finished work if it's urgent.'

'No, don't do that, I'll come to you. I'm not working at the moment so I've got plenty of time. And it isn't really urgent, I just—I wanted to talk to you. Can I pop over in the morning?'

Pop? From a hundred and thirty odd miles away? And why wasn't she working? 'Sure. Why don't you stay over till Tuesday, if you're free? We can catch up.' *And I can find out what the hell's going on that's so 'not urgent' that you have to come tomorrow morning.*

'Are you sure? It would be lovely but I've got the dog, don't forget. Can you cope with that? She's very good now—housetrained and all that, but I can't put her in kennels at such short notice.'

Had she mentioned a dog? Possibly, but it didn't matter. He had a secure garden. She'd be fine. The dog was the least of his worries.

'I'm sure we'll cope,' he said. 'Come. It'll be lovely to see you.'

'Thanks. When do you want me?'

Always...

He crushed the inappropriate thought. 'Whenever you're ready,' he said. 'Give me a call when you're an hour away, so I can be sure I'm at home. I'll see you tomorrow some time.'

'Great. Thanks, James.'

'No worries. Drive carefully.'

Ending the call, he ate the soft, squishy roll, drank his coffee and tasted neither. All he could think about was Connie and her non-urgent topic of conversation. He ripped the wrapper off the chocolate bar and bit into it absently.

What the hell did she want to talk to him about? He had no idea, but he was beginning to regret his invitation. He must have been crazy. His place was a mess, he had a zillion and one things to do, and catching up with Connie just wasn't on his agenda—especially not like this. The prospect of being alone with her for thirty-six hours was going to test him to the limit. Not that he wasn't looking forward to seeing her. Not at all.

Just—maybe a little too much...

Crushing the cup in his hand, he headed off back to the department, his thoughts and emotions tumbling.

Connie. His old friend, his ex-colleague, and his best friend's wife.

No. His best friend's *widow*. The woman he'd promised to take care of.

'When it happens, James—'

'If it happens—'

'When it happens—promise me you'll take care of her.'

'Of course I will, you daft bastard. It won't happen. It's your last tour. You'll be fine.'

Famous last words.

The ache of loss, still raw after two years, put everything back in perspective and gave him a timely reminder of his duties and responsibilities. It didn't matter what else he'd had planned, whatever his personal feelings for her, his duty to Connie came first and right now she needed him.

But apparently not urgently. Tomorrow would do.

Sheesh.

Savagely tossing the crushed cup into a bin, he strode through the door and headed back to work.

'Well. We're going to see James. What do you think of that, Saffy? Do you think he'll understand?'

Saffy thumped her tail once, head on Connie's foot, eyes alert as she peered up at her. Connie reached down a hand and stroked her gently, and Saffy groaned and rolled over, one leg lifted to reveal the vulnerable underside she was offering for a tickle.

'Hussy,' she crooned, rubbing the scarred tummy, and the dog's tail wagged again. She licked Connie's ankle, the contact of her warm, moist tongue cementing the already close bond between them. Almost as if she understood. No, of course she didn't, Connie told herself. How could she, even though Connie had told her everything there was to tell about it all in excruciating detail.

'Sorry, sweetheart,' she murmured, straightening up and getting to her feet. 'No time for cuddles, I've got too much to do.'

If she was going to see James tomorrow, she needed to pull herself together and get ready. Do some washing so she had something other than jeans and a ratty old T shirt to wear. Pack. Make sure the house was clean and tidy before they left.

Not that it was dirty or untidy, but now the decision was made and she was going to see him, to ask him the most monumental and massive favour, she needed to do something to keep herself busy or she'd go crazy.

She'd rehearsed her speech over and over again, gone through what she was going to say until she'd worn it out. There was nothing left to do but clean the house, so she cleaned it until it squeaked, and then she fell into bed and slept restlessly until dawn.

God, the place was a tip.

He'd been going to tackle it last night, but as usual he'd been held up by admin and hadn't got home until ten, so he'd left it till this morning. Now, looking round it, he realised that had probably been a massive mistake.

He blitzed the worst of it, made up a bed for her and went back downstairs.

Better. Slightly. If he ever had any regular time off he might stand a chance, but right now that was just a distant dream. He glanced at his watch. Ten to ten. Supermarket now, or later, after she'd arrived? She was an early riser but the journey would take her a good two hours.

Now, he decided, if he was quick, and ten minutes later he was standing there in the aisles and trying to remember what she liked. Was she a vegetarian?

No, of course she wasn't. He recalled watching her eating a bun crammed with roast pork and apple sauce at the Suffolk Show, the memory still vivid. It must have been the first year he'd been in Yoxburgh, and Joe had been on leave.

And he'd been watching her eat, his body throbbing with need as she'd flicked out her tongue and scooped up a dribble of apple sauce on her chin. He'd dragged his eyes away and found Joe staring at him, an odd expression on his face.

'Food envy,' he'd explained hastily, and Joe had laughed and bought him another roll from the hog roast stand.

He'd had to force himself to eat it, because he hadn't had

food envy at all, just plain old envy. He was jealous of Joe, jealous of his best friend for being so ridiculously happy with his lovely wife. How sick was that? How lonely and empty and barren— Whatever. She wasn't vegetarian, so he picked up a nice piece of fillet steak from the butchery counter, threw some other stuff into the trolley and headed home, wondering for the hundredth time what she wanted to say to him. She'd said she was ready to move on, and now it was in his head a disturbing possibility wouldn't go away.

Was there someone new in her life?

Why not? It was perfectly plausible. She was a beautiful woman, she was alone, she was free to do whatever she liked—but even the thought of her replacing the best friend a man could wish for, the kindest and most courageous man he'd ever known, made him feel sick.

Dismissing the pointless speculation, he drove down Ferry Road towards the little community grouped around the harbour mouth, turned onto the gravel track that led past a little string of houses to his cottage and pulled up on the drive next to a four-wheel drive he'd never seen before, just as his phone pinged.

Damn. He'd meant to be here, but she hadn't rung—or had she, while he'd been vacuuming the house?

Yup. There was a missed call from her, and a voicemail.

'I've arrived. Couldn't get you on the phone earlier, but I'm here now so I'm walking the dog. Call me when you get home.'

He dialled her number as he carried the bags into the kitchen and dumped them on the worktop, and she answered on the second ring, sounding breathless.

'Hi—did you get my message?'

'Yeah. Sorry I wasn't here, I went food shopping. I'm back now. Where are you?'

'On the sea wall. I'll be two ticks, I can see the cottage

from here,' she told him, so he opened the front door and stood on the porch step scanning the path, and there she was, blonde hair flying in the breeze, a huge sandy-coloured dog loping by her side as she ran towards him, her long limbs moving smoothly as she covered the ground with an effortless stride.

God, she was lovely.

Lovelier than ever, and that took some doing. His heart lurched, and he dredged up what he hoped was a civilised smile as he went to meet her.

She looked amazing, fit and well and bursting with energy. Her pale gold hair was gleaming, her blue eyes bright, her cheeks flushed with the sea breeze and the exertion as she ran up, her smile as wide as her arms, and threw herself at him. Her body slammed into his and knocked the breath from him in every way, and he nearly staggered at the impact.

'Hey, Slater!'

'Hey yourself, Princess,' he said on a slight laugh as his arms wrapped round her and caught her tight against him. 'Good to see you.'

'You, too.'

She hugged him hard, her body warm and firm against his for the brief duration of the embrace, and he hugged her back, ridiculously pleased to see her, because he'd missed her, this woman of Joe's. Missed her warmth and her humour, missed the laughter she carried with her everywhere she went. Or had, until she'd lost Joe.

Don't tell me you're getting married again—please, don't tell me that...

Swearing silently, he dropped his arms and stepped back, looking down at the great rangy hound standing panting at Connie's side, tongue lolling as it watched him alertly.

'So—I take it this is your rescued dog? I'd pictured some little terrier or spaniel.'

Connie winced ruefully. 'Sorry. Teensy bit bigger. This is Saffy—Safiya. It means best friend. Joe sort of adopted her in Afghanistan on his last tour. He was going to bring her home, but—well, he didn't make it, so I brought her back.'

Typical Joe, he thought with a lump in his throat. Big tough guy, soft as lights. And he'd just bet she'd been his best friend, in the harsh and desolate desert, thousands of miles from home. A touch of humanity in the inhumanity of war.

He held out his hand for Saffy to sniff. She did more than sniff it. She licked it. Gently, tentatively, coming closer to press her head against his shoulder as he crouched down to her level and stroked her long, floppy ears. A gentle giant of a dog. No wonder Joe had fallen for her.

He laughed softly, a little taken aback by the trusting gesture, and straightened up again. 'She's a sweetie,' he said, his voice slightly choked, and Connie nodded.

'She is. I had to bring her home.'

Of course she'd had to, because Saffy was her last link to Joe. If Joe had been soft, Connie was softer, but there was a core of steel in there, too. He'd seen plenty of evidence of that in the past few years.

He'd seen her holding herself together when Joe was deployed to Afghanistan for what was meant to be his final tour, and then again, just months later, when he came home for the last time in a flag-draped coffin—

'So, this is the new house, then,' she said, yanking him back to the present as he opened the gate and ushered her and Saffy through it.

He hauled in a breath and put the memories away. 'Hardly new. I've been here over two years. I'd forgotten you hadn't seen it.'

'No, well, things got in the way. I can't believe it's that long,' she said. She looked slightly bemused, as if the time had somehow passed and she'd been suspended in an emotional void. He supposed she might well have been. He had, for years. Still was in many ways, and it was a lonely place.

Take care of Connie.

Guilt ate at him. He should have been there more for her, should have looked out for her, emailed her more often, rung her. It had been months, and he'd just let it drift by. Too busy, as usual, for the things that really mattered.

There didn't seem to be anything else to say, so he took her into the house, looking at it with the critical eyes of a stranger and finding it wanting. Not the house, but his treatment of it. The house was lovely and deserved better than a quick once-over as and when.

'Sorry, it's a bit of a mess. I haven't done a great deal to it, but the people I bought it from left it in great condition so I just moved in and got on with other things. I've been so busy I haven't even unpacked the books yet.'

She looked around and smiled. 'I can see that. You haven't put any pictures up, either.'

'I've got the sea. I don't need pictures,' he said simply, and she turned and looked out of the window, feeling the calming effect of the breakers rolling slowly in, the quiet suck of the surf on the shingle curiously soothing.

'No, I suppose you don't,' she said. She glanced around again. The living space was all open, the seating area at the front of the house facing the sea, the full-width dining and kitchen area at the back overlooking the marshes and the meandering river beyond. There was an unspoilt beauty about the area, and she could absolutely see why he'd bought the cottage.

'It's lovely, James. Really gorgeous. I was expecting something tiny from the name.'

'Thrift Cottage? There's a plant called sea thrift—*Armeria maritima*. The garden's full of it. I don't know which came first but I imagine that's the connection. It was certainly nothing to do with the price,' he said drily. 'Coffee?'

She chuckled. 'Love one. I haven't had my caffeine fix yet today.'

'Espresso, cappuccino, latte, Americano?'

She blinked. 'Wow, you must have a fancy coffee machine.'

He grinned. 'Some things have to be taken seriously.'

'So do me a flat white,' she challenged, her eyes sparkling with laughter.

Typical Connie, he thought. Never take the easy route or expect anyone else to. He rolled his eyes, took the milk out of the carrier bag he'd just brought home and started work while she and the dog watched his every move, Connie from the other side of the room, Saffy from her position on the floor just close enough to reach anything he might drop. Hope personified, he thought with a smile.

'You do know I was a *barista* while I was at uni?' he offered over his shoulder, the mischievous grin dimpling his lean cheek again and making her mouth tug in response.

'I didn't, but it doesn't surprise me.'

She watched him as he stuck a cup under the spout of the coffee machine, his broad shoulders and wide stance reminding her of Joe, and yet not. Joe had been shorter, stockier, his hair a lighter brown, and his eyes had been a muted green, unlike James's, which were a striking, brilliant ice-blue rimmed with navy. She noticed the touch of grey at his temples and frowned slightly. That was new. Or had she just not noticed before?

'So how long did the drive take you?' he asked, turning to look at her with those piercing eyes.

'Just over two hours—about two fifteen? I had a good run but I had to stop to let Saffy out for a minute.'

She stepped over the dog and perched on a high stool beside him, and the light drift of her perfume teased his nostrils.

He could feel her eyes on him as he foamed the milk, tapping the jug, swirling the espresso round the warmed cup before he poured the milk into it in a carefully controlled stream, wiggling the jug to create a perfect rosetta of microfoamed milk on top of the crema.

'Here,' he said, sliding the cup towards her with a flourish, pleased to see he hadn't lost his touch despite the audience.

'Latte art? Show-off,' she said, but she looked impressed and he couldn't resist a slightly smug chuckle.

He tore open a packet of freshly baked cookies from the supermarket, the really wicked ones oozing with calories. He wouldn't normally have bought them, but he knew Connie was a sucker for gooey cookies. He slid them towards her as Saffy watched hopefully.

'Here. Don't eat them all.'

'Whatever gave you that idea?' she said innocently, her smile teasing, and he felt his heart lurch dangerously.

'I've never yet met a woman who could resist triple choc chip cookies still warm from the oven.'

Her eyes lit up. 'Are they still warm?' she said, diving in, and he watched in fascination as she closed her eyes and sank her teeth into one.

He nearly groaned out loud. How could eating a cookie be so sexy?

'Murgh,' she said, eyes still closed, and he gave a strained chuckle and trashed his own rosetta as his hand jerked.

'That good?' he asked, his voice sounding rusty, and she nodded.

'Oh, yes,' she said, a little more intelligibly, and he laughed again, set his own coffee down on the breakfast bar and joined her on the other stool, shifting it away from her a little after he'd taken a cookie from the bag.

Her eyes were open again, and she was pulling another

one apart, dissecting it slowly and savouring every bit, and he almost whimpered.

He *did* whimper. Did he? *Really?*

'Saffy, don't beg,' she said through a mouthful of cookie, and he realised it was the dog. He heaved a quiet sigh of relief and grabbed the last cookie, as much as anything so he wouldn't have to watch her eat it.

And then, just because they had to talk about something and anyway, the suspense was killing him, he asked, 'So, what did you want to talk to me about?'

Connie felt her heart thump.

This was it, her chance to ask him, and yet now she was here she had no idea—*no* idea—how to do it. Her carefully rehearsed speech had deserted her, and her mind flailed. *Start at the beginning,* she told herself, and took a deep breath.

'Um—did you realise Joe and I were having problems?' she asked tentatively.

'Problems?'

James stared at her, stunned by that. Problems were the last thing he would have associated with them. They'd always seemed really happy together, and Joe, certainly, had loved Connie to bits. Had it not been mutual? No, Joe would have said—wouldn't he? Maybe not.

'What sort of problems?' he asked warily, not at all sure he wanted to know.

'Only one—well, two, if you count the fact that I spent our entire marriage waiting for the doorbell to ring and someone in uniform to tell me he was dead.'

'I'd count that,' he said gruffly. He'd felt it himself, every time Joe had been deployed on active service—and it didn't get much more active than being a bomb disposal officer. But still, he'd never really expected it to happen. Maybe Connie had been more realistic.

'And the other problem?'

She looked away, her expression suddenly bleak. 'We couldn't have children.'

He frowned, speechless for a second as it sank in. He set his cup down carefully and closed his eyes. When he opened them she was watching him again, her bottom lip caught between her teeth, waiting for him to say the right thing.

Whatever the hell that was. He let out a long, slow sigh and shook his head.

'Ah, Connie. I'm so sorry. I didn't realise there was anything wrong. I always thought it was by choice, something you'd get round to when he'd finished that last tour.'

...except he never had...

'It was.' She smiled a little unsteadily, and looked away again. 'Actually, he was going to come and see you about it when he got home.'

'Me?' he asked, puzzled by that. 'I don't know anything about infertility. You're a doctor, you probably know as much about it as I do, if not more. You needed to see a specialist.'

'We had. It wasn't for that. We'd had the tests, and he was the one with the problem. Firing blanks, as he put it.' She grimaced a little awkwardly, uncomfortable revealing what Joe had considered a weakness, a failure, something to be ashamed of. 'I wanted him to tell you, but he wouldn't, not for ages. He was psyching himself up to do it when he got home, but it was so hard for him, even though you were so close.'

'We were, but—guys don't talk about that kind of thing, Connie, especially when they're like Joe.'

'I know. It's stupid, I feel so disloyal telling you because he just wouldn't talk about it. I would have told you ages ago, but he couldn't, and so nor could I because it wasn't my secret to tell.'

He sighed and reached out a hand, laying it over her arm and squeezing gently. 'Don't feel disloyal. I loved him, too, remember. You can tell me anything you need to, and you know it won't go any further.'

She nodded. 'I know. I just wish he'd felt he could tell you.'

'Me, too.' He sighed again and withdrew his hand. 'I'm really sorry, Connie. That must have been so tough to deal with.'

She looked down at her coffee, poking at the foam with the teaspoon, drawing little trails absently through the rosetta, and he noticed her cheeks had coloured a little.

She sucked in a slightly shaky breath. 'He was going to tell you, as soon as he got back. He wanted to ask you...' *Oh, just spit it out, woman! He can only say no!*

She sat up straighter and made herself look him in the eye, her heart pounding. 'He was going to ask you if you'd consider being a sperm donor for us.'

He stared at her blankly, the shock robbing him of his breath for a moment. He hauled it back in and frowned.

'Me?'

They'd wanted him to give them a child?

'Why me?' he asked, his voice sounding strangely distant. *Of all the people in the world, why me?*

She shrugged. 'Why not? I would have thought it was obvious. He doesn't have a brother, you were his best friend, he loved and respected you. Plus you're not exactly ugly or stupid. Who better?' She paused for a second, fiddled with her spoon, then met his eyes again, her own a little wary. 'Would you have said yes?'

He shook his head to clear it, still reeling a little from the shock.

'Hell, I don't know, Connie. I have no idea.'

'But—possibly?'

He shrugged. 'Maybe.'

A baby? Maybe not. Most likely not.

'Definitely maybe? Like, probably?'

Would he? He tried to think, but he was still trying to come to terms with it and thinking seemed too hard right then.

'I don't know. I really don't know. I might have considered it, I suppose, but it's irrelevant now, so it's hard to know how I would have reacted. But you would have been brilliant parents. I'm just so sorry you never had the chance. That really sucks.'

She'd shifted her attention to the cookie crumbs on the breakfast bar, pushing them around with her fingertip, and he saw her swallow. Then she lifted her head and met his eyes. Her whole body seemed to go still, as if every cell was holding its breath. And then she spoke.

'What if it wasn't irrelevant now?'

CHAPTER TWO

Was this why she'd wanted to see him? To ask him *this*?

He searched her eyes, and they didn't waver.

'What are you saying, Connie?' he asked quietly, but he knew already, could feel the cold reality of it curling around him like freezing fog.

He saw her swallow again. 'I wondered—I don't know how you'll feel about it, and I know Joe's not here now, but—James, I still really want a baby.'

He stared at her, saw the pleading in her eyes, and he felt suddenly drenched with icy sweat. She meant it. She really, really meant it—

He shoved the stool back abruptly and stood up, taking a step away on legs that felt like rubber. 'No. I'm sorry, Connie. I can't do it.'

He walked away, going out onto the veranda and curling his fingers round the rail, his hands gripping it so hard his knuckles were bleached white while the memories poured through him.

Cathy, coming into their bedroom, her eyes bright with joy in her pale face, a little white wand in her hand.

'I might've worked out why I've been feeling rough...'

He heard Connie's footsteps on the boards behind him, could feel her just inches away, feel her warmth, hear the soft sigh of her breath. Her voice, when she spoke, was hesitant.

'James? I'm sorry. I know it's a bit weird, coming out of the blue like that, but please don't just say no without considering it—'

Her voice cracked slightly, and she broke off. Her hand was light on his shoulder, tentative, trembling slightly. It burned him all the way through to his soul.

'James? Talk to me?'

'There's nothing to talk about,' he said, his voice hollow. 'Joe's dead, Connie. He's gone.' *They're all gone...*

Her breath sucked in softly. 'Do you think I don't know that? Do you really think that in the last two years I haven't noticed? But I'm still here, and I'm alive, and I'm trying to move on with my life, to rescue something from the wreckage. And you could help me do that. Give me something to live for. Please. At least think about it.'

He turned his head slightly and stared at her, then looked away again. 'Hell, Connie, you know how to push a guy's buttons.' His voice was raw now, rasping, and he swallowed hard, shaking his head again to clear it, but it didn't work this time any more than it had the last.

'I'm sorry. I know it's a bit sudden and unexpected, but— you said you would have considered it.'

'No, I said I *might* have considered it, for you and Joe. Not just for you! I can't do that, Connie! I can't just hand you a little pot of my genetic material and walk away and leave you on your own. What kind of person would that make me?'

'Generous? I'd still be the mother, still be the primary carer, whatever. What's the difference?'

'The difference? The *difference* is that you're on your own, and children need two parents. There's no way I could be responsible for a child coming into the world that I wasn't involved with on a daily basis—'

'So—what? You want to be involved? You can be involved—'

'What? No! Connie, no. Absolutely not. I don't want to be a father! It's not anywhere, anyhow, on my agenda.'

Not any more.

'Joe said you might say that. I mean, if you'd wanted kids you would have got married again, wouldn't you? But he said you'd always said you wouldn't, and he thought that might be the very reason you'd agree, because you might see it as the only way you'd ever have a child…'

She trailed off, as if she knew she'd gone too far, and he stared down at his stark white knuckles, his fingers burning with the tension. One by one he made them relax so that he could let go of the rail and walk away. Away from Connie, away from the memories that were breaking through his carefully erected defences and flaying him to shreds.

Cathy's face, her eyes alight with joy. The first scan, that amazing picture of their baby. And then, just weeks later…

'No, Connie. I'm sorry, but—no. You don't know what you're asking. I can't. I just can't…'

The last finger peeled away from the railing and he spun on his heel and walked off, down the steps, across the garden, out of the gate.

She watched him go, her eyes filling, her last hope of having the child she and Joe had longed for so desperately fading with every step he took, and she put her hand over her mouth to hold in the sob and went back to the kitchen to a scene of utter chaos.

'Oh, Saffy, no!' she wailed as the dog shot past her, a slab of meat dangling from her jaws.

It was the last straw. Sinking down on the floor next to the ravaged shopping bags, Connie pulled up her knees, rested her head on them and sobbed her heart out as all the hopes and dreams she and Joe had cherished crumbled into dust.

* * *

It took him a while to realise the dog was at his side.

He was sitting on the sea wall, hugging one knee and staring blindly out over the water. He couldn't see anything but Connie.

Not the boats, not the sea—not even the face of the wife he'd loved and lost. He struggled to pull up the image, but he couldn't, not now, when he wanted to. All he could see was Connie's face, the hope and pleading in her eyes as she'd asked him the impossible, the agonising disappointment when he'd turned her down, and it was tearing him apart.

Finally aware of Saffy's presence, he turned his head and met her eyes. She was sitting beside him, the tip of her tail flickering tentatively, and he lifted his hand and stroked her.

'I can't do it, Saffy,' he said, his voice scraping like the shingle on the beach. 'I want to help her, I promised to look after her, but I can't do that, I just can't. She doesn't know what she's asking, and I can't tell her. I can't explain. I can't say it out loud.'

Saffy shifted slightly, leaning on him, and he put his arm over her back and rested his hand on her chest, rubbing it gently; after a moment she sank down to the ground with a soft grunt and laid her head on her paws, her weight against him somehow comforting and reassuring.

How many times had Joe sat like this with her, in the heat and dust and horror of Helmand? He stroked her side, and she shifted again, so that his hand fell naturally onto the soft, unguarded belly, offered with such trust.

He ran his fingers over it and stilled, feeling the ridges of scars under his fingertips. It shocked him out of his grief.

'Oh, Saffy, what happened to you, sweetheart?' he murmured. He turned his head to study the scars, and saw feet.

Two feet, long and slim, slightly dusty, clad in sandals, the nails painted fire-engine-red. He hadn't heard her approaching over the sound of the sea, but there she was, and he couldn't help staring at those nails. They seemed so cheerful and jolly, so totally out of kilter with his despair.

He glanced up at her and saw that she'd been crying, her eyes red-rimmed and bloodshot, her cheeks smudged with tears. His throat closed a little, but he said nothing, and after a second she sat down on the other side of the dog, her legs dangling over the wall as she stared out to sea.

'She was injured when he found her,' she said softly, answering his question. 'They did a controlled explosion of an IED, and Saffy must have got caught in the blast. She had wounds all over her. He should have shot her, really, but he was racked with guilt and felt responsible, and the wounds were only superficial, so he fed her and put antiseptic on them, and bit by bit she got better, and she adored him. I've got photos of them together with his arm round her in the compound. His commanding officer would have flayed the skin off him if he'd known, especially as Joe was the officer in charge of the little outpost, but he couldn't have done anything else. He broke all the rules for her, and nobody ever said a word.'

'And you brought her home for him.'

She tried to smile. 'I had to. I owed it to her, and anyway, he'd already arranged it. There's a charity run by an ex-serviceman to help soldiers bring home the dogs that they've adopted over there, and it was all set up, but when Joe died the arrangements ground to a halt. Then a year later, just before I went out to Afghanistan, someone from the charity contacted me and said the dog was still hanging around the compound and did I still want to go ahead.'

'And of course you did.' He smiled at her, his eyes creasing with a gentle understanding that brought a lump to her throat. She swallowed.

'Yeah. Well. Anyway, they were so helpful. The money

wasn't the issue because Joe had already paid them, it was the red tape, and they knew just how to cut through it, and she was flown home a month later, just after I left for Afghanistan. She was waiting for me in the quarantine kennels when I got home at the end of December, and she's been with me ever since, but it hasn't been easy.'

'No, I'm sure it hasn't. Poor Saffy,' he said, his hand gentle on her side, and Connie reached out and put her hand over his, stilling it.

'James, I'm really sorry. I didn't mean to upset you. I just— it was the last piece of the puzzle, really, the last thing we'd planned apart from bringing Saffy home. We'd talked about it for so long, and he was so excited about the idea that maybe at last we could have a baby. He didn't know what you'd say, which way you'd go, but he was hoping he could talk you into it.'

And maybe he could have done, she thought, if James had meant what he'd said about considering it. But now, because Joe was dead, James had flatly refused to help her because she'd be alone and that was different, apparently.

'You know,' she said softly, going on because she couldn't just give up on this at the first hurdle, 'if you'd said yes to him and then he'd been killed in some accident, for instance, I would still have had to bring the baby up alone. What would you have done then, if I'd already had a child?'

'I would have looked after you both,' he said instantly, 'but you haven't had a child, and Joe's gone, and I don't want that responsibility.'

'There is no responsibility.'

He stared at her. 'Of course there is, Connie. I can't just give you a child and let you walk off into the sunset with it and forget about it. Get real. This is my flesh and blood you're talking about. My child. I could never forget my child.'

Ever...

'But you would have done it for us?'

He shook his head slowly. 'I don't know. Maybe, maybe not, but Joe's not here any more, and a stable, happily married couple who desperately want a baby isn't the same as a grieving widow clinging to the remnants of a dream.'

'But that's not what I'm doing, not what this is about.'

'Are you sure? Have you really analysed your motives, Connie? I don't think so. And what if you meet someone?' he asked her, that nagging fear suddenly rising again unbidden and sickening him. 'What if, a couple of years down the line, another man comes into your life? What then? Would you expect me to sit back and watch a total stranger bringing up my child, with no say in how they do it?'

She shook her head vehemently. 'That won't happen—and anyway, I'm getting older. I'm thirty-six now. Time's ebbing away. I don't know if I'll ever be truly over Joe, and by the time I am, and I've met someone and trust him enough to fall in love, it'll be too late for me and I really, really want this. It's now or never, James.'

It was. He could see that, knew that her fertility was declining with every year that passed, but that wasn't his problem. Nothing about this was his problem. Until she spoke again.

'I don't want to put pressure on you, and I respect your decision. I just—I would much rather it was someone Joe had loved and respected, someone I loved and respected, than an anonymous donor.'

'Anonymous donor?' he said, his voice sounding rough and gritty to his ears.

'Well, what else? If it can't be you, I don't know who else it would be. There's nobody else I could ask, but if I go for a donor how do I know what they're like? How do I know if they've got a sense of humour, or any brains or integrity—I might as well go and pull someone in a nightclub and have a random—'

'Connie, for God's sake!'

She gave a wry, twisted little smile.

'Don't worry, James. It's OK. I'm not *that* crazy. I won't do anything stupid.'

'Good,' he said tautly. 'And for the record, I don't like emotional blackmail.'

'It wasn't!' she protested, her eyes filling with tears. 'Really, James, it wasn't, I wouldn't do that to you. I wasn't serious. I'm really not that nuts.'

He wasn't sure. Not nuts, maybe, but—desperate?

'When it happens—promise me you'll take care of her.'

'Of course I will, you daft bastard. It won't happen. It's your last tour. You'll be fine.'

But he hadn't been fine, and now Connie was here, making hideous jokes about doing something utterly repugnant, and he felt the weight of responsibility crush him.

'Promise me you won't do anything stupid,' he said gruffly.

'I won't.'

'Nothing. Don't do anything. Not yet.'

She tilted her head and searched his eyes, her brows pleating together thoughtfully. 'Not yet?'

Not ever, because I can't bear the thought of you giving your body to a total stranger in some random, drunken encounter, and because if anybody's going to give you a baby, it's me—

The thought shocked him rigid. He jack-knifed to his feet and strode back to the house, his heart pounding, and after a few moments he heard the crunch of gravel behind him on the path.

Saffy was already there at his side, glued to his leg, and as he walked into the kitchen and stared at the wreckage of his shopping bags, she wagged her tail sheepishly, guilt written all over her.

A shadow fell across the room.

'Ah. Sorry. I was coming to tell you—she stole the steak.'

He gave a soft, slightly unsteady laugh and shook his head. 'Oh, Saffy. You are such a bad dog,' he murmured, with so much affection in his voice it brought a lump to her throat. He seemed to be doing that a lot today.

'She was starving when Joe found her. She steals because it's all she knows, the only way she could survive. And it really is her only vice. I'll replace the steak—'

'To hell with the steak,' he said gruffly. 'She's welcome to it. We'll just have to go to the pub tonight.'

Better that way than sitting alone together in his house trying to have a civilised conversation over dinner and picking their way through this minefield. Perhaps Saffy had inadvertently done them both a favour.

'Well, I could have handled that better, couldn't I, Saff?'

Saffy just wagged her tail lazily and stretched. James had gone shopping again because it turned out it was more than just the steak that needed replacing, so Connie was sitting on a bench in the garden basking in the lovely warm June sunshine and contemplating the mess she'd made of all this.

He'd refused her offer of company, saying the dog had spent long enough in the car, and to be honest she was glad he'd gone without her because it had all become really awkward and uncomfortable, and if it hadn't mattered so much she would have packed up the dog and her luggage and left.

But then he'd said 'yet'.

Don't do anything yet.

She dropped her head back against the wall of the cabin behind her and closed her eyes and wondered what he'd really meant by 'yet'.

She had no idea.

None that she dared to contemplate, anyway, in case a ray of hope sneaked back in and she had to face having it dashed all over again, but he'd had a strange look about him, and then he'd stalked off.

Run away?

'No! Stop it! Stop thinking about it. He didn't mean anything, it was just a turn of phrase.'

Maybe…

She opened her eyes and looked up at the house, trying to distract herself. It was set up slightly above the level of the garden, possibly because of the threat of flooding before the sea wall had been built, but the result was that even from the ground floor there were lovely views out to sea across the mouth of the estuary and across the marshes behind, and from the bedrooms the views would be even better.

She wondered where she'd be sleeping. He hadn't shown her to her room yet, but it wasn't a big house so she wouldn't be far away from him, and she felt suddenly, ridiculously uneasy about being alone in the house with him for the night.

Crazy. There was nothing to feel uneasy about. He'd stayed with them loads of times, and he'd stayed the night after Joe's funeral, too, refusing to leave her until he was sure she was all right.

And anyway, what was he going to do, jump her bones? Hardly, James just wasn't like that. He'd never so much as looked at her sideways, never mind made her feel uncomfortable like some of Joe's other friends had.

If he had, there was no way she would have broached the sperm donor subject. Way too intimate. It had been hard enough as it was, and maybe that was why she felt uneasy. The whole subject was necessarily very personal and intimate, and she'd gone wading in there without any warning and shocked his socks off.

It dawned on her belatedly that she hadn't even asked if there was anyone else who might have been a consideration in this, but that was so stupid. He was a fit, healthy and presumably sexual active man who was entitled to have a relationship with anyone he chose. She'd just assumed he wasn't in a relationship, assumed that just because he'd never mentioned anyone, there wasn't anyone.

OK, so he probably wasn't getting married to her, whoever she might be, but that didn't stop him having a lover. Several, if he chose. Did he bring them back here?

She realised she was staring up at the house and wondering which was his bedroom, wondering where in the house he made love to the *femme du jour*, and it stopped her in her tracks.

What was she *doing*, even *thinking* about his private life? Why the hell was she here at all? How had she had the nerve to ask him to do this?

But he'd said 'yet'...

She sighed and stopped staring up at the house. Thinking about James and sex in the same breath was *so* not the way forward, not if she wanted to keep this clinical and uninvolved. And she did. She had to, because it was complicated enough. She looked around her instead, her eye drawn again to the cabin behind her. It was painted in a lovely muted grey-green, set up slightly on stilts so it was raised above the level of the garden like the house, with steps up to the doors.

She wondered what he used it for. It might be a store room, but it seemed far too good to use as a glory-hole. That would be such a waste.

Home gym? Possibly, although he didn't have the sort of muscles that came from working out. He looked like more of a runner, or maybe a tennis player. Not that she'd studied his body, she thought, frowning at herself. Why would she? But she'd noticed, of course she had.

She dragged herself back to the subject. Hobbies room? She wasn't aware that he had any. James had never mentioned it, and she realised that for all she'd known him for years, she hardly *knew* him. Not really. Not deep down. She'd met him nine years ago, worked with him for a year as his SHO, seen him umpteen times since then while she'd been with Joe, but he didn't give a lot away, at least not to her. Never had.

Maybe that was how she'd felt able to come down here and ask him this? Although if she'd known more about how he ticked she could have engineered her argument to target his weak spot. Or had she inadvertently done that? His reaction had been instant and unmistakeable. He'd recoiled from the idea as if it was unthinkable, but then he'd begun to relent—hadn't he?

She wasn't sure. It would have helped if Joe had paved the way, but he hadn't, and so she'd had to go in cold and blunder about in what was obviously a very sensitive area. Pushing his buttons, as he'd put it. And he'd said no, so she'd upset him for nothing.

Except he hadn't given her a flat-out no in the end, had he? He'd said don't do anything *yet*. Whatever yet meant.

She sighed. Back to that again.

He didn't really need another trip to the supermarket. They could have managed. He'd just needed space to think, to work out what, if anything, he could do to stop Connie from making the biggest mistake of her life.

Or his.

He swore softly under his breath, swung the car into a parking space and did a quick raid of the bacon and sausage aisle to replace all the breakfast ingredients Saffy had pinched, then he drove back home, lecturing himself every inch of the way on how his responsibility to Connie did *not* mean he had to do this.

He just had to stop her doing something utterly crazy. The very thought of her with a total stranger made him gag, but he wasn't much more thrilled by the idea of her conceiving a child from a nameless donor courtesy of a turkey baster.

Hell, it could be anybody! They could have some inherited disease, some genetic disorder that would be passed on to a child—a predisposition to cancer, heart disease, all manner of things. Rationally, of course, he knew that no reputable clinic would use unscreened donors, and the checks were rigorous. Very rigorous. He *knew* that, but even so…

What would Joe have thought about it? If he'd refused, what would Joe and Connie have done next? Asked another friend? Gone to a clinic?

It was irrelevant, he told himself again. That was then, this was now, this was Connie on her own, fulfilling a lost dream. God knows what her motives were, but he was pretty sure she hadn't examined them in enough detail or thought through the ramifications. Somehow or other he had to talk her out of it, or at the very least try. He owed it to Joe. He'd promised to take care of her, and he would, because he kept his promises, and he'd keep this one if it killed him.

Assuming she'd let him, because her biological clock was obviously ticking so loud it was deafening her to reason. And as for his crazy reaction, that absurd urge to give her his baby—and without the benefit of any damn turkey baster—

Swearing viciously under his breath, he pulled up in a slew of gravel, and immediately he could hear Saffy yipping and scrabbling at the gate.

'Do you reckon she can smell the shopping?' Connie asked, smiling tentatively at him over the top, and he laughed briefly and turned his attention to the shopping bags, wondering yet again how on earth he was in this position. Why she hadn't warned him over the phone, said something, anything, some little hint so he hadn't been quite so unprepared when she'd just come out with it, though quite how she would have warned him—

'Probably,' he said drily. 'I think I'd better put this lot away in the fridge pronto. I take it she can't open the fridge?'

'She hasn't ever done it yet.'

'Don't start now,' he said, giving the dog a level stare immediately cancelled out by a head-rub that had her shadowing him into the kitchen.

Connie followed him, too, hesitating on the threshold. 'James, I'm really sorry. I didn't mean to put you in a difficult position.'

He paused, his hand on the fridge door, and looked at her over his shoulder. 'You didn't,' he said honestly. 'Joe did. It was his idea. You were just following up on it.'

'I could have let it go.'

'So why didn't you?'

Her smile was wry and touched with sadness. 'Because I couldn't,' she answered softly, 'not while there was any hope,' and he straightened up and shut the fridge and hugged her, because she just looked so damned unhappy and there was nothing he could do to make it better.

No amount of taking care of her was going to sort this out, short of doing what she'd asked, and he wasn't sure he would ever be able to do that, despite that visceral urge which had caught him off guard. Or because of it? Just the thought of her pregnant with his child…

He let her go, easing her gently away with his hands on her shoulders and creating some much-needed distance between them, because his thoughts were suddenly wildly inappropriate, and the graphic images shocked him.

'Why don't you stick the kettle on and we'll have a cup of tea, and then we can take Saffy for a walk and go to the pub for supper.'

'Are we still going? I thought you'd just been shopping.'

He shrugged. 'I didn't bother to get anything for tonight.

The pub seemed like a good idea—unless—is Saffy all right to leave here while we eat?'

She stared at him for a second, as if she was regrouping.

'Yes, she's fine. I've got a big wire travelling crate I use for her—it's a sort of retreat. I leave the door open all day so she can go in there to sleep or get away from it all, and I put her in there at night.'

'Because you don't trust her?'

'Not entirely,' she said drily. 'Still early days, and she did pinch the steak and the sausages.'

'The crate it is, then.' He smiled wryly, then glanced at his watch. 'Why don't we bring your luggage in and put it in your room while the kettle boils? I would have done it before but things ran away with us a little.'

Didn't they just? she thought.

He carried the dog's crate, she carried her overnight bag and the bag of stuff for Saffy—food, toys, blanket. Well, not a blanket, really, just an old jumper of Joe's she'd been unable to part with, and then when Saffy had come home she'd found a justification for her sentimental idiocy.

'Can we leave the crate down here?' she asked. 'She'll be fine in the kitchen, she's used to it.'

'Sure. Come on up, I'll give you a guided tour. It'll take about ten seconds. The house isn't exactly enormous.'

It wasn't, but it was lovely. There were doors from the entrance hall into the ground floor living space, essentially one big L-shaped room, with a cloakroom off the hallway under the stairs, and the landing above led into three bedrooms, two doubles and a single, and a small but well-equipped and surprisingly luxurious bathroom.

He showed her into the large bedroom at the front, simply furnished with a double bed, wardrobe and chest of drawers. There was a pale blue and white rug on the bare boards between the bed and the window, and on the edge of it was a comfy armchair, just right for reading in. And the bed, made up in crisp white linen, sat squarely opposite the window—perfect for lying there drinking early morning tea and gazing out to sea.

She crossed to the window and looked left, over the river mouth, the current rippling the water. The window was open and she could hear the suck of the sea on the shingle, the keening of the gulls overhead, and if she breathed in she could smell the salt in the air.

'Oh, James, it's lovely,' she sighed.

'Everyone likes this room.' He put her bag down and took a step towards the door. 'I'll leave you to settle in.'

'No need. I travel light. It'll take me three seconds to unpack.'

She followed him back out onto the landing and noticed another flight of stairs leading up.

'So what's up there?' she asked.

'My room.'

He didn't volunteer anything else, didn't offer to show it to her, and she didn't ask. She didn't want to enter his personal space. Not under the circumstances. Not after her earlier speculation about his love life. The last thing she needed was to see the bed he slept in. So she didn't ask, just followed him downstairs, got her walking boots out of the car and put them on.

'In your own time, Slater,' she said lightly, and he gave her one of those wry smiles of his and got off the steps and led her and Saffy out of the gate.

CHAPTER THREE

SHE PUT SAFFY on a lead because she didn't really want to spend half the evening looking for her if she ran off, but the dog attached herself to James like glue and trotted by his side, the lead hanging rather pointlessly across the gap between her and Connie.

Faithless hound.

'So, where are we going?' she asked, falling in beside them.

'I thought we could go along by the river, then cut inland on the other side of the marshes and pick up the lane. It'll bring us out on the sea wall from the other direction. It's about three miles. Is that OK?'

'Sounds good.'

The path narrowed on top of the river wall, and she dropped back behind him, Saffy still glued to his heels, and in the end she gave him the lead.

'You seem to have a new friend,' she said drily, and he glanced down at the dog and threw her a grin over his shoulder.

'Looks like it. Is that a problem?'

'No, of course not,' she said promptly. 'I'm glad she likes you. She does seem to like men, I expect because she's been used to them looking after her out in Helmand, but she'll have to get over it when we go home tomorrow. I hope it won't unsettle her.'

'Do you think it might?'

'I don't know. I hope not. She's doing so well.'

'Apart from the thieving,' he said drily, and she gave a guilty chuckle.

'Yeah, well. Apart from that.'

They walked in silence for a while by the muddy shallows at the edge of the river, and then as they turned inland and headed uphill, he dropped back beside her and said, 'So, how was Afghanistan? You haven't really told me anything about it.'

'No. It was a bit strange really. A bit surreal, but I'm glad I went. The facilities at Camp Bastion are fantastic. The things they do, what they achieve—for a field hospital it's unbelievable. Did you know it's got the busiest trauma unit in the world?'

'I'm not surprised. Most of them aren't in an area that has conflict.'

'No. No, they aren't. And I found that aspect really difficult.'

'Because of Joe?'

She nodded. 'Sort of. Because of all of them, really. I had second thoughts about going, after he died. I didn't know how I'd feel facing the stark reality of it, but I realised when the first wave of grief receded that I still wanted to go. There was so much I wanted to try and understand, such as why it was necessary, why he'd gone in the first place, what he'd been trying to achieve.'

'And did you?'

'No. No, I still don't understand, not really. I don't think I ever will and I'm not sure I want to. People killing each other, maiming each other—it all seems so pointless and destructive. There must be a better way than all this sense-less violence.'

'It must have been really hard for you, Connie,' he said, his voice gentle. 'Very close to home.'

She nodded slowly, remembering the shock of seeing the first casualties come in, the realisation that this was it, this was what really happened out there. 'It was. I'd seen videos, had training, but I hadn't really understood what it was like for him until then. Seeing the injured lads there, though, fighting so hard to save them—it brought it all home to me, what he'd gone through, the threat he'd faced every day, never knowing when or if it might happen to him. That was tough.'

'I'm sure. He mentioned you were talking about going. I got the feeling he didn't like it much.'

'No, he didn't. I don't think he wanted to be worrying about me while he was trying to do his job, and he'd tried to put me off when I joined the Territorial Army as a volunteer doctor four years ago, but I thought, if Joe can do it, so can I. Not in the same way, but to do something, to do some good—and I'm glad I did, even though it was tough, because it's an incredible experience as a doctor.'

They fell silent for a while, then she went on, 'It's amazing what they can do there, you know, saving people that in civilian medicine we simply couldn't save because we just don't get to them fast enough or treat them aggressively enough when we do.'

He followed her lead and switched the conversation to practical medical aspects. 'So what would you change about the way we do things here?'

'Speed. Blood loss. That's the real killer out there, so stopping that fast is key, and transfusions. Massive transfusions. We gave one guy a hundred and fifty units of whole blood, plasma, platelets—you name it. No mucking about with saline and colloids, it's straight in with the blood products. And total body scans, the second they're stable enough to go, so they can see exactly what's wrong and treat it. We should really be doing that with multiple trauma, because it's so easy to miss something when there's loads going on.'

He nodded. 'If only we could, but we just don't have the resources. And as for the time issue—we lose people so often because they just get to us too slowly.'

'Oh, they do. We have the golden hour. They have the platinum ten minutes—they fly out a consultant-led team, scoop them up and bring them back and they're treating them aggressively before the helicopter's even airborne. Every soldier carries a tourniquet and is trained to use it in an emergency, and it's made so much difference. They save ninety per cent of multiple trauma patients, where in the rest of the world we save about twenty per cent. And I realised that if Joe died despite everything they were able to throw at him, it was because he was unsaveable. That was quite cathartic.'

He nodded slowly. 'I can imagine it would be. So, will you go again?'

'No,' she said softly. 'I'm glad I went, because it helped me let go of Joe, but I've done it now, and I've said goodbye and I've left the TA. I need to move on. I have other goals now.'

A baby, for one.

He went quiet for a while, then turned his head and looked at her searchingly.

'So how come you aren't working at the moment?'

She gave him a fleeting smile and looked away again. 'I wondered if you'd ask that. I could blame it on Saffy, say she'd taken a lot of time, a lot of training, and in a way it's true, but really she's just an excuse. I guess I was—I don't know… Taking time out to regroup, maybe? I worked solidly for the first year after he died, and I didn't give myself time to think, and then I went off to Afghanistan and put even more pressure on myself. That was a mistake, and by the time I got back after Christmas I was wiped. I needed time just to breathe a bit and work out where I go from here. A bit of a gap year, in a way. So I took it—or a few months, anyway. Just to try and make some sense of it.'

She made herself meet his eyes again, and found a gentle understanding in them.'Yeah. I did that after Cathy died. Took a gap year and grabbed the world by the throat, trying to make sense of it.'

'Did it help?'

He thought back to the aching emptiness, the people he'd met who'd scarcely registered in the haze of grief that had surrounded him. 'No. I don't know. Maybe. Maybe not. It took me away from it, but when I came back it was still there, lurking in wait. The grief, the loneliness.'

It was the closest he'd ever got to talking about Cathy, so she pushed a little more, to see if he'd open up further.

'She had cancer, didn't she?'

The shadows in his eyes darkened. 'Yes. One minute she was fine, the next she was dying.'

Connie felt her heart ache for him. 'Oh, James. It must have been dreadful watching that.'

He could see her now, the image crystal clear, pale as a ghost against the crisp white sheets, trying to smile at him, the small, neat curve of her doomed pregnancy so prominent in that thin frame.

'It was,' he said simply.

They reached the lane then, and he led the way, walking in single file for a while, facing the oncoming traffic.

Convenient, she thought, since it meant they couldn't talk. Far from opening up, he'd shut down again, so she left him alone, just following on behind until they reached the sea wall again and turned left towards the harbour and the little community clustered around the river mouth.

As they drew nearer they passed a house, a sprawling,

ultra-modern house clad in cedar that had faded to silver. It was set in a wonderful garden on the end of the little string of properties, and there were children playing outside on the lawn, running in and out of a sprinkler and shrieking happily, and a woman with a baby on her hip waved to him.

He waved back, and turned to Connie as they walked on. 'That's Molly. She and her husband used to own my house. They outgrew it.'

'I should think they did. There were a lot of children there.'

'Oh, they're not all hers,' he said with a fleeting smile. 'The baby's theirs and she's got a son of about twelve, I think, and they've got another little one. The others will be her sister-in-law's. They didn't want to move away from here, but with two children and room for her painting they were struggling for space, as you can imagine, and then that house came on the market and David pounced on it.'

'It's an amazing house. They must have had a stash of cash somewhere or a lottery win.'

He chuckled, the sombre mood seeming to slip away. 'Oh, it didn't look like that when they bought it, but I don't think they're exactly strapped. David's a property developer and he part-owns a chain of boutique hotels in Australia. His father's a local building contractor, and they extended the house massively. She's got a great studio space and gallery there, and they've done a lovely job of it. They're nice people. Good neighbours.'

She wondered what it must be like to live in one place long enough to get to know your neighbours. She'd moved so much with Joe, shifting from one base to another, never putting down roots, and it hadn't been much better in her childhood. She envied James the stability of his life, even if he was alone. Not that she knew that for sure, she reminded herself.

He cut down off the sea wall to his garden gate and held it for her. 'Right, I need a shower, and then shall we go over to the pub? I haven't had anything but those cookies since breakfast and I'm starving.'

'Me, too, but I need to feed the dog. You take the bathroom first.'

'No need. I've got my own upstairs.'

She felt the tension she'd been unaware of leave her. So, no sharing a bathroom, no awkward moments of him tapping on the door or her being caught in the hall with dripping hair.

Heavens, what was wrong with her? This was *James*!

'Half an hour?' he suggested.

'That's fine. I'll feed Saffy first.'

He disappeared up the stairs, and she fed the dog and put her in the crate, not taking any chances while she was getting ready to go out. This would *not* be the diplomatic time to find out that Saffy could, indeed, open the door of the fridge.

She put her hair up in a knot and showered quickly, then contemplated her clothes. She hadn't really brought anything for going out, it hadn't occurred to her, but it was only the pub and she'd got a pretty top that would do. She put it on over her cropped jeans, let her hair down and then put on some makeup. Not much, just a touch of neutral eyeshadow, a swipe of mascara and a clear, shimmery lipgloss. Just enough to hide behind.

'Stupid woman,' she muttered. They were going to the local pub for a quick meal to make up for the fact that Saffy had stolen the steak. It wasn't an interview, and it sure as hell wasn't a date.

Not even remotely!

So why did she feel so nervous?

She looked gorgeous.

She wasn't dressed up, but she'd put on a little bit of makeup and a fine, soft jersey top that draped enticingly over her subtle curves.

She wasn't over-endowed, but she was in proportion, and when she leant forward to pick up her drink the low neckline fell away slightly, just enough to give him a tantalising glimpse of the firm swell of her breasts cradled in lace.

Fine, delicate lace, the colour of ripe raspberries.

He hauled his eyes away from her underwear and sat back, propping an ankle on the other knee to give his unruly body a little privacy. God, what was *wrong* with him?

'So, what are you going to eat?' he asked, studying the menu even though he knew it by heart.

'I don't know. What's good?'

'All of it. I eat here fairly often, and there's always something new on. The specials are worth a punt, but if you don't fancy anything on the board there's a good menu.'

She swivelled round to look at the board, arching backwards so she could get a better view, and the top pulled tight over those lace-clad breasts.

Raspberry lace, the fruit inside them ripe and soft and full, he thought, and almost groaned out loud.

'Do they do good puds?'

An image of her eating the cookies with such relish popped into his head, and gave a slightly strangled chuckle. 'Yes,' he said, feeling doomed. 'They do brilliant puds. Save room.'

'Just what I was thinking.'

'Yeah. It wasn't hard to read your mind. I can hear it from here.'

She turned back, the top sliding back into place and settling down, and he breathed a tiny sigh of relief.

Regret?

Hell, Slater, pull yourself together!

'I think I'll have the shell-on prawns.'

He might have known. Now he'd have to spend the whole meal watching her sucking her fingers while the juice ran down her chin. He was beginning to think the steak at home might have been easier...

'That was amazing. Thank you. I wish you'd let me pay.'

'Why? I invited you to stay.'

'And you bought steak,' she pointed out, still feeling guilty, 'and my dog ate it.'

He gave a wry smile. 'And I should have put it in the fridge.'

'OK, I give up, have it your way, I'll pay next time,' she said with a laugh, and they headed up the gravel track away from the pub, cut across to the sea wall and went back along the top. She paused for a moment, looking out over the estuary, absorbing the scene. It felt oddly romantic, standing there with him as the evening sun slanted across the marshes behind them and turned everything to gold. Absurdly romantic. Crazy. This was James—

'Slack water. The tide's just on the turn. Look—the boats are swinging at anchor.'

He pointed back upriver, and she nodded, watching the fishing boats and little cabin cruisers trying to make up their minds which way to point. 'It's so peaceful. Joe said it was lovely here. No wonder you bought the cottage.'

'It was just lucky it came up when I was looking. Properties down here are pretty rarely on the market, and they have a ridiculous premium, but I fell in love with it.'

'I'm sure. I can see why. Was the cabin there?'

'Oh, yes. I wouldn't have added it, I simply don't need it. Molly used to use it for paying guests. That was how she met David, apparently, and then after they were married she used it as her studio. I just sling the garden furniture in it for the winter, which seems a wicked waste. I put a bed in there in case I ever needed to use it, and there's even a small shower room, but I'm hardly short of guest rooms,' he said drily, 'and anyway, I don't seem to have time for entertaining these days. Life is more than a tad hectic at work.'

'So what's this staffing problem?' she asked.

'Oh, one of the ED consultants had a brain tumour last autumn and he's been off for months. He's only recently come back part time, and he's decided he wants to keep it like that, which would be bad enough without him going off on paternity leave any minute now, but that's just the usual ongoing nightmare. Finding someone to cover the other half of his rota permanently is much more of a problem. Decent well-qualified trauma specialists are hard to find; they aren't usually kicking about without a job, and even if they are, they don't want to work part time, and we're on a bit of limb here out in the back end of Suffolk.'

'Really?' she said, surprised. 'But it's gorgeous here, and anyway, you wanted to do it so why not other people?'

'It was a golden opportunity for me. I'd had a consultancy, it was a chance at a clinical lead job in a small department, a brilliant rung on the ladder—it was perfect for me, so perfect I might just stay here forever.'

And she guessed he didn't care where he lived because he had no ties. Fewer, even, than her, because she at least had a dog now. James had nothing.

They got back to the cottage and she took Saffy out for a little walk along the sea wall to stretch her legs, then settled down with the dog on the veranda, soaking up the last rays of the evening sun while James made the coffee.

He came out, slid the tray onto the table as he sat down and eyed her thoughtfully. 'You OK?'

'Mmm. Just basking in the sun. It's lovely here. I could stay forever just chilling out.'

'Well, if you haven't got any ties, why don't you stay on for a bit, have a break? God knows I've got the space.'

'A break from what? I'm not doing anything. Anyway, I

can't. I've got to go back to my friend's house and pack it up because she's home in a couple of weeks and I need to find myself a job and another house to live in. It's time to get back to reality and frankly I'm running out of money.'

He eyed her thoughtfully. He'd already told her that people of her calibre were hard to find, especially ones who would work part time. Would she consider it? Locum for him part time, and chill out the rest?

'Are you sure you're ready to work?'

'Yes. Absolutely.'

I am, she realised suddenly, and she felt as if a weight had been lifted off her. *I'm ready now, more than ready. Ready to move on, to start my life again in every way.*

'In which case, do you want the locum job?'

She sat bolt upright and turned to stare at him. 'What?'

'The locum job—the other half of Andy's job. Just for a while, to ease yourself back in. You could stay here, in the cabin if you wanted, if I give it a bit of a scrub. It would be perfect for you and Saffy, and when you felt ready or we got someone else, you could move on. It would give you time to work out what you're going to do, to look for a job properly without any haste, no strings, no rent, no notice period. Well, a week or two might be nice, but not if it compromised an opportunity, and you could have the cabin for as long as you want.'

She searched his face for clues, but there were none. 'Why are you doing this?' she asked, perplexed.

He laughed. 'Why? *Why?* Haven't you been listening? I can't get a locum for love or money. Andy's about to go off on paternity leave, and I'm already pretty much covering half his workload already. I can't do the other half. I need you, Connie, I genuinely need you. This isn't charity, we're desperate, and if you're really ready to start again, you'd be saving my life.'

She thought about it, considering it carefully. It would be so easy—too easy?

'Decent pay?'

'Yes, absolutely. It's a consultant's post. This is a straightforward offer, Connie, I'm not just being nice to you. There is just one condition, though.'

She searched his eyes, and they were serious, not a hint of a smile.

'Which is?'

He looked away. 'I can't do the baby thing,' he said, his voice oddly expressionless. 'I would help you if I could, but I can't, so please don't ask me again.'

She nodded slowly. No. She'd realised that. Just not why.

'Can you tell me why?' she asked softly. 'Just so I can understand? Because plenty of women have babies on their own and manage fine, so that just doesn't make sense to me that that's the reason.'

'It does to me,' he said firmly.

'Why? I would have been bringing up the baby mostly anyway, even if Joe was still alive. Is it because you don't trust *me*?'

'Oh, Connie, of course I trust you, but you couldn't just hand your baby over to me and let me get on with it, could you? So how can you expect me to do it for you?'

'Because you don't want a baby,' she said, as if it was obvious. 'You've said that. You said you don't want a child, that it's never going to be on your agenda. You don't want to be involved, but that's fine, because it would be *my* baby! All you'd have to do is—well, you know what you'd have to do,' she said, blushing furiously and looking away. 'I'd be the one to carry it, to give birth to it, to bring it up—'

'No. It would be *our* baby, my son or daughter,' he told her, the words twisting his insides. 'I would insist on being involved right from the beginning, whether I wanted to or not, and I can't do that. Please, Connie, try and understand. It's not that I don't trust you, I just don't want the emotional involvement and the logistics of it are a nightmare. We'd have to live near each other, which probably means I couldn't stay here, and I like it here. I'm settled. It's taken me a long time to reach this point, and I don't want that to change. I just want peace.'

She nodded slowly, her eyes filling. 'No—no, I can see that. I'm sorry. It's a lot to ask, to be that involved with me, I see that.'

He sighed. 'It isn't that. And anyway, there's still the possibility that another man will come along and snap you up. Look at you, Connie—you're gorgeous. You'll find someone, someday, and I don't know how I'd feel about another man being involved with bringing up my child if you got married again.'

'We've had this conversation. I won't get married again.'

'You don't know that.'

She gave him a keen look that seemed to slash right to the heart of him. 'You seem to.'

He looked away. 'That's different.'

'Is it? You don't seem to have moved on in the nine years I've known you, James. You're still single, still shut down, still alone, and it's not because you're hideous or a lousy catch. You're not. Women must be throwing themselves at you. Don't tell me you don't notice. Or is there someone? A woman in your life? I didn't even think of that before, but is that why? Because there's some woman lurking in the wings who might not like it?'

'There's no woman in my life, Connie,' he said quietly, feeling curiously sad about it all of a sudden. 'I don't do relationships. They get demanding. People have expectations, they want more than I'm prepared to give, and I can't and won't meet them. So, no, there's nobody who's got any right to have an opinion. It's entirely my decision and that's the way it's staying. I'm not interested in dating.'

'Why?'

Because they're not you.

He closed his eyes briefly. 'This is irrelevant. The point is, there's more to bringing up children than I've got time to commit to, and I don't want to go there. I don't know if we'll feel the same way about things, and we have to be able to compromise when we disagree, trust each other's judgement. We have to like each other, even when the chips are down and the gloves are off, and I don't know if we can do that.'

That shocked her. 'You don't like me?' she asked, feeling gutted, because it was the one thing that had never occurred to her, but he shook his head instantly.

'Connie, don't be ridiculous, of course I like you. I've always liked you. It's just such a significant thing, so monumental, and I just don't think I can do it. And I don't want you building your hopes up, allowing yourself to imagine that this is all going to work out in the end, because it's not. So, there you have it. You wanted to know why I can't help you. That's why.'

She lifted her shoulders slightly. 'So that's it, then. I go down the anonymous donor route,' she told him simply.

He held her eyes for a moment, then looked away, hating the idea, unwilling to confront the reality of her doing what she'd said. Watching another man's child grow inside her, knowing it could have been his.

No. That was never going to happen. The immediate future was bad enough, though, the prospect of being close to Connie for weeks or maybe even months with this ridiculous longing for her, this burning need occupying his every waking thought. Could he do it without losing his mind?

'Fair enough. It's your decision. So, will you still take the job?'

He could feel her eyes on him, and he turned his head and searched them.

'Yes. Yes, I will. Why not? I need a job and somewhere to live. You need a locum, I'm certainly qualified enough, and the cabin would be brilliant. It would be great for Saffy, and it would give us both privacy and enough space to retreat if we get on top of each other. It would be perfect.'

He didn't want to think about them getting on top of each other; the images it brought to mind were enough to blow his mind. But she was right, it would be perfect for her and the dog, and it would solve his staffing crisis. And despite him telling her he wouldn't talk about it and couldn't do it, it would give him a chance to get to know her, to understand her motivations for wanting a baby.

So he could give her the child she so desperately wanted?

Panic clawed at him. Hell, what on earth was he getting himself into? The very thought of his child growing in her body made his chest tighten with long-buried emotions that he really didn't want to analyse or confront. But...

'So?' she prompted. 'Do we have a deal?'

He met her eyes, and she saw the tension in his face, the reluctance, the hesitation, and something else she didn't really understand, some powerful emotion that scared her slightly because it was the closest she'd ever come to seeing inside his soul. It was so raw, so elemental, and she was about to tell him to forget it when he nodded his head.

Just once, slowly.

'OK. Do the locum thing, but I don't want to hear another word about this baby idea. OK?'

'OK. So—can I look at this cabin?'

He gave a short huff of laughter. 'Um—yeah, but it's not exactly pristine. I haven't even opened the door for months.'

'Well, no time like the present,' she said cheerfully, putting her mug down. 'Come on. Where's the key?'

'Right here.'

He unhooked it from the back of the kitchen door and went down the steps and across the lawn, put it in the lock and swung the door open, flicking on the light to dispel the gathering dusk.

'Wow.'

He looked around and winced. Maybe he should have left the light off. 'I'll clear it out and give it a good clean. It's a tip.'

'No, it's fine. OK, it's a bit dusty, but it's lovely! Oh, James, it'll be perfect!'

He studied it, trying to see it through her eyes, but all he could see was the garden furniture stacked up against the wall and the amount of work he'd have to do to clean it up.

'I don't know about perfect, but you're right, it would be ideal for you and the dog. We could easily rig up a small kitchen area, a kettle and toaster, something like that. I can get you a small fridge, too.'

'Are you sure?'

Was he? Probably not, but he'd said he'd do it now so how could he change his mind and let her down? The enthusiasm in her eyes was enough to cripple him.

'Yes, I'm sure,' he said gruffly. 'When do you want to start?'

Well, she wasn't getting what she'd come for, but he'd taken a lot of the stress and worry out of the next few weeks at a stroke, and she supposed she should be thankful for that.

And she'd be working with James again, after all this time. She'd never thought she'd do that again, and the prospect was oddly exciting.

She'd loved working with him nine years ago. He'd been a brilliant doctor and a skilful and patient mentor and she couldn't wait to work with him again. And she was looking forward to getting back to normality, to real life. Not the strange and somehow dislocated life of an army wife trying to keep her career going despite the constant moves, or the empty and fruitless life of a woman widowed far too young and unfulfilled, but real life where she could make her own decisions.

She'd thought about it all night, lying awake in that beautiful bedroom listening to the sound of the sea sucking on the shingle, the rhythm curiously soothing. She'd had to go down and let Saffy out in the middle of the night, and once she'd settled her she'd curled up in the chair in the bedroom window staring out over the moonlit sea and hoping she wouldn't let him down.

Not that there was any reason why she should, of course. She was a good doctor, too, and she had confidence in herself. And if he didn't want to give her a child, felt he couldn't do it—well, he had the right to do that. It was a shame, though, because he was perfect for the job. Intelligent, good looking, funny, kind to animals, he could make amazing coffee…

He'd make someone a perfect husband, if only he wasn't so set against it. What a waste. But that was his business, his decision, his choice to make. And when it came to the baby thing, there were other ways, other avenues to explore.

Except maybe, of course, if she was working alongside him, he might change his mind—

She'd stopped that train of thought right there, gone back to bed and tried to sleep, but it had been pointless and she'd got dressed and come downstairs shortly before six, let Saffy out again and made herself a cup of tea, taking it out onto the veranda and huddling up on the bench waiting for James to wake up.

She'd agreed to come back down to Yoxburgh in two weeks, when Andy was due off on paternity leave, and all she had to do was go back to Angie's house and pack her things and come back. She didn't have much to pack. Most of her stuff was in store, flung there in haste after Joe died when she'd had to move out of the married quarters; she still had to go through it properly, but that task would keep until she had somewhere permanent.

Somewhere for her and a baby?

She pressed a hand to her chest and sucked in a breath, and Saffy got to her feet and came and put her nose against her arm, nuzzling her.

'Oh, Saffy. I wonder where we'll end up?' she murmured, and then she heard sounds behind her and James appeared in a pair of jeans and bare feet, looking tousled and sleepy and more sexy than a man of forty-two had any right to look.

Sheesh. She yanked her eyes away from his bare chest and swallowed hard.

'Morning,' she managed, and he grunted.

'Coffee?'

'Please. Just a straight, normal coffee.'

'That's all you get at this time of day. It's too early for party tricks.'

He walked off again, going back into the house and leaving her on the veranda, and she let out the breath she'd been holding and stared up at the sky. Wow. How had she never *noticed* before?

Because you were in love with Joe. Why would you notice another man? You had a husband who was more than man enough for you!

But—James was every bit as much a man as Joe had been, in his own way, and anyway, she had noticed him, all those years ago when she'd first met him. She'd asked about him hopefully, and been told about Cathy. Not that anyone knew very much, just that his wife had died and he didn't talk about it.

Didn't talk about anything except work, really, and didn't date as far as anyone knew, but then one weekend she'd been out with friends and bumped into him in a bar, and he'd introduced her to Joe.

And that was that. Joe with his wicked smile and irrepressible sense of humour had swept her off her feet, and she'd fallen hook, line and sinker. Now she was back to square one, noticing a man who still wasn't interested, who was still shut down, closed off from life and love and anything apart from his work.

A man she'd tried to talk into agreeing to something that he was obviously deeply reluctant about—

'Hey, what's up?'

He set the coffee down on the table in front of her and she looked up at him, searching his eyes for the reticence that had been there last night, but there was none, just gentle concern, so she smiled at him and reached for her coffee, telling herself she was relieved that he'd pulled a shirt on.

'Nothing,' she lied. 'I'm fine—just a bit tired. I didn't sleep very well—it was too quiet and all I could hear was the sound of the sea.'

'I can't sleep without it now,' he said wryly, dropping down beside her on the bench and fondling Saffy's ears. 'So, how was your night, Saffy? Find anything naughty to do in the cage?'

'She was fine. I came down at three and let her out because I could hear her whining, but I think she just wanted reassurance.'

'I heard you get up.'

So he hadn't slept, either. Wondering what he'd let himself in for?

Nothing, she reminded herself. They were just going to work together, and the baby conversation—well, it was as if it had never happened. They'd just opened the door on the subject, that was all, and he'd shut it again.

Only, maybe, it would never be the same again. Whatever

happened now, that door had been opened, and she sensed that it would have changed something in the dynamic of their relationship.

'Connie? I'm sorry I can't help you.'

How did he know what she was thinking? Could he read her mind? Or perhaps, like her, it was the only thing *on* his mind?

She nodded, and he reached out a hand—a large, square hand with strong, blunt fingers—and laid it gently over her wrist.

'Whatever happens, whatever you decide to do, I'll always be here for you,' he said quietly. 'I promised Joe I'd take care of you if anything happened to him, and I will, and if you decide to take the clinic route and have a baby, I'll still be here, I'll still support you in your decision even if I don't agree with it. You won't ever be alone. Just—please, don't be hasty.'

'Oh, James…'

Her eyes filled with tears, and she put her coffee down and sucked in a shaky breath.

He stared at her in dismay. Hell. Now he'd made her cry.

'Hush, Connie, hush,' he murmured, gathering her against his chest. 'It's OK. I didn't mean to make you cry. Come on, now. It's all right. It'll be OK.'

'Why are you so damn nice?' she said unsteadily, swiping tears out of her eyes and wondering why his chest felt so good to rest her head against. She could stay there all day in his arms, resting her face against the soft cotton of his shirt, inhaling the scent of his body and listening to the steady thud of his heart while he held her. It had been such a long time since anyone had held her, and it had been him then, too, after Joe's funeral.

He'd held her for ages, letting her cry, crying with her, and nobody had held her since. Not really. She'd had the odd hug but nothing like this, this silent support that meant more than any words.

But she couldn't stay there all day, no matter how tempting, so she pulled herself together, swiped the tears away again and sat up.

'So what about this breakfast then?' she asked, her voice uneven, and he gave a soft laugh and leant back, his arm along the bench behind her.

'Drink your coffee and let me have mine. I can't function this early, I need a minute. And don't talk. Just sit and relax and stop worrying. I can hear your mind from here.'

Sound advice. She didn't think it had a hope in hell of working, but she was wrong. The distant sound of the shingle sighing on the beach, the drone of bees in the honeysuckle, the whisper of the wind in the tall grass beyond the garden— all of it soothed her, taking away the tension and leaving her calm and relaxed.

Or was that the touch of his hand on her back, the slow, gentle circling sweep of his thumb back and forth over her shoulder blade? She closed her eyes and rested her head back against the wall of the house, and felt something that had been coiled tight inside her for so long slowly give way.

CHAPTER FOUR

HE WATCHED HER sleep, his arm trapped behind her, unable to move in case he disturbed her.

And he didn't want to disturb her, because as long as she was sleeping he could watch her.

Watch the slight fluttering of her eyelashes against her faintly flushed cheeks, still streaked with the dried remnants of her tears. Watch the soft rise and fall of her chest with every breath, and hear the gentle sigh of air as she exhaled through parted lips that were pink and moist and so damn kissable it was killing him.

He looked away, unable to watch her any longer, unable to sit there with his arm around Joe's wife and lust after her when she'd been entrusted to his care.

And he'd actually agreed to let her come and live with him and locum in the department? He must have been mad. He'd have to sort the rota so that they worked opposing shifts—not that that would help much, but at least she was living in the cabin rather than the house. And that was essential because if he didn't keep his distance, he wasn't sure he could keep these deeply inappropriate feelings under wraps.

And he needed to start now.

He shifted his hand a fraction, turning his thumb out to take it off her shoulder blade, and she rolled her head towards him, those smoky blue eyes clear and unglazed.

She hadn't been asleep at all, apparently, just resting her eyes, but now they were open and she smiled at him.

'Can I speak yet?' she asked cheekily, her mouth twitching, and he laughed and pulled his arm out from behind her, shifting slightly away to give himself some much-needed space.

'If you can manage not to say anything contentious.'

'I don't know what you mean.'

That taunting smile playing around her mouth, she sat up straighter, moving away from him a little more, and he had to remind himself that that was good.

'I was going to say, if I'm going to be working with you here, it might be an idea if I knew what I was signing up for.'

He nodded, knowing exactly what kind of exquisite torture *he* was signing up for, but the exit door on that had slammed firmly shut already so analysing why he'd done it was purely academic. He was already committed to the emotional chaos and physical torment that was bound to come his way with having her underfoot day in, day out. He must have been mad to suggest it.

'Sure. Want a guided tour of the hospital?'

'That would be good. Can we have breakfast first? I'm starving.'

He gave a soft huff of laughter and stood up, taking the empty coffee cup from her and walking back inside, and she watched him go and let out an almost silent groan.

How could she be so *aware* of him? OK, it had been a while, but—James? Really? Not that there was anything wrong with him, far from it, but there was more than good looks and raw sex appeal in this. There was his relationship with Joe—*her* relationship with Joe—and she knew for him that would be a massive issue.

And Joe had made him promise to take care of her? Trust him. Trust Joe to pile that kind of responsibility on his friend, but she reckoned he would have become her self-appointed guardian anyway regardless of what Joe might have said, because he was just like that, so she'd just have to learn to live with it and make very, very sure he got no hint of her feelings.

Not that she knew what they were, exactly.

A flicker of interest?

OK, more than a flicker, then, a lot more, but of what? Lust?

No. More than that. More than a flicker, of more than lust. And that was deeply scary. This situation was complicated enough without this crazy magnetic attraction rearing its head.

She got to her feet and stuck her head round the kitchen door. 'Want a hand?'

'No, I'm fine.'

'Right. I'll take Saffy for a quick run. Ten minutes?'

'Barely. Don't be longer.'

'I won't.'

She shoved her feet into her abandoned trainers, put Saffy's lead on and escaped from the confines of James's garden. She ran along the river wall this time, retracing their footsteps of the day before beside the remains of the old rotting hulks, their ribs sticking up like skeletons out of the mud of the little natural inlets in the marshy river bank.

The smell was amazing—salt and mud and fish, all mingled together in that incredible mix that reminded her of holidays in Cornish fishing villages and sailing in the Solent in her childhood.

Wonderful, evocative smells that brought back so many happy memories. And the sounds—amazing sounds. The clink of halliards, the slap of wavelets on the undersides of the moored boats, the squeak of oars in rowlocks, the putter of an outboard engine.

And the gulls. Always the gulls, wheeling overhead, keening their sad, mournful cry.

The sunlight was dancing on the water, and the tide had just turned, the boats swinging round so they faced down-river as the water began surging up the estuary with the rising tide. She stood and watched for a moment as the last of the boats swung round and settled on their moorings.

Just twelve hours, she thought, since they'd watched this happen together. Twelve hours ago, she'd had no idea of what her future held, just a flat no to her request for a baby and a massive question mark hanging over her next job, next home, all of it. Yet in the past twelve hours all that had become clearer, her immediate future settled and secure if not in the way she'd hoped.

Unless he changed his mind? Unlikely, but just in case, she'd make sure she kept a lid on her feelings and kept them to herself, and then maybe...

She glanced at her watch, and yelped. She was going to be late for breakfast, and he'd told her not to be longer than ten minutes. She had three to get back, and she made it with seconds to spare.

He was propped up in the doorway, arms folded, legs crossed at the ankle, and his lips twitched.

'Close,' he said, glancing at his watch, and she smiled, hands propped on her knees, her breath sawing in and out.

'Sorry. I was watching the tide turn. I could watch it all day.'

'Well, four times, anyway. Scrambled or fried?'

She straightened up, chest heaving, and grinned, oblivious of the effect she was having on him. 'Scrambled.'

Like his brains, he thought desperately, watching her chest rise and fall, the wild tangle of blonde hair spilling over her shoulders, the faint sheen of moisture gilding her glowing skin—

'Can I do anything?'

'Yes,' he said blandly. 'Get the dog out of the kitchen. She's eyeing up the sausages.'

They left, and he braced his hands on the worktop, breathed in and counted to ten, then let the air out of his lungs on a whoosh and turned his attention to the eggs.

Working with her, all day, every day, and having her here at home? For months?

It was going to kill him.

'This is such an amazing building.'

'Isn't it? It's all a front, of course, all this beauty, and it hid a hideous truth. Apparently it used to be the pauper lunatic asylum.'

'How frightfully politically correct.'

He grinned wryly. 'Not my words. That's the Victorians for you. Actually it was a workhouse taking advantage of the inmates, and I'd like to be able to say it's moved on, but in the last few months I've wondered.'

'Ah, poor baby. That'll teach you to be clinical lead.'

He rolled his eyes and punched her arm lightly. 'Do you want this job or not?'

'Is this a formal interview?'

He laughed. 'Hardly. Any qualified doctor with a pulse would get my vote at the moment. The fact that you've got all the necessary and appropriate qualifications and outstanding experience to back them up is just the cherry on top. Trust me, the job's yours.'

'I'm not sure I'm flattered.'

'Be flattered. I'm fussy who I work with. That's why there isn't anyone. We're round here in the new wing.'

He drove round the corner of the old building and pulled up in a marked parking bay close to the ED, and her eyes widened.

'Wow. That's a bit sharper. I did wonder if we'd be working by gas light.'

'Hardly,' he said with a chuckle. 'We're very proud of it—of the whole hospital. It was necessary. People living on the coast were having to travel long distances for emergency treatment, and they were dying—back to your platinum ten minutes, I guess. We can treat them much quicker here, and if we have to we can then refer them on once they're stable. That said we can do most stuff here, but it's not like Camp Bastion.'

'Hopefully it doesn't need to be,' she said quietly, and he glanced down and saw a flicker of something wounded and vulnerable in her eyes and could have kicked himself.

'Sorry. I didn't mean to drag it all up.'

'It's OK, it's never far away.' She gave him a too bright and very fleeting smile. 'So, talk me round your department, Mr Clinic Lead Slater.'

He took her in via Reception so she could see the triage area where the walking wounded were graded according to severity, and then went through into the back, to the row of cubicles where the ambulance cases were brought directly.

'We've got four high dependency beds where we can keep people under constant observation, and we can accommodate three patients in Resus at any time. It's not often idle.'

They stood at the doors of Resus and watched a team working on a patient. It looked calm and measured. A man looked up and smiled at James through the glass, waggling his fingers, and he waved back and turned to her. 'That's Andy. He's been damn lucky. He had an awake craniotomy and had to talk through it to make sure his speech centre wasn't damaged when they removed the meningioma, but the post-op swelling gave him aphasia. He lost his speech—nothing else. He could understand everything, all the words were on the tip of his tongue, he just couldn't find them, but of course he couldn't work until he got his speech back, and he was tearing his hair out for weeks.' He grinned wryly. 'So was I, because there was no guarantee he ever would recover completely.'

'You still are, aren't you? Tearing your hair out, trying to replace half of him?'

He shrugged. 'Pretty much. It's a bit frustrating trying to get anyone decent all the way out here, but he's brilliant and getting anyone as good as him is just not possible on a part-time contract. And no,' he said with a smile, holding a finger up to silence her, 'before you say it, that's not a criticism of you, because I know you've got bigger fish to fry and you aren't here for the long haul. I wish to God you were. You'd solve all my problems at a stroke.'

Well, not quite all. Not the one of having enough distance between them so that he wasn't being constantly reminded of just how damned lovely she was and how very, very inaccessible.

Not to mention asking the impossible of him…

The door to Resus opened and Andy came out, his smile a little strained. 'Hi. Did you get my text?'

'Your text?' he said, getting a bad feeling.

'Yes. Lucy rang. She says she's in labour and she doesn't hang about. I'm just about to bail, I'm afraid.'

He swore silently, closed his eyes for a moment and then opened them to find Connie smiling knowingly.

'Yes,' she said.

He let out something halfway between a laugh and a sigh and introduced them. 'Connie, this is Andy Gallagher. Andy, this is Connie Murray. I worked with her several years ago, and she was obviously so inspired by me she became a trauma specialist.'

Andy eyed her hopefully. 'Tell me she's our new locum.'

'She is, indeed, as of—well, virtually now. Say hello to her very, very nicely. She wasn't due to start for a fortnight.'

'Oh, Connie—I'm so pleased to meet you,' Andy said fervently, his shoulders dropping as a smile lit up his face. 'I thought I was about to dump a whole world of stuff on James, so to know you're here is such a relief. Thank you. From the bottom of my heart. And his,' he added with a grin. 'Probably especially his.'

This time James gave a genuine laugh. 'Too right. You'll be out of here in ten seconds, if you've got any sense, and utterly oblivious to the chaos you're leaving in your wake, which is exactly how it should be. Go. Shoo. And let us know the minute it's born!'

'I will!' Andy yelled over his shoulder, heading out of the department at a run.

James let his breath out on a low whistle and pushed open the door of Resus. 'You guys OK in here, or do you need me?'

'No, we're all done. He's on his way to ICU. They're just coming down for him.'

'OK, Andy's gone but I'm around, page me if you need me. Pete's on later, and I'll be in tomorrow morning first thing. Oh, and this is Connie Murray. She's our new locum, starting tomorrow. Be really, really nice to her.'

They all grinned. 'You bet, Boss,' one of them said, and they all laughed.

He let the door shut, turned to Connie and searched her eyes, still not quite able to believe his luck.

'Are you really OK with this?'

'I'm fine,' she said, mentally running through the logistics and counting on her fingers. 'Look, it's eleven o'clock. I can get home, grab my stuff and be back here by eight tonight at the latest. That'll give me three hours to pack and clean the house, and it won't take that long.' She hoped. 'Can you cope with Saffy if I leave her? I can't get her and all my stuff in the car.'

'Sure. She can help me scrub out the cabin.'

'Yeah, right. Just don't let her run off,' she warned as they walked briskly back to the car.

'I won't. Don't worry, Connie, the dog's the least of my problems. You saw that cabin.'

She ignored him. 'Put her in the crate if you have to go back to the hospital,' she said as she put on her seat belt. 'She's used to it. And she has a scoop of the dry food twice a day, morning and evening, so you might need to feed her if I'm held up in traffic—'

He stopped her, his hand over her mouth, his eyes laughing. 'Connie, I can manage the dog. If all else fails, I'll bribe her with fillet steak.'

She left almost immediately when they got back to the cottage, and as she was getting in the car he gave in to impulse and pulled her into his arms and hugged her.

'Thank you, Connie. Thank you so much. I'm so, so grateful.'

'I'll remind you of that when I'm driving you crazy,' she said with a cheeky grin, and slamming the door, she dropped the clutch, spraying gravel in all directions. 'See you later!'

'Drive carefully,' he called after her, but she was gone, and he watched her car until she'd turned out onto the road and headed away, the imprint of her body still burned onto his.

'Well, Saffy,' he said softly as he went back into the garden and shut the gate firmly. 'It's just you and me, old thing, so no running off. Shall we go and have a look at this cabin?'

It was worse than he'd thought.

Dirtier, dustier, mustier. Oh, well, he could do with a bit of hard physical graft. It might settle his raging libido down a bit after that innocent hug.

He snorted. Apparently there was no such thing as far as his body was concerned.

He threw open all the windows and the doors, took everything including the bed outside and blitzed it. He vacuumed the curtains, washed the windows, mopped the walls and floors, slung the rug over the veranda rail and bashed it with a broom to knock the dust out before he vacuumed it and returned it to the now dry floor, and finally he reassembled it all, stripped the bedding off the bed upstairs and brought it all down and made up the bed.

And through it all Saffy lay there and watched him as if butter wouldn't melt in her mouth. He trusted her about as far as he could throw her, but she seemed content to be with him, and once it was all tidy and ready for Connie's return, he took her out for a walk, picking up his phone on the way.

And he had a message, a text with a picture of a new baby. Very new, a mere two hours old, the caption reading, 'Daniel, eight pounds three ounces, both well'.

He felt something twist inside him.

'Congratulations!' he texted back, and put the phone in his pocket. Saffy was watching him closely, head cocked on one side, eyes like molten amber searching his face.

'It's OK, Saffy,' he said, rubbing her head, but he wasn't sure it was. Over the years countless colleagues had had babies, and he'd been happy for them. For some reason this baby, this time, felt different. Because the possibility was being dangled in front of his nose, tantalising him?

The possibility of being a father, something he'd thought for the past eleven years that he'd never be? He'd said no to Connie, and he'd meant it, but what if he'd said yes? What if he'd agreed to give her a child?

A well of emotion came up and lodged in his chest, making it hard to breathe, and he hauled in a lungful of sea air and set off, Saffy trotting happily at his side as he broke into a jog.

He ran for miles, round the walk he'd taken Connie on yesterday, but with a detour to make it longer, and Saffy loped easily along at his side. He guessed she ran with Connie—another thing they had in common, apart from medicine? Maybe.

He wondered what else he'd find. Art? Music? Food he knew they agreed on, but these were irrelevancies. If he'd agreed to her suggestion, then she'd be bringing up his child, so he would have needed to be more concerned with her politics, her attitude to education, her ability to compromise. It didn't matter a damn if they both liked the same pictures or the same songs. It mattered if she thought kids could be taken out of school in the term time to go on holiday, something he thought was out of the question. How could you be sure they wouldn't miss some vital building block that could affect their entire future?

And what on *earth* was he doing worrying about that? He'd said no, and he'd meant it! He had! And anyway, there were bigger things to worry about. Things like his ability to deal with the emotional minefield that he'd find himself in the moment her pregnancy started to manifest itself—

'What pregnancy?' he growled, startling Saffy so that she missed her stride, and he ruffled her head and picked up the pace, driving on harder to banish the images that flooded his mind.

Not images of Cathy, for once, but of Connie, radiant, glowing, her body blooming with health and vitality, the proud swell of her pregnancy—

He closed his eyes and stumbled. Idiot.

He stopped running, standing with one hand on a fence post, chest heaving with emotion as much as exertion. This was madness. It was hypothetical. He'd said no, and she was going to a clinic if she did anything, so nothing was going to happen to her that involved him.

Ever.

But that just left him feeling empty and frustrated, and he

turned for home, jogging slowly now, cooling down, dropping back to a walk as they hit the sea wall and the row of houses. And then there was Molly, out in the garden again with David and their children, and he waved to them and Molly straightened up with a handful of weeds and walked over.

'So who's your friend?' she asked, openly curious as well she might be, because he hardly ever had anyone to stay, and certainly never anyone single, female and as blatantly gorgeous as Connie.

'Connie Murray. She's a doctor. I've known her for years, she was married to a friend of mine.'

'The one who died? Joe?'

He nodded. 'She's going to be here for a while—she's taking the locum job I've been trying to fill, and she'll be living in the cabin.' He got that one in quick, before Molly got any matchmaking ideas, because frankly there was enough going on without that.

But it didn't stop the little hint of speculation in her eyes.

'I'm glad you've got someone. I know you've been working crazy hours, we hardly ever see you these days.' She dropped the weeds in a bucket and looked up at him again. 'You should bring her to my private view on Friday.'

'That would be nice, thanks,' he said, fully intending to be busy. 'I'll have to check the rota, though.'

'Do that. And change it if necessary. No excuses. You've had plenty of warning. We told you weeks ago.'

He gave a quiet mental sigh and smiled. 'So you did.'

She laughed and waved him away. 'Go on, go away. We'll see you on Friday at seven. Tell her to wear something pretty.'

He nodded and turned away, walked the short distance to his house while he contemplated that sentence, and let Saffy off the lead in the garden.

She found her water bowl on the veranda while he was

doing some stretches, drank noisily for a moment and then flopped down in the shade under the bench and went to sleep, so while she was happy he ran upstairs and showered, then on the way down he gathered up Connie's things from her bedroom, Molly's words still echoing in his head.

Tell her to wear something pretty.

Like the top she'd worn last night which was lying on the chair, together with the raspberry red lace bra and matching lace shorts that sent his blood pressure into orbit? Or then there were her pyjamas. Thin cotton trousers and a little jersey vest trimmed with lace. They were pretty, but nothing like substantial enough to call pyjamas, he thought, and bundling them up with the other things, he grabbed her wash bag out of the bathroom and took them all down to the cabin.

Saffy was still snoozing innocently, so he topped up her water bowl, filled a glass for himself and drained it, then put the kettle on to make tea and sat down with the paper and chilled out.

Or tried to, but it seemed he couldn't.

Connie would be back in a very few hours, and from then on his space would be invaded. He wasn't used to sharing it, and having her around was altogether too disturbing. That lace underwear, for example. And the pyjamas. If he had to see them every morning—

He got up, prowling round the garden restlessly, and then he saw the roses and remembered he'd been going to put flowers in her room yesterday, but he'd run out of time.

So he cut a handful and put them in a vase on the chest of drawers and went back to reading the paper, but it didn't hold his attention. The only thing that seemed to be able to do that was Connie.

And going to Molly's private view with her just sounded altogether too cosy. And dangerous. He wondered what pretty actually meant, and how Connie would interpret it. He was rather afraid to find out.

But how the hell could he get out of it?

It didn't take long to pack up her things.

Much less than the three hours she'd allowed, and because she'd cleaned the house so thoroughly on Sunday there was nothing much to do, so she was back on the road by three-thirty and back in Yoxburgh before six.

She wondered if James would be around, but he was there, sitting on the veranda in a pair of long cargo shorts with Saffy at his feet, reading a newspaper in the early evening sun.

He folded it and came down to the gate, leaning on it and smiling as she clambered out of the car and stretched.

'You must drive like a lunatic.'

She laughed softly and shook her head. 'That was Joe. I'm not an adrenaline junkie. There was practically nothing to do.'

And not that much in the way of possessions, he thought, looking at the back of her small SUV. Sure, it was packed, but only vaguely. She handed him a cool box out of the front footwell. 'Here, find room for that lot in the fridge,' she said, locking the car and coming through the gate to give Saffy a hug. 'Hello, gorgeous. Have you been a good girl?'

Saffy wagged her tail and leaned against her.

'She's been fine. We went for a run.'

'Oh, she will have enjoyed that! Thank you. She loves it when we run.'

'She seemed to know the drill.'

'What, don't stop in front of you to sniff something so you fall over her? Yeah. We both learned that one the hard way.'

He laughed and carried the cool box up to the kitchen, shocked at the lightness in his heart now she was back, with her lovely smile and sassy sense of humour.

'So how did you get on with the cabin?' she asked, following him up the steps to the kitchen.

'OK, I suppose. It's clean now, but I'm sure you'll want to do something to it to make it home.'

He turned his head as he said that, catching a flicker of something slightly lost and puzzled in her expression, and could have kicked himself.

Home? Who was he kidding? She hadn't had a proper home for ages now, not since she'd met Joe. They'd moved around constantly from one base to another, and she'd had to move out of the married quarters pretty smartly after he'd died. By all accounts she'd been on the move ever since, living in hospital accommodation in the year after Joe died, then out in Afghanistan, then staying with a friend. It was only one step up from sofa-surfing, and the thought of her being so lost and unsettled gutted him.

But the look was gone now, banished by a smile. 'Can I put my stuff straight in there?'

'Sure. I'll put Saffy in her crate, so she doesn't run off while the gate's open. The door's not locked.'

Connie opened the cabin door, and blinked. The dust was gone, as was the stack of garden furniture, and it was immaculate. He'd made the bed up with the linen she'd had last night, and her pyjamas were folded neatly on the pillow, her overnight bag on the bed. She stuck her head round the bathroom door and found her wash things on the side, and when she came back out she noticed the flowers on the chest of drawers.

Roses from the garden, she realised, and a lump formed in her throat. He hadn't needed to cut the roses, but he had, to make her welcome, and the room was filled with the scent of them.

It was the attention to detail that got to her. The careful way he'd folded her pyjamas. The fact that he'd brought her things down at all when it would have been so easy to leave them there.

'I hope you don't mind, I moved your stuff in case you were really late back, so you didn't have to bother.'

'Mind? Why should I mind?'

And then she remembered she'd left yesterday's clothes on the chair—her top, her underwear. Yikes. The red lace.

Don't be silly. He knows what underwear looks like.

But she felt the heat crawl up her neck anyway. 'It looks lovely,' she said, turning away so he wouldn't see. 'You've even put flowers in here.'

'I always put flowers in a guest room,' he lied, kicking himself for doing it in case she misinterpreted the gesture. Or, rather, rumbled him? 'I would have done it yesterday but I ran out of time. Give me your car keys, I'll bring your stuff in.'

She handed them over without argument, grateful for a moment alone to draw breath, because suddenly, with him standing there beside her and the spectre of her underwear floating in the air between them, the cabin had seemed suddenly airless.

How on earth was she going to deal with this? Thank God they'd be busy at work, because there was no way she could be trusted around him without him guessing where her feelings were going, and there was no way she was going to act on them. He was a friend, and his friendship was too important to her to compromise for something as fleeting and trivial as lust.

'So where do you want this lot?'

He was standing in the doorway, his arms full, and she groped for common sense.

'Just put everything down on the floor, I'll sort it out later.'

She walked past him, her arm brushing his as he turned, and she felt a streak of heat race through her like lightning.

Really? *Really?*

This was beginning to look like a thoroughly bad idea…

CHAPTER FIVE

'SUPPER AT the pub?'

She straightened up from one of the boxes and tried to read his eyes, but they were just looking at her normally. Odd, because for a second there—

'That would be great. Just give me a moment to sort out some work clothes for tomorrow and I'll be with you.'

'Do you want the iron?'

She laughed. 'What, so I make a good impression on the boss?'

He propped himself up on the doorframe and grinned mischievously. 'Doesn't hurt.'

'I think I'll pass. I'll just hang them up for now and do it when we've eaten—if I really have to. Have you fed Saffy?'

'Yes, just before you got back. She seemed to think it was appropriate.'

'I'll bet,' she said with a chuckle, and pulling out a pair of trousers and a top that didn't cling or gape or otherwise reveal too much, she draped them over the bed and gave up. 'Right, that'll do for tomorrow. Let's go. I'm starving, it's a long time since breakfast.'

'You haven't eaten since breakfast? You're mad.'

'I just sort of forgot.'

'You emptied the fridge. There was food in your hands. How could you forget?'

Because she'd been utterly distracted by the thought of what she was doing? Because all she could think about was that she was coming back here to James, taking the first step towards the rest of her life?

'Just call me dozy,' she said, and slinging a cardi round her shoulders in case it got cold, she headed for the door.

They took Saffy with them and sat outside in the pub garden, with the lead firmly anchored to the leg of the picnic bench in case a cat strolled past, and he went in to order and came back with drinks.

'So, what time are we starting tomorrow?' she asked, to distract herself from the sight of those muscular, hairy legs sticking out of the bottom of his shorts. Definitely a runner—

'Eight, technically, but I'd like to be in by seven. You can bring your car and come later if you like. I'll sort you out a parking permit.'

'I can do seven,' she said. 'I'll have to walk Saffy first, and I'll need to come back at lunchtime to let her out and give her a bit of a run so I'll need my car anyway, if you can sort a permit for me that soon. Will that be all right?'

'That's fine. I don't expect you to work full time, Connie. I know you've got the dog, I know you haven't worked since you got her and I know I can't leave her indefinitely. I expect HR will want to check all sorts of stuff with you before they let you loose on a patient anyway, so there's no point in being too early. I take it you've brought the necessary paperwork?'

'Oh, sure. I've got everything I need to show them. So, did you hear from Andy? Is there any news?'

'Ah. Yes. He sent me a text.'

'And?'

'It's a boy,' he said, the words somehow sticking in his throat and choking him. 'Daniel. Eight pounds three ounces. Mother and baby both doing well.'

'Did he send a picture?'

'Of course.' And she would want to see it, wouldn't she? He pulled his phone out of his pocket and found the text, then slid it across to her. 'There.'

'Oh—oh, James, he's gorgeous. What are the others?'

'Girls. Three girls. Emily, Megan and Lottie.'

'And now they've got their boy. Oh, that's amazing. They must be so thrilled.'

'Yeah.' He couldn't bring himself to speculate on their delight, or debate the merits of boys or girls. It was all too close to home, too close to the reason she was here—and the very reason he didn't want her here at all.

No, that was a lie. He did want her here. Just—not like this. Not for why she'd come, and not feeling the way he did, so that he had to be so damn guarded all the time in case he gave away how he felt about her. And if he could work *that* one out for himself he'd be doing well, because frankly at the moment it was as clear as mud.

'So, tell me about this friend you've been staying with,' he said, changing the subject without any pretence at subtlety, and after a second of startled silence, she cleared her throat.

'Um. Yeah. Angie. Long-time friend. We worked together a couple of times. She's been in Spain for a few months visiting family but she's back in a week or so—I really ought to write to her and thank her for lending me the house. It's been a lifesaver. Getting a rented place with a dog is really hard, especially a dog like Saffy.'

She pricked up her ears at her name, and James reached down and rubbed her head. She shifted it, putting her chin on his foot and sighing, and he gave a wry chuckle.

'I can imagine. I thought you and Joe had bought somewhere?'

'We had. It's rented out, on a long lease. The tenant's great and it pays the mortgage.'

'So why not live there?'

She shrugged. 'It was where we were going when he came out of the army. It was going to be our family home, where we brought up our children.'

And just like that, the subject reared its head again. James opened his mouth, shut it again and exhaled softly.

'Don't say it, James. I know we aren't talking about it, I was just stating a fact.'

'I wasn't going to.'

'Weren't you?'

He shrugged. The truth was he hadn't known what to say, so he'd said nothing.

'Two sea bass?'

He sat back, smiled at the waitress and sighed with relief.

'Saved by the bass,' Connie said drily, and picking up her knife and fork, she attacked her supper and let the subject drop.

HR wanted all manner of forms filled in, and it was driving her mad.

She was itching to get to work now, if only to settle her nerves. She'd been away from it too long, she told herself, that was all. She'd be fine once she started. And then finally the forms were done.

'Right, that's it. Thank you, Connie. Welcome to Yoxburgh Park Hospital. I hope you enjoy your time with us.'

'Thanks.'

She picked up her bag and legged it, almost but not quite running, and made her way to the ED. She found James up to his eyes in Resus, and he glanced up.

'Cleared for takeoff?' he asked, and she nodded.

'Good. We've got an RTC coming in, nineteen year old male pedestrian versus van, query head, chest and pelvic injuries and I haven't got anyone I can spare. Do you feel ready to take it?'

She nodded, used to being flung in at the deep end as a locum. 'Sure. Where will you be, just in case I need to check protocol?'

'Right here. Don't worry, Connie, I won't abandon you. I won't be much longer here.'

She nodded again, and he pointed her in the direction of the ambulance bay. She met the ambulance, took the history and handover from the paramedics, and by the time they were in Resus she was right back in the swing of it.

'Hi, there, Steve,' she said to the patient, holding her face above his so he could see her without moving. 'I'm Connie Murray, and I'm the doctor who's going to be looking after you. Can you tell me where you are?'

'Hospital,' he said, but his voice was slurred—from the head injury, or the morphine the paramedics had given him? She wasn't sure, but at this stage it was irrelevant because until she was sure he wasn't going to bleed out in the next few minutes the head injury was secondary.

'OK. Can you tell me where it hurts?'

'Everywhere,' he mumbled. 'Legs, back—everything.'

'OK. We'll soon have you more comfortable. Can we have an orthopaedic consultant down here, please? This pelvic fracture needs stabilising, and can we do a FAST scan, please? We need a full trauma series—do we have a radiographer available? And a total body CT scan. I need to know what's going on here.'

She delegated rapidly, and the team working with her slipped smoothly into action, but throughout she was conscious of James at the other end of the room keeping an ear open in case she needed backup.

The X-rays showed multiple fractures in his pelvis, and the FAST scan had shown free fluid in his abdomen.

She glanced up and he raised an eyebrow.

'Do we have access to a catheter lab? I think he's got significant vascular damage to the pelvic vessels and I don't want to wait for CT.'

'Yes, if you think it's necessary. What are his stats like?'

'Awful. He's hypotensive and shocky and the ultrasound is showing free fluids in the abdomen. He's had two units of packed cells and his systolic's eighty-five and falling. We need to stop this bleed.'

'OK. Order whatever you need. I won't be a tick.'

He wasn't. Moments later, he was standing opposite her across the bed, quietly taking his cues from her and nodding to confirm her decisions.

And when they'd got him stable and shipped him off to the catheter lab for urgent vascular surgery prior to a CT scan to check for other injuries, he just smiled at her and nodded. 'You've learned a lot since I last saw you in action.'

'I'd hope so. It's been more than eight years.' Years in which she met, married and lost his best friend.

'I always said you had promise. It's nice to see you fulfilling your potential.'

Crazy that his praise should make her feel ten feet tall. She knew she was good. She'd worked with some of the best trauma surgeons in the world, she didn't need James to tell her.

And yet somehow, those few words meant everything to her.

'Want me to talk to the relatives?' he asked, but she shook her head.

'No, I'm fine with it. Come with me, though. I might need to direct them to where they can wait.'

'OK.'

They spoke to the relatives together; she explained the situation, and James filled in the details she'd missed—the name of the orthopaedic surgeon, where the ward was, how long it might take, what would happen next—and then as they left the room he looked up at the clock and grinned.

'Coffee?'

'I've only just started work!'

'You can still have coffee. I'm the boss, remember? Anyway, it's quiet now and it won't last. Come on. I reckon we've got ten seconds before the red phone rings.'

'How far can we get?'

'Out of earshot,' he said with a chuckle, and all but dragged her out of the department.

They ended up outside in the park, sitting on a bench under a tree, and she leant back and peeled the lid off her cappuccino and sighed. 'Bliss. I'm going to like working here.'

He snorted rudely. 'Don't run away with the idea that it's always like this. Usually we don't have time to stop.'

'The gods must be smiling on us.'

James laughed and stretched out his legs in front of him, ankles crossed. 'Don't push your luck. How did you get on with HR?'

'I've got writer's cramp.'

He laughed again and took a long pull on his coffee. 'That good, eh?'

'At least. I hate paperwork.'

'So don't ever, ever find yourself winding up as clinical lead,' he said drily, just as his pager bleeped. He glanced at it, sighed and drained his cup. 'Duty calls.'

'Really?' She sighed, took a swallow of her coffee and burnt her tongue.

'That's why I never have a cappuccino at work,' he said, getting to his feet. 'It takes too long to cool down. Bring it with you. I can hear a siren.'

And just to punctuate that, his bleep went off again.

She followed him, coffee in hand, and she almost—almost—got to finish it by the time it all kicked off again.

He sent her home at one to let Saffy out, and she walked back in to the news that the pedestrian had died of his head injury.

'You're kidding me,' she said, the colour draining from her face. 'Oh, damn it. Damn it.'

And she walked off, back rigid, her face like stone. He couldn't follow her. He was up to his eyes, about to see a relative, but as soon as he was free he went to look for her.

He found her under the tree where they'd had their coffee, staring blindly out across the grass with the drying tracks of tears down her cheeks.

'Why did he have to die?' she asked angrily. 'My first patient. Why? What did I do wrong, James?'

He sat down next to her and took her hand in his. It was rigid, her body vibrating with tension.

'You didn't do anything wrong. You know that.'

'Do I?' she said bitterly. 'I'm not so sure.'

'Yes, you are. We can't save everyone.'

'But he died of a head injury. All I was worried about was stopping him bleeding out, and all the time it was his head I should have been thinking about.'

'No. His pelvic injury was horrific. If you'd sent him for CT before he was stable, he would have bled out and died anyway. You did what you had to do, in the order you had to do it, and he didn't make it. It was a no-win situation. Not your fault. I wouldn't have done anything different, and neither would Andy.'

'But he was nineteen,' she said, her voice cracking. 'Only nineteen, James! All that wasted potential—all the effort and time put into bringing him up, turning him into a young man, wiped out like that by some idiot—'

'He had headphones in his ears. He wasn't listening to the

traffic. It wasn't the van driver's fault, and he's distraught that he hit him. He's been hanging around waiting for news, apparently, and he's devastated.'

Connie turned her head and searched his eyes. 'It was Steve's fault? Are you sure?'

'Apparently so, according to the police. And it certainly wasn't your fault he died.'

She looked away again, but not before he saw the bleakness in her eyes. 'It feels like it. It feels like I let him down.'

'You didn't, Connie. You did your best with what you were given, that's all any of us can do.' He pressed her hand between his, stroked the back of it with his thumb. 'Are you OK to go back in there, or do you need some time?'

'No. I'm fine,' she said, even though she wasn't, and tugging her hand back she got to her feet and walked away.

He followed slowly, letting out his breath on a long sigh, and found her picking up a case in cubicles. He said nothing, just laid a hand on her shoulder briefly and left her to it, and at five he found her and told her to go home.

'James, I'm fine.'

'I don't doubt it, but you're supposed to be part-time and Saffy's been in the cage long enough. Go home, Connie,' he said gently. 'I'll be back at seven.'

She went, reluctantly, because she didn't want to be alone, didn't want to go back to the empty house and think about the boy she'd allowed to die.

Instead she worried about Saffy, because the cabin was in full sun and she should have thought of that. Another layer of guilt. What if the dog was too hot? What if she'd collapsed and died?

She hadn't. She let her out of the crate the moment she got home, and Saffy went out to the garden, sniffed around for a few minutes, had a drink and flopped down under a tree in the shade.

Connie poured herself a drink and joined her, fondling her ears and thinking about her day.

She was still angry with herself for losing Steve, but she knew James was right. She'd done everything she could, and you couldn't save everyone. She knew that, too. She'd had plenty of evidence.

She went into the cabin and changed into shorts and a sleeveless vest, slid her feet into her trainers and took Saffy for a run. Anything to get away from the inside of her head.

She went the other way this time, up the sea wall, along the lane and back along the river, and as she reached the beginning of the river wall she saw another runner up ahead of her.

It stopped her in her tracks for a moment, because he'd lost one leg below the knee and was running on a blade. Ex-military? Possibly. Probably. So many of them ended up injured in that way.

Or worse. She'd spoken to the surgeon who'd gone out to Joe in the helicopter, and he'd told her about his injuries. And she'd been glad, then, for Joe, that he'd died. He would have hated it.

The man veered off at the end of the path, and she carried on at a slower pace, cooling down, then dropped to a steady jog, then down to a walk as they reached the end of the path.

Molly was there with the children, the baby in a buggy, a little girl of three or four running giggling round the grass chasing a leggy boy of twelve or so. Happy families, Connie thought as Molly smiled at her.

'Hi there. You're Connie, aren't you? It's nice to meet you properly. So, are you coming on Friday to my private view?'

She stared blankly, and Molly rolled her eyes.

'He hasn't mentioned it, has he?' Connie shook her head, and she tutted and smiled. 'Men. He probably hasn't even told you I'm an artist. Seven o'clock, Friday night, our house. We'd love to see you.'

'Thanks. I'd love to come. I love art exhibitions, even though I can hardly hold a pencil. I haven't seen the rota yet, but if I'm not on, it would be great. Thank you.'

'I told James to change the rota. He'd better have done it. And I also told him to tell you to wear something pretty.'

She blinked. 'Pretty? How pretty?'

'As pretty as you like,' Molly said, deadpan, but there was a subtext there Connie could read a mile away, and she wondered if Molly was matchmaking. She could have saved her the trouble. James wasn't interested in her. He wasn't interested in anything except work. He certainly wasn't interested in babies.

'I'll see what I've got,' she said, and towed Saffy away from the little girl who'd given up chasing her brother and was pulling Saffy's ears gently and giggling when she licked her. 'I'd better get back, I need to feed the dog, but I'll see you on Friday and I'll make sure James changes the rota.'

'Brilliant. We'll see you then.'

She walked away, glancing back in time to see the runner with the blade join them. David? Really? He swept the little girl up in his arms and plonked her on his shoulders, and her giggle followed Connie up the path, causing an ache in her heart.

They looked so happy together, all of them, but it obviously hadn't been all plain sailing. Was it ever? And would she find that happiness, or a version of it, before it was too late?

Maybe not, unless James changed his mind, and frankly she couldn't really see that happening. She trudged up the steps to the veranda and took Saffy in to feed her.

'So how was the cabin last night?' he asked as she plonked the salad bowl down on the newly evicted garden table. 'You haven't mentioned it so I imagine it wasn't too dreadful. Unless it was so awful you can't talk about it?'

'No, not at all, it was fine. Very nice, actually. It's good to have direct access to the garden for Saffy, although I have to admit she slept on the bed last night. I'm sorry about that.'

'I should think so. Shocking,' he said, his eyes crinkling with amusement.

Connie frowned. 'She's not supposed to,' she said sternly. 'She's supposed to have manners.'

The crinkles turned to laughter as he helped himself to the salad. 'Yeah. I'm sure she is. She's not supposed to steal, either, but I wouldn't beat yourself up over it. The family dog slept on my bed his entire life, and then his successor took over.'

'Well, I don't want Saffy doing that. She's too big and she hogs the bed.'

'She can't be worse than Joe. I remember sharing a tent with him in our teens. Nightmare.' And then he looked at her, rammed a hand through his hair and sighed sharply. 'Sorry. That was tactless.'

'True, though. He did hog the bed. At least the dog doesn't snore.' She twiddled her spaghetti for a moment, then glanced up at him. 'James, about earlier. I know it wasn't my fault Steve died. I was just raw. It was just—so wrong.'

'It's always wrong. Stuff happens, Connie. You know that.'

She held his gaze for a long time, then turned slowly away. 'I know. I'm sorry I got all wet on you.'

'Don't be. You can always talk to me.'

'You can talk to me, too,' she pointed out, and he looked up from his plate and met her eyes. His smile was rueful.

'I'm not good at talking.'

'I know. You weren't nine years ago, and you haven't got better.'

'I have. Just not at the talking.'

'I rest my case.'

'Physician, heal thyself?'

She held his eyes. 'Maybe we can heal each other.'

His gaze remained steady for an age, and then he smiled sadly.

'I wish.'

'Will you tell me about her?' she asked gently. 'About how she died?'

Could he? Could he find the words to tell her? Maybe. And maybe it was time he talked about it. Told someone, at least, what had happened.

But not yet. He wasn't ready yet.

'Maybe one day,' he said gruffly, then he got up and cleared the table, and she watched him go.

Would he tell her? Could he trust her enough to share something so painful with her?

It was a nice idea. Something from cloud cuckoo land, probably. There was no way James would have let anyone in in the past, and she wasn't sure he'd changed that much.

He stuck his head back out of the kitchen door.

'Coffee?'

'Lovely. I'll have a flat white, since you're offering.'

She heard the snort as his head disappeared back into the kitchen, and she smiled sadly. She could hear him working, hear the tap of the jug, the sound of the frother, the sound of Saffy's bowl skidding round the floor as he fed her something. Probably the leftover spaghetti. She'd like that. She'd be his slave for life if she got the chance.

The light was fading, and he paused on the veranda, mugs in hand. 'Why don't you put Saffy on a lead and we'll take our coffee up on the sea wall? It's lovely up there at night.'

It was. The seagulls were silent at last, and all they could hear was the gentle wash of the waves on the shingle. The sea was almost flat calm, and the air was still.

Saffy lay down beside him, her nose over the edge of the wall, and they sat there side by side in the gathering dusk drinking their coffee and listening to the sound of the sea and just being quiet.

Inevitably her mind went back over the events of the day, and sadness came to the fore again.

'How are Steve's parents going to feel, James?' she asked softly. 'How will they get over it?'

'They won't. You don't ever get over the loss of a child. You just learn to live with it.'

It was too dark to read his expression but his voice sounded bleak, and she frowned.

He'd never had a child. She knew that. And yet—he sounded as if he understood—really understood, in the way you only could if you'd been through it. Or perhaps he knew someone who had.

And maybe he was just empathetic and she was being ridiculous.

She was about to change the subject and tell him she'd seen David and Molly when he started to speak again.

'It's probably time I told you about Cathy.'

She sucked in a quiet breath. 'Only if you want to.'

He made a sound that could have been a laugh if it hadn't been so close to despair, but he didn't speak again, just sat there for so long that she really thought he'd changed his mind, but then he started to talk, his voice low, hesitant as he dug out the words from deep inside.

'She wasn't well. She felt sick, tired, her breasts were tender—classic symptoms of early pregnancy, so she did a test and it was positive.'

'She was pregnant?' she whispered, and felt sick with horror. 'Joe never told me that—!'

'He didn't know. He was away at the time and I didn't tell anyone. Anyway, there wasn't really time. She was nearly twelve weeks by the time she realised she was pregnant, and she was delighted, we both were, but she felt dreadful. By sixteen weeks I thought she ought to be feeling better. She'd been to see the doctor, seen the midwife, been checked for all the normal pregnancy things, but she was getting worse, if anything. So she went back to the doctor, and he referred her to the hospital for tests, and they discovered she'd got cancer. They never found the primary, but she was riddled with it, and over the next six weeks I watched her fade away. She was twenty-two weeks pregnant when she died.'

Too soon for the baby to be viable. She closed her eyes, unable to look at him, but she could hear the pain in his voice, in every word he spoke, as raw as the day it had happened, and the tears cascaded down her cheeks.

His voice was so bleak, and she could have kicked herself. He'd lost a child, albeit an unborn one, and she felt sure he still grieved for it. No wonder he hadn't wanted to help her have a baby. How must he have felt when she'd blundered in and asked him to help her?

Awful.

He must have been plunged straight back there into that dreadful time. Not that it was ever far away, she knew from experience, but even so.

She shook her head, fresh tears scalding her eyes. 'I'm sorry,' she said softly, 'so, so sorry. I should never have asked you about the baby thing. If I'd known about Cathy, if I'd had the slightest idea that she was pregnant, I would never have asked you—never—'

His hand reached out in the darkness, wiping the tears from her cheeks, and he pulled her into his arms and held her.

'It's OK. You weren't to know, and I'm used to it, Connie. I live in a world filled with children. I can't avoid the subject, try as I might.'

'No. I guess not, but I'm still sorry I hurt you so much by bringing it up.'

'But you did bring it up, and because of that you're here,

and maybe you're right, even if I can't make that dream come true for you, maybe we can help each other heal.'

'Do you think so?' she asked sadly, wondering if anything could take away a pain that great.

'Well, I'm talking to you now. That's a first. I didn't tell anyone. I didn't want their pity. I didn't want anything. I lost everything on that day. My wife, my child, my future—all at once, everything was gone and I wanted to die, too. There was no way I could talk about it, no way I could stay there. I had nothing to live for, but I was alive, and so I packed up the house, sold it, gave everything away and went travelling, but it didn't really help. It just passed the time, gave me a bit of distance from it geographically and emotionally, and I worked and partied my way around the world. And all the time I felt nothing. A bit of me's still numb, I think. I guess you can understand that.'

She nodded. 'Oh, yes. Yes, I can understand that. It's how I felt after Joe died—just—nothing. Empty. Just a huge void. But at least you had the chance to say goodbye. That must have been a comfort.'

'No. Not really,' he said softly, surprising her. 'I didn't even have the chance to say hello to our baby, never mind goodbye, and with Cathy—well, you can't ever really say goodbye I don't think, not in any meaningful way, because even though you know it's happening, you still hope they might be wrong, that there's been a mistake, that there'll be a miracle cure. You just have to say the things you need to say over and over, until they can't understand any more because the drugs have stolen them from you, and then you wait until someone comes and tells you they've gone, and even then you don't believe it, even though you were sitting there watching it happen and you knew it was coming.'

She nodded. 'I did that with Joe,' she told him softly. 'I didn't watch him die, but from the moment I met him I waited for it, knowing it was coming, unable to say goodbye because I kept hoping it wouldn't be necessary, that it wouldn't happen, and in the end it took almost seven years. I always knew I'd lose him, just not when, so I never did say goodbye.'

He sighed and took her hands with his free one, folding them in his, warming them as they lay in her lap. 'I should never have introduced you. You could have been happily married to someone else, have half a dozen kids by now, not be here like this trying to convince me to give you the child you wanted with Joe.'

'I won't ask you again. I feel dreadful—'

'Shh.' He pressed a finger to her lips, then took it away and kissed her, just lightly, the slightest brush of his lips on hers. 'It's OK, Connie. Truly. I'd rather you'd come to me like that than call me one day and tell me you'd been to a clinic and you were pregnant. At least this way I'm forewarned that it's on the cards.'

'I'm sorry you don't approve.'

'It's not that I don't approve, Connie. I just don't want you to make a mistake, to rush into it.'

'It's hardly a rush. We started trying four years ago. That's a lot of time to think about it.'

'I wish I'd known.'

'I wish you'd known. I wish we'd known about Cathy. Maybe we could have helped you.'

'We'll have to look after each other, then, won't we?'

Could they? Maybe. She sucked in a breath and let it go, letting it take some of the pain away.

'Sounds like a plan. I saw Molly's husband today, by the way, out on a run,' she went on, after a long and pensive silence. 'I didn't know he'd lost his leg. Is he ex-army?'

'No. He got in a muddle with a propeller in Australia.'

'Ouch. Some muddle.'

'Evidently. He doesn't let it hold him up much, though. I

run with him sometimes and believe me, he's pretty fit. Oh, and incidentally, Molly's having a private view on Friday. She wants us to go.'

'Yes, she mentioned it. She said she'd told you to tell me.'

'Sorry. Slipped my mind,' he said, but she had a feeling he was lying.

'So, how's the rota looking for Friday?' she asked lightly.

He turned his head, the moon coming out from behind the clouds just long enough for her to see the wry grin. 'Don't worry, I'll be there and so will you. And Molly said wear something pretty, by the way.'

She grinned back at him, feeling the sombre mood slip gently from her shoulders, taking the shadows of the past with it. 'Is that you or me?' she teased.

He chuckled, his laugh warm, wrapping round her in the darkness of the night just like the arm that was still draped round her shoulders, holding her close. 'Oh, I think you do pretty rather better than me,' he said softly, and she joined in the laughter, but something in his voice made her laugh slightly breathless.

She looked up at him, their eyes meeting in the pale light of the moon, and for an endless moment she thought he was going to kiss her again, but then he turned away and she forced herself to breathe again.

Of course he hadn't been going to kiss her! Not like that. Why on earth would he do that? He didn't have anything to do with women, he'd told her that, and certainly not her.

'I'll try not to let you down,' she said, her voice unsteady, and his wry chuckle teased her senses.

'Oh, you won't let me down, Connie,' he said softly, and she swallowed hard.

Was he flirting with her? Was she with him? Surely not. Or were they? Both of them?

She gave up talking after that in case it got her into any

more trouble, just closed her eyes and listened to the sea, her fingers still linked with his, his other arm still round her, taking the moment at face value.

One day at a time. One hour at a time.

Or even just a stolen ten minutes on a dark, romantic night with an old friend. Maybe more than an old friend.

Right now, tonight, she'd settle for that.

CHAPTER SIX

HE FELT SLIGHTLY shell-shocked.

He'd come home that evening uncertain of what he'd find after the rough start she'd had, and he'd walked into a warm welcome, food ready for the table, and company.

Good company. Utterly gorgeous company, if he was honest. She'd been for a run, she said, and she'd obviously showered because she smelled amazing. Her hair had drifted against him at one point, and he'd caught the scent of apples. Such a simple thing, but it made his gut tighten inexplicably.

It had been so long since anyone other than his mother or the wife of a friend had cooked for him—except, of course, that Connie *was* the wife of a friend.

Only this evening it hadn't felt like it, not really. It had felt more like two old friends who were oddly drawn to each other, sharing a companionable evening that had touched in turn on trivia and tragedy and somehow, at points, on—romance? Innuendo? A little light flirtation?

The food had been simple but really tasty, and they'd sat there over it and talked about all sorts of things. Friendship, and Joe's sleeping habits and the dog's, and how he ought to talk more. How they could help each other heal.

He still wasn't sure about the possibility of that. Some wounds, surely, never truly healed. Acceptance, he'd discovered after a while, was the new happy, and that had seemed enough—until now. And suddenly, because of Connie, he was wondering if there might be more out there for him than just this endless void.

With her?

No. That was just fantasy. Wasn't it? He didn't know, but he'd felt comfortable with her in a way he hadn't felt comfortable with anyone for years, possibly ever, and it wasn't because the subjects were comfortable, because they weren't.

They'd talked about Steve and how his parents would be feeling, and then somehow he'd found himself able to tell her about Cathy and the baby. He still couldn't quite believe that, couldn't believe he'd let her in, shared it so easily.

And it had been easy, in a way. Easier than he'd thought, although it had made her feel guilty. Still, at least now perhaps she'd understand his reluctance to discuss the baby thing, the emotional minefield that it meant for him, and it would help her understand his refusal.

Then they'd talked about Molly's private view, and her looking pretty, and he'd flirted with her. What had he been thinking about? He must have been mad, and he'd come so close to kissing her. Not the light brush of his lips on hers. That didn't count, although it had nearly killed him to pull away. But properly.

He let his breath out on a short sigh and closed his eyes. Too close. Thankfully it had been dark, just a sliver of moonlight, so maybe he'd got away with it, but Friday was going to be a trial, with her all dressed up.

He was actually looking forward to it—not to the art, he'd meant what he'd said about not needing pictures, but to seeing Connie wearing whatever she'd decided was 'pretty'.

Hell, she'd look pretty in a bin bag. She couldn't help it. The anticipation kept him on edge all night, humming away in the background like a tune stuck in his head, and when he slept, she haunted his dreams, floating through them in some gauzy confection that left nothing to the imagination.

He got up at six, had a cold shower to dowse his raging hormones and met her in the kitchen. In her pyjamas, if you could call them that, which totally negated the effects of the shower.

'You're up early,' he said, noticing the kettle was already on.

'I've been up for ages. I couldn't sleep.'

'Worrying about work?'

'No. Saffy snoring on the bed. I take back what I said about Joe, she's much worse. She really has no manners.'

He laughed then, glancing down at Saffy who was lying on the floor and watching him hopefully. Better than studying Connie in her pyjamas. It was going to kill him, having this encounter every morning.

'I haven't done anything about getting you a kettle and toaster,' he said, changing the subject abruptly. 'I'll order them today.'

'Don't do that, I've got both of them in storage. I've got all sorts of things in storage, I just haven't dealt with them. They don't give you long to move out of married quarters, and I just packed everything up and got it out of the way.'

He eyed her thoughtfully. 'Maybe you need to deal with it.'

She nodded. 'Probably. I would, if I had anywhere to put the stuff.'

'You could bring it here. Put it in a spare room. I have three, after all. You're welcome to at least two.'

'Are you sure?'

'Why not?'

'I don't know. It just seems an imposition.'

'It's no imposition. How much is there? Is it furniture as well?'

'Oh, no, I put the decent stuff into our own house and gave

the rest away. It's just personal stuff, really.' She looked troubled, and he wondered whose stuff. Joe's?

'Think about it,' he said, reaching for a pair of mugs and sticking them in front of the kettle. 'Tea or coffee?'

'Oh—tea. It's way too early for coffee. Are you going to work already?'

'Might as well. Why don't you come in at nine? There's always a rush then in Minors. I could do with someone reliable in there if you wouldn't mind.'

She gave him a wry smile. 'Is this because you feel you can't use me on the front line after Steve?'

He rolled his eyes. 'Connie, I *know* I can use you on the front line, but I need someone I can trust in Minors. And I can call you if I need to. And I will, believe me.'

'Promise?'

He met her eyes, saw the challenge in them and smiled. 'Promise.'

'Thank you. Have you made that tea yet?'

She thought she'd be bored, but actually working in Minors was busy, varied and interesting, and she found herself enjoying it.

And then he rang her, just when she was beginning to think he'd lied.

'We've got an RTC, two vehicles, mother and child in a car, and a van driver, all trapped. They need a team on site and we need to leave now. I'm in the ambulance bay.'

Her heart skipped. 'I'm on my way.'

She passed the fracture case she was dealing with to the SHO and met James in the ambulance bay. He handed her a coat that said 'DOCTOR' on the back in big letters, and they ran for the door.

'So what do we know?' she asked as the rapid response car pulled away, sirens blaring.

'Not a lot. Three casualties, one's a small child. It's not far away.'

It wasn't, ten minutes, tops, but it was a white knuckle ride and she was glad when they got there. The police were already in attendance, and an officer came over as they pulled up and got out.

'The woman in the car might have chest injuries, she's complaining of shortness of breath and pain, and we can't get to the child but it's screaming so it's alive. The car's rolled a couple of times but it's on its wheels. She swerved to avoid a cyclist and hit the van and it flipped her over into a field.'

'And the van driver?' James asked briskly. She could see him eyeing the scene and weighing up their priorities, and they could hear the child crying already.

'He's conscious, breathing, trapped by one leg but not complaining. She was clearly on the wrong side of the road and going too fast. Oh, and she's pregnant.'

Connie saw the blood drain from his face.

'Right. Connie, come with me,' he said tautly. 'The van driver'll keep till the ambulance gets here. Let's look at the mother and child. Can we get in the car?'

'Not yet. The fire crew's on its way.'

'Right.'

He wasn't impressed by what they found. It was a mess. All the windows were shattered, and the roof was bent and twisted. It wasn't going to be quick or easy to open the doors, but they could probably get in if they had to.

He crouched down and peered through the shattered glass of the driver's door, and his heart rate kicked up another notch.

The woman was pale, very distressed and covered in blood from superficial glass injuries, and he reached a hand in and touched her shoulder, smiling reassuringly—he hoped—as she turned back to face him.

'Hi there. I'm James Slater, I'm a doctor. Can you tell me your name?'

'Judith. Judith Meyers.'

'OK, Judith. Can you tell me how you're feeling? Any pain, shortness of breath, numbness, tingling?'

'Can't breathe. Banged my knee. Please, look after my little boy. Get him out—please, get him out!' She pressed her hand to her chest and gave a little wail of distress, and then tried to open the door.

'I can't get out,' she sobbed, her breath catching, and there was a blue tinge to her lips.

Damn. He straightened up and tugged the door. Nothing.

'Right, I need this door open now. Where the hell is the fire crew?' he growled.

'I can see them, they'll be here in seconds,' the police officer told him.

'Good.' He tried the handle again, tugged the door harder but it wouldn't give, and he glanced across the dented roof and saw Connie leaning in the back window.

'How does it look your end?' he called, and she pulled her head back out and shrugged.

'He's still restrained by the car seat, seems OK, moving well but I can't really assess him without getting in there. He's yelling well, though.'

He smiled thinly. 'I can hear that. Just hang on, the fire crew'll be here in a tick. Do what you can. OK, Judith, we're going to get the door open soon so we can get a better look at you, and we'll get your baby out as soon as we can, but yelling's good. What's his name?'

'Zak,' she said unevenly, her breathing worsening, and he frowned and checked her air entry again.

'OK, Connie, we've got a— Connie? What are you doing?' he asked, pointlessly, because he could see exactly what she was doing. She'd crawled into the car through the broken window and she was running her hands over Zak's limbs, oblivious to the broken glass and shattered debris on the back seat. She was going to be cut to ribbons.

'Checking the baby. He seems fine. Hey, Zak, you're all right, Mummy's just there.'

'Can you get him out?'

'Yes. He's moving well, no obvious signs of injury. Frankly I think he just needs a cuddle more than anything at the moment. He's fighting to get out but I'll need someone to take him from me. How's mum?'

'Reduced air entry on the left. Query pneumothorax. I need to fit a chest drain. Can you help me from there?'

'Not easily. Can you do it on your own?'

'I can if you can hold stuff.'

'Sure. I can do that. I'm going deaf but hey.'

By that time the fire crew was there and managed to wrench the driver's door open so he had better access, and Connie was leaning through the gap between the seats to help him when someone yelled.

'Clear the vehicle, Doc,' the fire officer in charge said quietly in his ear. 'Fuel leak.'

His heart rate went into hyperdrive, and he felt sick. He turned his head so Judith couldn't lipread. 'I can't move her yet. I need to secure her airway, get a spinal board on her and lift her out.'

'Not before we've made it safe.'

He ducked out of the car for a second. 'I can't leave her, she'll die. They'll both die, her and her unborn baby, and the baby'll die in the next few minutes if I can't secure that airway,' he said bluntly. 'Just do what you have to do and leave me to do the same.'

He stuck his head back in and met Connie's challenging eyes. 'Out,' he said, but she just shook her head.

'I'll get Zak out. Here, someone, take the baby carefully,

please!' she said, and freeing little Zak, she lifted him up to the window and handed him over, then with a wriggle she was next to him on the passenger seat, sitting on another load of broken glass and debris.

'Right, what can I do?'

'You need to get out—'

'Shut up, Slater. You're wasting time. Where's the cannula?'

He was going to kill her.

Right after he'd hugged her for staying to help him save Judith's baby. He hoped.

They'd got Judith out in the nick of time, and just moments after they'd loaded her into the ambulance the car had gone up. If it had happened sooner—

'Hey, Slater, why the long face?'

He just stared at her expressionlessly. 'Your cuts need attention.'

'Later. I'm not finished with Judith. How's Zak?'

'He's fine. Check her over, make sure the baby's all right and get an X-ray of those ribs if you can.'

'James, I can manage,' she said firmly, and turned her attention to Judith as they wheeled her into Resus.

'Hi, Judith, remember me? Connie? I'm taking you over now from James Slater, the clinical lead, because he's looking after Zak, OK? You don't need to worry about him, he seems fine but James just wants to check him out.'

'I want to see him!' she sobbed hysterically. 'Please, let me see Zak. I need to know he's all right.'

'He's all right,' James said from behind her. 'Don't worry, Judith, I'll just look at him and do a few tests and then I'll bring him over to you. You just lie still and let Connie check you over.'

Fat chance. She stopped fighting the restraints, but moved

on to another worry that was obviously eating holes in her, her hand grabbing at Connie and hanging on for dear life. 'How's the baby?' she asked, her eyes fixed on Connie's. 'Tell me it's all right, please. It has to be all right.'

'I'm going to do an ultrasound now. Cold gel coming.' She swept the head of the ultrasound over Judith's bump, and the sound of the baby's strong, steady heartbeat filled Resus.

Judith sobbed with relief, and behind her Connie heard James let out a ragged sigh.

'There you are,' Connie said with more confidence than she felt, her legs suddenly like jelly. 'Good and solid. Let me just get a look at the placenta—it's fine, no obvious signs of bleeding. How many weeks are you?'

'Thirty-one tomorrow.'

'So even if you did go into labour the baby's viable now. We just need to make sure that you don't if possible, so I want you to lie here and relax as much as you can, and I'll get an obstetrician to come down and look at you.'

She checked her thoroughly, did a full set of neuro obs, and the neck X-rays came back clear and so did the ribs.

'Any back ache? Leg pain?'

'No. Only from lying flat, and no leg pain.'

'We'll log-roll her to check and then she can come off the spinal board,' James said, appearing at her side with the little boy in his arms. 'Here, Judith, have a cuddle with your little man for a moment. He's fine.'

'Mumum,' he said, reaching out to her, and James laid him carefully down in his mother's arms.

Then he glanced up and met Connie's eyes, and she smiled at him, searching his face.

'OK?' she said softly, and his mouth twisted in a cynical smile.

'Apart from being ready to kill you,' he said, so softly that only she could hear, but it didn't faze her, it was exactly how Joe would have reacted.

She held his eyes for a moment, just long enough to say she understood, and he frowned and looked down at the mother and child snuggled up together.

'I don't want to break up the party, but could I have Zak, Judith? We need to take you off the board and check your back.'

'Oh—yes, of course. Sorry, I'm being so pathetic but I just can't believe we're all all right.'

'Don't worry, I'd expect you to be concerned. I'd worry much more if you weren't.'

Her back was fine, and apart from a few cuts and bruises and the pneumothorax, so was the rest of her. More or less.

'There's a bruise on her temple,' Connie told James, and he knew instantly that she was thinking of Steve and his head injury.

'I think we'll keep her here under observation overnight, check her head injury, keep an eye on the baby, unless you want to do it in Maternity?'

He glanced past her with a smile, and she looked up as a man in scrubs approached.

'Do what in Maternity?'

'Observe a pregnant patient overnight. Minor head injury, pneumothorax from seat belt injury, a few cuts and bruises, thirty-one weeks tomorrow, rolled the car. We've just got back from freeing her.'

'Yikes. OK. Shall I take a look at her?'

'Please. Connie, this is Ben Walker. Ben, Connie. Want to talk him through it?'

She shook his hand, introduced him to Judith and filled him in on her findings. He was gentle, reassuring and happy to have her for the night.

'Just to be on the safe side,' he said with a smile. 'I'll make sure we've got an antenatal bed for you when they're ready to transfer you.'

He turned back to James with a grin. 'So, met little Daniel Gallagher yet?'

James ignored the odd sensation in his chest. 'No. How is he?'

'Fine. Gorgeous. Lovely healthy baby. Fighting fit. They're still here—he was a little bit jaundiced so we've kept them in till this afternoon. You ought to pop up and say hello.'

He could feel that his smile was strained, but there was nothing he could do about it. 'I think we're probably a bit busy. I'm sure I'll see him soon enough. We'll send Judith up as soon as we're done with her.'

'Do that. Cheers. Nice to meet you, Connie.'

'You, too.'

Connie watched him go out of the corner of her eye, most of her attention on James. Wall to wall babies today, or so it seemed, and he wasn't enjoying it one bit. It was right what he'd said last night, he couldn't avoid it, he was surrounded by children in one way or another, and so was she. They just had to deal with it, but it didn't make it easy.

She did the paperwork for Judith's transfer, handed little Zak over to the woman's harassed husband when he arrived and then went over to James.

'Anything else I can do?'

He shook his head. 'Just get your cuts seen to,' he said tightly.

'You're welcome.'

He sighed. 'Thank you, Connie. Really, thank you. Now, please, get your cuts seen to.'

She did. They were worse than she'd realised, little nicks all over her legs and bottom from the car seats, but she wasn't worried about herself. She'd seen his face in the car, seen the tension in his shoulders in Resus until they'd heard the baby's heartbeat. He wasn't alone, everyone in there had been worried for them, and if she hadn't known about Cathy she probably wouldn't have thought anything of it, but there was just something else, another element to his concern that underlined his lingering grief.

And Andy's baby. He'd definitely not wanted to go up and see it. OK, so they probably were busy, but even if they hadn't been he wouldn't have gone. Because it hurt too much?

She changed into scrubs, because her trousers were ruined, and went back to work to carry on with her fractures and squashed fingers and foreign bodies up the noses of small children, but he was at the back of her mind for the rest of the day.

'How are the cuts?'

'I'll live.'

He snorted. 'Not for want of trying, you crazy woman. You should have got out when I told you.'

'What, and leave a pregnant woman stuck in a car that was about to blow? Not to mention you. No way was I going anywhere without both of you, so save your breath, Slater.'

'Damn you, Connie,' he growled, and with a ragged sigh he hauled her into his arms and hugged her hard. 'Don't ever do that to me again.'

'What, stand up to you?'

'Put your life in danger.'

'Don't get carried away, I didn't do it for you,' she said, leaning on him because it felt so good and she'd been worried sick about him underneath the calm.

'I know that.'

He rested his head against hers and let out a long, slow sigh. 'Thanks for staying. You were good with her. She was pretty hysterical.'

'She was scared. All I did was reassure her and try and keep her calm.'

'And you did it well. You were really good. Calm, methodical, systematic—and you didn't waste any time.'

'Well, I wonder who I got that from?' she teased, and he gave a soft huff of laughter. 'It's true,' she protested. 'I modelled myself on you. I always loved watching you work. You're funny, warm, gentle, cool as a cucumber—and terrifyingly efficient.'

He lifted his head and stared down into her eyes. 'Terrifyingly?'

'Absolutely. You were a brilliant role model, though.'

'You were a pretty good student.'

'Then I guess we're both pretty marvellous.'

He laughed softly, then the laughter died and he stared down at her mouth.

It was the lightest kiss. Fleeting. Tender, like the kiss of the night before.

The kiss of a friend?

Probably not, but it was over so soon she couldn't really assess it. She just knew it was too short.

He stepped back, dropping his arms and moving away from her, and she swayed slightly without his support.

He frowned at her. 'Have you eaten?'

'Um—no. I wasn't really hungry. I had some chocolate.'

'Nice balanced diet. Good one, Connie.'

'What about you? It's late, James. Surely you've eaten something at work?'

He shook his head. 'I'll have some cheese on toast. Want some?'

'Yeah. Just a slice.'

She followed him into the kitchen, Saffy following hopefully at her heels, and perched on the stool and watched him as he made bubbly cheese on toast, and then afterwards he found some ice cream and dished it up, and they all ate it in silence.

Too tired to talk? Or was the kiss troubling him as much as it was troubling her?

'Is there any more of that ice cream left?'

'A scraping.' He opened the freezer and handed her the plastic container. 'Here. Be my guest. Coffee?'

'Mmm. Can we take it on the wall?'

He made coffee, she scraped the ice cream off the sides of the container, licked the spoon one last time and put it in the dishwasher, and they headed to the sea wall with Saffy in tow.

'So what are you wearing tomorrow night?' he asked, trying not to think too hard about the flimsy thing in his dream and failing dismally. That kiss had been such a bad idea.

She slurped the froth off her coffee and licked her lips. 'Dunno. Define pretty in this part of the world. What do your dates wear?'

He laughed at that. 'I have no idea, Connie. You're asking the wrong person. I thought I'd told you that. I don't date, I never go out except for dinner with friends occasionally. I have absolutely no idea what women wear these days.'

She turned and studied him curiously. 'You don't date at all?' Not even for sex, she nearly asked, but shut her mouth in the nick of time.

'Not any more. After Cathy died I went a bit crazy, sort of tried to lay her ghost, but I just ended up feeling dirty and disappointed and even more unhappy, so I gave up. So, no, I don't date. Not even for that, before you ask. I was just scratching an itch, and frankly I can do that myself and it's a lot less hassle.'

Wow. She thought about that. Thought about his candid statement, and felt herself colouring slightly. It wasn't the fact, it was his frankness that had—well, not shocked her, exactly, but taken her by surprise. Which was silly, because Joe had never been coy and she'd never blushed before. Maybe it was because it was James and his sex life they were suddenly and inexplicably talking about. She changed the subject hastily.

'So—dress? Long linen skirt and top? Jeans and a pretty top? Or I've got a floaty little dress that's rather lovely, but it might be too dressy.'

Gauze. Pale, oyster pink gauze, almost the colour of your skin, with dusky highlights over the nipples and a darker shadow—

He cleared his throat. 'I don't know. It's an art exhibition. Something arty, maybe? Molly will probably wear some vintage creation.'

Please don't wear gauze.

'So who will be there?'

'Oh, all sorts of people. David's family and the people he works with, his old friends, some of the doctors. They asked me to spread the word and gave me some invitations to hand out, but how many of them will come I don't know. Andy and Lucy Gallagher probably won't, with a three day old baby, but they might because they were seriously interested, and Ben and Daisy wanted to come because they've done up their house and they're looking for artwork for it. Otherwise I'm not sure. The movers and shakers of Yoxburgh society, I imagine.'

She gave a little splutter of laughter. 'Does Yoxburgh society have movers and shakers?' she asked, slightly incredulously.

'Oh, yeah. David's probably one of them. His family own that hotel and spa on the way in, near the hospital site. The big one with the Victorian facade.'

'Wow. That's pretty smart.'

'It is. Ben and Daisy got married there and it was lovely.'

'Is that the Ben I met today?'

'Yes. Daisy's an obstetrician, too, but I think she's pretty much on permanent maternity leave and she's loving every minute of it, apparently. They've got two little ones and Ben's got an older daughter.'

Another happy family twisting the knife. Yet it was interesting, she thought, that all of his friends seemed to be family-orientated. To replace his own family? He had no one. Like her, he was an only child, and he'd lost both his parents in his twenties, and then he'd lost Cathy and the baby. And if that wasn't enough, he'd lost Joe, his closest friend. He must be so *lonely*, she thought. She knew she was. It was why she'd brought Saffy home, and part of the reason she wanted a baby, to have someone of her own to love.

'Why are you frowning? You look as if you disapprove.'

'No. Not at all. I was thinking about my clothes,' she lied glibly.

But Saffy was lying propped against him, her head on his lap, and he was fondling her ears absently as he sipped his coffee and stared out over the darkening sea. Maybe she should give Saffy to him? She seemed to adore him. At least that way he wouldn't be alone. Or she could stay with him, and they could live together and have a family and all live happily ever after.

And she was in fantasy land again.

'I could sit here all night,' she said to fill the silence, and he gave a slightly hollow laugh.

'Sometimes I do. You know, on those nights when you can't sleep and things keep going round and round your head? I don't know what it is—the sound of the sea, maybe. It just seems to empty out all the irrelevancies, like when you clean up your computer and get rid of all the temporary files and other clutter, the cookies and all that rubbish, and everything seems to run faster then, more efficiently. Only the stuff that really matters is left.'

She wondered what that was, the stuff that was left, the stuff that really mattered to him now.

'Interesting theory. I might have to try it.'

'Do. Be my guest.'

She laughed softly. 'Nice idea, but I'll take a rain check. If I'm going to look pretty tomorrow night, I need my beauty sleep or I'll look like a hag and frighten off all the potential buyers. Molly wouldn't like that.'

He chuckled and stood up, shifting Saffy out of the way, and the dog shambled to her feet and stretched, yawning and wagging her tail and looking lovingly up at him.

'No way,' he said firmly. 'I'm not sharing my bed with a dog. I've done enough of that in my time.'

'Are you sure? I'm happy to lend her to you.'

Her voice was wry and made him chuckle. 'No, thanks. Although I did wonder about her being shut in the crate all day.'

'It's not all day. And I don't like it, either, but what else can I do?'

'I could build her a kennel outside, and a run,' he suggested. 'She'd have access to water, then, and she wouldn't have to cross her legs till you get home.'

'She might bark.'

'But she doesn't, does she? I've never heard her bark.'

'No, but I can't guarantee it, and I wouldn't want to annoy your neighbours,' she said, but she was seriously tempted to take him up on it. 'I could buy a kennel if you didn't mind making her some kind of run. It would have to be pretty strong.'

'I know that. Leave it with me. I'll think about it.'

They paused at the foot of the veranda steps and he stared down at her, his eyes in shadow. 'Are your cuts really all right?'

'Why, are you offering to dress them?'

Why on earth had she said that?

He frowned. 'Do they need it?'

'No. Really, James, I'm all right. They're just little nicks. Tracy had a look for me.'

He nodded, looking relieved. 'OK. Well, keep an eye on them. I'll see you tomorrow. Come in at nine again. It seems to work.'

'OK. Thanks.'

'You're welcome.'

His face was still in shadow, so she couldn't read his expression, but she could feel his eyes on her, and for a moment she wondered if he was going to kiss her again. Apparently not.

'Goodnight, Connie,' he said eventually, his voice soft and a little gravelly. 'Sleep tight.'

'And you. 'Night, James.'

She took Saffy into the cabin. By the time she'd finished in the bathroom, Saffy was ensconced on the bed, so she turned out the light and stood at the window for a minute, watching the house through a gap in the curtains.

He was in the kitchen. Every now and then he walked past the window and she could see him. Then the light went off, and she watched the progress of the lights—the landing, then a thin sliver of light across the roof from his bathroom. Then that went off, leaving a soft glow—from his bedroom?

After a few minutes that, too, went off, plunging the house into darkness. She pressed her fingers to her lips and softly blew him a kiss.

'Goodnight, James,' she whispered. 'Sleep tight.'

And pushing Saffy out of the way she crawled into bed, curled on her side and tried to sleep.

It was a long time coming.

CHAPTER SEVEN

HE SPENT HALF the night wondering why the hell he'd kissed her again and the other half dreaming about her flitting around in the garden in that scrap of gauze he couldn't get out of his mind.

He really, really wasn't thrilled when the alarm went off, but by the time he'd washed and dressed and gone down to the kitchen, Saffy was waiting for him on the veranda, tail wagging, and there was a little plume of steam coming from the kettle.

He stuck his head out of the door and found Connie with her feet up on the veranda rail, dressed in another pair of those crazy pyjamas, her nose buried in a mug.

'More tea?' he asked, and she shook her head, so he made himself a lethal coffee and took it out and sat himself on the bench beside her. Her feet were in sun, the bright clear sun of an early summer's morning, slanting across the corner of the house and bathing them in gold.

Her toenails had changed colour. They were greeny-blue today, and pearly, the colour changing according to the angle of the light, and the sun made them sparkle dazzlingly bright.

'Interesting nail varnish.'

'Mmm. I thought I'd go arty, for tonight,' she said, grinning at her toes. 'Cool, aren't they?'

'I don't think they'd suit me.'

'Well, we've already established I do pretty better than you.'

Their eyes locked for a moment, something—an invitation?—glimmering in hers for the briefest instant. Surely not. Really, he needed more sleep. He grunted and stretched his legs out, turning his attention to his coffee as a potential means of keeping his sanity. 'So, about this dog run.'

'Really? It's a lot of effort, and where would you put it?'

'I've been thinking about that. There's a little store room under here. I could divide it off so there was a kennel one side and a store the other, and build a run off it against the fence. What do you think?'

'Are you sure? Because I do worry about her and that would be amazing. I'd pay for all the materials.'

'OK. It shouldn't take much. We'll have a look at it after work.'

'No we won't, because we're going out. You hadn't forgotten, had you?'

Fat chance. How could he forget, with 'pretty' haunting his every waking moment and tantalising him in his sleep? Never mind those kisses he couldn't seem to stop giving her.

'Of course I haven't forgotten.' He downed his coffee and went back into the kitchen, grabbed a banana, slung his jacket on and headed out of the door.

'I'll see you later,' he muttered, running down the steps, and she dropped her feet to the veranda floor and wriggled them back into her flip-flops as she watched him go. He looked hunted, for some reason. Because of the private view?

She had no idea, but it was the last thing they'd talked about and he'd taken off like a scalded cat.

'Fancy a run, Saffy?' she asked, and Saffy leapt to her feet, tail lashing. 'That's a yes, then,' she said, and pulled her clothes on, locked up the cabin and the house and headed off.

She went on the sea wall for a change, and ran along to the end of the sea defences, then up a long set of steps to the top of the cliff and back down towards the harbour through the quiet residential streets.

She'd never been along them before, but it was obviously where the movers and shakers lived, she thought with a smile, and she wondered how many of them would be coming tonight.

She felt a tingle of anticipation, and realised she was actually looking forward to it. It was ages since she'd been out, ages since she'd had an occasion to dress up for, and she was determined to enjoy herself. And if she had anything to do with it, James would enjoy himself, too.

He felt ridiculously nervous.

He didn't know what to wear, so in the end he wore a lightweight suit with a silk shirt. No tie, because that would be overdoing it, but a decent silk shirt, open at the neck because it was a warm night.

Maybe not as warm as he felt it was, though. That was probably because he was waiting for Connie to come out of her cabin, and he was on edge.

She'd left him out something to eat, and he hadn't seen her since he'd got home. Saffy was in the garden, though, so he sat on the veranda and watched the cabin door and waited.

Was it all right?

She'd settled on a knee-length dress with a flirty hem in a range of sea colours from palest turquoise to deep, deep green, and it was soft and floaty and fitted like a dream. She'd bought it last year for a friend's wedding and she'd thought it would be perfect for tonight, but now she wasn't sure.

What if she'd overdone it? There was no long mirror in the cabin, so she'd had to make do with peering at the one in the shower room and trying to angle her head to see herself, but she couldn't. Not adequately.

And it was five to seven, and James was on the veranda, watching her door and tapping his fingers on the bench.

She took a steadying breath, slipped her feet into her favourite strappy sandals with killer heels, because, damn it, why not, and opened the door.

'Does this count as pretty?'

He felt his jaw drop.

He'd seen her looking beautiful before, lots of times, when she'd been with Joe. At their engagement party. On her wedding day. At a ball they'd all attended. Hell, sitting on the deck in her pyjamas this morning she'd nearly pushed him over the edge.

But this…

'I think you'll do,' he said, his voice sounding strangled.

Her face fell. 'Do?'

He got up and went to the top of the steps, looking down at her as she walked towards him and climbed the steps on incredibly sexy, utterly ridiculous heels that showed off her legs to perfection, and stopped just beneath him.

'Connie, you look—' He closed his eyes, then opened them again and tried to smile. 'You look beautiful,' he said, and his voice had handfuls of gravel in it.

'Oh.' She laughed, and her whole body relaxed as the laugh went through her. 'I thought, for a minute—you looked so—I don't know. Shocked.'

'Shocked?'

Try stunned. Try captivated. Try completely, utterly blown away.

'I'm not shocked,' he said. 'I just—'

He didn't like it. Damn. He was just being nice. 'Look, I can go and change. There isn't a mirror in there, but it's probably a bit much. A bit too dressy. I just don't have a lot to choose from, and—well, Molly did make a point—'

'Connie, you look fine,' he said firmly. 'Utterly gorgeous. Believe me. There's nothing wrong with the way you look. You're lovely. Very, very lovely.'

'Really?'

Her eyes were soft and wide, and he so badly wanted to kiss her again. 'Really,' he said, even more firmly. 'Let me just put Saffy away and then we'd better go.'

He called the dog, put her in her crate in the cabin and breathed in the scent of Connie. It had been diluted in the garden, drifting away on the light sea breeze, but in the confined space of the cabin the perfume nearly blew his mind.

'Good girl, Saff,' he said, closing the door on her. She whined, and he promised her he'd make her a run, then closed the cabin door and braced himself for an evening in Connie's company.

Torture had never smelt so sweet.

It was already buzzing by the time they got there.

She'd heard lots of cars going past on the gravel road, and so she wasn't surprised. And she wasn't overdressed, either, she realised with relief. All the women were in their designer best, diamonds sparkling on their fingers, and the men wore expensive, well cut suits.

None of them looked as good as him, though, and she felt a shiver of something she hadn't felt for years.

'Connie, James, welcome!' David said, pressing glasses of champagne into their hands. 'Just mingle and enjoy—the pictures are all over the place, and there's a pile of catalogues lying around somewhere on a table. Just help yourselves. And there are some canapés coming round.'

'Wow,' she said softly as he moved away, and James raised an eyebrow.

'Indeed. The movers and shakers,' he murmured.

She suppressed a giggle, the bubbles of the champagne already tickling her nose. 'I ran past some pretty smart houses this morning up on the clifftop. I guess they're here.'

'Undoubtedly. His friends are pretty well connected. Ah—Andy and Lucy *are* here. Come and say hello.'

Not only were they there, she realised as he made the introductions, they had the baby with them, snug in the crook of Andy's arm, and her heart turned over.

James leant over and kissed Lucy's cheek, his smile looking entirely genuine if you ignored the tiny tic in his cheek. 'Congratulations. How are you? I didn't really expect to see you here so soon.'

'Oh, I'm fine,' Lucy said, positively glowing. 'My parents are here helping us out for a few days, and we really wanted to come, so we thought we'd sneak out while the going was good. And I'm really glad, because I get to meet Connie and say thank you for stepping in like that so I can have Andy at home.'

'Oh, you're welcome,' Connie said with a laugh, liking Lucy instantly. 'It's nice to be back at work. I've had a sabbatical and I was beginning to feel a bit redundant.'

'Oh, well, glad to be of service,' Lucy said with a chuckle. 'And this is Daniel, the cause of all the trouble.'

'Oh, he's so beautiful,' she whispered, and she felt her eyes fill with tears. 'Sorry. Babies always do that to me,' she said with a light laugh, but she could feel James watching her.

'Oh, good,' Andy said. 'You can hold him while I dig out my chequebook. Lucy's found a picture and I need to pay for it. Here.'

And he reached over and gave her little Daniel. Just like that, her arms were full of new baby, closing round him automatically and cradling him close, and she felt the threatening tears well again. 'Hello, little guy,' she crooned softly, breathing that wonderful new baby smell and welling up again. It just felt so *right*. 'Aren't you gorgeous?'

James felt his heart squeeze just looking at them together. *She should be a mother,* he thought suddenly. *She's born for it. It could be my child, but if I stop her, it'll be someone else's, and how will that feel?*

'So how do you two know each other?' Lucy asked, and James dragged his eyes off Connie and the baby before he went crazy.

'We worked together nine years ago, and we've kept in touch.'

He noticed Lucy's eyes flick to Connie's wedding ring, and winced inwardly, but he didn't say any more, and neither did Connie. She was absorbed by the baby, utterly focused, and she just looked so damned *right* holding him that he could hardly think straight, never mind make small talk or fend off gossip. Not that Lucy was a gossip, but he didn't feel it was up to him to broadcast Connie's personal circumstances.

'All done.'

Connie looked up at Andy and smiled ruefully. 'Does that mean you want him back?'

'Afraid so, having gone to all that trouble to get him.'

So she handed him back, releasing him reluctantly, her arms feeling suddenly desperately empty and unfulfilled.

And then she glanced at James and saw a muscle clench in his jaw, and she thought, *I'm not alone. He feels it, too. The ache. The need. The emptiness. Only how much worse is it for him?*

'So what do you think of the exhibition?' Lucy asked.

James shrugged. 'I don't know, we've only just arrived.'

'Well, you'd better go and look, the red dots are going on faster than a measles epidemic,' Andy said with a grin.

'Oh, I don't do pictures. It would require finding a hammer and a nail to put it on the wall, and that would mean unpacking the boxes.'

Andy laughed, and James was still smiling, but it was lingering there in his eyes, she thought. The emptiness.

He still wants a child, she realised with sudden clarity. *He wants one, but he doesn't know how to move on.* But maybe, once he'd got to know her—maybe she'd be able to do something about that…

'Well, hi.'

'Ben! Nice to see you. How's our patient?'

'Fine. Doing well.'

'Are you two going to talk shop?' Lucy asked pointedly, but Connie just grinned.

'No, we three are. Sorry. So how is she? How's the head injury?'

'A nice shade of purple, and so's her knee, but she's fine. This is Daisy, by the way.'

She was scintillating.

She mingled with everyone with the confidence of someone totally at ease with herself, smiling and laughing and waving her hands all over the place to illustrate what she was saying. Which was great, because it meant he didn't need to stand right next to her all night, breathing in that intoxicating perfume and threatening to disgrace himself.

'So, what do you think?'

He turned round to Molly. 'Great exhibition. Really good.'

'I meant of Connie.'

'Connie?'

'Oh, James, come on, you haven't taken your eyes off her. Doesn't she look beautiful?'

Well, he could lie, or make some excuse, or drop his drink. Or he could just be honest.

'Yes. She does. It's the first time I've seen her look happy in ages. Thanks for inviting her. She's really enjoyed dressing up, I think. She's even got crazy matching nail varnish on her toes.'

Molly chuckled. 'Not that you noticed, of course.'

'Of course not. Why would I? I'd better go and rescue her, that guy's getting a bit pushy.'

'He's harmless, James. I'm sure she can cope,' Molly murmured, but *he* couldn't. Couldn't cope at all with the good-looking bastard oozing charm all over her like some kind of vile slime, and the words she'd said to him less than a week ago were echoing in his head. Words about pulling some random stranger in a club. Or at an art exhibition?

Fighting off the red mist, he made his way over to her, smiling grimly.

'There you are,' he said, slipping his hand through her arm, and he stuck his hand out. 'James Slater.'

The man blinked, introduced himself as Tony and made himself scarce. Excellent.

Connie turned slowly and looked up at him. Not that far up, not now, because she was teetering on those skyscrapers that messed with his head and they brought her up almost to eye level with him.

'So what was that all about?' she asked, laughter dancing in her eyes.

'He was flirting outrageously.'

'Yes. He was. And I was perfectly happy letting him make a fool of himself. It was quite fun, actually.'

At which point James began to wonder if he was making a fool of his own self. Very probably. He tried not to grind his teeth. 'I thought he might be annoying you.'

'In which case I would have told him where to go. James, I've lived on an army base for years,' she said patiently, her eyes laughing at him. 'Several of them. And in every one there was someone like that. I can deal with it.'

He nodded. Of course she could. He'd seen her doing it

years ago, for God's sake, handling the drunks on a Friday night in the ED. Tony whoever was nothing. 'Sorry. I didn't mean to come over all heavy, I just…' He shrugged, and she shook her head slowly and smiled at him.

'You're crazy. Come with me. There's a picture I want to show you.'

She tucked a hand in his arm and led him through to another room. It was quieter in there, and she pulled him to one side and then turned him.

And there, on the wall opposite them, was a blur of vibrant colour. It radiated energy, and for a second he couldn't work out what it was. And then the mist seemed to clear and he could make out the figure of a runner, smudged with speed, the power almost palpable, and at the bottom was a fine, curved line.

'It's called Blade Runner,' she said softly. 'Isn't it amazing? As if she's tapped into his soul.'

'Amazing,' he echoed. 'It's incredible. It must be David.'

'I would think so. It's not for sale.' Connie let him stand there for a minute, then she tugged his arm. 'Come on. There are others. Have you looked at them?'

He shook his head. 'No. No, not really.' *Because he'd been watching her. Picturing her with a baby in her arms. Picturing her pregnant. Fantasising about getting her that way—*

'You should. Your walls are crying out for colour, for movement. And these are fantastic.'

He stopped thinking about Connie then and started to look at them, really look at them, and he was blown away.

'Wow. I love this one,' Connie said, pausing in front of a very familiar scene. At least he thought it was familiar, but Molly's work was blurred and suggestive rather than figurative, and he wasn't entirely sure.

'It looks like the marshes from my veranda.'

'Gosh, yes. I think you're right—what does it say?'

'"Mist over the ferry marshes",' he told her. 'I'm sure it is. I recognise the pattern of the landscape.'

'It's the view out the back here, she paints it all the time. She loves it,' David said in passing, and gave him another drink. He took it without thinking. So did Connie, and by the time they'd worked their way round the exhibition again, they'd had another two. At least.

Realising he'd lost count, he took a closer look at Connie and sighed inwardly. She was tiddly. Not drunk, certainly not that, but gently, mildly inebriated. At the moment. And frankly, so was he.

'I think it's time to go home,' he murmured.

'Really?'

'Really.' The crowd was thinning out, Andy and Lucy with their tiny baby were long gone, and he figured that he just about had time to get Connie home before the last glass entered her system and pushed her over the edge.

'Fabulous exhibition. I love every single one,' she told Molly fervently. 'I want them all, but I haven't got any money, and more importantly I haven't got any walls or I might have to start saving.'

Molly laughed. 'Thank you. I'm glad you like them. And you'll have walls one day.'

'I've got walls right now that need pictures,' James said, surprised to realise that he meant it. 'Can I come and see you tomorrow?'

'Sure. We're opening the door at ten. Come before then. Both of you, come for coffee.'

'That'll be lovely. Thanks.' He kissed her cheek, shook David's hand and ushered Connie out of the door.

'Can we walk by the sea?' she asked, so he led her up onto the sea wall, her hand firmly anchored in his.

'Oooh. That's a bit steep. When did that happen?' she asked, eyes rounded, and giggled.

'When you had all that champagne,' he told her wryly, and she laughed and tucked her arm in his and they walked arm in arm along the sea wall until they reached his house. Then she looked down at the bank.

'Hmm. We walked along the road before, didn't we?'

'We did.'

'Oh.'

If it was anybody else, he would have thought it was staged, but Connie wasn't that artful. He shook his head and hoisted her up into his arms, and she gave a little shriek and wrapped her arms around his neck.

'What are you doing?'

'Carrying you down the bank so you don't break your ankle in those crazy shoes.'

'Don't you like my shoes?' she asked, lifting one foot up and examining it thoughtfully, and he turned his head and looked at her leg and groaned softly.

'Your shoes are fine,' he said a little abruptly, and put her down. She slid down his front, ending up toe to toe with him, their bodies in contact from chest to knee.

Dear God.

'James?' she whispered.

She was so close her breath teased his cheek, and it would take only the tiniest movement of his head to bring their lips into contact.

He moved, brushed his mouth against hers. Pulled back, then went in again for more, his hands tunnelling into her hair, his tongue tracing her lips, feeling them part for him. He delved, and she delved back, duelling with him, driving him crazy.

She whimpered softly, and he pulled away, resting his head on hers and breathing hard, stopping now while he still could.

'More,' she said, and he shook his head.

'Connie, no. This is a bad, bad idea.'

'Is it?'

'Uh-huh.'

'What a shame.' She hiccupped, and looked up at him, her eyes wide in the moonlight. 'Do you think we might be just a teeny, tiny bit drunk?' she asked, and then giggled.

He closed his eyes, the imprint of her body against his burning like flames, the touch of her lips branding him forever. 'Just a teeny, tiny bit,' he agreed. 'Come on, Connie, it's time you went to bed.'

And he turned her and pointed her in the direction of the cabin, unlocked the door and pushed her in.

Quickly, before he did something that couldn't be undone, something he'd regret for the rest of his life.

Something like cup that beautiful, laughing face in his hands once more and bend his head and kiss her again, only this time, he knew, he wouldn't stop...

How ironic. And what a brilliant way to find out that he was ready to move on.

With his best friend's widow.

Great move, Slater, he told himself in disgust. He picked up a pebble off the sea wall and hurled it into the water. Or tried to. The tide was too far out, and he missed by miles.

That was champagne for you.

Or the distracting realisation that you were about to make a real idiot of yourself.

Even more disgusted, he threw another one, and this time he was angry enough that it made its mark.

Better.

So he did it again.

She was woken by Saffy scratching at the door.

'Saff, no, it's too early, come and lie down,' she pleaded, her head thrashing, but Saffy wanted out, and she wasn't giving up. She whined, then gave a soft bark, and Connie stumbled out of bed and opened the door.

James was on the veranda, sitting there in the pre-dawn light, a mug cradled in his hands.

'Is that tea?' she asked, her throat parched and her head pounding.

'You need water,' he told her, and dropped his feet to the deck and stood up. 'Gallons of it.'

She walked barefoot across the dewy grass and climbed the steps gingerly. 'I want tea.'

'Water first,' he insisted, handing her a glass.

'I wasn't that bad,' she protested, but a sceptical eyebrow flickered and she scowled at him. 'I wasn't!'

'No. To quote you, you were only a teeny, tiny bit drunk.'

'Oh, God,' she moaned, and slumped down onto the bench and put her head in her hands. 'Did I disgrace myself?'

'No. You were lovely,' he said, his internal editor clearly on holiday, and she dropped her hands from her face and straightened up, turning slowly to look at him.

'I was?'

'Well, of course you were.'

She smiled and leant back, picking up the glass. 'Phew. For a moment there I thought I might have made a fool of myself.'

He chuckled. 'You didn't, but probably only because I got you out of there in time.'

'You didn't *have* to carry me home,' she pointed out, which answered the question of how much she remembered. More than he'd expected, probably. The kiss?

'I didn't. I just carried you down the bank.'

'Yeah. Crazy shoes. I bought them after Joe died. He was only three inches taller than me, and they're five inch heels. And I love them soooo much.'

'I don't know how the hell you walk in them.'

'Carefully,' she said with a little laugh. 'So—I've drunk

the water. Can I please have tea now? Because I do have a teensy little headache.'

'I'll just bet you do,' he grumbled, getting to his feet again. 'What did your last servant die of?'

And then he stopped in his tracks, swore viciously and turned back to her. Her eyes were wide with shock, all laughter gone, and he could have kicked himself.

'Ah, hell, Connie, I'm sorry—I didn't mean—' He swore again, and dropped his head against the doorframe, banging it gently. OK, maybe not so gently. 'I'm really sorry. That was inexcusable. I can't believe I said it.'

'Hey. It's all right,' she said softly. 'It was just a silly remark. We all do it. And it's exactly the sort of thing Joe used to say to me. I'll forgive you if you get me tea and stop making wisecracks about my hangover. Done?'

'Done,' he said, sending her a wry, apologetic smile. 'Do you want anything to eat?'

'It's a bit early.'

'Not if you've been up all night.'

'Survivors' breakfast?' she said, and there it was again, the spectre of Joe between them, and this time it was her fault.

I can't do this, he thought. *I can't just be with her feeling like this with Joe hanging over us. And I'm not sure I can cope with the idea of giving her a baby. Ever. I can't even cope with thinking about it because I want it so much. How did I get myself in this mess?*

Easy. He'd been forced into a corner by the staffing crisis, and he'd been so desperate for help that Connie had seemed like the answer to his prayers, so he hadn't let himself think about it too hard. The trouble was, she was hoping he'd be the answer to hers, or at least give her the answer to her prayers in the form of a baby, and he really wasn't sure he could. Not in the way she wanted, anyway, just a clinical donation of his

DNA. Not when the real alternative was growing more and more compelling by the second—

'Something like that,' he said mildly. 'Bacon sandwich?'

'Oh, amazing! That would be so good.'

'Coming up.'

And he retreated to the kitchen, dragging the task out far longer than necessary while he tried to work out if she'd remembered the kiss or if she was just avoiding the subject like him.

'Are you growing that tea?' she asked, appearing in the doorway in those inadequate pyjamas, and he slid the mug towards her, fished the bacon out of the pan and dropped it on the bread and hesitated, sauce bottle in hand.

'Ketchup or brown sauce?'

'Neither. As it comes. Unless you've got fresh tomato?'

He gave an exaggerated sigh, got a tomato out of the fridge and sliced it, and handed her the sandwich. 'Right. I'm going for a run,' he said, and left the kitchen before his body gave him away. He was going to cut those pyjamas up, he vowed, plodding up the stairs and turned the corner into his bedroom, to come to a dead halt.

'Connie! Your dog's up here, in my bed, and she's eating my trainers!'

Saffy was in disgrace.

They'd been his favourite running trainers, he said, and she felt racked with guilt.

'I'm really sorry—I'll buy you a new pair,' she promised, but of course that didn't help him, he wanted to go for a run there and then, and so he wore his old ones and came back with blisters. He had, however, taken Saffy with him, and she came back panting, as if the run had been further and harder than she was used to.

'Poor Saffy. Did he wear you out, darling?' she crooned, and he laughed.

'Poor Saffy?' he said with studied sarcasm. 'She's had a great time. She chased the seagulls, and played on the beach with a Labrador, and she's had brilliant fun.'

'You let her off the lead?' she squawked.

'Don't sound so horrified, she was fine.'

But she was horrified, because the only time she'd tried it, it had taken her all day to find the wretch. But that was her, and this was James, and Saffy worshipped him. Even to the point of wanting to eat his smelly old trainers.

'I'm going to shower. Try and make sure she doesn't eat anything else while I'm gone,' he said drily, and so just to be on the safe side she took Saffy back into the cabin with her and put her in the crate while she had a shower herself.

'So, jeans and a T, or my blue dress, Saffy?' She looked at the options, debated for a second and then grinned at Saffy. 'Blue dress. Excellent choice. It's going to be a hotty.'

She pulled on the sundress, found some flip-flops and slid her feet into them, and went out to find James with his head in the store under the veranda. The kennel?

Oops, she thought. Poor old Saffy really was in trouble!

'Is this a work party? Because if so I probably ought to change, only I thought we were going up to Molly and David's this morning.'

He pulled his head back out of the doorway and thumped it on the head of the frame. 'Ouch. No, it's not a work party,' he said, and then looked at her stupidly for a moment.

She looked—well, she'd been beautiful last night, elegant and sophisticated and downright stunning. Now, she just looked plain lovely, the dress that barely brushed the top of her knees leaving those gorgeous legs exposed to taunt him again, and he wanted to walk over to her, scoop her up in his arms and carry her up to bed.

Which was *so* not going to happen!

'I thought I'd investigate the possibilities before she eats anything else of mine,' he said, trying not to sniff the air to see if she'd used that same shampoo. She didn't have the perfume on, he was sure of that, because even in the garden he would have been able to smell it.

'And?'

And? And what? 'Um—yes, it'll work,' he said hastily, retuning. 'We'll do it later. So, are you ready to go?'

CHAPTER EIGHT

THE PICTURES WERE every bit as good in the cold, sober light of day as they had been last night with the clever lighting, but there was nothing there that just said, Buy me.

'There are some others,' David said. 'We ran out of wall space. Come and have a look.'

He took him through into Molly's studio, and immediately he was captivated by a canvas propped up on the easel.

'Oh, wow.'

It was a view across the harbour mouth, painted from the vantage point of the sea wall, he thought, looking out. The sea was a flat, oily calm, the skies threatening, and it was called 'Eye of the Storm'.

He loved it. Loved everything about it. The menace. The barely leashed power. The colours in the lowering sky.

'She got drenched doing the sketches for that,' David said with a chuckle.

'It was worth it.'

'What was worth what?'

He turned and smiled at Connie. 'Getting drenched.'

'Wow. I can see why. That sky looks pretty full.'

'It was a lot emptier a few minutes later,' Molly said drily. 'I had to retreat to the bedroom to carry on. I painted it standing at the window in the attic bedroom at your house, James, and I never finished it because I couldn't seem to get the sea right. I got it out again the other day and it sort of fell into place. Do you want another coffee?'

'No, thanks. I think I want to buy this picture. Kind of poetic, taking it home. I might even hang it in the bedroom, since my sitting room is still a work in progress. I know it's not in the exhibition, but is it for sale?'

He found the hammer and some picture hooks, buried in the back of the tool shed under the veranda, and he took Connie inside to help him hang it.

'So, where?'

'Sitting room?'

He looked around, but there wasn't anywhere obviously right for it. The books were still in boxes and he wasn't sure if the furniture worked where it was, and just then sorting it out and unpacking the books and getting to grips with it seemed too big a task.

'No. Bedroom. Come and help me place it.'

So not a good idea, he thought the moment they were in there. The walls seem to close in, the air was sucked out of the room and the bed grew until it filled all the available space.

'So—' He cleared his throat and looked around a trifle desperately. 'Whereabouts would you put it?'

'I don't know. You want to be able to see it from the bed, don't you?'

'Probably.'

And before he could breathe she was there, sitting cross-legged at the top of the bed, bossing him about.

'Try there.'

Try what where? The only thing he wanted to do was crawl onto the bed beside her and kiss her. Drag her into his arms and slide that blue dress off over her head and kiss her from top to toe—

Focus!

'Here?'

'No. Angle's wrong. Try that side—that's better. Down a bit. Perfect.'

And she scrambled off the bed and took the picture from him. 'You look at it. Go and lie on the bed and look at it.'

Really? Right there, where she'd just been? Where he'd been fantasising about kissing her?

'Is it really necessary—? OK, OK,' he grumbled, defeated by that challenging stare, and he threw himself down on the bed, propped himself up on the pillows and was immediately swamped by the scent of her. Had she *bathed* in the perfume? Sprayed it on her legs? Sheesh!

'Well? My arms are aching.'

'Um—yeah, that's really good.' He swung his legs off the side, found a pencil and went over to mark the top of the picture so he could put a hook in the wall, but she was just there, so close, and the urge to lean into her, to take the picture from her and put it down and kiss her nearly—so nearly—overwhelmed him.

He reached past her and marked the wall before he lost it completely. 'OK,' he said, and she stepped back so he could put the hook in, then she settled the picture on it.

'Great,' she said. 'One down, however many more to go.'

'What?'

Connie turned to look back at him; she was already heading down the stairs to get away from the image of him lying sprawled on his bed where she'd imagined him so many times. She simply hadn't done him justice.

'The rest of the house,' she explained. 'The sitting room needs at least three pictures—unless you have one huge one.'

'I can't afford a huge one. This one was bad enough.'

'I'm sure she'd do a bulk discount. There was that fabulous one of the marshes. It would go really well in there.'

She left him standing there staring at her, and ran down

the stairs and out onto the veranda. She needed fresh air. The window had been open in his room but—well, clearly on a hot day the heat rose to the top of the house. There couldn't be any other explanation, or not one she wanted to consider.

Not James! she told herself. *You can't fall for James! You'll just break your heart. You can't just have a trivial affair with him, and you know he doesn't want more than that! Hell, he doesn't even want that, and especially not with you. If he did, he wouldn't have stopped after that kiss. So, keep out of his bedroom, keep out of his way, just—keep out of his life! It's not safe, not at all. He's not in the market for anything permanent, and if you mess this up he won't even be your friend. Don't do it!*

'Coffee?'

'Mmm. Flat white, if you've got the milk, please. And good and strong.'

'Coming up.'

She spent the next few minutes lecturing herself along the same lines, until James appeared on the veranda again with her coffee. Interesting, she thought as he put it down in front of her a few moments later. The rosetta was a mess.

'Losing your touch?' she teased, trying to introduce a light note, but he avoided her eyes.

'I knocked my hand on the kettle,' he said, but he sounded evasive and she just—wondered…

He was a man, after all, and she knew she wasn't exactly ugly, and she'd been sitting on his bed. And he'd already admitted that he didn't have a woman in his life and hadn't for ages. And he'd kissed her.

Was it mutual, this insane and crazy attraction?

Surely not. It wasn't her. Probably any half-decent woman with a pulse would make him think twice if she was sitting on his bed. It hadn't even occurred to her, and it probably should have, but it wasn't happening again. No, no, no, no, no!

She drank her coffee without a murmur and got out of his hair the moment it was done.

'Wow. What are you doing?'

'Making the kennel—what does it look like?'

Like he'd emptied the shed out all over the garden, was what, but she had the sense not to say so. 'Want a hand?'

He hesitated, then nodded. 'It might be useful. Steadying things, you know.'

'I'll put Saffy in her crate out here so she can watch us. I don't think she needs to get involved with this lot.'

'Probably not. Do you want a cold drink before we start?'

'That would be good. I wouldn't mind a sandwich, either. Have you eaten?'

'No. I've got some ham and salad, and a few cartons of soup in the fridge. Want to make us something?'

'Sure.'

She changed into her scruffiest clothes, because there was no way this was going to be anything other than a hot, dirty, sweaty job, and then threw together some lunch before they started.

'In your own time, Slater,' she said, carrying it all out to the table in the garden next to Saffy, and he washed his hands and joined her.

'Looks good. It's a long time since we had breakfast.'

'Yeah. Bacon and tomato sandwich, ham salad sandwich with tomato soup—do you see a pattern emerging? Maybe I need to go shopping later this afternoon and stock up the fridge.'

'Only when this run's made. I'm not having anything else chewed up. I loved those trainers.'

'Oh, Saffy,' she said slowly. 'Are we in trouble?'

'Too right.' He swiped the tail end of his sandwich around

his empty soup bowl and sat back with a sigh. 'That was good. Thanks.'

'Tea?'

'If you insist.'

'I do. You need liquids.'

'Says she, the queen of dehydration.'

'I was not dehydrated.'

He snorted softly and got up. 'Call me when it's made. I want to see if I've got enough wood to make a doorframe.'

It took them ages. Far longer than he'd anticipated, and he'd had to go shopping twice for materials, but finally Saffy had a kennel with a run, and his possessions were safe.

The only downside was that he'd had to spend the afternoon with Connie, and every second of it had been exquisite torture. She might have changed, but she was still wearing that perfume, and working in the confined space of the kennel had been enough to push him over the brink.

He'd kept bumping into her, her firm-yet-soft body close enough to him that he could feel the warmth coming off it, and then every now and then he'd shift or she'd reach up and they'd bump. Just gently. Just enough to keep his hormones simmering on the brink of meltdown.

He banged in the last nail and threw the hammer down. 'Right, that's it, I'm calling it a day. If that's not good enough, I give up.'

'What are you talking about? It's fantastic. Brilliant. Saffy, come on, come and have a look at what James has made you.'

She was wary, but with a little coaxing she went inside and had a sniff around. 'She might feel happier if her crate was in there, with the door open,' Connie suggested, so he wrestled it through the narrow doorway and set it down at the back, and Saffy went straight in it and lay down, wagging her tail.

'Excellent. Job done,' Connie said, and gave him a high

five. She was laughing, her whole face lit up, and he felt a huge ache in the centre of his chest.

'Great. Let's clear up the tools and have a drink.'

'How about something fizzy?'

'Didn't you have enough of that last night?' he asked mildly, and she gave him a level look.

'I meant fizzy water, or cola or something. Not champagne.'

'Ah. Well, I have spring water.'

'Perfect.' She emerged from the kennel, he put the last of the tools away and then she remembered the parlous state of the fridge. 'Damn.'

'What?'

'I forgot to go shopping.'

He shrugged. 'We can go to the pub. It'll be a good test for Saffy. We'll leave her in here, sit outside at the pub and listen. If she barks or howls continuously, I'm sure we'll hear her.'

'I'm not sure I want to know,' Connie said drily, feeling a twinge of apprehension.

'Oh, man up. She'll be fine. She'd better be, after all we've done for her.'

Connie just raised a brow. 'Man up?' she said, trying not to laugh. 'Really?'

'Technical term.'

'I have met it.'

He grinned and threw her one of Saffy's toys. 'Here. I'll get her water bowl.'

She was fine.

They had a peaceful, undisturbed meal at the pub.

Undisturbed, that was, by Saffy. Connie, though, was ridiculously aware of James the entire time. His soft, husky laugh, the crinkles round his eyes, the bones of his wrist—

there didn't seem to be a thing about him that didn't interest or absorb her.

And that was deeply distracting.

It was such a shame, she thought as she went to bed that night after shutting Saffy outside in her new quarters, that if she eventually had a child it wouldn't be his.

But the sudden ache of longing at the thought, low down in her abdomen, nearly took her breath away. She pressed one hand to her mouth, the other to the hollow, empty ache inside, and blinked away the tears that inexplicably stung her eyes.

No! She couldn't fall in love with him! Not really, truly in love with him, and that's what it was suddenly beginning to feel like. She couldn't let herself, she had far too much to lose. He would never be in it for the long haul, and she'd lose her heart, lose a friend she treasured, and lose her only chance to have a child. Because if she fell in love with him, truly, deeply in love with him, how could she ever consider having any other man's child inside her body, when all she longed for was his?

Far, far too late for common sense to intervene, she realised just what an incredibly stupid mistake this all was. She ought to cut her loses and go. But she couldn't leave, she thought desperately. Not while there was still hope. Maybe if she stayed, if they got to know each other better, explored this attraction, then at some point in the future maybe—

She was clutching at straws, dreaming up a happy-ever-after that could never be! She was deluding herself, and she really, really should know better.

She turned over, thumped the pillow into shape and made herself relax. She ached all over, not just in that hollow place inside that craved his child, and tomorrow was going to be hard enough without a sleepless night, so she slowed her breathing, tensed and relaxed all her muscles in turn, and finally fell asleep, only to dream of James.

* * *

He ended up on the sea wall again at stupid o'clock in the morning.

He'd crept out the front so he didn't disturb Saffy, and he was sitting there staring blindly out over the water and wondering what had happened to the amazing, relaxing properties of the waves because frankly they didn't seem to be working any longer.

Mostly because when he'd gone to bed, he could still smell the lingering essence of Connie's perfume on the pillows, and his mind was in chaos.

He couldn't believe how much he wanted her. He told himself it was lust. He told himself it was just physical, she was a beautiful woman, it had been so long that frankly any half-decent-looking woman would have the same effect.

He knew he was lying.

It was Connie. He'd felt it for years, off and on, but because Joe had been there he'd managed to keep it down, keep it under control. Not now. Now, it was driving him crazy, and tomorrow he was going to go into work and change the rota so they didn't have to work together so much.

Or, more to the point, be at home together so much.

But first, he was going to see David and Molly about that picture of the marshes for the blank wall in his sitting room. At least clearing the room up ready for it would give him something to do for the day, even if he couldn't have the picture till the exhibition closed.

He got stiffly to his feet, stretched his arms out and groaned softly. He ached all over from the unaccustomed physical exertion of building Saffy's run.

He wondered if Connie ached, and immediately an image of him massaging her long, sleek limbs filled his mind, running his oiled hands up her back and round over those slender but surprisingly strong shoulders and then down, round her ribs, under her breasts—

He swore, quietly and viciously, stabbed a hand through his hair and headed back to the house. Sleep wasn't an option, he realised, so he went into the sitting room, unearthed the boxes of books and unpacked them, putting them on the empty shelves that had mocked him for the last two and a bit years.

Better, he thought, and it had only taken him a little over an hour. They weren't sorted, but they looked a lot better than they had, and he could always move them. And it was pointless spending a small fortune on a picture to hang it up in a room that was so obviously unloved.

He debated cleaning the room properly, but tomorrow would do. He'd dusted the shelves, put the books on. That would do for tonight. And anyway, he needed something to do tomorrow to keep him out of Connie's way.

Connie. Always it came back to Connie.

He gave in to the urge and went back up to his bedroom, lay down in the cloud-soft bedding and went to sleep, wrapped around in Connie's perfume. It was almost like lying in her arms...

'Wow, that looks amazing!'

She stood in the opening between the kitchen and the living space and stared in astonishment at the transformation. There were books on the shelves, he'd rearranged the sofas and it actually looked lived-in rather than as if the removal men had just walked out the door. 'What time did you get up?'

'Two,' he said, trying to ignore the pyjamas. 'I've been back to sleep since for a while.'

'I'm glad to hear it. Want a cup of tea?'

'Yeah, why not? Have I got time for a shower?'

'Sure. You won't be long, will you? I'll make it now.'

He'd like to be long. He'd like to be long enough that she went and got dressed into something he was less excruciatingly conscious of, but that clearly wasn't going to happen. He paused in the doorway. 'How was Saffy last night, by the way?'

'Fine. I've let her out, she's sniffing round the garden at the moment. Thank you so much, James. I actually had room to stretch my legs out.'

He laughed. 'Happy to oblige,' he said, and hit the stairs. 'Don't make it too strong, I've already had a lot.'

He had. There were three teabags lying on the side, and she picked them up and put them in the bin. He always did that. So idle. No. Not idle, she corrected herself, remembering how hard he'd worked yesterday. He just had odd little habits. She made the tea, wiped the worktop down and went into the sitting room to study it.

Saffy followed her, looked at the sofas and then at her, and lay down on the floor.

'Wise move,' she said, and Saffy's tail banged the floor.

'What's a wise move?'

'Saffy. She eyed the sofas.'

'Did you?' The tail thumped again.

'So where are you putting the picture?' she asked him.

'I don't know. I'm not sure yet. I can't have it till after the exhibition, so I thought I'd work out where I want everything else. The first thing I'm going to do is give the place a thorough clean, now I've got it more or less straight.'

'I'll give you a hand.'

He almost groaned with frustration. 'You don't need to—'

'Oh, come on, you spent all day yesterday making the run for Saffy. It's the least I can do. Here, drink your tea while I get dressed, and we'll get started.'

So much for his escape plan.

* * *

He went to the hospital in the afternoon, and savaged the rota.

He had to leave most of the coming week alone, but the following week onwards he chopped to shreds. He spoke to the other key people who would be affected, shifted whatever he could and managed to minimise their contact really quite successfully.

And if it all got too much at home, there was always a massive stack of admin with his name on it. He could always come back in. If necessary he could invent a few meetings.

He gave his desk a jaundiced look. Locked in the drawers for confidentiality were a stack of files.

So—Connie, or admin?

Admin won, which was testament to his desperation, and it only kept him going till six that evening, at which point he gave up. Six on a Sunday, when he wasn't even supposed to be working, was more than late enough.

He locked the files away, headed home and walked in to the smell of roasting chicken.

'Hey, smells good.'

'Saffy thinks so.'

She unravelled herself from the sofa and wandered through to the kitchen looking sun-kissed and delectable, and he had to forcibly stop himself from kissing her. 'So how's your day been?'

'Tedious. I had to rework the rota and do some admin. I've moved us around—we're really short of suitably qualified people in the next few weeks, so I've split us up a bit so one or other of us is there. I know it's not ideal, but I'll only be here or doing admin in the department, and it'll be better for Saffy.'

She nodded. 'OK. And if the offer's still open, I might go and collect all the stuff that's in store and sort it out. You've only got me down part-time on the rota, haven't you?'

'Yes.'

'So when you aren't here and I am, I can go through it all. And I can have the kettle and toaster in the cabin, so that if it's raining I can make tea without coming over here.'

Except in practice she'd been over here all the time, and it had never been an issue—well, not for her. Still, it was an excuse to get the things and start to go through them, and maybe it was because of James dealing with his boxes, but she suddenly just wanted to clear up all the loose ends and get it sorted out.

'Are you sure?' he asked, watching her closely. 'I just remember going through Cathy's stuff. It can be a bit gut-wrenching.'

'I'm sure it can, but it has to be done, and I'm ready now.'

'Well, go for it. You can always stop and put it all away if it gets too much. And I won't charge you storage.'

He smiled, a wry quirk of his lips that said so much, and she felt warmed inside. He was such a good friend. She had to protect that friendship at all costs.

'Thank you,' she said humbly. 'So—roast, mashed, boiled or jacket?'

'Excuse me?'

'Potatoes. With the chicken.'

'Um—roast. Always.'

She smiled. 'Thought you'd say that. I'll put them in.'

It worked well.

He did a little more shuffling that week, and it ended up panning out nicely, so that Saffy wasn't shut away for too many hours in her run, both of them had some personal time alone and there was enough company to make the place feel homely.

Actually, he realised, it was great. She'd got the stuff out of storage and started working through it, and everything was going fine. And since he'd washed his sheets, the hormones weren't such an issue, either. She didn't wear perfume at work or if they weren't going out anywhere, and life settled down into a regular and almost cosy routine.

And then he had a job application in from someone who sounded perfect. A woman with two children whose husband had taken himself off to another country with his second wife and left her literally holding the babies.

He phoned her, and she came in that afternoon to look round and impressed his socks off.

She wanted part time, her mother was in Yoxburgh, and she was going nowhere. She was young, younger than Connie, and it would be her first consultancy, but her CV and references were stunning. And she could start whenever he pressed the button. He just had to put it to the hospital board, get her a formal interview and it would all be set in motion.

It was like a dream come true—but it meant that he didn't really need Connie beyond the end of Andy Gallagher's paternity leave, and a bit of him felt gutted because he loved working with her.

But she wasn't there forever, he knew that. She wanted to go off and have her baby and start her new life somewhere else, and there was nothing here to keep her now.

Nothing except him, and he knew that didn't count.

He went home and found her sitting in a welter of Joe's possessions with Saffy snoozing on the floor at her side.

'How are you doing?' he asked, sitting down cross-legged on the floor opposite her and scratching behind Saffy's ears.

'OK. There's a lot of rubbish—paperwork that's meaningless now, irrelevant stuff about our army accommodation and so forth. I'll never need it, but it's got personal information on it.'

'Want to borrow my shredder?'

'Oh, please.'

He went and got it, and they spent an hour shredding documents. Then finally he called a halt.

'Stop now. I need to talk to you.'

She stopped, her heart hitching for some reason. He sounded so—serious? 'About?'

'I've had a suitable applicant for the job.'

'Wow.' She stood up on legs that trembled slightly, picked up the bag of shreddings and followed him downstairs, Saffy trailing after them. 'What's he like?'

'She. Very good. Divorced, two kids—twins. Dad walked. I interviewed her today.'

'And?'

'She's nice. Really nice. Open, friendly, efficient—little bit nervous, but that's to be expected. I need to get it rubber stamped, but we've been looking for someone for three months now without success, so I'm sure it won't be an issue.'

She nodded, trying to be practical, trying not to cry for some crazy reason. 'Good. Well, for you. For Andy, too. Takes away the guilt.'

'And you?'

She shrugged. 'I knew it was short term. I guess it's just going to be shorter than I'd expected. I had hoped I'd have a bit longer to find a permanent job and somewhere to live, but I'm sure I'll find something. When can she start?'

'Now. She's free, so as soon as the formal interview's taken place and she's officially accepted, she can start.'

She stared at him across the kitchen, feeling the bottom drop out of her stomach. 'Oh. Right. So I haven't got time.'

'Well, you don't have to leave here, you know that, but the job will go. I'm really sorry. I honestly thought it would take months and I'm really grateful to you for what you've done.'

She shrugged, her shoulders lifting a little helplessly, and he felt a complete heel, but what could he do? It was only the truth. The job was taken, he didn't need her.

Not in that way, and he wasn't even going to think about the other.

'Don't worry about it. I'll be fine. I'll find a job, I always do. And I'll get out of your hair, just as soon as it's all rubber stamped and she's ready to go.'

'If you find something else you want to go to, if there's a job that comes up with your name on it, I don't expect you to give me any notice, Connie. You can leave whenever you like,' he said, and she felt her heart break a little more.

'Oh. Right. Well, I'll start packing.'

'But you haven't got anywhere to go to! I'm just saying, do it in your own time, don't worry about fitting in with me.'

'But you're right, there's nothing here, I might as well get myself out into the job market.'

'Connie, there's no rush. Sleep on it, give yourself time to work out what to do next.'

What's to sleep on? You want me out! Out of your home, out of your department, out of your life!

'Good idea. I'm tired. We'll talk tomorrow. Saffy, come on, James is going to bed.'

And she all but dragged the reluctant dog out of the door and down the steps and into her cabin. She got the door shut— just—before the little sob broke free, but it had a friend, and then a whole posse of them, and she shut herself in the shower room, turned all the taps on and sobbed her heart out.

Then she blew her nose, washed her face and put her pyjamas on.

She didn't need James. She could do this. She could still have a baby, still have her dream without the complication of knowing the father.

Simpler all round—except her dream had changed, and she'd realised that she didn't just want a baby, any baby. She wanted James's baby. And she wanted James.

God, what a mess.

She put Saffy out for a moment, and when she ran back in, she jumped straight up onto the bed, circled round and lay down in a perfect pattern of earthy footprints on the immaculate white bedding.

Tough.

Connie got into bed, shunted Saffy over a little and curled on her side, the dog behind her knees, and wondered what on earth she was going to do and where she was going to go.

She had no idea. She was out of options. The tenant in her house was there for the next six months, at least, and there was nobody else she could ask. Not with Saffy.

She'd have to get onto it first thing in the morning, try and find somewhere to go, somewhere to rent.

And a job?

God, it was all so complicated. It had been complicated since the day she'd agreed to have Saffy, and it just got worse. She needed a job, she needed a home and she didn't need James telling her she didn't need to work any kind of nominal notice period because he wanted her out of the house.

He hadn't said that, to be fair, but it felt like that.

And then she had a brilliant idea.

She'd apply for the job. Formally, properly. She'd find herself somewhere to live nearby, somewhere she could keep Saffy, and she'd go down the anonymous donor route, and then James would be close enough to help out if necessary, and she wouldn't lose his friendship, and it would be fine.

She just had to get him to agree.

There was no sign of her in the morning, and Saffy's run was hanging open.

Unlike Connie's curtains, which were unusually firmly shut.

He stood on the veranda and hated himself. It wasn't his fault that this woman had turned up when she had. It was nobody's fault. But it was his fault that they'd reached this point, that he hadn't given Connie a flat-out no right at the beginning so that she'd moved on with her life already.

And now she'd retreated into a cocoon, and he felt like the worst person in the world.

He made tea and took it over to the cabin.

'Connie?'

No reply, just a scuffle and the sound of Saffy's toenails clattering on the wooden floor as she came to the door.

'Connie? I've made you tea.'

He knocked and opened the door, to find her sitting up in bed, huddled in the quilt and watching him warily. She had her phone in her hands. Looking for a job?

'Are you OK?'

'Of course I'm OK. Put the tea down, I'll get it in a minute.'

Go away, in other words.

'Has Saffy been out?'

'Yes. I'm afraid she trashed the quilt cover.'

He glanced down and saw a crazy pattern of muddy paw-prints all over it. 'It'll wash,' he said, although he doubted it, but the quilt cover was the least of his worries. Connie looked awful.

Tired, strained, her eyes red-rimmed, her back ramrod straight.

He put the tea down and left her to it, plagued by guilt and unable to change anything for the better.

He'd gone.

She'd hoped to catch him before he left for work, but he'd been too quick off the mark. Damn. She hadn't wanted him going to the hospital board before she had a chance to talk to him about it, so she took Saffy for a quick run, showered and dressed in work clothes and drove to the hospital.

'Anyone seen James?' she asked.

'He's not in the ED but he's around somewhere—want me to page him?'

'Please. Tell him I'm in the ED.' And hopefully it wasn't already too late.

The phone didn't ring. Had he not taken his pager? No, that wasn't like him. Just ignored it? Maybe he was in a meeting—with the chief exec?

He walked in, just as she was ready to give up.

'Connie. Hi. I gather you're looking for me.'

'Have you got a minute?'

'Sure. I'll just make sure Kazia's all right. We've got a patient with a head injury waiting for a scan but he's stable.'

He stuck his head into Resus. 'You all OK for a few more minutes?'

'Sure. No change.'

'Thanks, Kaz. Page me if you need me.'

He turned to Connie. 'My office, or do you want to get a coffee and sit outside?'

'Your office,' she said. She wanted this to be formal, in a way. A little bit official. And an office seemed the place to do that.

'OK.'

He led her in, shut the door and offered her a chair, then sat down opposite her. 'So. Talk to me.'

'I want the job.'

He felt his jaw sag slightly.

'Job?'

'Yes. The part-time consultant post in the department. I want to make an official application, and I want you to interview me.'

He sat back in his chair, fiddling with a pen to give him time, straightening the notepad, lining up the small ring-stained mat he used to protect the top of the desk.

'No,' he said in the end, because it was the only word that
came to mind that wasn't unprintable.

'No?' She sat forward, her face shocked. 'Why no? I'm
good, James. Whatever this other woman's got, I've got more,
and I've thought it through. This is a sensible decision. I want
a child, I have a dog already, I can't work full-time. You said
you'd support me in my decision about the baby, and if I'm
here in Yoxburgh, that makes it easy for all of us. I understand you don't want the fatherhood thing, that's fine, but I've
thought it all through. I'll sell the house and buy one here,
and I'll have a stable base, friends in the area—this is just
the perfect answer.'

'No, Connie. I can't do it. I can't offer you the job because
I've already offered it to the other woman. I offered it to her
yesterday and I can't retract it. And anyway, I've spoken to
the board and they've agreed. They're interviewing her now,
as we speak. I'm really, really sorry.'

So was she. If only she'd thought this through sooner, mentioned it earlier—but she'd thought she'd had time, and she
hadn't. Her time had run out, and it was over.

Just as well, perhaps. She'd get away, leave him behind her,
start again. Good idea. Maybe one day it would feel like it.

She got to her feet, her legs like rubber, her eyes stinging.

'It's OK. It's not your fault. I understand. I hope it works
out well. Goodbye, James.'

And she walked out of his office, through the department—why hadn't she agreed to coffee outside in the park?—
and out of the doors.

Her frustration and anger at herself for not doing this in
time sustained her all the way back to his house, and then
she opened the gate to be greeted by Saffy wagging her tail,
waiting to be let out of her run.

The run James had made for her out of the kindness of
his heart.

Damn.

She let Saffy out, went into the cabin and started packing. There wasn't much, and it didn't take her long. She took the kettle and the toaster, because she'd need them, and all her clothes and bits and pieces, and she stacked them as tightly as she could in the car.

Saffy's crate went in next, packed around with as much as possible, until she was left only with a box or two of things in the spare bedroom. She'd got rid of a lot of the stuff, and this was all that was left that was still unsorted.

Well, she wasn't doing it now. She was getting the hell out of here before James came home, because she really didn't think she'd be able to hold it together when she saw him again.

She'd been doing so well, and now she felt lost again.

Don't think about it!

She scooped up the last two boxes, carried them downstairs and out to the car, and with a little repacking she even got them in. She could hardly see out of the car, but that was fine. She had wing mirrors. She'd manage.

Wherever she was going.

Where *was* she going? She had no idea, none at all, and it was already lunchtime.

Back towards Nottingham?

She had friends down in Cornwall, but that was too far and she couldn't expect them to help. But there was nobody in the world who'd tolerate Saffy in the way that James had.

Nobody else who'd build her a run and not mind when she stole the fillet steak or trashed the sheets with her muddy paws or ate his favourite trainers.

There was only one option open to her, and it broke her heart, but in many ways it was the right answer.

She'd leave Saffy with James.

CHAPTER NINE

HE HAD THE day from hell.

He couldn't leave, but Connie's face was etched on his mind and he was hardly able to concentrate.

What had he done? He could have told her about the other applicant, could have offered her the chance, but he'd wanted her out of his life because she was upsetting it, messing it all up, untidying it. He'd been trying to make life easier for himself, because the thought of having her working there with him indefinitely, driving him mad on a daily basis with her crazy pyjamas and her lace underwear, was unthinkable.

And now she was going, and he realised he didn't want her to. He didn't want her to go at all. And she'd said goodbye.

Hell. He had to go home to her.

He pulled his phone out of his pocket, called Andy and drummed his fingers until he answered.

'I need a favour. Is there any way you can cover for me? I need to go home urgently.'

'What, now? No, that's OK, I think. Lucy's here.' He heard him talking to Lucy, then he came back. 'That's fine. I'll come now. Give me ten minutes.'

'Thank you,' he said, but Andy had gone, without prevaricating or asking any awkward questions. Still, ten minutes was a long time and he just hoped to God nothing kicked off in the meantime which meant he couldn't leave.

He was there in five.

'I'll be as quick as I can,' he promised.

'Don't worry. Just go.'

'Thank you.'

He drove home on the back roads because there was less traffic, his heart in his mouth.

'Please be there, please be there, please be there—'

She was, her car on the drive, the door hanging open. He pulled up beside it and swore. It was packed to the roof with all her worldly possessions. Except Saffy. There was a crate-shaped hole in the back, but no crate, no dog, no sign of her.

She must be taking her for a last walk, he thought, but her keys were in the ignition, and his heart started to race.

Where was she?

The cabin was locked, the curtains open, the bed stripped. The house was unlocked, though, so he searched it from top to bottom, but there was nothing. No clue, no sign, no hint of what was going on. He even looked under the beds and had to stop himself from being ridiculous, but—where had she gone?

'Connie?'

He yelled her name, again and again as he raced through the house, but all that greeted him was silence. So he rang her, and her phone rang from the car. From her handbag, lying there in the gap between the two front seats, squashed in.

Had Saffy run off at the last minute? Unsure what to do, where else to look, he locked her car, pocketed the keys and went up onto the sea wall. Nothing. He could see for miles, and there was nothing, nobody.

Nobody with a sandy-coloured, leggy dog with dangling ears and a penchant for stealing, anyway.

He looked the other way, went up to his attic for a higher view of the river wall, but there was nothing there, either. All he could do was wait.

So he did. He made himself a cup of tea that he felt too sick to drink, took it out onto the veranda and waited.

And then he heard it.

A sob.

Faint but unmistakeable, from under him.

The kennel. Idiot! He hadn't searched the kennel!

He took the steps in one, crossed the run in a single stride and ducked his head through the entrance. 'Connie?'

'I couldn't leave her,' she said brokenly, and she started to sob again.

'Oh, Connie. Leave who? Why?'

'Saffy. James, where can I take her? How can I? I don't even have a home—'

Her voice cracked on the last word, and he squashed himself into the crowded kennel, dragged Connie into his arms and wrapped her firmly against his chest.

'Crazy girl. You don't have to go anywhere.'

'Yes, I do. I have to make a life. I have to start again, make something of my future, but I can't do it with this stupid great lump of a dog, so I was going to leave her here, because I thought, you promised Joe you'd take care of me, and he loved Saffy too, and I know you do, so I thought maybe you could look after her instead, but I can't leave her—'

The sobs overwhelmed her again, and he pressed his lips to her hair and held on tight. His eyes were stinging, and he squeezed them shut, rocking her gently, shushing her, and all the time Saffy was licking his arm frantically and trying to get closer.

He freed a hand and stroked her. 'It's OK, Saffy, it's all right,' he said, his voice cracking, and Connie snuggled closer, her arms creeping round him and hanging on.

'Oh, Connie, I'm sorry,' he said raggedly. 'So, so sorry. I don't want you to go, and if I'd only known you wanted the job I could have done something, but I'm not letting you go anywhere like this. Come on, come out of here and blow your nose and have a cup of tea and we'll talk, because this is crazy.'

'I can't just stay here,' she said, still hanging on to him and not going anywhere. 'You don't need me, you don't want me…'

Oh, hell.

'Actually, that's not true,' he admitted quietly. 'I do.'

'You do?' She lifted her head, dragging an arm out from behind him to swipe a hand over her face. 'I don't understand.'

'Neither do I, but I know I can't let you go. I can't do what you came here to ask me. I've dug deep on this one, and one of the reasons I just can't give you a baby and then step back is because my feelings for you are very far from clear.'

She went utterly still. 'I don't understand.'

His smile felt twisted, so he gave up on it. 'Nor do I. I don't know how I feel about you, Connie. I know I want you. You have to know that, up front, but you're a beautiful woman and it's not exactly a hardship. But whether that has the capacity to turn into anything else, I don't know. We've both got so much emotional baggage and Joe may be an obstacle that neither of us can get over, but I just know I can't lose you forever without giving it a try, seeing where it takes us.'

She said nothing. She didn't move, didn't speak, just clung on to him, her eyes fixed on his face, but her breathing steadied and gradually some of the tension went out of her.

'Connie?'

She tilted her head up further, and in the dim light he could see the tear tracks smudged across her face.

'Can we start by getting out of here?' she said. 'It's all a little bit cosy and I'm not sure about the spiders.'

He gave a hollow chuckle and unravelled himself, standing up as far as he could and ducking through the doorway, and she followed him out, Saffy squashing herself between them, her eyes anxious.

Poor dog. She felt racked with guilt.

She put her hand down to Saffy and found his there already. He turned it, and their fingers met and clung.

'Did you say something about tea?' she said lightly, and he tried to smile but it was a pretty shaky effort. She didn't suppose hers was a whole lot better.

'If you like.'

'I like.'

'I'll make it. You go and wash your face. I'll see you in a minute.'

She looked awful. Her eyes were so red and puffy they were nearly shut, and her cheeks were streaked with tears and dirt from being in the kennel, and her clothes were filthy.

What on earth did he see in her? He must be mad. Or desperate.

No. He was single by choice. A man with as much going for him as James wouldn't lack opportunity. And he wanted to explore their relationship?

She closed her eyes and sucked in a shaky breath. This was about so much more than just giving her a baby. This was everything—marriage, a family, growing old together—all the things she might have had with Joe, but had lost. The things he might have had with Cathy and their baby.

He was right, they had a hell of a lot of emotional baggage, but if they could make it work—

She let herself out of the cloakroom and went back to the kitchen.

'Out here,' he called, and she went and sat next to him, exactly over the spot where he'd held her while she'd cried, and Saffy leaned against their legs and trapped them there.

'Do you think she's telling us we can't go anywhere until

this is sorted?' she asked, a little hitch in her voice, and James gave a quiet laugh.

'Maybe. Seems like a sensible idea.'

'Mmm.' She sniffed, still clogged with tears. 'So—what now?'

'Now? Now I suggest we unpack your car, settle Saffy back in and then I go back to work. I called Andy in, but I can't really leave him there for hours. Just—promise me you'll be here when I get back.'

'I'll be here. Where else can I go?'

'If you really want to, I'm sure there's somewhere. And for the record, I would have had Saffy for you. Not because of Joe, or you. Just for herself.'

Her eyes filled again and she blinked hard and cleared her throat. 'Will you please stop making me cry?' she said, and he hugged her, his arm slipping naturally around her shoulders and easing her up against his side.

'Oh, Connie, what are we going to do?'

'I don't know. I'm totally confused now. I thought you didn't want a relationship, I thought you were happy on your own.'

'Not happy,' he corrected softly. 'Just—accepting. I couldn't imagine falling in love like that again, and maybe I never will, but maybe it doesn't have to be like that. Maybe we're both so damaged that we can't ever love like that again, but it doesn't mean we can't be happy with someone else, someone who doesn't expect that level of emotion, someone who can accept our scars and limitations. Maybe it would only work with someone equally as hurt, someone who could understand.'

Which would make them ideal for each other.

Would it work? Could it work?

She took a deep breath. 'I guess there's only one way to find out.'

'Shall we unpack your car?'

'I'll do it,' she said. 'You go back to work. I won't go anywhere, I promise.'

He went—reluctantly—and she sat a little while longer, trying to make some kind of sense of the developments of the day.

She didn't even know how she felt about a relationship with him. It had seemed so unlikely she hadn't ever really let herself consider it, but—a couple? Not just an affair, but a real relationship?

She tried to get her head around it, and failed. Unrequited lust she could understand, but happy ever after? Could he do it? What would he be like as a partner? People who'd been single a very long time found it hard to be part of a couple, to give and take and compromise.

Could she? Joe had been away so much she'd been pretty self-sufficient. Could she cope with someone having a say in her life?

'I don't know,' she said out loud. Saffy lifted her head and stared up at her, and she rubbed her chest gently. 'It's OK, Saff. We'll be all right. We'll find a way.'

She wasn't sure how, if this thing with James didn't work, but it seemed they were still friends, at the very least, and she wanted to make sure that continued. It had to. Friends, she'd learned over the years, were infinitely precious. She only had a few, and James, it seemed, was one of them. The best.

She eyed her car. She ought to unpack it, really, but she'd stripped her bed and put the sheets in the washing machine; they were done, so perhaps she should hang them on the line before she started?

'Oh, Saffy, we're OK, the pawprints came out. That's a good job, isn't it?' Saffy wagged her tail, tongue lolling, and Connie shut her back in the run and emptied the car.

There was no point putting the stuff that had been in stor-

age back in James's spare bedroom. There was so little left—
had only ever been so little of any consequence, really—that
she put it into the cabin with everything else.

And all the time there was a little niggle of—what? Anticipation? Apprehension? Excitement?—fizzing away inside
her. Should she cook for him? If there even was anything in
the fridge. She wasn't sure. She'd look later, she decided,
after she'd sorted herself out, but by the time she'd unpacked
her things, hung up her clothes, found her washbag and had
a shower, he was home.

And the butterflies in her stomach felt like the images she'd
seen of bats leaving a cave in their thousands.

She'd put her stuff in the cabin.

All of it, by the looks of things, because the car was empty
and there was no trace of her possessions in the house. He
went up to his bedroom to check, and it was untouched since
he'd changed his clothes before he'd gone back to work.

He stood there, staring at it, and tried to analyse his feelings. Mixed, he decided. A mixture of disappointment—physical, that one, mostly—and relief.

His common sense, overruling the physical disappointment, pointed out that it was just as well. Too early in their
relationship to fall straight into bed, too easy, too fast, too
simple. Because it wasn't that simple, sleeping with Connie.
Not after Joe.

Inevitably there would be comparisons. He knew that. He
wasn't unrealistic. And he wasn't sure he wanted to be compared to his best friend. He didn't want to be better in bed,
but he sure as hell didn't want to be worse.

He swore softly, sat down on the edge of the bed and stared
at the picture of the estuary that Molly had painted here in
this room.

The Eye of the Storm.

Was that what this was? The eye of the storm? The lull before all hell broke loose again in his life?

'James?'

He heard her footsteps on the landing, and went to his bedroom door. She was wearing jeans and a pretty top, and from where he was standing he had a perfect view of her cleavage. 'Hi. I'm just going to change, and then I thought we could go out for dinner if you like.'

'That would be lovely,' she said with a wry smile. 'I've just looked in the fridge and it's none too promising.'

He chuckled. 'Give me ten minutes. I'll have a quick shower and I'll be with you.'

A cold one. He retreated, the updraught through the stairwell wafting the scent of her perfume after him, so that it followed him back into the room. He swallowed hard. Damn his common sense. Just then, the other side of the coin looked a lot more appealing.

Dinner?

As in, supper at the pub, or dinner? Formal, dressy, elegant? Because jeans and a floaty little cotton top wouldn't do, in that case.

But he came down the stairs bang on time in jeans and a crisp white cotton shirt open at the neck with the cuffs turned back, and she relaxed. She didn't feel ready for a formal dinner. Not yet. Too—what? Romantic? Laden with sexual expectation?

'So—Chinese, Indian, Thai, Tex-Mex, English gastro pub or fish and chips out of the paper? You choose.'

She laughed, feeling another layer of tension peel away. 'Gastro pub?' she suggested. 'It's a lovely evening. It would be nice to eat outside, if we can. And if you want to drink, I don't mind driving, or we could go to the Harbour Inn and sit outside so we can walk.'

'We've done that, and I don't need more than one glass. I'll drive. There's a lovely pub just a few miles up the river. We'll go there. Have you fed Saffy?'

'Yes. She's ready to go in her run.'

He rubbed the dog's head. 'How is she? Has she settled down?'

'I think so. She was a bit clingy until I'd unpacked everything and put it all away in the cabin but then she was fine. Oh, by the way, I put the rest of the stuff from storage in the cabin, too, so your spare bedroom's yours again. There wasn't much, and it'll make it easier to sort out. I can pick at it, then.'

'Good idea,' he said, stifling the regret. 'Right, shall we?'

It was a lovely pub, as he'd said.

The setting was wonderful, down on the edge of the river bank and miles from anywhere, or so it seemed. The river was wide at that point, and there were lots of boats moored on the water.

'It's buzzing, isn't it?' she said, slightly surprised, and he smiled.

'Wait till you taste the food. It'll all make sense then,' he said.

'It makes sense now,' she pointed out. 'Look at it. It's gorgeous here.'

They sat outside at a picnic table, side by side, and watched the boats come and go, sipping their drinks and reading the menu and just chilling out. It had been a gruelling day for both of them, and the quiet moment by the river was just what they needed, she thought.

She scanned the menu again, her mind slightly numb with all that had happened, her concentration shot. 'I can't decide.'

'We can come again. It's not life or death, it's just food and it's all good.'

'But I'll just get food envy,' she said, and he thought instantly of the time he'd watched her eat that hog roast roll, the apple sauce squeezing out and dribbling down her chin.

'We could always share.'

'Dangerous.' Hell, had he really said that? He hoped she hadn't heard—or caught the tiny eye roll he'd done at his impulsive comment.

Both.

She scrunched her lips up and gave him a wry grin. 'You're right. You might come off worst.'

'Never. I fight for my food.'

She smiled and put her menu down. 'Me, too. I'll go for the sea bream fillet on samphire.'

He put his menu down. 'I'll have the same. That way you won't be tempted.'

She pouted, and he chuckled softly, hailed the waitress and placed their order.

'Wine?'

'Oh—I'll have a small glass of whatever.'

'Two of the sauvignon blanc, then,' he said, handing back the menus, and he cradled his mineral water, propped his elbows on the table and leant against her.

She leant back, resting her head against his, and sighed.

'You OK?' he asked quietly. He felt her nod.

'Yup. You?'

'I'm OK.'

'Good.'

They sat there until their food arrived, in contact from shoulder to knee, feeling the way forward. From where he was sitting, it felt pretty good.

More than good.

And it smelt amazing—or, rather, she did. She'd put that perfume on again, and it had been teasing his senses ever since he'd got in the car.

He would have joined in, for once, but the only cologne

he had was some Joe had given him for Christmas the year before he'd died. He hadn't opened it until now and it didn't seem like the time to break it out, when he was contemplating seducing his widow. She'd have to make do with clean skin.

'That was amazing.'

He smiled, his eyes crinkling at the corners. Funny how she'd never really registered just how gorgeous his eyes were. Not just the colour, that striking ice-blue with the navy rim, but the shape of them, the heavy, dark lashes, the creases at the corners, the eloquent brows.

They said so much, those eyebrows. She could often tell exactly what he thought of something just from the tiny twitch that gave him away. She'd seen it in the ED, when someone had been trying to lie about how they'd injured themselves. She could always tell if he thought it was a pile of steaming manure.

And if he was troubled, or concentrating, they crunched together, but in a different way.

So complex, the facial muscles. So revealing.

He glanced across at her as he fastened his seat belt. 'Will that still go round you?'

'Cheeky,' she said without rancour. 'It would have been rude not to have a pudding. Anyway, I was starving. I hadn't eaten all day.'

'Really?' He shot her a quick glance, surprised, but then realised he hadn't had much, either. And nothing since he'd spoken to her in his office that morning.

He drove her home, parked the car and looked at her.

'Coffee?'

'Is that *coffee* coffee, or go upstairs with you?' she asked, hoping he'd say no.

Something happened to his brows, but she couldn't quite work out what. 'That's *coffee* coffee,' he said, firmly, and she felt her shoulders drop because all the way home she'd been beginning to get tense.

She smiled, the tension sliding out of her like a receding tide. 'Yes, please. Can we have it on the sea wall?'

'Sure.'

They took Saffy, and as usual she sat in between them, her head on her front paws, hanging slightly over the edge of the wall. He lifted one of her ears and laid it across his thigh and stroked it rhythmically, and Connie chuckled.

'I swear, if a dog could purr,' she murmured, and he laughed softly.

'She's just a hussy. No wonder you couldn't leave her.'

'No. I wanted to burn my boats with you, but I just couldn't. Even if I'd left her, I couldn't have walked away. Not completely.'

'No. I'm glad you didn't.' He stopped stroking Saffy's ear and held out his hand, and she placed hers in it. His hard, warm fingers closed around it gently and he lifted it to his lips and kissed the back of it, drifting his lips over her knuckles.

It sent a shiver through her, a tingle of something electric and rather beautiful. Something she'd almost forgotten.

He turned his head slowly and she met his eyes, holding his gaze for an age. Their hands fell softly to his lap, and he straightened her fingers out over Saffy's ear, so she wasn't really touching him, but she was.

It was utterly harmless, totally innocent, and yet not, and the air seemed trapped in her chest so she could only breathe with the very top of it, just very lightly, a little fast.

His eyes fell to her cleavage, watching the rapid rise and fall, and then they dragged back up to meet her eyes again.

Even in the darkness, with only the soft light from the front of the cottage to illuminate them, she could see that his pupils had gone black. His mouth was slightly open, his chest moving in time with hers, and the tension was coming off him in waves.

She eased her hand out from under his and turned away, breaking the spell, and they sat there in silence, the heat simmering between them, and gradually their breathing returned to normal.

'So am I coming to work tomorrow?'

'You're down on the rota.'

'What time?'

He cursed himself inwardly for changing the rota so they never saw each other, but maybe, with the sizzle he'd just felt between them, that was just as well.

'Eight o'clock. I'm on from one till nine.'

'OK. Will you take Saffy for a run for me?'

'Of course I will.'

'Thanks.' She picked up her cup and turned her head to face him. 'I'm going to turn in now. Don't bother to get up. You take your time. I'll see you tomorrow. And thank you for a lovely evening.'

'My pleasure. Sleep well, Connie.'

And then, to his surprise, she leant over and kissed him. Just the lightest brush of her lips, not like the last kiss they'd shared but the first, and then she was gone, walking away, leaving his mouth tingling and tasting of regret.

She did sleep, to her surprise. She slept like a log, and woke in the morning feeling refreshed and ready for the day.

He greeted her on the veranda with a cup of tea and a slice of hot, buttered toast, and she ate it, said goodbye to Saffy and at the last minute leant over and kissed his cheek.

He hadn't shaved, and the stubble grazed her skin deliciously. 'See you later,' she murmured, and he nodded.

'Call me if you need to, if it gets too chaotic.'

'Are you implying I can't cope?' she asked cheekily as she went through the gate.

'I wouldn't dare,' he said, laughing, and watched her go.

Gorgeous, he thought, as she flicked her hair back over her shoulder and stuck her sunglasses on her head to anchor it. Utterly, unaffectedly gorgeous.

And if he'd thought that this was in any way going to be easier than ignoring his feelings, he was finding out just how wrong he was.

He sighed heavily. If only she hadn't been Joe's woman, he would have kissed her last night. She'd been all but hyperventilating when he'd brushed her knuckles with his lips, and if it hadn't been for Joe he would have slid his hand around the back of her neck and eased her closer and kissed her till she whimpered. And that would have been it, because this time they were stone cold sober and knew exactly where it was leading.

He sighed again.

So near, and yet so far.

They passed in Reception at lunchtime, him on the way in, her on the way out.

'Good shift?'

'Yes, fine. No problems.'

'Good. I'll see you later. Don't wait for me to eat, I won't be back till after nine.'

'OK. I'll have something ready for you.'

'Star.'

He winked. No kisses here, not in front of the others, she realised, and she was glad, really. This was all too new, too precious, too fragile. It could so easily go wrong.

She drove home, changed into her running gear and took Saffy out. Not for long, because James had taken her once

already, but just for a gentle lope along the sea wall as a reward for being good shut up in her run.

Then she showered and made herself a sandwich and a
cup of tea and went back into the cabin. Those last two boxes
of stuff were all that was left, and she had time now to deal
with them.

She put the tea down on the bedside table, took a bite of
the sandwich and opened the first box.

Correspondence. All sorts of stuff, out of the top drawer
of Joe's desk. She'd just emptied it out, stacked it all together
and packed it, and she had no idea what it was.

A will, for one thing, she realised.

There had been a copy with the solicitors who'd done the
conveyancing on their house, so in many ways it was redundant. She checked it, and it was the same, leaving everything to her.

Letters. Letters from his sisters, from his mother, from her,
grouped together in elastic bands, kept out of sentiment. There
had been more of those that had been sent home to her when
he'd died, but she'd never looked at them. And then, leafing
through them, she found two others she'd never seen before.

One to her, one to James.

To be opened in the event of his death.

Trembling, her fingers not quite brave enough to do this,
she slit the envelope open, pulled out the single handwritten
sheet and spread it out on her lap.

My darling Connie,
If you're reading this, then I guess it's caught up with
me at last. I'm so sorry. I've been waiting for it for a
long time now, dreading it, expecting it, hoping I was
wrong, and I know you have, too.

I hope you're OK, that my family are taking care of
you and making sure you're all right. I'm sure you're

not, not really, but you will be. It takes time, but you'll get there, and when you do, I want you to go out and grab life with both hands.

You've been an amazing wife, a wonderful partner and a really good friend, loyal and supportive and understanding, even when you didn't agree with my choices. I'm just so sad that we've never had a family, that the baby I know you've longed for has never come, that I've let you down, but you'll have a chance now to find that happiness with someone else, and I want you to take it. Don't hold back because of me. I want you to be happy, to be a mother, if that's what you'd like, but I can't bear to think of you all alone without me, so don't be. Don't be sad, don't be lonely. If the chance for happiness arises, take it.

I've left a letter for James. Make sure he gets it. He promised me, the last time I saw him, that he'd take care of you when I died, and I know that whatever happens, he'll do that because he's that kind of person. I've always wondered, though, what would have happened to you two if he'd never introduced us. I know Cathy's death tore him apart. I don't know the details, but he's shut himself down and I know he's lonely, but I'm sure he could love again if the right person came along, and maybe you're the right person for him, have been all along.

There's always been something between you, some spark. I've noticed it sometimes and been jealous, but why should I be, because I've been the one privileged to share my life with you, and I always trusted you both implicitly.

I know I shouldn't meddle, shouldn't matchmake, but I can't think of a single person more worthy of you, no one I'd entrust your happiness to the way I would to

James, and maybe this would give you both a chance at happiness, a chance to be parents, to have the family I know you've both longed for.

I love you, my darling. Completely, unreservedly, to the depths of my soul, and I always will. But life moves on, and time heals, and I want you to be happy.

Goodbye, sweetheart.
All my love,
Joe x

She closed her eyes, the tears spilling down her cheeks, and she let them fall. She didn't sob. She just sat there while the tears flowed, his voice echoing in her head as he said goodbye.

She was still sitting there motionless when James got home, the sandwich long gone, stolen by Saffy when supper didn't seem to be forthcoming.

CHAPTER TEN

She was in the cabin. He walked in and saw her, and something about her stillness alarmed him. He went over to her and sat down on the bed beside her, taking her lifeless hand in his.

'Connie?'

'I found a letter,' she said, her voice hollow. 'From Joe. There's one for you.'

She handed him the envelope.

'If it's anything like mine, you might want to read it on your own,' she said, and she folded the closely written sheet that was lying on her lap. It was smudged with tears, creased from the pressure of her hands, and she laid it gently down on the bedside table and got up and walked away.

Not sure at all that he wanted to read it, James slit the envelope.

Dear James,
I know you won't want to hear a load of sentimental crap, but there are times when it's necessary and this is one of them.

I asked you to take care of Connie for me when I died. If you're reading this, it's happened, and I hope she's giving you a chance to do that. Whether she is or not, I know you'll be keeping an eye on her if only from a distance.

You've been the best friend a man could ask for. Too good to me, I've thought from time to time. You gave me Connie, for a start, and she's filled my life with joy, but I sometimes wonder if you cheated yourself when you did that. There's always been something there between you. I've seen you watching her, but I know I've always been able to trust you to do the decent thing, and I trust you now. I trust you not to use her, but I also trust you to love her if that's the way it goes.

I know you won't hurt her deliberately. I never have, but my choice of career and my inability to give her the family she's longed for have both hurt her deeply and it grieves me.

I know Cathy's death hurt you, too, very deeply, but maybe together you can find happiness. If not together, then I hope you both find it another way, because of all the people in the world, I love you two the most and I want you to be happy.

If it's right for you, then please feel free to love her as she deserves, as you deserve. You have my blessing.
Your friend
Joe

Hell.

He put the letter down, folding it carefully and putting it with Connie's, and then he got to his feet and went to find her.

She was on the sea wall, and she was waiting for him. He sat beside her, on the other side of Saffy, and she looked up at him searchingly.

'Are you all right?'

He closed his eyes because it hurt simply to look at her. 'I'll live,' he said, hoping it was true, because for the first time since Cathy had died, he really wanted to. 'How about you?'

She smiled a little wanly. 'Me too. What did he say?'

'I've left it on your bedside table.'

She turned to look at him again, her eyes searching in the dim light. 'Did you read mine?'

'No—God, no, Connie. Of course not.'

No. Of course he hadn't. It simply wasn't like him to do that.

'He wants me to be happy,' she said. 'And I think he's matchmaking.'

Beside her, she heard James huff softly. Not a laugh, not a sigh, something in between, a recognition of the character of the man they'd both loved and lost.

'I know he's matchmaking—or at least facilitating. He gave us his blessing, Connie.'

She nodded slowly. 'It makes a difference.'

'It does. It makes a hell of a difference. I've been feeling guilty, thinking of you as Joe's woman, but it's what he wants, if it's right for us. He wants us to be together. He's given us permission, Connie, handed us to each other and bowed out. I don't think I'd be that bloody noble.'

She laughed, the same little noise he'd made, something closer to a sob. She heard him sigh softly.

'Or maybe I was. When Cathy died I felt as if my life had ended. There was nothing in it, nothing worth having, and chasing round the world for God knows how long didn't seem to make it any better, so I came home and still there was nothing.

'And then you came into my life, bright and funny, clever, quick-witted and warm—so warm. In another life, I would have grabbed the chance, but it was then, and I was broken, and so I introduced you to Joe. And I've never regretted it, before you ask. I loved seeing you together. You made him happy, and for that I'm truly grateful, because at the end of the day we're still alive and he isn't, and he deserved that happiness and so did you.'

She didn't say anything. She couldn't speak. She just sat there beside him, and their hands found each other over the top of Saffy's shoulders and clung.

It was pitch dark by the time they moved.

The sky had clouded over, the moon obscured, and he made her wait there while he went back to the house and turned on the lights.

She heard him stumble, heard the dog yelp and him swear softly, and then the lights were on and he was back there, holding out his hand to help her up.

She got stiffly to her feet, her body cold with lack of food and movement, and he led her back to the house, his arm slung loosely round her shoulders, holding her by his side.

'You're freezing. When did you last eat?' he asked, and she shrugged.

'I made a sandwich about three. I had a bite or two, then I opened the letter. I guess Saffy had the rest. I haven't fed her.'

He made a soft sound with his tongue and fed the dog, fed them both some toast slathered with butter and honey, and poured two glasses of wine.

'What's that for?' she asked, and he laughed, if you could call it that.

'Dutch courage?'

She blinked. 'Am I so scary?'

'You are when I'm going to ask you to come to bed with me.'

She felt her jaw sag slightly, and then she laughed. Softly at first, and then a little hysterically, and then finally she stopped, pressing her fingers to her mouth, tears welling, unbearably touched by his nervousness.

'Are you sure?' she asked.

'As sure as I can be. I don't know if I can love you like Joe wants me to, I have to tell you that, but, my God, I want to try, Connie. I've wanted you for so long, and you've been out of reach in every conceivable way, but now you're not, maybe, and I want you so much it hurts.'

She nodded. 'Me, too. I've always liked you, always felt I could trust you, known that you were decent to your bones, but just recently my body's woken up again and it's like I've seen you for the first time, only I haven't. I've always known you oozed sex appeal, it just wasn't aimed at me so it didn't register. But now...'

'Is that a yes, then?'

'It could be. Just—talking of conceivable...'

'Don't worry. I'm not going to get you pregnant, Connie. Not by accident. If and when we reach that point, it'll be by choice.' He smiled wryly. 'I went shopping yesterday, after I left work. Just in case.'

He drained his wine glass, stood up and held his hand out to her.

'Coming?'

She smiled. Not coquettishly, not the smile of a siren, but gently, with warmth. 'I hope so.'

Heat flared in his eyes, and he gathered her against his chest with a ragged sigh. 'Ah, Connie,' he whispered, and his lips found hers and he kissed her. Tentatively at first, and then more confidently, probing the inner recesses, his tongue duelling with hers, searching, coaxing until her legs buckled and she staggered slightly.

'Bed,' he said gruffly. 'Now.'

'Saffy,' she said, and he stopped, swore, shut the dog away with an extra biscuit and was back to her in seconds.

'The cabin's unlocked.'

He ran back and locked it.

It was closer, but the letters were in there, and this first time together they needed to be alone without the ghost of Joe smiling over them.

However graciously.

They ran upstairs hand in hand, right to the top, and then he stopped and turned her towards him and undressed her. He would have done it slowly but she was wearing that blue dress again and he lifted it over her head, leaving her standing there in that lace bra and the tiny, fragile little cobweb shorts that had tantalised him so much. He'd put on the bedside light, and its soft glow gilded her body and nearly brought him to his knees.

'You're wearing that raspberry red lace again,' he groaned, and she smiled, a little uncertain this time.

'It's comfortable.'

'I don't care. I think you've worn it long enough,' he said, and turning her away from him, he unfastened the catch of her bra and slid the straps off her shoulders, catching her soft, firm breasts in his hands as they spilled free.

He dropped his head against hers, his mouth raining kisses down the arch of her neck, over her collar bone, under her ear—anywhere he could reach. It didn't matter. Every brush of his lips, every touch of his tongue made her gasp and shudder. He slid his hands down her sides, but she pushed him away and turned, her mouth finding his as her fingers searched his shirt for buttons.

He was still in his work clothes, she realised. The shirt was nothing special, just a normal shirt, so she grasped the front of it and tore it open, buttons pinging in all directions. And then she giggled mischievously.

'I've always wanted to do that.'

'Have you?' he said, and took his trousers off himself, just to be on the safe side.

'Spoilsport.'

'Vandal.'

He kicked off his shoes, stripped off his boxers and socks and trousers in one movement and held out his hand.

'Come to bed with me, Connie,' he said, his eyes suddenly serious. 'I need to make love to you and I don't think I can wait any longer.'

She went with him, toppling into the bed in a tangle of arms and legs, hungry mouths and searching hands. So hungry. So searching.

So knowing. Knowing, clever hands that explored her body inch by inch. She'd thought he was in a hurry, but there was nothing hurried about his thorough exploration.

'James—please,' she begged, and he lifted his head and touched her lips with his fingers. She could taste herself on him, and she moaned softly, rocking against him.

'Please—now, please...'

He left her briefly, then he was back, his eyes glittering with fire and ice, his body vibrating with need.

'James,' she begged, and then he was there, filling her, stroking her, pushing her higher, higher, his body more urgent, his touch more demanding, until finally he took her over the brink into glorious, Technicolor freefall.

His body stiffened, pulsing deep within her, and then as the shockwaves ebbed away he dropped his head into the hollow of her shoulder and gathered her gently against his chest, rolling them to the side.

They lay there in silence for a moment, scarcely moving, and then he turned his head and kissed her.

'You OK, Connie?' he murmured, and she lifted her head and met his eyes and smiled.

'I'm fine. More than fine. You?'

He smiled back. 'Oh, I'm fine, too. I'm so fine I think I must be dreaming.'

'Not unless it's the same dream.'

He hugged her, then let her go and vanished to the bathroom and left her lying there staring out of the roof window at the night sky. The clouds had cleared, she thought. There was moonlight on the side of the reveal that had been in shadow.

He came back to bed and turned off the light, pulling her into his arms, and they lay together staring at the stars and watching the moon track across the sky, and they talked.

They talked about Joe, and Cathy, but about other things, too. How he'd lost his parents, how she had, what he should do with the garden, and about her career.

'I'm sorry I put you in a difficult position,' she said quietly. 'I know you didn't have a choice, not if you'd offered her the job. I just didn't want to hear it. I can't afford to hear it, if the truth be told, because my money's running out fast and I need to work.'

'Not necessarily. Not yet, at any rate. If this works for us, if we don't get sick of each other and decide we can't tolerate the other one's appalling habits—'

'What, like leaving a little heap of teabags on the side?' she teased, and he laid a finger over her mouth and smiled.

'If we don't get sick of each other, then it's not an issue. If we do, if one of us thinks it isn't working for them, then I'll support you until you find a job. Don't worry about the money, Connie. I promised Joe I'd look after you, and one way or the other, you're stuck with me.'

'Thank you.' She smiled tenderly, and leant over and kissed him, her lips gentle. 'I can think of worse fates.'

They both had irritating habits, it turned out.

He left the teabags in a heap, she was bordering on OCD with the arrangement of the mugs in the cupboard. Handles on the left, and God help anyone who put them away wrong.

She squashed the toothpaste in the middle, he didn't put the lid on.

But they muddled through, and the nights took away any

of the little frustrations encountered along the road to adjustment.

Work was going well, too. Annie Brooks, the new doctor, had started, and Connie was doing only occasional shifts and researching career options and training Saffy in her free time.

The career thing was a bit difficult, because she didn't really know where she should be looking for a job.

Living with James was great, the sex was amazing, they seemed to get on fine at work—but emotionally he still hadn't given her a hint of his feelings, of how he thought it was going, of how their relationship might pan out long-term.

And she wanted to know. Needed to know, because she was falling in love with him, she was sure, and she didn't want to fall too far if he was going to pull the plug on them. She'd tried to hold back some of herself from Joe, but it hadn't worked. She thought it had, but then he died and she realised she'd been fooling herself. She wasn't going to let herself do the same thing with James.

And then one day towards the end of August they were down at the little jetty, and James was pointing out things on the other side of the river. Saffy was at his side, patiently waiting for him to throw her stick again, and then it happened.

One minute they were standing on the dock, the next a boat went past and sent up a wave that knocked Saffy off her feet.

She fell into the churning water and was swept out, right into the middle of the current.

'Saffy!' she screamed, and then to her horror James kicked off his shoes and dived in after her. 'Noooo!' she screamed. 'James, no, come back! What are you doing?'

He went under briefly, then re-emerged a little further downstream.

'He'll be all right, love. Tide's going out, and Bob's gone to fetch them.'

'Bob?'

'The harbourmaster. Don't worry. It'll be all right.'

Would it? She didn't think so. He went under again, and then came up, dragging Saffy by the collar, just as Bob got to him. Terrified, still unable to believe her eyes, she watched as Bob pulled Saffy's body into the boat.

'That's a goner,' someone said, and her breath hitched on a sob.

'Get him out,' she pleaded silently. 'Please, get him out.'

'He'll be all right now. He's got a rope wrapped round his wrist. Don't you fret.'

Fret? She was beside herself as the boat pulled up at the jetty and someone dragged James out of the water.

'Get the dog out of the boat,' he snapped, and hauling her onto the wet boards of the jetty, he pumped down hard on her chest. Connie fell to her knees beside him, numb with shock.

'What can I do?' she asked, and he met her eyes, his own despairing.

'Nothing. I'm going to swing her.'

And grabbing the big dog by the back legs, he lifted her up and swung her over the side of the jetty to drain her lungs.

Nothing happened for a moment, and then water poured out.

He dropped her back on the jetty, clamped her mouth shut and breathed hard down her nose. Her chest inflated, and he blew again, and then again, and suddenly she coughed and struggled up, and his face crumpled briefly.

'It's OK, Saffy,' he said gently, holding on to her for dear life. 'It's OK.'

But it was too much for Connie.

'No, it's not OK,' she yelled, losing it at last now she knew they were both safe. 'That could have been you lying there with filthy water pouring out of your lungs, scarcely breathing! I've lost one man with a death wish, I'm not going to lose another one. You could have told me you were an idiot before I let myself fall in love with you!'

And spinning on her heel, she ran back towards the cottage, tears of rage and fear and relief pouring down her face, blinding her so that she ran smack into something.

Someone?

'Connie?'

David. It was Molly's David, her blade runner, gripping her shoulders and holding her upright, and she fell sobbing into his arms.

'Connie, whatever's happened? I heard all the commotion—what is it? Where's James?'

'He went in the river,' she said raggedly. 'Saffy was swept in, and he went in after her.'

'Where is he?' he asked, starting to run.

'He's out, David. He's out of the water. He's fine. I'm just—so angry.'

'And Saffy?' he asked, coming back.

'I think she'll be all right. She didn't breathe. She had water in her lungs, and he got it out, but his stupid heroics—'

She broke off and clamped her mouth shut so she didn't make an even bigger fool of herself, but it was too late, apparently, because James was coming now, Saffy walking unsteadily at his side, and at the sight of him she started to cry again.

'Did you mean it?' he asked, stopping right in front of her. In front of everyone.

'Mean what? That I'm angry with you? You'd better believe it.'

'That you love me.'

The crowd went utterly silent.

'Well, of course I love you, you idiot,' she ranted. 'Why else would I put up with your teabags?'

He laughed, his face crumpling after a second. 'God

knows, but I love you, too,' he said, then reached for her, dragging her up against his sodden chest and kissing her as if his life depended on it.

Against her leg she could feel Saffy shivering, and in the cheering crowd someone said, 'What was that about teabags?'

'Time to go home,' he said firmly, and tucking her under his arm, he walked slowly back, Saffy on one side, the woman he hoped to spend the rest of his life with on the other.

'We need to rub her dry and keep her warm,' he said, bringing towels for Saffy into the kitchen.

'Let me do that,' Connie said, taking a towel. 'You need a shower and some dry clothes on before you catch your death.'

'I'm fine. Call the vet. She'll need antibiotics after that.'

Saffy staggered to her feet again and went out onto the veranda and retched, bringing up more of the murky water, and then she came back, lay down beside them and licked his hand.

His eyes filled, and he blinked hard and rubbed her with a towel until she stopped shivering.

Connie was kneeling beside Saffy, keying a number into the phone and muttering about him catching his death of cold, and he sat back on his heels and looked at her. 'Can I ask you something?'

'What?' she said, holding the phone to her ear.

'Will you marry me?'

She stared at him, her jaw sagging slightly, and put the phone down on the floor before she dropped it. 'Marry you?'

'Yes. You know, big dress, diamond ring, honeymoon, babies—'

Her heart started beating harder, so loud now it almost deafened her. 'Babies?' she asked, just to be sure she'd heard it right.

'Absolutely. Definitely babies. I can't wait.'

Her breath left her in a rush. 'Neither can I.'

'So—is that a yes?'

She laughed—or was it a sob? He wasn't sure, but she was in his arms, saying, 'Yes, yes, yes,' over and over again until he actually began to believe it.

'Good. We'll talk in a minute.' And he picked up the handset from the floor.

She stared at him, listening to someone saying, 'Hello? This is the vet surgery. Did you call?'

Oh, no! Had they heard? She felt hot colour surge into her cheeks, and he smiled at her, his eyes laughing. 'Yes. Sorry about that, we got a little distracted. Can you come out on a house visit, please? We've got a rather large dog who nearly drowned in the river. I think she needs looking at urgently.'

He gave them the details, hung up and tucked her in closer beside him. 'I'm sorry I scared you. Tell me you've forgiven me.'

'No, I won't,' she said, snuggling up to his side and ignoring the rank smell of river water that clung to his sodden clothes. 'I don't know if I ever will. I thought I was going to lose you, James. I was so scared.'

'I'm sorry. I didn't think. I just saw her go in, and I couldn't let her die. Not Saffy, not after all she's been through, all she means to you, to Joe. You would have been devastated. She's our family, Connie. And I knew the tide was going out. It's when it's coming in it's so dangerous, because the denser sea water sinks under the river water where they meet and it drags you under.'

'And if you hadn't known that? Would you still have dived in?'

He shrugged. 'I don't know. Probably not. I might have nicked a boat and gone after her, but even on an outgoing tide, the current's really strong. I do know it's dangerous. I'm not an adrenaline junkie, Connie, not like Joe. I want to grow old with you, and see our children graduate and have babies of their own. I have no intention of dying. Not now. Not now I've got something worth living for. Some*one* worth living for.'

Saffy lifted her head and laid it on his lap, and he stroked her gently. 'Poor old girl. Two someones.'

Connie leant over and pressed a kiss to the dog's now warm flank. 'Thank you for rescuing her. You're right, I would have been devastated if we'd lost her.'

'I know that. I'm sorry I frightened you.'

'Don't do it again. Ever.'

'I won't.'

'Good.'

Two hours later, after the vet had been and Saffy was declared fit enough to stay at home to recover from her experience, they were all upstairs in his bedroom.

Saffy was snuggled up on an old quilt on the sofa by the window, snoring softly, and James and Connie were in bed, emotionally exhausted but happy. They'd showered to get rid of the smell of the river water which by then had been cling-ing to both of them, and now they were lying propped up on the pillows watching Saffy's chest rise and fall and letting the drama of the day subside.

'I love you,' she murmured, and he bent his head and pressed a warm, gentle kiss to her hair.

'I love you, too. I've loved you for years.'

She turned her head then and looked up at him. 'Really?'

'Really. I didn't let myself think about it before but you've always been more to me than just a friend. That was one of the reasons I couldn't just say yes to giving you a baby the way you asked, because I wanted so much more. I wanted to do it properly, like this, in the context of a permanent lov-ing relationship, and anything less just seemed wrong, as if it would cheat all of us.'

'Oh, James…'

She lifted her hand and cradled his cheek, touching her lips to his, and he eased her closer, deepening the kiss, feeling the warmth of her soothing him.

It was like coming home, and he couldn't quite believe it.

'So—about these babies,' he murmured against her lips, trailing a daisy chain of kisses over her cheek and down towards the hollow of her throat.

She arched her head back, the soft sigh whispering in his hair. 'Mmm—want to make a start?'

She felt his smile against her skin.

'You read my mind,' he said softly, and kissed her all over again.

* * * * *

A KNIGHT FOR NURSE HART

LAURA IDING

This book is dedicated to Senior Editor
Sheila Hodgson, for giving me a chance five
years ago and buying my first book.
Thanks for being so supportive.

CHAPTER ONE

"RAINE! You're here? Working Trauma again?" Sarah greeted her when she walked into the trauma bay fifteen minutes before the regular start of her shift.

Emergency nurse Raine Hart smiled at her co-worker. "Yes, I'm back. Working in the minor care area for a few weeks was a nice reprieve and a lot less stress. But I confess I've missed being a part of the action."

"Well, we sure missed you, too. And I'm so glad you came in early," Sarah said, quickly changing the subject from Raine's four-week hiatus from Trauma to her own personal issues. "I have to leave right away to pick-up my son, he's running a fever at the day care and there's a new trauma coming in." Sarah thrust the trauma pager into her hands as if it were a hot potato. "ETA is less than five minutes."

"No problem." Raine accepted the pager, feeling a tiny thrill of anticipation. She hadn't been lying, she really had missed the excitement of working in the trauma bay. She scrolled through the most recent text message from the paramedic base. Thirty-year-old female with blunt trauma to the head with poor vital signs. Not good. "Sounds like it's been busy."

"Crazy busy," Sarah agreed. "Like I said, we missed you. Sorry I have to run, but I'll see you, tomorrow."

"Bye, Sarah." Raine clipped the pager to the waist-band of her scrubs, and swept a glance over the room. It looked as if Sarah had everything ready to go for the next patient. She was secretly relieved to start off her first trauma shift with a new admission. She'd rather be busy—work was a welcome distraction from her personal problems. Raine was thankful her boss had kept her real reason for being away from Trauma a secret, telling her co-workers only that she'd been off sick, and then reassigned to Minor Care to work in a less stressful environment on doctor's orders. After three weeks in Minor Care, she was more than ready for more intense nursing.

So here she was, back in the trauma bay. Raine took a deep breath and squared her shoulders, determined to keep the past buried deep, where it belonged.

She could do this, no problem.

"No sign of our trauma patient yet?" a low husky, familiar voice asked.

She sucked in a harsh breath and swung around to stare at Dr. Caleb Stewart in shocked surprise. According to the posted schedule, Brock Madison was supposed to be the emergency physician on duty in the trauma bay tonight. Obviously, he and Caleb must have switched shifts.

"Not yet." Her mouth was sandpaper dry and she desperately searched for something to say. Caleb looked great. Better than great. Better than she'd remembered. But she hadn't been prepared to face him. Not yet. She hadn't seen him since they'd decided to take a break from their relationship just over a month ago.

She couldn't ignore a sharp pang of regret. If only she'd tried harder to work things out. But she hadn't.

And now it was too late.

Thankfully, before he could say anything more, the doors of the trauma bay burst open, announcing the arrival of their patient. Instantly, controlled chaos reigned.

"Becca Anderson, thirty years old, vitals dropping, BP 86 over 40, pulse tachy at 128," the paramedic standing at the patient's head announced. "Her GCS was only 5 in the field, so we intubated her. She probably needs fluids but we've been concerned about brain swelling, and didn't want to make her head injury worse."

Raine took her place on the left side of their trauma patient, quickly drawing the initial set of blood samples they'd need in order to care for Becca. Luckily, the rhythm of working in Trauma came back instantly, in spite of her four-week absence. Amy, one of the other nurses, came up on the right side to begin the initial assessment. One of the ED techs cut off the patient's clothes to give them better access to any hidden injuries.

"Raine, as soon as you're finished with those labs, we need to bump up her IV fluids and start a vasopresser, preferably norepinephrine," Caleb ordered. "Shock can kill her as much as a head injury."

"Left pupil is one millimeter larger than the right,"

Amy informed them. "I can't feel a major skull fracture, just some minor abrasions on the back of her scalp. It's possible she has a closed cranial trauma."

Raine's stomach dropped at the news. Patients with closed cranial trauma had the worst prognosis. When the brain swelled there was no place for it to go, often resulting in brain death. And Becca was too young to die.

Suddenly, she was fiercely glad Caleb was the physician on duty. Despite their differences, she knew he'd work harder than anyone to make sure their patient survived. Determined to do her part, Raine took her fistful of blood tubes over to the tube system to send them directly to the laboratory. En route, she noticed two uniformed police officers were standing back, watching the resuscitation. It wasn't unusual to have law enforcement presence with trauma patients, so she ignored them as she rushed back to increase their patient's IV fluids and to start a norepinephrine drip.

"We need a CT scan of her head, stat. Any other signs of internal injuries?" Caleb demanded.

"Bruises on her upper arms," Raine said, frowning at the dark purple spots that seemed to match the size and shape of fingertips. She hung the medication and set the pump to the appropriate rate as she talked. "Give me a minute and we'll roll her over to check her back." She finished the IV set-up and took a moment to double-check she'd done everything correctly.

"I'll help." Caleb stepped next to Raine, adding his strength to pulling the patient up and over onto her side, so Amy could assess the patient's backside. Caleb was close, too close. She bit her lip, forcing herself not to overreact at the unexpected warmth when his arm brushed against hers.

Memories of the wonderful times together crashed through her mind and she firmly shoved them aside. Their relationship was over. She wasn't the same person she'd been back then.

And they had a critically ill patient to care for.

"A few minor abrasions on her upper shoulders, nothing major," Amy announced. Raine and Caleb gently rolled the patient onto her back.

"She's the victim of a domestic dispute," one of the police officers said, stepping forward. "Her husband slammed her head against the concrete driveway, according to witnesses."

Dear God, how awful. A small-town girl at heart, Raine had moved to the big city of Milwaukee just two years ago after finishing college. But she still wasn't used to some of the violent crime victims they inevitably cared for. She tried to wipe the brutal image from her mind.

"Raine?" Caleb's voice pierced her dark thoughts. "Call Radiology and arrange for a CT scan."

She nodded and hurried to the phone. Within minutes, she had Becca packed up and ready to go.

"I'm coming with you," Caleb said, as she started pushing the cart towards the radiology suite next door. Thankfully the hospital had had the foresight to put the new radiology department right next to the emergency department. "I don't like the way her heart rate is continuing to climb. Could be partially due to the norepinephrine, but it could also be her head injury getting worse."

She couldn't argue because Becca's vital signs were

not very stable. Usually the physicians only came along on what the nurses referred to as road trips, for the worst-case scenarios.

As Becca's blood pressure dropped even further, Raine grimly acknowledged this was one of those times she would be glad to have physician support.

She was all too aware of Caleb's presence as they wheeled the patient's gurney into the radiology suite. There were unspoken questions in his eyes when he glanced at her, but he didn't voice them. She understood—this was hardly the time or the place for them to talk about the mistakes they'd made in the past. About what might have been.

She kept her gaze focused on their patient and the heart monitor placed at the foot of her bed. They were only part way into the scan when Becca's blood pressure dropped to practically nothing.

"Get her out of there," Caleb demanded. The radiology tech hurried to shut down the scanner so they could pull the patient out from the scanner opening. "Crank up her norepinephrine drip."

Raine was already pushing buttons on the IV pump. But then the pump began to alarm. She looked at the swollen area above the patient's antecubital peripheral IV. "I think her IV is infiltrated."

Caleb muttered a curse under his breath and grabbed a central line insertion set off the top of the crash cart the radiology tech had wisely brought in. "Then we'll put a new central line in her right now."

"Here?" the radiology tech asked incredulously.

Caleb ignored him. Raine understood—they couldn't

afford to lose another vein. A central line would be safer in the long run. Anticipating his needs, she quickly placed sterile drapes around the patient's neck, preparing the insertion site as Caleb donned sterile gloves. Luck or possibly divine intervention was on his side when he hit the subclavian vein on the first try.

"Here's the medication," Raine said, handing over the end of the IV tubing she'd disconnected from the non-working IV.

The moment Caleb connected the tubing, she administered a small bolus to get the medication into her patient's bloodstream quicker, since the woman's blood pressure was still non-existent and her heart rate was dropping too. For a moment, Raine held her breath, but their patient responded well and her blood pressure soon returning to the 80s systolic. Caleb anchored the line with a suture and then quickly dressed the site.

But they weren't out of the woods yet. Worried, she glanced at Caleb. "Should we complete the scan?" she asked.

He gave a curt nod, his expression grave. One of the things she liked best about Caleb was that he didn't build a wall around himself to protect his emotions. He sincerely cared about his patients. "We have to. The neurosurgeons are going to need to see the films in order to decide whether or not to take her to surgery."

The radiology tech didn't look very happy at the prospect, but took his place to continue running the scan. Raine and Caleb together slid the patient back onto the exam table. She was startled when he took her arm, and instinctively pulled away. She winced when she realized what she'd done, knowing he'd done nothing to deserve her reaction. Her issues, not his.

His stormy gray eyes darkened with hurt confusion but she avoided the questioning look he shot her way. She felt bad about hurting him again, but at that moment her patient's heart monitor alarmed so she was forced to go over to adjust the alarm limits. The ten-minute exam seemed excruciatingly long, but they finally finished the procedure.

Caleb didn't say anything as they pushed the gurney back to the trauma bay. The moment they arrived, he crossed over to page the neurosurgeon to discuss the best course of action for their patient.

"Becca?" Raine glanced over at the shrill voice. She saw Amy bringing in a woman who looked to be a few years younger than their patient. "Oh, my God, Becca. What did he do to you?"

Raine had to turn away from the crying woman who clutched their patient's hand.

"Her sister, Mari," Amy said in a low tone. "I had to let her in because I'm betting Becca will be going to the OR ASAP."

"Of course you did," Raine said, but her voice sounded far away, as if she was speaking through a long tunnel. She'd wanted to be busy, but maybe she'd been overconfident. Maybe she wasn't ready for the trauma room just yet. Maybe she should have stayed longer in the minor care area of the ED, where they didn't deal with anything remotely serious.

Her eyes burned and she fought the need to cry right along with Mari. She turned away, to give them some privacy and to pull herself together. She went over to the computer to look up Becca's most recent labs.

"Raine? Are you all right?" Caleb asked, coming up to the computer workstation.

"Of course." She subtly loosened her grip on the edge of the desk and forced herself to meet his gaze, hoping he couldn't tell how emotionally fragile she was. It was far too tempting to lean on Caleb's strength. To confide in him. If things had been different...

But they weren't. Reminding herself that she needed to find her own strength to work through her past, she waved a hand at the computer screen. "Did you see these latest results? Her electrolytes are way out of whack."

He gave her an odd look, but then nodded. "Get her prepped for the OR. Dr. Lambert wants her up there ASAP."

"Okay." Raine abandoned her computer and jumped to her feet. She hurried over to Becca's bedside and told Amy and Mari the news.

Within moments she and Amy transported Becca up to the OR, releasing her into the hands of the neurosurgeons. There was nothing else they could do for now but wait.

Raine tried to push Becca's fate out of her mind since she and Caleb had done everything she could for the patient. But concentrating on her job wasn't easy. Especially when she could feel Caleb's gaze following her as she worked.

She could tell he wanted to talk. The very thought filled her with dread. She couldn't talk to him now, no matter how much she wished she could.

It was too late. She'd missed her chance to take his

calls weeks ago. Better now to focus her energy on moving forward rather than rehashing the past.

What she and Caleb had once shared was over.

"Dr. Stewart?" He glanced up when Raine called his name. "I think you'd better check Mrs. Ambruster's chest X-ray. Her breathing has gotten dramatically worse."

Caleb scowled at the formal way she addressed him. They'd dated for almost two months, had shared more than one passionate kiss. He knew it was his fault that she'd requested a break from their relationship but, still, hadn't they moved well beyond the *Dr. Stewart* stage?

"Sure." A surge of regret washed over him. Seeing Raine again made him realize he'd never gotten over her. Not completely. If only he'd handled things differently. If only he hadn't been such an ass.

He'd heard she'd moved over to the minor care area because she'd needed a break from Trauma. He knew full well she'd really needed a break from him.

And he'd missed working with her, more than he'd wanted to acknowledge.

He gave himself a mental shake. This wasn't the time or the place. He crossed over to the patient, who had come in with vague flu-like symptoms that he was beginning to suspect was something much more complicated. Using the closest computer terminal, he pulled up the patient's chest X-ray. Raine was right, the patient's breathing must be severely compromised as the X-ray looked far worse. He suspected the large shadow was a tumor and likely the cause of a massive infiltrate on the right side of her lungs, but she would need more of a work-up to be sure. "How much O2 do you have her on?"

"Six liters."

He frowned. "Crank her up to ten liters per minute and prepare for a thoracentisis."

Raine did as he asked, although he noticed she gave him a wide berth whenever he came too close.

He was troubled by the way Raine was acting. He regretted the way he'd overreacted that night and had tried to call her several times to apologize but she hadn't returned his calls. Did she still blame him? Was it impossible for her to forgive him?

Seeing her tonight brought his old feelings back to the surface. Along with the same sexual awareness that had shimmered between them from the very first time they'd met.

But as much as that sensation was still there, something was off. He'd noticed right from the start of their shift how her usual enthusiasm was missing. Maybe it was just the seriousness of their domestic violence patient, but they'd shared tough shifts before. Somehow this was different, especially the way she seemed to avoid him whenever he came too close.

Maybe she was worried he'd ask her out again. And he had to admit, the thought had crossed his mind. More than once. Sure, he'd made a stupid mistake before, but didn't he deserve a second chance?

Apparently, Raine wasn't willing to grant him one.

He turned to their elderly patient, focusing on the procedure he needed to do. He put on a face mask and then donned sterile gown and gloves, while Raine prepped the patient. He lifted the needle and syringe in his hand and gently probed the space between the fourth and fifth ribs. He numbed the area with lidocaine and then picked up the longer needle used to aspirate the fluid. Slowly, he advanced the needle.

He hit the pocket of fluid and held the needle steady while the site drained. Once he'd taken off almost a liter of fluid, their patient's oxygen saturation improved dramatically.

"Place a dressing over this site, would you?" he asked Raine. "And we need to send a sample of this fluid to Pathology." Stepping back, he stripped off his sterile garb. Once she'd gotten the specimens sent to the lab and the patient cleaned up, he went back in to talk to the husband and wife.

"Mrs. Ambruster, I'm afraid your chest X-ray shows something abnormal and I believe whatever is going on is causing fluid to build up in your lungs."

The elderly couple exchanged a look of dismay. "What is it? Cancer?" her husband asked.

Caleb didn't want to lie but at the same time he didn't honestly know for certain what the problem was. He was impressed by the mutual love and respect this elderly couple displayed toward each other, something missing from his own family life. He tried to sound positive. "That is one possibility but there are others that could be less serious. I'm not a thoracic surgeon, but I'd like to refer you to one. I can arrange for you to see someone first thing in the morning if you're willing."

The Ambrusters agreed and he made the arrangements with the thoracic surgery resident. By the time he wrote the discharge orders for Mrs. Ambruster, the oncoming shift had arrived.

He was free to go home. But he didn't want to leave, not without talking to Raine.

He found her in the staff lounge, but stopped short when he realized she was crying. Immediately concerned, he rushed over. "Raine? What's wrong?"

"Nothing." She quickly swiped at her eyes, as if embarrassed by her display of emotion.

"Raine, please. Talk to me." He couldn't hide the desperate urgency in his voice.

There was a slight pause, and he found himself holding his breath when she finally brought her tortured gaze up to meet his. "Becca died. She never made it out of surgery."

Caleb grimaced beneath a wave of guilt. Here he'd been worried about himself when Raine was grieving over their patient. "I'm sorry, Raine. I didn't know."

"Doesn't matter. We did what we could."

The despair in her tone tugged at his heart. He wanted to reach out to her, but knew he'd given up that privilege when he'd accused her of cheating on him.

He wanted to apologize. To explain he now knew he'd been wrong, but where to start?

"I have to go," Raine muttered, swiping at her face and attempting to brush past him.

"Wait." He reached out to grasp her arm. "Please don't go. Let's talk. About us. About where we went wrong."

"There's no point. What we had is over," she whispered, wrenching from his grasp. The hint of dark desperation shadowing her eyes hit hard. She hesitated only for a moment, before ducking out of the room.

Shocked, he could only stare after her. Something was definitely wrong. This wasn't just Raine wanting to take a break from their relationship. There was something more going on.

He'd screwed up before, but he wouldn't give in so easily this time. He was determined to uncover the truth.

CHAPTER TWO

RAINE drove home, wishing she hadn't lost control like that in front of Caleb. It was her own fault that he had no idea what she'd been through. No one did. She been too embarrassed, too ashamed. Feeling too guilty to tell anyone.

She was determined to get over the past, and she knew that moving forward was the best way to accomplish that. And if she regretted taking a break from her relationship with Caleb, she had no one to blame but herself.

Caleb had trust issues. But instead of trying to work through them, she'd broken things off. And then, when he'd tried to call to make up, she hadn't returned his calls.

Because by then everything had changed.

She'd thought she'd put the past behind her. But obviously she'd jumped back into the trauma environment a little too quickly. She'd taken off work completely for a week, and then had taken a three-week assignment in the minor care area, trying to ease herself back into the stressful working environment the way her counselor had suggested. Obviously, she had a way to go before she'd be back to her old self.

She pulled into her assigned parking space in the

small lot behind her apartment, threw the gearshift into park and dropped her forehead on the steering-wheel with a deep, heavy sigh.

Who was she trying to kid? She'd never be the person she had been before. Hadn't her counselor drilled that fact into her head? There was no going back. The only option was to move forward.

Firming her resolve, she climbed from the car and headed up to her second-story apartment. She smiled when her cat, Spice, meowed softly and came running over to greet her, rubbing up against her leg with a satisfied purr. She picked up the cat and buried her face in the soft fur. She'd adopted Spice from the local shelter a few weeks ago and had not regretted it. Coming home to an empty apartment night after night had been difficult. Spice made coming home much easier. And the cat gave her someone to talk to.

She threw a small beanbag ball past Spice—the goofy cat actually liked to play fetch like a dog—and tried to unwind from the long shift. But the relaxation tips her therapist had suggested didn't help and she still had trouble falling asleep. She'd taken to sleeping on her sofa, and as she stared at the ceiling, she thought about her counselor's advice to confide in someone. She knew her counselor might be right, but she just couldn't make herself take that step.

If she told one of her friends what had happened, they'd look at her differently. With horror. With pity. Asking questions. She shivered with dread. No, she couldn't stand the thought of anyone knowing the gory details. Especially when she couldn't remember much herself.

The one person she might have confided in was Caleb. If he'd trusted her. Which he didn't.

The events of that night when he'd looked at her with frank disgust still had the power to hurt her. She'd gone out to a local pub with a group of ED staff nurses and physicians after work. Jake, one of the new ED residents, had flirted with her. She hadn't really thought too much about it until the moment she'd realized he'd had too much to drink. He'd leaned in close, with his arm around the back of her chair, trying to kiss her.

Before she could gently, but firmly push him away, Caleb had walked in. She'd blushed because she knew the situation looked bad, but he hadn't given her a chance to explain. Instead, he'd accused her of seeing Jake behind his back.

She'd seen the flash of hurt in his eyes, but at the same time she hadn't appreciated Caleb's willingness to think the worst of her. She'd talked to him the next day, and had tried to explain. But when he'd sounded distant, and remote, she'd given up, telling him it might be best to take a break from their relationship for a while.

She'd been stunned when he'd agreed.

Pounding a fist into her pillow, she turned on the sofa and tried to forget about Caleb. With everything that had happened, she'd put distance between herself and her friends.

Her closest friend, Elana Schultz, had recently married ED physician Brock Madison. In the months since their wedding she hadn't seen as much of Elana. They were still friends, but Elana had a new life now with Brock.

When Elana had assumed Raine had taken the job in Minor Care to avoid Caleb, she hadn't told her friend any different.

It was better than Elana knowing the truth.

The next morning Raine's phone woke her from a deep sleep. She patted the mound of linens on her sofa, searching for her cellphone. "Hello?"

"Raine? It's Elana. I just had to call to tell you the news."

"News?" Elana's dramatically excited tone brought a smile to her face. She pushed a hand through her hair and blinked the sleep from her eyes. "What news?"

"We heard the baby's heart beat!" Elana exclaimed, her excitement contagious. "You should have seen the look on Brock's face, he was so enthralled. He brought tears to my eyes. You'd never guess he once decided to live his life without children."

"He was delusional, obviously," Raine said dismissively. "And that was long before he met you. I'm so excited for you, Elana. Did you and Brock change your mind about finding out the baby's gender?"

"No, we still want the baby's sex to be a surprise. But my due date is confirmed—five months and one week to go."

Raine mentally calculated. It was the seventh of June. "November fifteenth?"

"Yes, give or take a week. Brock is painting the baby's room like a madman—he's worried we won't have everything ready in time," Elana said with a laugh. "I keep telling him there's no rush."

"Knowing Brock, he'll have it ready in plenty of

time." Raine tried to hide the wistful tone of her voice. Watching Elana and Brock together was wonderful and yet painful at the same time. They were so in love, they glowed.

If only she were worthy of that kind of love. She pushed aside the flash of self-pity. "Do you have time to meet for lunch?" she asked.

"Oh, I'm sorry Raine. I'd love to, but I agreed to volunteer at the New Beginnings clinic this afternoon. Can I take a rain-check?"

"Sure." Raine forced lightness into her tone. The New Beginnings clinic was a place where low-income patients could be seen at no cost to them. She'd volunteered there in the past, but not recently. "No problem. Take care and I'm sure I'll see you at work one of these days."

"I know, it's been for ever, hasn't it?" Elana asked. Raine knew it was exactly one month and three days since they'd worked together. Since her life had irrevocably changed. "You've been working in the minor care area and I've been cutting back my hours now that I'm pregnant. The morning sickness has been awful. Brock is being a tad overly protective lately, but I'm not going to complain. I'm scheduled to work this weekend."

"Great. I'm working the weekend, too and I'm back on the schedule in the trauma bay. I'll see you then." Raine hung up the phone, feeling a bit deflated. Not that she begrudged her friend one ounce of happiness. Elana had gone through some rough times, too.

Elana had moved on from her painful past, and Raine was sure she could too. One day at a time.

Since the last thing she needed was more time on her

hands, Raine forced herself to climb out of bed. There was no point in wallowing in self-pity for the rest of the day.

She needed to take action. To focus on the positive. She'd taken to volunteering at the animal shelter on her days off, as dealing with animals was somehow easier lately, than dealing with people.

It was time to visit her furry friends who were always there when she needed them.

Caleb pulled up in front of his father's house and swallowed a deep sigh. His father had called to ask for help, after injuring his ankle after falling off a ladder. His father was currently living alone, as his most recent relationship had ended in an unsurprising break-up. Caleb was relieved that at least this time his father had been smart enough to avoid marrying the woman. With four divorces under his belt, you'd think his father would learn. But, no, he kept making the same mistakes over and over again.

Leaving Caleb to pick up the pieces.

He walked up to the house, frowning a bit when he saw the front door was open. He knocked on the screen door, before opening it. "Dad? Are you in there?"

"Over here, Caleb," his father called out. His father's black Lab, Grizzly, let out a warning bark, but then came rushing over to greet him as he walked through the living room into the kitchen. He took a moment to pet the excited dog, and then crossed over to where his father was seated at the table, with his ankle propped on the chair beside him. "Thanks for coming."

"Sure." He bent over his father's ankle, assessing the

swollen joint, tenderly palpating the bruised tissue around the bone. "Are you sure this isn't broken?"

"Told you I took X-rays at the shelter, didn't I?" his father said in a cantankerous tone. "It's not broken, it's only sprained. Did you bring the crutches?"

"Yes, they're in the car." But he purposely hadn't brought them in. He'd asked his father to come into the ED while he was working, but did he listen? No. His father had taken his own X-rays on the machine he used for animals. Caleb would rather have looked at the films himself.

"Why did ya leave them out there? Go get 'em."

Caleb propped his hands on his hips and scowled at his father. "Dad, be reasonable. Take a couple of days off. Being on crutches around animals is just asking for trouble. Surely the shelter can do without you for a few days?"

"I told you, there's some sort of infection plaguing several of the new animals. I retired from my full-time veterinary practice last year, didn't I? I only go to the shelter three days a week and every other Saturday. Surely that's not too much for an old codger like me." His dad yanked on the fabric of his pants leg to help lift his injured foot down on the floor. "If you won't drive me, I'll arrange for a cab."

Caleb closed his eyes and counted to ten, searching for patience. He didn't remember ever calling his dad an old codger, but nevertheless a shaft of guilt stabbed deep. He'd promised to help out more, but hadn't made the time to come over as often as he should have. "I said I'd take you and I will. But, Dad, you have to try taking it easy

for a while. Every time I stop by I find you doing something new. Trying to clean out the gutters on that rickety
old ladder was what caused your fall in the first place."

"Well, someone had to do it."

This time Caleb counted to twenty. "You never asked
me to help you with the gutters," he reminded his father,
striving for a calm tone. "And if you'd have waited, I
could have done the job when I came over to mow your
lawn on the weekend."

His father ignored him, gingerly rising to his feet,
leaning heavily on the back of the kitchen chair to keep
the pressure off his sore ankle. Grizzly came over to
stand beside him, as if he could somehow assist. "I'm
going to need those crutches to get outside."

Arguing with his father was about as effective as
herding cats. His father simply ignored the things he
didn't want to deal with. "Sit down. I'll get them." Caleb
strode back through the house, muttering under his
breath, "Stubborn man."

He grabbed the crutches out of the back of the car and
slammed the door with more force than was necessary.
He and his father had always been at odds and the
passing of the years hadn't changed their relationship
much. Caleb's mother had taken off, abandoning him at
the tender age of five. One would think that fact alone
would have brought him and his dad closer together. But
his father hadn't waited very long before bringing home
future stepmothers in an attempt to replace his first wife.
At first the relationships had been short-lived, but then
he'd ended up marrying a few.

None of them stayed very long, of course. They left,

just like his mother, for a variety of reasons. Because they realized being a vet didn't bring in a boat-load of money, especially when you were already paying alimony for a previous marriage. Or they found someone else. Or simply got bored with playing step-mom to someone else's kid.

Whatever the reason, the women his father picked didn't stick around. Carmen was the one who'd stayed the longest, almost three years, but in the end she'd left, too.

Yeah, his father could really pick them.

"Here are the crutches," he said as he entered the kitchen. "Now, be patient for a minute so I can measure them. They have to fit your frame."

For once his father listened. After he'd adjusted the crutches to his father's height, the older man took them and leaned on them gratefully. "Thanks," he said gruffly.

"You're welcome." Caleb watched his father walk slowly across the room, making sure he could safely use them. Grizz got in the way once, but then quickly learned to avoid them. Crutches weren't as easy to use as people thought, and Caleb worried about his father's upper-arm strength. But his father was still in decent shape, and seemed to manage them well enough. Reluctantly satisfied, he followed his father outside, giving Grizz one last pat on the head.

The shelter was only ten miles away. Neither one of them was inclined to break the silence as Caleb navigated the city streets.

He pulled up in front of the building and shut the car. "I'll come inside with you," he offered.

"Sure." His father's mood had brightened the closer

they'd gotten to the shelter, and Caleb quickly figured out the elder man needed this volunteer work more than he'd realized.

More guilt, he thought with a slight grimace. He held the front door of the building open, waiting for his father to cross the threshold on his crutches before following him in.

"Dr. Frank! What happened?"

Caleb froze when he saw Raine rushing toward his father. She didn't seem to have noticed him as she placed an arm around his father's thin shoulders.

"Twisted my ankle, that's all. Nothing serious." His father patted her hand reassuringly. "Now, tell me, Raine, how's Rusty doing today? Is he any better?"

"He seems a little better, but really, Dr. Frank, should you be here? Maybe you should have stayed at home to rest." Raine lifted her gaze and he knew she'd spotted him when she paled, her dark red hair a stark contrast to her alabaster skin. "Caleb. What are you doing here?"

"Dropping off my father." He couldn't help the flash of resentment at how friendly his father and Raine seemed to be. She had never mentioned working at the animal shelter during those two months they'd dated. But here she was, standing with her arm protectively around his father, as if they were life-long buddies.

A foreign emotion twisted in his gut. Jealousy. For a moment he didn't want to acknowledge it. But as he absorbed the camaraderie between his father and Raine, he couldn't deny the truth.

His father had grown closer to Raine in the time since she'd pushed him away.

* * *

Raine couldn't believe that Dr. Frank was actually Caleb's father. She'd never really known if Frank was the retired vet's first or last name, and hadn't asked. They'd had an unspoken agreement not to pry into each other's personal lives. But now that she saw the two of them in the same room, the resemblance was obvious. Dr. Frank's hair was mostly gray, whereas Caleb's was dark brown, but the two men shared the same stormy gray eyes and aristocratic nose. Of course, Caleb was taller and broader across the shoulders but his dad was no slouch. In fact, she thought Dr. Frank was rather handsome, all things considered.

Caleb would age well, if his father's looks were any indication. And for a moment regret stabbed deep. As much as she needed to move forward, it was difficult not to mourn what might have been.

"What time do you want me to pick you up?" Caleb asked his father.

"I can give Dr. Frank a ride home if he needs one," she quickly offered.

Caleb's eyebrows rose in surprise, as if he suspected she had some sort of ulterior motive. Was he assuming she was trying to get back into his good graces by helping his father? If things were different, she might have been tempted.

"That's very kind of you, Raine," Dr. Frank said. She could have sworn the older man's gaze was relieved when he turned back toward his son. "There's no need for you to come all the way back out here, Raine will drive me home. Thanks for the ride, Caleb. I'll see you this weekend, all right?"

"Yeah. Sure." For a moment Caleb stared at her, as

if he wanted to say something more, but after a tense moment he turned away. She had to bite her lip to stop herself from calling out to him as he headed for the door. "See you later, Dad," he tossed over his shoulder.

He didn't acknowledge Raine as he left. And even though she knew it was her fault, since taking a break from their relationship had been her idea, she was ridiculously hurt by the snub.

Trying to shake off the effects of her less than positive interaction with Caleb, she faced Dr. Frank. "So, are you ready to get to work?"

Caleb's father's glance was sharp—she should have known he wouldn't miss a thing. "Do you and my son know each other?"

She tried to smile. So much for their rule to stay away from personal things. "Yes, we both work in the emergency department at Trinity Medical Center," she admitted. "Caleb is a great doctor, everyone enjoys working with him."

"Everyone except you?"

She flushed, hating to think she'd been that transparent. Especially when she liked working with Caleb. Too much for her own good. "I like working with him, but I'm thinking of changing my career to veterinary medicine," she joked, in an attempt to lighten things up. "Maybe you'll give me some tips, hmm? Come on, let's head to the back. I think I should take a look at that ankle of yours."

"Caleb already looked at it." Dr. Frank waved her off. "I'm more interested in the animals. I'm going to need you to bring them to me in the exam room as my mobility is limited."

"No problem." Raine wanted to help, but as he deftly maneuvered the crutches, she realized he was doing fine on his own.

Dozens of questions filtered through her mind, but she didn't immediately voice them. Caleb obviously hadn't mentioned her to his father during the time they'd been seeing each other, which bothered her. Especially since he hadn't even talked about his father very much.

What else didn't she know about him? And why did it matter? What she and Caleb had was over. For good. No matter how much she missed him.

Dr. Frank didn't notice her preoccupation with his son. His attention was quickly focused on the sick animals.

She brought Rusty into the room, the Irish setter puppy they'd rescued three weeks ago. She'd fallen for Rusty in a big way, especially when everyone teased her that Rusty's dark red coat was the same color as her hair. But unfortunately the lease on her apartment didn't allow dogs, which was why she'd taken Spice, the calico cat, instead.

But when she did have enough money saved to buy a house, she planned on adopting a dog, too. Hopefully one just as sweet tempered and beautiful as Rusty.

"There, now, let me take a listen to your heart," Dr. Frank murmured as he stroked Rusty's fur. The dog had been in bad shape when he'd been picked up as a stray, and he'd shied away, growling at men, which made them think he might have been abused. Raine didn't know how long he'd been on the streets, but he'd been dangerously malnourished when he'd arrived. And he'd been sick with some sort of infection that had soon spread to the animals housed in the kennels near him.

She held the dog close, smiling a little when he licked her arm. "You're such a good puppy, aren't you?"

"He's definitely doing better on the antiviral meds we've been giving him," Dr. Frank announced, finishing his exam. "Let's move on to Annie, the golden retriever."

Volunteering at the shelter had saved her from losing her mind in her dark memories. Raine found she loved working with the animals. The hours she spent at the shelter flew by. She barely had enough time to run home to change, after dropping off Dr. Frank, before heading off to work.

As she entered the emergency department, she saw Caleb standing in the arena. When his gaze locked on hers, her stomach knotted with tension. Was she really up for this? Working in Trauma with Caleb? She quickly glanced around, looking for the charge nurse, determined to avoid being assigned to his team.

Unfortunately, there were only two trauma-trained nurses on duty for the second shift, so she had no choice but to work in the trauma bay. And, of course, Caleb was assigned to the trauma bay as well.

Her stomach continued to churn as she took report from the offgoing nurse. As they finished, a wave of nausea hit hard, and she put a hand over her stomach, gauging the distance to the bathroom.

She swallowed hard, trying to figure out what was wrong. Could she have somehow gotten the virus that seemed to be plaguing the animals at the shelter? She'd have to remember to ask Dr. Frank if animal-to-people transfer was even possible.

Sipping white soda from the nearby vending machine helped and Raine tried to concentrate on her work. They'd transferred their recent patient up to the ICU but within moments they'd received word that Lifeline, the air-rescue helicopter, had been called to the scene of a crash involving car versus train.

Sarah, the other trauma nurse on duty, was restocking the supplies so Raine used the few moments of free time to head into the bathroom.

As she fought another wave of nausea, she leaned over the sink and thought of Elana. This must be how her friend had felt with her horrible bouts of morning sickness.

Her eyes flew open at the implication and she stared at her pale reflection in shock. Could it be? No. Oh, no. She couldn't handle this.

Her knees went weak and she sank down onto the seat of the commode. Counting backwards, the sickness in her stomach threatened to erupt as she realized it had been just over four weeks since her last period.

CHAPTER THREE

DEAR God, what if she was pregnant?

No, she couldn't be. There was just no way she could handle this right now. Especially considering the circumstances under which she might have conceived. She shied away from the dark memories.

She didn't have time to fall apart. Not when there was a serious trauma on the way. Car versus train, and the train always won in that contest. She took several deep breaths, pulling herself together with an effort.

She couldn't think about this right now, she just couldn't. It was possible she had flu, nothing more. She had to stop jumping to conclusions. She'd been through a lot of stress lately. Far more stress than the average person had to deal with. There were plenty of reasons for her period to be late. And it wasn't really late. She could get her period any day now.

But the nagging fear wouldn't leave her alone.

She used the facilities and then splashed cold water on her face in a vain attempt to bring some color back to her cheeks. She stopped in the staff lounge to rummage for some crackers to nibble on as she made her way back to the trauma bay.

The pager at her waist beeped. She glanced at the display. *Thirty-five-year-old white male with multiple crushing injuries to torso and lower extremities. Intubated in the field, transfusing four units of O negative blood. ETA five minutes.*

Five minutes. She took another sip of white soda and finished the cracker. She couldn't decide if she should be upset or relieved when the cracker and white soda combination helped settle her stomach.

"What's wrong?" Caleb demanded when she entered the trauma bay a few moments later. "You look awful."

"Gee, thanks so much," she said sarcastically. "I really needed to hear that."

"I'm sorry, but I wanted to make sure that you're okay to work," Caleb amended. "The trauma surgeon has requested a hot unload. We need to get up to the helipad, they're landing in two minutes."

"I'm okay to work," she repeated firmly, determined to prove it by not falling apart as she had last night. Every day was better than the last one—hadn't her counselor stressed the importance of moving forward? She was living proof the strategy worked. "Let's go."

She and Caleb took the trauma elevators, located in the back of the trauma bay, up to the helipad on the roof of the hospital. At first the confines of the elevator bothered her, but she inhaled the heady scent of Caleb's aftershave, which pushed the bad memories away and reminded her of happier times. When they reached the helipad, they found the trauma surgeon, Dr. Eric Sutton, was already standing there, waiting. Lifting her hand to shield her eyes against the glare of the sun, Raine watched as the air-rescue chopper approached. The noise of the aircraft made it impossible to speak.

When the helicopter landed, they waited until they saw the signal from the pilot to approach, ducking well below the blades. The Lifeline transport team, consisting of a physician and a nurse, helped lift the patient out of the back hatch of the chopper.

"He's in bad shape, losing blood fast," the Lifeline physician grimly informed them. "In my opinion, you need to take him directly to the OR."

"Sounds like a plan. We can finish resuscitating him there," Dr. Sutton agreed. "Let's go."

In her year of working Trauma, she'd only transported a handful of patients directly to the OR. They all squeezed into the trauma elevator around the patient, Greg Hanson. She kept her gaze on the portable monitor, trying to ignore the close confines of the elevator as they rode back down to the trauma OR suite located on the second floor, directly above the ED.

The elevators opened into the main hallway of the OR. The handed the gurney over to the OR staff who were waiting, taking precious moments to don sterile garb before following the patient into the room.

"Caleb, I need a central line in this guy—he needs at least four more units of O neg blood," Sutton said.

They fell into a trauma resuscitation rhythm, only this time the trauma surgeon had taken the lead instead of Caleb. As Eric Sutton was assessing the extent of the patient's crushing leg wounds, she and Caleb worked together to get Greg Hanson's blood pressure up to a reasonable level.

She didn't know the circumstances about why Greg Hanson's car had been on the railroad tracks and as she hung four more units of blood on the rapid infusor, she found herself hoping this hadn't been a suicide attempt.

Being in close proximity to Caleb put all her senses on alert. But when his shoulders brushed against hers, she didn't flinch. She tried to see that as a sign she was healing.

"Here," she said, handing him the end of the rapid infuser tubing once he'd gotten the central line placed. "Connect this so I can get the blood started."

Caleb took the tubing from her hands, his fingers warm against hers. Eric and the OR nurse were prepping the patient's legs to begin surgery and the anesthesiologist was already putting the patient to sleep, but for a fraction of a second their gazes clung, as if they were all alone in the room.

"Great. All set," Caleb said, breaking the nearly tangible connection. "Start the blood."

She turned on the rapid infuser, rechecking the lines to make sure everything was properly connected. She took four more units of blood, confirmed the numbers matched, and then set them aside to be hung as soon as the other four had been transfused into their patient. She could see by the amount of blood already filling the large suction canisters that he was going to need more.

"Draw a full set of labs, Raine," Caleb told her.

She did as he asked, handing them over to the anesthesia tech, who ran them to the stat lab. She began hanging the new units of blood when the current bags were dry.

"I think we have things under control here," the anesthesiologist informed them a few minutes later. Taking a peek over the sterile drape, she could see Dr. Sutton was already in the process of repairing a torn femoral artery.

She was loath to leave, feeling as if there was still more they could do. But now that the anesthesiologist had put the patient to sleep, he'd taken over monitoring the rapid infuser, along with the anesthesia tech.

They really weren't needed here any longer.

Caleb put a hand on her arm, and she glanced up at him. The warmth in his gaze made it seem as if the last four weeks of being apart hadn't happened. "Come on, we need to get back down to the trauma bay."

"All right," she agreed, following him out of the OR suite. Outside the room, they stripped off the sterile garb covering their scrubs.

"Good work, Raine," Caleb told her, as they headed down to the trauma bay.

"Thanks. You too," she murmured, sending him a sideways glance. From the first time she'd met Caleb, there had been an undeniable spark between them. An awareness that had only intensified as they'd worked together.

His kisses had made her head spin. There was so much about him that she'd admired. And a few qualities she didn't.

Working together just now to save Greg Hanson's life had only reinforced how in sync they were. They made a great team.

Professional team, not a personal one, she reminded herself.

The nauseous feeling returned and she glanced away, feeling hopelessly desperate.

Impossible to go back and change the mistakes and subsequent events of the past, no matter how much she wished she could.

Caleb couldn't seem to keep his gaze off Raine. The adrenalin rush that came from helping to save a patient's life seemed to make everything around him stand out in sharp definition. Especially her. Raine's dark red hair, her pale skin, her bright blue eyes had beckoned to him from the moment they'd met.

She was so beautiful. His fingers itched to stroke her skin. Memories of how sweetly she'd responded to his kisses flooded his mind. Along with a stab of regret. If only he'd have handled things differently, they might have been able to make their relationship work.

His fault. She'd pushed him away, but it was all his fault. Because he'd jumped to conclusions.

Raine had tried to talk to him, but he hadn't been very receptive. And then Jake had come to apologize. Confessing that he'd had too much to drink and had made a pass at Raine.

So he'd called her back, prepared to apologize, but she'd refused to take his calls.

He wished, more than anything, that she'd talk to him. Allow him to clear things up between them. But instead she'd gone to work in the minor care area, located at the opposite end of the ED from the trauma bay.

He and Raine made a great team on a professional level. He shouldn't dwell on the fact they couldn't seem to make the same connection on a personal one.

"Where's my brother? Greg Hanson?" a frantic voice asked, as they walked past the ED patient waiting area.

Caleb stopped to address the young man. "He's in surgery. We can let the trauma surgeon, Dr. Eric Sutton, know you're here waiting for him."

"Surgery?" The man's expression turned hopeful. "So he's going to make it?"

"I'm sorry, but it's a little too early to say for sure, although I think he has a good fighting chance," Caleb told him. He glanced at Raine, who gave a nod of encouragement.

"His vital signs were stabilizing when we left," she added.

"Good, that's good." The young man sighed. "Greg's wife and baby are being examined to make sure they didn't sustain any injuries. He risked his life to save them. His wife, Lora, panicked when her van got stuck on the railroad tracks. She didn't want to leave because the baby was in the back seat. He pulled her out of the car first, and then yanked the baby out just as the train hit."

He heard Raine's soft gasp. "Dear heavens," she murmured.

Caleb grimly agreed. The guy was a hero, and he could only hope the poor guy didn't suffer irreparable damage to his legs as a result of his actions. "Are his wife and baby both here?"

"The baby's at Children's Memorial, my wife is over

there with their daughter now. Lora's here, the doctor is seeing her now. As soon as they're medically cleared, we'll all be here waiting to hear about Greg's condition."

"I'll let the trauma surgeon know," Caleb promised.

"Thank you," the young man said gratefully.

He and Raine returned to the trauma bay. He made the call up to the OR, leaving a message with the OR circulating nurse about Greg's family. She passed the word on to Eric Sutton, who reassured them he'd come to the waiting room to talk to the family as soon as he was finished.

Satisfied, he hung up the phone. There was a lull in the action. Trauma was either busy or slow, and he found himself looking once again for Raine.

They needed to talk. He just couldn't let her go without a fight. Maybe it was crazy, but the awareness still shimmering between them made him believe in second chances.

He found her in the staff lounge, sipping a soda. She looked surprised to see him.

"I was surprised to see you earlier today. You never mentioned working at the animal shelter while we were going out," he said, being careful to sound casual and not accusatory.

She met his gaze briefly, before glancing away. "No, I didn't. I've only been volunteering at the animal shelter for the past month or so."

The past month. Since their break-up. For some reason, the timing bothered him.

"Your dad is a sweetheart," she continued, staring down into the depths of her soft drink. "He's a great vet, really wonderful with animals. Everyone at the shelter loves him."

Strange, Raine had never struck him as being an animal lover, although now that he knew she was, he wondered what else he hadn't known about her.

And why did it matter now?

"Yeah, my dad has quite the female fan club," he said dryly. "Just ask any of his ex-wives."

She frowned at him and he immediately felt guilty for the lame joke.

"My dad is a great guy," he amended. "He does have a special talent for working with animals."

Raine nodded thoughtfully. And then she suddenly jumped to her feet. "Look, Caleb, I'm sorry things didn't work out between us on a personal level. But at least we know we can work together, right? We helped save Greg's life. Surely that counts for something."

Her words gave him the opportunity he needed.

"Raine, I'm sorry. I shouldn't have accused you of seeing Jake behind my back."

She stared at him with wide blue eyes. "Why were you so ready to believe the worst?" she asked in a low voice.

He swallowed hard, knowing she deserved the truth. "I had a bad experience with being cheated on in the past," he finally admitted. "I walked in and found my fiancée in bed with another man."

"I see." She frowned and broke away from his gaze.

Did she? He doubted it. "Look, Raine, I know now that I overreacted. Jake explained everything."

She brought her gaze, full of reproach, up to his. "So did I, remember? The next day, when I called you?"

He didn't know what to say to that, because what she said was the truth. She had tried to explain, but he hadn't believed her.

"You listened to Jake, but you didn't listen to me," Raine murmured, her blue eyes shadowed with pain. "I guess that sums everything up right there."

Panic gripped him by the throat. "Raine, please. Give me another chance."

She sighed and rubbed her temples. "It's too late, Caleb. There were a lot of other signs that you didn't trust me, but I tried to ignore them. The way you kept asking me where I was going and who I was going to be with. The night with Jake only solidified what I already knew."

"I learned my lesson," he quickly protested. "I promise, this time I'll trust you."

But she was already shaking her head. "It's not that easy, Caleb. Trust comes from within. You have to believe with your whole heart."

His whole heart? Her words nagged at him. Because he cared about Raine a lot. But had he loved her? He'd thought things were heading in that direction, but now he wasn't so sure.

Those feelings of intense betrayal, when he'd seen her with Jake, had haunted him. Had made him think the worst about her.

He remembered how Raine had tried to explain how thrilled and relieved she'd been to be away from the overbearing scrutiny of her three older brothers. At first she'd teasingly accused him of being just like them.

But then she'd become more resentful.

And he'd accused her of cheating on him.

No wonder she'd wanted a break.

Still, he wanted another chance. Even though there was something different about her. A shadow in her eyes that hadn't been there before. The Raine he'd worked with tonight didn't seem to be the same person she'd been a month earlier.

Because of him?

Caleb's stomach twisted with regret. He hadn't told her about his mother abandoning him and his father, taking off to follow her dream of being a dancer. Or the string of stepmothers and almost stepmothers. Obviously, he should have.

"Raine, I'm sorry. I know I don't deserve another chance, but—" He stopped when their pagers went off simultaneously.

Sixty-nine-year-old male passed out at home, pulse irregular and slow, complaining of new onset chest pain. ETA three minutes.

"How about we focus on being friends?" she said. "Excuse me, but I need to make sure everything is ready for our new patient." Raine brushed past him to head towards the trauma room.

He followed more slowly, watching as Raine and Sarah double-checked the equipment and supplies they had on standby.

They didn't have to wait long. When the doors from the paramedic bay burst open, he was assailed by a strange sense of déjà vu as the paramedic crew wheeled in their new arrival.

Raine's sudden gasp made him frown. And in the next second he understood as he recognized the patient too.

His father.

CHAPTER FOUR

RAINE glanced at Caleb, worried about his reaction. She couldn't imagine how it would feel to have your father being wheeled into the trauma bay.

She grabbed the closest ED tech. "Ben, run to the arena and ask Dr. Garrison to come over." She stepped up to put the elderly vet on the heart monitor. Caleb couldn't function as his father's physician. Especially when Dr. Frank's face was sweaty and pale, his eyes closed and his facial muscles drawn, as if he was in extreme pain.

Caleb surprised her by stepping up and taking control. "He's still bradycardic. Raine, start oxygen at two liters per minute. Send a cardiac injury panel and then we'll run a twelve-lead EKG."

"He'll need something for pain, too." The paramedic had placed the oxygen on, so she concentrated on drawing blood, knowing they needed the results stat in order to determine if he should go straight to the cardiac cath lab. But Dr. Frank's pain was her next priority.

"Dr. Garrison can't come," Ben announced when he returned from the arena, a tad short of breath himself. "He's about to deliver a baby."

"A baby?" Raine echoed in shocked amazement. Good grief, could things get any worse? She shot a quick glance at Caleb before giving his father two milligrams of morphine. And then called for the EKG tech.

"I'm fine," Caleb said in a low tone, answering her unspoken question. "We're going to need to call the cardiologist anyway, since I'm sure my father is having an acute myocardial infarct."

"Can't you…just call it…a heart attack?" his father asked in a feebly sarcastic tone.

"Dr. Frank, you need to try to relax," Raine urged, putting a reassuring hand on his arm. "We don't know for sure that you're having a heart attack, but we're going to do all the preliminary tests just in case."

The vet ignored her, his gaze locked on his son. "I should have…told you."

Raine glanced up at Caleb, who'd come up to stand beside his father. She continued to record vital signs as they spoke.

"Should have told me what?" Caleb asked urgently. "Have you had chest pain before?"

"No. Dizzy spells." Caleb's father spoke in short phrases, his breathing still labored. Raine cranked up the oxygen to five liters per minute as his pulse ox reading was only 89 percent. "I got dizzy-and fell off…the ladder."

Caleb's breath hissed out between his teeth. But his tone was surprisingly gentle. "Yes, you should have told me."

"Denial…can be…very powerful." His father's eyes were shadowed with regret.

Raine stepped in with a bright smile, trying to ease the tension between father and son. "Well, thank heavens you're here now. Don't worry, Dr. Frank, we're going to take good care of you."

"You're…a sweet girl…Raine."

Caleb's smile was strained. "Dad, Geoff Lyons is the cardiologist on call, he should be here to see you shortly. How's your chest pain? Any better?"

"Not much," his dad answered.

"Raine, start him on a nitroglycerine drip. If that doesn't help, we'll give him another two milligrams of morphine."

She was already crossing over to the pharmaceutical dispensing machine to fetch a bottle of nitroglycerine and more morphine.

The phone rang and she could hear Caleb crossing over to answer it. She listened as he repeated the critical troponin level of 2.4 and gave his name before hanging up.

His father was more alert than he let on. "Guess I've…earned a trip…to the cath lab."

"Yes." Caleb glanced up in relief when Dr. Geoff Lyons walked in.

"What's going on?" Geoff asked.

Raine gave Dr. Frank more morphine as Caleb and Geoff discussed the results of the EKG and the lab work. She stayed by his side as Dr. Lyons made arrangements for Caleb's dad to be transferred to the cardiac cath lab.

"You'll be fine," Raine told him reassuringly, as she connected him to the transport monitor.

"I'll see you after the procedure, Dad," Caleb added.

"Caleb…take care of Grizz for me," his father whispered.

"I will. I'll run and get him after my shift." Caleb squeezed his father's hand and then stepped back.

"Is there someone else we should call?" Raine asked him softly, as the cardiac team whisked Caleb's dad away. "Your mom? Brothers or sisters?"

"No." Caleb gave a deep sigh. "My dad isn't married at the moment and he's recently broken up with his current lady friend, Sharon. My mother took off years ago, and she has her own family now."

The way he spoke of his mother, so matter-of-fact, wrenched her heart. He'd never mentioned his mother leaving before. What sort of mother abandoned her son? No wonder Caleb found it hard to believe in women. "I'm sorry," she said helplessly.

"Not your fault." Caleb brushed her sympathy aside as if determined to make her believe he was over it. "We'd better get ready for the next patient."

"The next patient?" She stared at him as if he'd lost his mind. "Caleb, your father is having a heart procedure. I'm sure one of the physicians would be willing to cover for you."

"I'm fine. There's nothing I can do until after his procedure is over anyway." His dark, stormy gray eyes warned her not to say anything more, before he turned and walked away.

Caleb was determined to finish his shift, even though his thoughts kept straying to his father.

He didn't blame his dad for not telling him about the dizzy spells. Rather, he was upset with himself. He should have forced his father to go in to be checked out when he'd fallen off the ladder in the first place.

If he'd have listened to his gut instinct, it was possible

he could have prevented the additional damage to his father's heart.

He could feel Raine's concerned gaze following him as they worked on their next patient, an abdominal stabbing sustained during a bar fight. The tip of the blade had just missed the diaphragm, which was lucky as that meant his breathing wasn't impaired, but Caleb was certain either the stomach or the intestines had been hit.

"Raine, we need to explore the depth of the wound," he informed her.

She nodded her understanding and quickly began prepping the area with antimicrobial solution before spreading several sterile drapes around the wound. Once he'd donned his sterile gear, he reached for a scalpel. "Hold the retractor for me, will you? Like this."

She did as he asked, opening the wound so he could see better. The damage wasn't as bad as he'd expected, although the laceration in the small intestine meant the patient would need surgery. He irrigated the wound with sterile saline to help clean it out. "Okay, that's all we can do here. Put a dressing over this, would you? I need to get in touch with the general surgeon on call. This guy needs a small bowel resection."

Once he'd gotten their stab patient transferred to the care of the general surgeon, he checked his watch, wondering how his father was doing. A good hour had passed since he'd been taken up to the cardiac cath lab.

"Caleb? There's a phone call for you." Raine's expression was troubled as she handed him the receiver.

The display on the phone indicated the call was from

the OR, not the cath lab. Was this regarding his stab-wound patient? "This is Dr. Stewart."

"Caleb, it's Geoff Lyons. I'm sorry to tell you that your father's condition took a turn for the worse. We had to abort the attempt to place a stent. I called a cardiothoracic surgeon in for assistance. Dr. Summers has taken him to the OR for three-vessel cardiac bypass surgery."

Raine watched the blood drain from Caleb's face and feared the news wasn't good. When he hung up the phone, she crossed over to him. "What's wrong? Your father?"

"In the OR, having cardiac bypass surgery." Caleb's expression was grim. "They couldn't get the stent placed and his condition grew very unstable, so they called in the surgeon."

"I'm sorry," she murmured, feeling helpless. "Do you want me to call Dr. Garrison to cover you? There's only about an hour and a half left of the shift."

"I'll talk to him," Caleb said. She was somewhat surprised he'd given in. Of course, there was a huge difference between having a cardiac cath procedure and full-blown open-heart surgery.

Dr. Joe Garrison agreed to cover and luckily the steady stream of trauma calls seemed to dwindle. At the end of her shift, she transferred her last patient to the ICU and then was free to go.

Raine couldn't bring herself to head home, though. Instead, after she swiped out, she went to the OR waiting room to find Caleb.

He was sitting with his elbows propped on his knees,

his head cradled in his hands. He looked so alone, she was glad she'd come.

"Hey," she said, dropping into the seat beside him. "Have you heard anything?"

He lifted his head to look at her, his forehead furrowed with lines of exhaustion. "Not really, other than a quick call to let me know this could take hours yet. Is your shift over already?"

"Yes, and don't worry, it was relatively quiet. Not a problem at all for Dr. Garrison to cover."

Caleb nodded. "I'm glad. I was just thinking about whether or not I should leave for a while to pick up Grizz. I'm sure he'll need to go outside soon."

"I can run and let him out if you like," she offered. "I'd take him home with me, but my apartment doesn't allow dogs."

"Thanks, but I need to get him moved into my house anyway, now that Dad's going to be in the hospital for a while." Caleb rubbed the back of his neck and slowly stood.

She stared at him, wondering about this sudden urge to pick up the dog. Was he looking for an excuse to get away from her?

And, really, could she blame him? He'd asked for a second chance, but she'd refused.

But they could still be friends, couldn't they?

"Do you want some company?" she asked lightly.

He hesitated for a moment, and then nodded. "Sure."

Okay, so maybe Caleb wasn't looking for an excuse to avoid her. She had to stop second-guessing his motives. She stood and followed him to the parking structure where all the ED employees parked. "Do you want me to drive?"

He shook his head. "I'll drive."

She wasn't surprised—her brothers would have said the exact same thing. She didn't understand the macho need to drive, but figured it had something to do with wanting to be in control. She slid into the passenger seat, remembering the last time she'd ridden with Caleb.

On their last date before the Jake fiasco. A romantic dinner and a trip to the theater to see *Phantom of the Opera*. She'd never enjoyed herself more.

Regret twisted like a knife in her heart.

Caleb didn't say anything on the short ride to his father's house. She pushed aside her own tangled emotions, understanding that at this moment, Caleb was deeply worried about his father. And she certainly couldn't blame him.

She was worried too.

"Your dad is strong, Caleb. He's going to pull through this just fine."

He glanced at her and nodded. "I know. It's just…" His voice trailed off.

"What?" she asked.

He let out a heavy sigh. "My dad and I don't see eye-to-eye on a lot of things, but that doesn't mean I don't love him. I just wish I would have told him that before he left to go to the cardiac cath lab. I should have said the words."

Her heart squeezed in her chest. She reached out to lightly touch his arm. "He knows, Caleb. Your dad knows how much you love him."

He didn't respond, but pulled into his father's driveway. She'd been there earlier that day, when she'd driven Dr. Frank home from the animal shelter. He got out of the car and she followed him into the dark house.

"Hi, Grizz." Caleb smiled a bit when the dog greeted them enthusiastically, trying to lick both of them in his excitement to see them.

"Grizz, you're just a big old softie, aren't you?" Raine said, stroking his wiggling body.

"Will you take him out into the back yard for me?" Caleb asked. "I need to get all his stuff packed into the car as he's coming home with me."

"Sure. Come on, Grizz," she called, walking through the house, flicking on lights as she went. The back door was in the kitchen, and she followed the dog outside, waiting patiently while he took care of business.

He bounded toward her soon afterwards and she stroked his silky fur. "I bet you're already missing Dr. Frank, aren't you?" she murmured. "Don't worry, I'm sure Caleb is going to take good care of you."

She took Grizz back inside the house to find Caleb lugging a forty-pound bag of dog food out to his car.

"All set?" she asked as he closed the trunk.

"Yes." He opened the back passenger door. "Come on, Grizz, you get the whole back seat to yourself."

The ride to Caleb's house didn't take long and when she followed him inside, she was assaulted by memories. Good memories. Painfully good memories. She averted her gaze from the sofa where she and Caleb had very nearly made love.

She wished more than ever she'd made love to Caleb that night. Now it was too late.

She put a hand to her stomach, surprised to note her earlier attack of nausea seemed to have gone away. Determined to hope for the best, she told herself that was a good thing. Maybe the sickness was nothing more than a touch of flu.

Grizz paced around Caleb's house, sniffing at everything with interest. When he'd finished exploring his new surroundings, and apparently deemed them acceptable, he made himself comfortable by flopping on Caleb's sofa.

She heard Caleb sigh, but he didn't make Grizz get down. Instead, he reached over to scratch the silky fur behind his ears. "I'll be back later, Grizz, okay?"

The dog thumped his tail on the sofa in agreement.

Raine followed Caleb back outside to his car. The ride back to the hospital was quiet.

When he'd parked the car, he turned toward her. "Thanks for coming with me, Raine."

"You're welcome." She tilted her head curiously, wondering if he was wanting to get rid of her. "Ready to head inside to see if there's any news on your dad?"

He took the key from the ignition and flashed a tired smile. "Raine, it's well after midnight. I appreciate everything you've done, but I'm sure you're exhausted. It's fine if you'd rather head home."

Slowly she shook her head. No matter what had transpired between her and Caleb in the past, there was no way in the world she could just walk away. Not now. She opened her passenger side door with determination. "Let's find out how he's doing, okay? Then I'll head home."

Caleb didn't protest when she followed him inside, riding the elevator up to the waiting room. She wanted to believe he was glad to have her around, but suspected he was just too tired to argue.

The desk in the waiting room was empty. Apparently the volunteers who usually manned the area had already gone home for the night.

She stood off to the side, while Caleb picked up the phone to call up to the OR.

"This is Caleb Stewart. Is there any news on my father, Frank Stewart?"

Raine couldn't hear what was said on the other end of the line, but when Caleb nodded and murmured thanks, before hanging up, she couldn't help asking, "Is he still in surgery?"

"Yeah. They're finished with the main portion of the procedure, and they're starting to close him now. They estimate he'll be in the ICU within the hour."

The knotted muscles in her neck eased. "That's good news."

"Yeah, although apparently he ended up having his aortic valve replaced too, in addition to the repairs to his coronary arteries." Caleb scrubbed a hand over his face. "But he's hanging in there, so I'm going to keep hoping for the best."

She watched as he crossed over to take a seat. He glanced up in surprise when she followed. "Raine, I don't expect you to hang out here with me indefinitely."

They may have dated for two months, but he obviously didn't know her very well. Why was he so anxious to believe the worst about her? Just because he'd been cheated on in the past? Was it possible he was incapable of trusting her at all? Maybe. But no matter what had transpired between them, she couldn't have left him alone in that waiting room if her life had depended on it.

She dropped into the seat beside him, curling her legs underneath her. "I'm not leaving, Caleb. I'm staying."

CHAPTER FIVE

CALEB glanced over at Raine sitting in the waiting-room chair, her eyes closed as she'd finally given in to her exhaustion. He stared at her, watching her sleep, trying to figure her out.

After not seeing her for the past month, it was scary how easily they'd ended up here together. He almost reached out to brush a strand of hair away from her eyes, but stopped himself just in time. He didn't want to read too much into her actions, but he couldn't help from wondering if her staying here with him meant she was willing to give him another chance.

And would he mess things up again, if she did?

He let out a heavy sigh, wishing he knew the answer to that one. Raine was beautiful, smart and funny. He'd enjoyed just being with her. But he couldn't blame the demise of their relationship solely on her. He owned a big piece of the problem.

Trust didn't come easy. And he didn't have a clue how to fix the tiny part of him that always held back. The tiny part of him that always doubted.

The tiny part of him that constantly expected and saw the worst.

The door to the waiting room swung open, distracting him from his reverie. An older man dressed in scrubs, a surgical mask dangling around his neck, emerged through the doorway. He recognized him as Dr. Steve Summers, one of the cardiothoracic surgeons who operated out of Trinity Medical Center.

"Raine?" Caleb reached over to gently shake her shoulder to wake her up.

At his touch, she bolted upright and recoiled from him, her eyes wide and frightened as she frantically looked around the room. "What?"

He frowned, bothered by her reaction. Had he interrupted a bad dream? He gestured to the CT surgeon who was approaching. "The doctor is here."

"Caleb Stewart?" the cardiothoracic surgeon asked, as he crossed over to shake his hand. "Steve Summers. I thought your name was familiar. I recognize you from the ED. Your father has been transferred to the ICU. I had to replace his aortic valve along with three of his coronary arteries. His heart took a bad hit and he lost a fair amount of blood, but seems to be holding his own at the moment."

Caleb knew that was a tactful way of saying his father was still in a critical condition. He'd used the same lines with family members himself. "How long do you think he'll need to stay in the ICU?"

"At least a day or two." Steve glanced curiously at Raine, no doubt recognizing her too, but then turned back to Caleb. "If he stays stable over the next couple of hours, I'll take him off the ventilator. The sooner we can get him breathing on his own, the shorter his recovery time should be."

"Can Caleb go up to see him?" Raine asked.

"Sure. Just give the nurses a couple of minutes to get things settled, and then you can head up." The surgeon flashed a tired smile. "I'm sure he's going to do just fine."

Caleb wished he could be as sure, but he nodded anyway and shook the surgeon's hand gratefully. "Thanks again."

The surgeon returned the handshake before turning to leave. He glanced at Raine. "Do you want to come upstairs to the ICU with me?"

She hesitated, her arms crossed defensively over her chest, her expression uncertain. "I'd be happy to come up if you like, but I don't want to intrude. He's your father. I'm just an acquaintance."

The way she backed off made him question her motives for staying in the first place. Maybe this was her way of telling him she was willing to be there for him, but only up to a point? She had told him they should just try being friends. It was possible she didn't want to come along because they weren't formally dating.

He swallowed the urge to ask her to come along, respecting the distance she apparently wanted to keep. Especially considering Raine had already gone above and beyond, sitting here with him while he'd waited to hear how his father had fared. Besides, it was already two in the morning and he understood she needed to get home. "Are you sure you're okay to drive?" he asked instead.

"Absolutely. I'm awake now." Her lopsided smile

tugged at his heart. "Tell your dad I'm thinking about him and that he needs to get better soon, all right?"

"Sure." His fingers itched to touch her, to pull her close, seeking comfort in her warm embrace. But they were colleagues. Maybe even friends. Nothing more. "Take care."

"You too, Caleb," she said softly.

They left the waiting room together, but then parted ways, heading in opposite directions. For a long moment, he watched her heading toward the parking structure, fighting the desperate need to call her back.

Cursing himself for being a fool, he turned away, heading toward the elevator to go up to the critical care unit.

It felt strange to walk into the busy unit as a visitor rather than as a physician. When he approached his father's room, his footsteps slowed.

As a doctor, he'd known what to expect. But seeing his dad so pale, connected to all the machinery, it made his breath lodge in his throat. He took a moment to watch his father's vital signs roll across the screen on the monitor hanging over his bed. The numbers were reassuring, so he softly approached his father's bedside.

The bitter taste of regret filled his mouth. He reached down and took his father's hand in his. "I love you, Dad," he whispered.

His father's eyes fluttered open, his gaze locking on his. Caleb blinked away the dampness of tears and leaned forward, holding his father's gaze. "The surgery is over and you're doing fine, Dad," he assured him, knowing his father couldn't speak with the breathing tube in his throat. "I took Grizz to my house, so you don't need to worry about a thing. Just rest and get better soon, okay?"

His father nodded and then his eyes drifted shut, as if that brief interaction had been all he could manage. Caleb squeezed his father's hand again, and then slowly released it.

Part of him wanted to stay, but there was really no purpose. In fact, he had to get home to take care of Grizz, as he'd promised. His father needed to rest, anyway. There was nothing more he could do here.

Regretfully, he turned away. His dad was a fighter. He was sure his dad would feel better in the morning.

Caleb went home, surprisingly glad when Grizzly dashed over to greet him. He hadn't realized what a difference it made to come home to a pet rather than an empty house.

"Hey, Grizz, were you afraid I wasn't coming back?" He scratched the dog behind the ears. He let the dog outside and then made his way into the bedroom. Grizz followed, tail wagging, glancing around the new environment.

"I bet you miss him, don't you, boy?" Caleb murmured. Grizzly laid his head on the edge of the bed, staring up at him with large soulful brown eyes. "I know. I miss him, too."

It was true, he realized. He did miss his father. But, truth be told, he missed what he and Raine had once had together even more.

Raine had the next day off, so she didn't see either Caleb or Dr. Frank. But she called the ICU and was told Caleb's father was in serious but stable condition. Raine knew if she wanted more details, she'd have to ask Caleb.

Or visit Dr. Frank for herself.

She kept busy at the animal shelter, glad to see the animals were doing much better. Everyone was concerned about Dr. Frank, so she told them enough to satisfy their curiosity without violating his privacy.

The next day, Friday, she was scheduled to work, so she went to the hospital an hour early to sneak up to Dr. Frank's room for a quick visit. Normally, the ICU only allowed immediate family members to come up, but her hospital ID badge worked to open the doors so she was able to walk in.

She found Caleb's father's room easily enough.

"Hi, Raine," Dr. Frank greeted her with a tired smile. "How are you? How are things at the shelter?"

"They're fine. In fact, I brought you pictures. See?" She took several glossy photos out of her purse and spread them out over his bedside table, knowing he'd appreciate them more than a handful of balloons and a sappy card. "Rusty, Annie, Ace and Maggie all miss you."

Dr. Frank's smile widened when he saw the pictures of his favorite dogs at the shelter. There were dozens of animals at the shelter, but since she couldn't take pictures of them all, she'd focused on the dogs who'd been sick, so he could see how much better they were doing. "They're beautiful, Raine. Thanks. I wish I had a picture of Grizzly, too."

"I'm sure Caleb is taking good care of him," she said reassuringly. No matter how much Dr. Frank missed his dog, there was no way she was going to ask Caleb if she could stop by to take a picture of Grizz.

That would be taking their new-found fragile truce a little too far.

"He is. I just miss him," Dr. Frank said in a wistful tone.

"Everyone at the shelter hopes you get better soon. I didn't tell them much, only that you were in the hospital and doing fine."

The older man lifted a narrow shoulder. "I don't mind if they know about my surgery. Seems like they'll figure out something is wrong when I'm not able to work for several weeks."

"Okay, I'll let them know. When are you getting out of here?" Raine asked, changing the subject with a quick glance around his room. "I thought they were transferring you out of the ICU to a regular floor sometime soon."

"That's the plan." Dr. Frank's gaze focused on something past her shoulder so she turned round, in time to see Caleb walking into the room. Her heart lurched a bit in her chest but he wasn't smiling. She hadn't seen him in the past twenty-four hours, and had no idea why he might be upset.

Her stomach churned, the nausea that came and went seemingly at will, returning with a vengeance. Since the nausea hadn't been as bad over the past day or so, she'd convinced herself the sensation had been nothing more than her over-active imagination. Or a touch of flu.

Now she wasn't so sure. Suddenly her stomach hurt so badly she could barely stand upright. She swallowed hard and prayed she wouldn't throw up her breakfast.

Fighting for control, she pushed away the desperate fear and worry. Enough playing the denial game. She needed to stop avoiding the possibility. She'd go and buy a stupid pregnancy test so that she knew for sure what was going on.

Everything inside her recoiled at the thought of being pregnant.

"Hi, Dad, you look much better today," Caleb said, crossing over to his father's bedside. He frowned a little when he glanced at Raine. "Are you all right?"

"Fine," she forced herself to answer cheerfully, when she felt anything but. Of course he'd noticed something was wrong. She wished Caleb was a little less observant. "Just hungry. I didn't eat anything for lunch. I'm going to get going now, so I can eat before my shift." She knew she was babbling, but didn't care. She wanted to get out of there, fast. "Take care, Dr. Frank, I'll let everyone at the shelter know you're doing better."

"All right. Thanks for the pictures, Raine." Caleb's dad looked better, but it was obvious he still tired easily. Just her short visit seemed to have worn him out.

She edged toward the door. "Bye, Caleb."

"See you later," he said as she practically ran from the room.

Raine sought refuge in the nearest ladies room, bending over and clutching her stomach until the urge to throw up passed. She didn't have time now, before work, but she was going to have to get a home pregnancy test soon.

Tonight.

And if it was positive, she'd deal with that news the

same way she'd dealt with everything else that had happened.

Alone.

Raine was glad she was able to avoid the trauma room for her Friday night shift. The patients seen in the arena certainly needed care, but it wasn't the life-and-death action that the trauma bay held.

But moving to the arena didn't help her escape Caleb.

"You're working tonight?" she asked, when he walked in, hoping her dismay didn't show. The nausea she'd felt earlier hadn't gone away.

Caleb shrugged. "I'll need to take some time off once my dad is discharged from the hospital, so I figured I should work now."

Since his logic made sense, she couldn't argue. "He seems to be doing much better," Raine said.

"Yeah, he is." Caleb raked his fingers through his hair. "I guess they bumped me out of Trauma for tonight. Brock Madison is covering the trauma bay instead."

Probably in deference to what he was going through with his dad. Something she should have figured out for herself, before switching to work in the arena.

Elana had called off sick, so they were a little short-handed, but Raine didn't mind. If she could find a way to keep her emotions under control and her stomach from rebelling, she'd be fine.

Their sickest patient was a woman with congestive heart failure, who'd been taken into the arena when she'd first arrived, but then had quickly needed more care. They would have moved her to the trauma bay, except that they were busy with traumas, which meant they had to manage her here.

"Raine, have you sent the blood gases yet?" Caleb asked.

"Yes." She frowned, glancing at the clock. "The results should be back by now. I'll call the lab."

She made the phone call, gritting her teeth in frustration when the lab claimed they'd never got the specimen. She hung up the phone and turned toward Caleb. "The sample got lost in the tube system. I'll have to redraw it."

"That's fine." He kept his attention focused on the chart.

The night they'd saved Greg Hanson's life they'd been completely in sync. Now that companionable relationship seemed to have vanished. Her stomach lurched again, and she concentrated on drawing the arterial blood gas sample from Mrs. Jones, trying to ignore it.

"Yvonne?" she called out to the middle-aged female tech working on their team. "Will you run this to the lab? I don't want this one to get lost, too."

"Sure." Yvonne willingly took the blood tube from her hands.

"Thanks." She took another sip of her white soda, before logging into the system to document the latest set of vital signs. In the lull of waiting for the lab results, she escaped for a few minutes, seeking refuge in the staff lounge.

Closing her eyes, she tried to focus on staying calm. But the more her nausea plagued her, the more she tensed up. She took several deep breaths, pulled up her legs and rested her forehead on her knees.

She couldn't keep up the pretense much longer. She needed to know if she really was pregnant, and soon. She shouldn't have put it off as long as she already had. She should know by now that denial didn't work.

Hadn't Caleb's dad said something to that effect? About how denial was a powerful thing? After everything she'd gone through, she should know by now that denial was a death-trap. Better to face the things you were afraid of head-on.

Dr. Frank's heart attack had distracted her from her personal problems. Being with Caleb had certainly helped. She missed being with him, more than she'd ever imagined she would. Had she made a mistake in not confiding in him? Would their relationship have survived? Maybe. But even the thought of telling him made her nausea spike. No, it was better that she'd broken things off.

Her fault, not his. And there was no going back. Thinking about what might have been was nothing but foolish fantasy.

Even if Caleb could learn to trust her. Which was doubtful.

Especially now that the damage had been done.

"Raine?" Yvonne poked her head into the staff lounge. "There you are. Dr. Stewart is looking for you."

She pasted a smile on her face, hoping she didn't look as awful as she felt. "Okay, I'm coming."

Caleb glanced up when she approached. "We have her blood gases back and Margaret Jones needs to be transferred up to the medical ICU. You need to make the arrangements." His face was drawn into a slight scowl.

"Next time I'd appreciate you telling me who's covering while you're on break."

"I was only gone ten minutes," she snapped. The surge of anger was a welcome respite from soul-wrenching desperation. "But, rest assured, I'll be sure to tell you every time I need to use the restroom so you'll know exactly where I am."

He stared at her for a long moment, before he let out a heavy sigh. "You're right, I was out of line. I'm sorry. Just call up to give report, will you? Our patient in room two, Jerry Applegate, with sutures over his left eye, is also ready to be discharged. I need you to move fast. I'm being asked to clear our patients out as the waiting room is full."

His apology diffused her annoyance. She needed to pull herself together.

She didn't want to lose the collaborative working relationship she and Caleb had managed to maintain in spite of their break-up. Especially not when their friendship seemed a bit tenuous.

She worked quickly to get Mrs. Jones transferred up to the medical ICU. As soon as that transfer was completed, she discharged Jerry Applegate, the man who'd had a few too many beers at the local tavern and had fallen and cut his eye. He'd sobered up the moment Caleb had placed the first suture. She began to ask him about the possibility of alcoholism, but he mumbled something about a retirement party, looking so embarrassed she ended up giving him the teaching materials on the subject rather than her usual spiel before sending him on his way.

The disinfectant used to clean his room wasn't even dry when the triage nurse called.

"We have a female assault victim," the triage nurse informed her. "I'm bringing her back to room two right away."

Raine didn't remember dropping the phone, but soon she realized the buzzing in her ears was actually the phone beeping because it was off the hook. Glancing down, she saw it was lying on its side. She fumbled a bit with the effort of picking up the receiver and placing it back in its cradle.

A female assault victim. Her mind could barely comprehend the news. She took a deep breath and let it out slowly. Surely this wasn't the same circumstances. No, it was more likely a result of some sort of domestic dispute. Like poor Becca. Tragic, yes, but not the same situation at all.

Yet she couldn't seem to make her feet move. She couldn't do this. She couldn't. Her stomach tightened painfully. She needed to find someone else to care for the patient. Anyone. If only Elana hadn't called in sick, her friend would have taken over in a heartbeat.

"Raine?" Yvonne poked her head out from behind the doorway of room two, her eyes wide with compassion and alarm. "I need you. Right away."

Oh, God. A quick glance at the other teams in the arena proved everyone was busy. There was no one to take her place. Four weeks had passed but at this moment it seemed as if it had only been four days.

Dread seeped from her pores as Raine forced herself to walk into the room. A young woman, about her age, was seated on the hospital bed, clutching the edges of a blanket she'd wrapped tightly around herself.

Numbly, Raine took the clipboard Yvonne shoved into her hands and glanced at the paperwork. The girl's name was Helen Shore and she was twenty-five years old. Dragging her gaze back to her patient, she noted the girl looked disheveled, her blonde hair tangled up in knots, her face pale and her mascara smudged beneath her eyes.

Pure instinct and compassion took over. Ignoring her own feelings and the persistent nausea, she stepped forward, keeping her tone low and soothing as she addressed the patient. "Helen, my name is Raine, and I'm a nurse. Can you tell me what happened?"

The girl's eyes filled with tears. "I don't know what happened. I can't remember. *I can't remember!*"

"Shh, it's okay." Raine crossed over to put a supporting arm around the girl's shoulders. She knew, only too well, exactly how Helen felt. The void where your memory should have been threatened to swallow you whole. Her own horrific experience had happened a month ago, but she was suddenly reliving every detail.

She pushed the fears away, trying to keep focused on Helen. The girl was her patient. The poor young woman had come here for help. "Do you have bruises? Do you hurt anywhere?"

Helen nodded, tears making long black streaks on her cheeks. "When I woke up…my clothes were off. And…was hurt. I think—I might have been raped."

CHAPTER SIX

THE room spun dizzily and Raine's knees buckled. She grabbed the edge of the bed, holding herself upright out of sheer stubbornness. But her mind whirled, drawing parallels matching the horrific experience she'd endured with this poor girl's situation.

She swallowed hard and tried to gather her scattered thoughts. She needed to get a grip. This wasn't about her. She needed to focus on the patient. Helen.

"Yvonne, please find Dr. Stewart, will you?" Raine wasn't sure how she managed to sound so calm. "I need him to approve some orders."

"Of course." Yvonne ducked from the room.

Helen tightened her grip on the blanket, her eyes wide and frightened in her face. "Is Dr. Stewart a man? Because I don't want him to examine me unless he's a woman."

The disjointed protest didn't make much sense, but Raine understood exactly what Helen was trying to tell her.

"Dr. Stewart is a man, but he won't examine you," she explained gently. "We have nurses, female nurses, who have special training as sexual assault experts to do that. Dr. Stewart does need to write the orders, though.

We'll need to draw some blood so we can run lab tests, to see if you have any drugs in your system."

"Drugs? I don't do drugs. Oh..." Helen's face paled and her eyes filled with fresh tears. "You mean he gave me something? Is that why I can't remember?"

Rohypnol was the drug they'd found in her bloodstream. But there were various date-rape drugs on the streets. She'd spent hours searching through the information on the internet. Even alcohol could be used to encourage a woman to do something she normally wouldn't do.

There were plenty of men who would take advantage of the opportunity.

Her skin felt cold and clammy, and she tightened her grip on the edge of Helen's bed in an effort to keep her mind grounded in reality. Thankfully the patient was too traumatized to realize there was something wrong with her nurse. Raine tried to speak calmly through the dull roaring in her ears. "We won't know until we get the test results back. When did this happen?"

"Last night, late. We closed the bar. But I didn't wake up until a couple hours ago. I slept all day. I never sleep all day."

Most likely because of the drugs. Especially if they were mixed with something else. "And were you drinking alcohol, too?"

"Yes." Helen dropped her chin to her chest, as if she couldn't bear to make eye contact. "Cosmo martinis."

The potent beverage may have been enough, but Raine didn't think so. Helen's total lack of memory sounded more like a date-rape drug than just alcohol alone. Men used it specifically so that the women they preyed upon couldn't remember anything incriminating.

To hide the extent of their crime.

"We need to contact the police," Raine said softly, knowing Helen wasn't going to like having to retell her story to the authorities. She wanted to say something reassuring, but couldn't think of a thing.

She knew better than most, there was no easy way to get through everything facing Helen from this point forward. Especially if there were long-term ramifications, like becoming pregnant.

Her patient didn't have a chance to respond to the news because at that moment the glass door slid open and Caleb walked in.

"Dr. Stewart, this is Helen Shore," Raine said, maintaining her professionalism with an effort. "We believe she's been sexually assaulted. We need an order for a drug screen and the SANE nurse." She stared at a spot over his left ear, hoping he couldn't tell how she was barely hanging onto her composure.

"Already done," he said. "Yvonne filled me in and the SANE nurse has already arrived. As soon as you're ready for the exam, she'll come in."

Raine froze. Oh, God. No. There was no way she could stay, not for this. She forced herself to meet his gaze. "Will you ask Yvonne to accompany Helen during the exam?"

He flashed a puzzled look, but nodded. "Sure."

Thank heavens. Raine released her death grip on the bed and walked towards the door.

But she didn't quite make it to the opening before her world went black.

* * *

Caleb reached out and grabbed Raine, hauling her upright before she hit the floor.

She was out cold, her head lolling against the crook of his arm, her dark red hair and smattering of freckles creating a stark contrast against her pale skin.

"What the—?" He swung her limp body into his arms and carried her to the only open bed they had on their team, room five. There was a minor burn patient from the waiting room slotted to be admitted in there, but he didn't care. At the moment Raine took priority. Gently, he set her on the bed.

Within seconds her eyelids fluttered open and she stared up at him in confusion. "What happened?"

"You tell me," he muttered, his voice grim. He was glad she'd come round so quickly, but couldn't help the sharp flash of concern and annoyance at how she obviously wasn't taking very good care of herself. He hadn't liked the awful way she'd looked awful earlier in his dad's room and now this. "You fainted. When's the last time you had something to eat?"

She winced and avoided his direct gaze. "I… um…ate before my shift."

He didn't believe her. "Take a break. Now." Caleb dragged a hand through his hair. She'd taken ten years off his life when she'd crumpled like a rag doll.

"I'm fine," she protested, pushing up on her elbows to sit upright. She ran a hand over her forehead and he could see the faint sheen of sweat dampening her fingertips. Her pulse was racing and her blood pressure was probably non-existent. "I never faint."

"Could have fooled me," he said, stepping forward

to put a hand on her shoulder to keep her in place. "Give yourself a few minutes' rest before going back to work, would you? I'd rather arrange for someone to come in to give you a full physical exam. Please don't take this the wrong way, but you look like hell."

Her eyes widened in horror at the suggestion. "No. I'm fine. I don't want an exam."

"Raine." He stared at her until she met his gaze. "I'm not kidding. Tell me what's going on. What's wrong?"

"Nothing." She avoided his gaze in a way that made him grind his teeth in helpless frustration. Why wouldn't she open up to him? Talk to him? "I swear I just had a physical exam not too long ago. I'm fine."

He stared at her, willing her to open up about what was going on. But she sat up, swinging her legs over the edge of the bed as if to prove she was fine. "I'll be all right in a few minutes. In the meantime, I'll ask Ellen or Tracey to cover for me."

He couldn't force her to stay, but that didn't mean he was particularly happy when she stood on shaky legs. He stayed within reach, watching to make sure she didn't fall again.

It was ridiculous to be hurt by her decision. Raine couldn't have made her feelings any clearer. She didn't want or need his help.

There were no second chances. At least for him.

Biting back a curse, he told himself to let her go. Raine's issues, whatever they entailed, weren't his concern. She was making it clear they didn't have a personal relationship any more. And he had plenty of his own problems to deal with. Like his father, who was almost as stubborn as Raine.

Gingerly, she walked toward the door as if testing the strength in her legs, still looking as if a mild breeze would blow her over.

"Raine," he called, as she crossed the threshold. She glanced at him over her shoulder. "I'm here if you need to talk. Or if you just want someone to listen."

Stark desolation flashed in her eyes, but just as quickly it was gone. "Thanks, but I'm fine. Really. I'll be back in twenty minutes."

This time when she left, he didn't bother trying to stop her.

In Raine's absence, Caleb took control of the patients in their team, including taking on the job of calling the police for the young sexual assault victim.

Their patient care tech, Yvonne, had remained glued to the young woman's side throughout the rape kit exam and even when the police arrived to question her. He didn't complain, even knowing that without Yvonne's help, patients moved slowly through the department.

He kept his distance from Helen Shore, knowing from past experience that most assault patients were far more comfortable with female caregivers. But as he worked, he couldn't get the shattered expression on the young woman's face out of his mind.

Victims of crimes were the most difficult patients to care for. Sexual assaults were right up there next to child abuse, at least in his opinion. Getting angry wasn't exactly helpful to the patients, though, so he schooled his features so that his true disgust and rage toward the assailant didn't show. None of this was the victim's fault.

He could only hope the evidence they obtained would help the police find the bastard who'd hurt her.

When Raine returned, she looked marginally better. Maybe she had finally eaten something. Her face was still lined with exhaustion, though, and he couldn't help wondering why. She looked much worse tonight than she had the night she'd stayed with him in the waiting room. Telling himself that he'd done all he could to open up to her, and that the next move was hers, didn't help. He had little choice but to turn his attention to the matter at hand.

She jumped into the fray without hesitation, quickly picking up on the patient care issues that still needed to be addressed.

"Have we had the drug screen results back yet on Helen Shore?" he asked, when Raine brought him the discharge paperwork on their burn patient.

Her eyes darkened momentarily. "I don't know. I'll check."

He signed the paperwork and then glanced towards Helen's room. The police were still in there, taking her statement. He wasn't sure how much longer they would be, but it didn't really matter since he wasn't about to hurry her out the door.

"Drug screen is positive for flunitrazepam," Raine said, returning to the workstation with a slip of paper in her hand.

Flunitrazepam was the generic name for Rohypnol, the infamous date-rape drug. They wouldn't have the results from the rape kit for several days, but this pretty much sealed poor Helen's fate. There was no doubt in his mind that her rape kit would turn out positive. He sighed and took the results from Raine. "All right. I'll let the patient know."

"I'll go with you." Raine hovered near his elbow as he entered the room. The police officers, one male and one female glanced up at him curiously.

"I have your drug screen results," Caleb said, ignoring the police and focusing on the patient. "Would you rather the officers leave, so I can tell you privately?"

The male police officer looked like he was about to protest, but he needn't have worried, because Helen was already shaking her head.

"No, go ahead," Helen said in a voice barely above a whisper. "They'll need to know either way."

"I'm sorry, but you tested positive for Flunitrazepam, also known as Rohypnol." He handed the drug result to Helen, who barely glanced at it before handing it to the female police officer.

"So there's no mistake," Helen whispered. "He did this on purpose."

"I'm afraid so." Caleb wished there was something he could say or do to make her feel better.

"That's the second case of Rohypnol from the After Dark nightclub in the past few months," the female officer said in disgust. "Could be the same bastard."

Beside him, he heard Raine suck in a harsh breath. And then suddenly she was gone. When he finished in Helen's room, he found her out at the desk working on the computer.

"We have a new admission coming in, new onset abdominal pain," she told him as if nothing was wrong.

"Okay, let me know once you get a set of vitals and a baseline set of labs. Could be his gall-bladder."

"Sure." The forced cheerfulness in her tone bothered him.

But it wasn't until much later, that he realized why. That the shattered look in Helen Shore's eyes reminded him too much of the haunted expression in Raine's.

Raine could barely concentrate as she prepared a summary report for the on-coming shift. Her assault and Helen's may have been by the same person. The idea was staggering. She hoped and prayed the police would find the guy, and soon.

After she finished with report, she gave a small sigh of relief. At last, her interminable shift was over. All she needed to do was to finish up the discharge paperwork on Helen Shore and she could leave.

Taking a deep breath, she entered Helen Shore's room. Yvonne had left the patient's bedside at eleven, since there was currently a hospital ban on over-time. Helen had dressed in her clothes but clutched the blanket around her shoulders, like a lifeline. Raine could relate, and she had no intention of taking it away from her.

"I have your discharge paperwork, Helen." Raine approached her bedside and handed her the slip of paper listing her follow up appointment for the next week. "Do you have any questions before you go?"

Helen slowly shook her head. "No. The other nurse told me she wouldn't have the rest of my test results for a few days. Not that it matters, much," she added bitterly. "I doubt the police will ever find the guy."

"They will." Raine injected confidence in her tone, even though she held the same doubts. She pulled up a chair to sit beside her. "Helen, you need to seek professional help in order to get through this. I know the name of a good therapist, if you don't have one."

"The social worker gave me a list." Helen stared morosely down at her hands. "But what good is talking about it? Doesn't change what happened."

"No, it won't." Raine empathized with the young woman's helpless anger. Especially if it was possible the same guy attacked them both. The After Dark nightclub should be forced to close until this bastard was caught. Even the police didn't believe it was a co-incidence. Detective Carol Blanchard had promised to be in touch if she had any evidence, but so far Raine hadn't heard a thing.

She gathered her scattered thoughts. "There are support groups, however. Other young women like yourself, who've been through the same thing." Raine had attended one of the support group meetings, but hadn't found it particularly helpful. She offered the option though, because everyone coped differently.

And she was hardly the expert in coping strategies. She'd thought she was doing so well.

Only to fall completely apart, tonight.

"I'm afraid to go home," Helen admitted in a low voice. "He knows where I live. What if he comes back?"

Raine understood. She'd experienced the exact same fear. In fact, she hoped to move once her lease was up. And she'd been sleeping on the sofa with Spice, unable to face her bed. "Do you have someone to stay with you?"

"I could ask my sister."

Raine gave a nod of encouragement. "I think that's a good idea. And add a deadbolt lock to your door if you don't have one already. Literature shows that date-rape perpetrators don't go back to the same victims, but it doesn't hurt to be extra-careful."

"I will, thanks."

She leaned over and covered the woman's hand with hers. "Remember, Helen, you're not alone. Try the support group, or talking to a therapist. Unfortunately, date rape is more common than the average person realizes."

Helen lifted her head to meet her gaze. "Sounds like you've had some experience with this," she said.

For a moment Raine longed to blurt out the truth. But she was supposed to be the nurse, helping and supporting the patient, not the other way around. The words stuck in her throat. "I—I've cared for other patient's in similar circumstances," she murmured evasively. "And I can imagine what you're going through. Please take care of yourself, okay?"

"Okay."

Raine walked with her outside to the parking lot where she'd left her car. She stared after Helen for a long moment, before turning to head back inside to swipe out. She couldn't wait to get out of there.

Caleb stood behind her and she caught herself just in time to prevent herself from smacking into him.

"Did you need something?" she asked testily. She wasn't in the mood for a confrontation. Not now. She wanted to go home.

"Yeah. Do you have a minute?"

"Not really. I need to go inside to swipe out." She tried to sidestep him, but Caleb didn't take the hint, turning and following her inside to the nearest time clock where she could swipe her ID badge, formally ending her shift.

She suppressed a sigh and faced him. "Caleb, couldn't we do this some other time? I really don't feel well. I've been sick to my stomach. I think I'm catching some flu bug or something."

"Stop it, Raine. I know the truth."

Her jaw dropped and she stared at him. He knew? How was that possible? No one knew. Except her boss, and Theresa had promised not to say a word.

Had she inadvertently said something when she'd passed out?

"You do?"

"Yes." He crossed his arms over his chest and stared at her. "And I'm not letting you go until you agree to talk to me about it."

CHAPTER SEVEN

RAINE stared at him in shock. To hear him blurt out so bluntly that he knew the truth was staggering. "No. I…can't talk about it. I'm sorry." She turned away, heading for the employee parking lot, wanting nothing more than to go home, to recover from her emotionally draining shift.

But once again Caleb followed her outside. She tried to think of something to say to make him go away. But her mind was blank. And one glimpse at the stubborn set of his features told her he wasn't going to let her go easily.

"You shouldn't drive when you're this upset." He took her arm, steering her towards where his car was parked.

For a moment she tensed beneath his touch, wanting to pull away, but then her shoulders slumped with exhaustion. She simply didn't have the energy to fight. Going along with him was easier than arguing. He opened the passenger door of his car and gestured for her to get inside.

She did, without uttering a single protest.

He slid behind the wheel, glancing at her, but not saying anything. The silence should have been oppressive but, oddly enough, she took comfort in his presence. Maybe because taking care of Helen had brought her suppressed fears to the surface.

He pulled out of the parking lot and headed towards his house, without bothering to ask if she was okay with his decision.

She didn't protest. She was secretly glad he hadn't taken her back to her apartment. Her imagination tended to work overtime there.

"How's your father doing?" she asked when he pulled into the driveway.

He glanced at her. "Better. Still in pain, but overall much better."

"I'm glad," she murmured.

After parking the car, he headed up to his house and unlocked the door. She followed him inside, smiling a bit when Grizzly greeted her enthusiastically.

For a moment she buried her face against his silky fur, hanging onto her self-control by a thin thread. She'd been in Caleb's house often while they'd dated. After her emotionally draining shift, the welcome familiarity of Caleb's house soothed her soul.

She'd missed him. Desperately. They'd shared some very good times, before she'd realized the extent of his inability to trust. And then it was too late. She'd made a terrible mistake.

"Grizz likes you," Caleb said, watching her pet the dog as he made a pot of coffee. "He's not that excited when I come home, more like disappointed that I'm not my father."

She didn't know how to respond, worried she'd burst into tears if she tried. Back when things had started to get more intense between them, she'd wondered what it might be like to share Caleb's home with him. She glanced around, liking the way Caleb's kitchen overlooked the living area, the cathedral ceiling providing a spacious feel. She took a seat on the butter-soft deep blue leather sofa. Grizzly followed her, sitting on his haunches in front of her and placing his big head on her lap. His soulful eyes stared up at her adoringly, wordlessly begging for attention. She pressed her face to the silky fur on the top of his head.

The sharp stab of regret pierced deep.

Caleb brought in two mugs of steaming coffee. She could smell the enticing scent of the vanilla creamer she loved. With a guilty start, she realized he must have bought it with her in mind, anticipating a night in the not-too-distant future when she might stay over.

And if things had been different, they might have spent the night together. More than once.

Her stomach churned. The nausea surged up with full force. Desperately, she swallowed hard.

There was no point in wishing for something she couldn't have. Caleb hadn't really trusted her before, there was no way that would change now.

And, really, she couldn't blame him.

He settled into the easy chair across from her, as if he didn't dare risk getting too close. She wrapped her hands around the coffee mug, seeking warmth despite the humid summer evening, wondering why he'd brought her here.

His gaze bored into hers. "Raine, I'm sure you'd feel better if you talked about it."

The hot coffee scalded her tongue. She stared into the

depths of her mug, not wanting to admit he was right. "I doubt it."

"Raine, what can I say to convince you? You stayed with me when my father was having surgery—at least let me help you now. As a friend."

She sighed, knowing he was right but somehow unable to find the words to tell him what had happened. She was afraid, so very afraid of seeing the same flare of disgust in his eyes.

"Did you meet someone else? Is that it? Is that what you're afraid to tell me? What happened? Did he move too fast for you?"

She blinked. Another guy? Was that really what he thought?

"I know you, Raine," he continued, obviously on a roll. "You're a passionate woman, but you're also sweetly innocent. He's a rat bastard for taking advantage of you. I can imagine exactly how it happened. A goodnight kiss went too far, and he pushed you into a level of intimacy you weren't ready for."

Dear God. He didn't know the truth. *He didn't know.*

Her mind whirling, Raine wasn't sure how to respond. Slowly, she shook her head.

"Come on. I know something happened." He set his coffee mug aside, untouched. "That's why you acted so strangely with our sexual assault patient. Because you were close to experiencing the same thing. Isn't that right? Dammit, tell me." The pure agony in his tone hit hard.

"No. You've got it all wrong," she said, sinking further into the sofa cushions, wishing she could close her eyes and disappear.

He let out a harsh laugh. "Yeah, right. That's why you have that haunted expression in your eyes. Don't protect the bastard."

Suddenly she couldn't take the pretence. Couldn't continue acting as if everything was fine when it was anything but. Unfortunately, the scenario he'd described might be closer to the truth than he realized. Except for one important fact.

"I'm not protecting anyone," she said finally. "I don't even know who he is."

"What do you mean?" Caleb frowned in confusion. "How can you not know?"

"Because I was given Rohypnol." She forced the truth out past the lump in her throat. "You were right, Caleb. Is that what you want to hear? You were right not to trust me. I flirted with a stranger and I paid the price."

Caleb stared at her, his eyes full of horror.

She forced herself to finish. "You want to know what happened? I'll tell you. I was sexually assaulted by a man I can't remember."

Raine's confession stabbed him in the chest, ripping away his ability to breathe. He'd known she was holding something back, but this was worse. So much worse than what he'd imagined. His mind could barely comprehend what she was telling him.

Raine had been assaulted. By a stranger.

Appalled, he jumped to his feet, unable to sit still. "My God. I…didn't know. Why didn't you tell me?" he asked in a strangled tone.

She hunched her shoulders and shivered. He wanted

to cross over to her, to put his arms around her and hold her tight, but obviously that was the last thing she'd want.

No wonder he'd seen the same shattered expression in her eyes that had been mirrored in their patient's eyes. He'd suspected some guy had pushed her into something, but he hadn't imagined this. Not that she'd been given Rohypnol and raped. He still could hardly believe it. The confession shimmered in the air between them, forcing him to keep his distance, even though it pained him.

"I couldn't," she whispered. "I haven't told anyone."

She hadn't told anyone? Why in heaven's name not? He paced the length of the great room, jamming his fingers helplessly through his hair. He needed to remain calm when all he wanted was to wrap his hands around the bastard's throat, squeezing until he begged for mercy. He was so angry he could barely see. How on earth had she managed? Especially all alone?

Raine shivered again, the uncontrollable movement capturing his gaze. He swallowed a curse and went into his bedroom. He grabbed the blanket off his bed and carried it into the living room. Wordlessly, he draped it around her slim shoulders, trying not to touch her.

"Thank you," she murmured, pulling the blanket close.

The fury he'd buried threatened to break loose. He didn't know how she could sit there so calmly. He wanted to rant and rave, to throw things. He curled his fingers into fists and he began pacing again, still reeling at the news.

He felt sick, realizing she'd gone through the horror all alone rather than seeking comfort from him. And he understood exactly why.

Because he hadn't believed her when she'd called to apologize after he'd seen her with Jake. And she'd assumed he wouldn't believe her about this as well.

He wanted to smack his head against the wall for being so stupid. For not listening to her when she'd called him the next day. Why had he believed Jake, when he hadn't believed Raine?

Grizz must have realized something was wrong, because the black Lab whined and then abruptly jumped up on the sofa, settling against Raine and placing his large head in her lap. He almost told the dog to get down from the furniture.

But when Raine hugged Grizz close, seemingly grateful for the comfort of the dog's presence, he couldn't bear to yell at Grizz to get down. The dog wasn't a threat to her, not in the way a man might be.

The way he would be? He remembered the way she'd tended to keep distance between them the first few times they'd worked together.

But not afterwards. Not when they'd sat in the waiting room together, waiting for news about his father.

He couldn't stand the thought that she might be afraid of him.

"Raine." He stared at her, hating feeling so helpless. "I don't know what to say."

"You don't have to say anything," she said, her voice muffled by Grizzly's fur. "It's enough that you know the truth."

He clenched his jaw and swung away, so she wouldn't see the simmering anger in his eyes. It wasn't enough to know the truth, not by a long shot. He wouldn't be satisfied until the bastard was caught. Helpless guilt grabbed him by the throat.

If he hadn't let his mistrust get the better of him, maybe he could have handled things differently. He knew now he should have given her the benefit of doubt.

And now it was too late to go back, to fix the mistakes he'd made.

The last thing he wanted right now was to do or say anything that could possibly hurt her. Or scare her.

Control. He needed to maintain control. He couldn't think about how she must have gone into the hospital, seeking help. Being examined. Talking to the police.

No wonder she'd fainted.

His imagination was worse than knowing the truth. How was she coping when he couldn't keep the awful images out of his mind? Another man's hands on her. Forcing her to have sex. Taking what she hadn't freely given.

Ruthlessly, he shoved the horrible images away.

"I'm sorry," he said finally. "I should have been there with you. You shouldn't have had to go through that alone."

She didn't answer. When he glanced back at her he could only see her face, the rest of her body was buried beneath the blanket and Grizz. Her eyes had closed, her mouth had relaxed and her lips were slightly parted in sleep.

Caleb let out a deep breath and collapsed in the chair opposite. He scrubbed his hands over his face.

He tried to tell himself he must not have handled things too badly if Raine was comfortable enough to fall asleep on his living-room sofa. Either that or he'd under-estimated the comfort provided by Grizz.

Hell, he'd convince his dad to give her the dog if only she'd smile again.

Smile. Yeah, right. He didn't know how in the world she'd recover from this. How did any woman put something like this behind them?

Broodingly, he watched her sleep, his gaze caressing the curve of her cheek, the silkiness of her hair. He remembered with aching clarity, their last embrace. Their last kiss.

He grimaced and closed his eyes, drowning in the bitter-sweet memories. The sexual chemistry between them had sizzled. During their kisses goodnight, it had taken every ounce of willpower he'd possessed to slow things down. Each night the heat had grown more passionate between them. And he couldn't deny that he'd always been the one to pull back, before either of them had got too carried away.

Even though they'd only dated for two months, he'd suspected he was falling for her. And that had caused him to overreact to everything she'd done. He hadn't been able to find a way to stop himself from constantly questioning her.

His selfish fears had pushed her away at the moment she'd probably needed him most.

He opened his eyes and looked at Raine, mourning the loss. His fault. What had happened to Raine was largely his fault. And now there was no going back.

Whatever feelings she might have had toward him were likely gone. What he hadn't destroyed had likely been demolished by her assailant.

Picking up his mug of coffee, he took a sip, grimacing at the cold temperature. His gaze burned with deep regret as he watched her sleep.

Raine opened her eyes, momentarily confused for a moment about where she was. Grizzly let out a deep sigh beside her. She blinked, realizing she was still on Caleb's sofa, suffocatingly warm as a result of being sandwiched between the blanket and the large dog.

She might be sweltering, but she'd also slept the entire night through without waking up. For the first time since the night of the assault.

She'd felt safe with Caleb. And Grizzly.

Feeling better than she had in a long time, she gingerly sat up, surprised to find Caleb asleep in the easy-chair across from her. So both the man and the dog had watched over her. She winced a bit, realizing that the way Caleb's head lay at such an awkward angle he would probably wake up with a severe crick in his neck.

His eyes shot open, startling her.

She licked suddenly dry lips, smoothing a hand self-consciously over her tangled hair. "Good morning."

"Morning." He straightened in the chair, twisting his head from side to side, stretching the tense muscles. "Are you hungry? We didn't eat anything for dinner last night."

Her stomach rumbled and for the second time in as many minutes she was surprised to discover her nausea was absent and her appetite had returned. "Yes, as a matter of fact, I am. Do you want help?"

Caleb shook his head. "No, I'll throw something together. Omelets okay?"

"Sure." The inane conversation helped keep things in perspective. Caleb had always been a nice guy, of course that hadn't changed. But she couldn't lie to herself. She'd caught the fleeting glimpse of appalled horror in his gaze when she'd finally confessed the truth. Luckily, there was no sign of his aversion now.

She untangled her legs from the blanket. "I'll, uh, need to borrow your bathroom for a minute."

"Help yourself. This will take a few minutes, anyway." Caleb seemed to be giving her distance, letting the dog out as she went past him towards the bathroom.

Ten minutes later, feeling slightly more human after washing up a bit, Raine returned to the kitchen. Caleb had changed his clothes too, looking ruggedly handsome in his casual jeans and T-shirt. He was busy pouring the egg mixture into the pan, and then added ham, cheese and mushrooms.

She smoothed a hand over her badly wrinkled scrubs, feeling awkward as Caleb cooked for her. "Are you sure you don't need help with anything?"

"I'm sure. Why don't you sit down at the table? The coffee should be ready in a minute." After a few minutes he pulled plates out of the cupboard, slid two fluffy omelets onto them and carried them over to the table.

For long moments they ate in silence. When the coffee was ready, he poured them each a mug, laced hers with the vanilla-flavored creamer and brought them to the table.

"Thanks," she said, accepting the cup. "I guess I should apologize for falling asleep on you."

"No, you shouldn't." His tone was tense, but his gaze

was uncertain as he glanced at her. "I'm glad you felt comfortable enough to sleep here."

She glanced away, hating the awkwardness that loomed between them.

"Besides, did you really think Grizz was going to let you leave without a fight?" Caleb asked lightly. "He was in doggy heaven, sleeping on the sofa beside you."

A smile tugged at the corner of her mouth, especially when Grizzly's head perked up at his name. "I didn't mind. He was wonderful company."

Caleb took a sip of his coffee, eyeing her over the rim. "You honestly haven't told anyone else? Not even your brothers?"

Her smile faded. She shook her head. "Especially not my brothers."

Caleb frowned. "Elana?"

"No. She and Brock have been so happy, planning the nursery for the new baby, that I couldn't find a way to tell her." She forced herself to meet his gaze. "I've been too embarrassed. Too ashamed to tell anyone."

"You have nothing to be ashamed of, Raine," he said with a frown.

Too bad she didn't really believe him. "I've been seeing a counselor and talking to her has helped," she said instead.

He nodded encouragingly. "That's good."

She set her fork down, not really in the mood to talk about this any more. "Thanks for breakfast, Caleb, but I really should get going."

Caleb didn't pick up on her hint. "Do the police have any leads on this guy?"

"Not that I know of," she admitted.

"They must have something to go on," he pressed. "Surely you remember some of the men who were there that night."

Her stomach cramped and she put a hand over it, as the nausea returned. Like it always did when she thought about how she'd acted that night at Jamie's bachelorette party, dancing and flirting with the various players and fans of the rugby team who had come in to celebrate their win, buying rounds of drinks for their group.

One of whom could have drugged her. Assaulted her.

Had he fathered a child, too?

CHAPTER EIGHT

"RAINE?" She glanced up when Caleb called her name, staring at him blankly when he leaned forward, his gaze full of concern. "You're awfully pale. Are you all right?"

"Fine," she forced herself to answer, willing the nausea away. Telling Caleb the truth had felt good last night, but now she was beginning to regret giving in. Why did he feel the need to keep talking about what had happened? There was no reason to keep harping on it. She wasn't ready to give him every excruciating detail.

As Helen had said, talking about it didn't change what had happened.

And if he knew everything, he'd realize he might have been right to accuse her of wanting other men. Hadn't she attended the bachelorette party that night, flirting like crazy, in an effort to prove she was over Caleb?

Grizz came over to lick her fingers, as if he could sense her distress, and she stroked his silky ebony fur, trying to summon a smile. "If you don't mind, I'd rather not talk about that night. It's been really hard, but I'm trying to move past what happened to me."

Instantly, Caleb's face paled, his gaze stricken. "I'm sorry. I should have realized…"

His self-recrimination wasn't necessary. Being treated differently was part of the reason she'd chosen not to say anything to anyone. She lifted her chin. "I don't want your pity, Caleb. I've been trying to move forward in my life. To focus on all the positive things I have to be grateful for, rather than dwelling on the negative."

He frowned a little and rubbed the back of his neck. "Pity is not at all what I'm feeling right now. I admire you. I think you're amazing, Raine. Truly."

His sincere, earnest expression eased some of the tension in her stomach. "I'm not. Obviously, taking care of Helen proves I still have a long ways to go. But each day gets a little better. At least, it had been, until last night."

If anything, he paled more. "Because you told me? Telling me made it worse for you?"

"No," she hastened to reassure him. "Because of Helen. I *fainted*, for heaven's sake. I thought I was handling trauma fairly well, even though taking care of Becca had been really hard. We saved Greg Hanson, which helped immensely. I thought I'd gotten over the worst, but then Helen came in and I lost it."

"You handled the stress all far better than anyone could expect." He frowned a little. "I knew you'd taken a temporary position in the minor care area. This was the reason?"

"Yeah. I couldn't take off work for more than a week and still pay my rent, so I asked Theresa, my boss, to put me in Minor Care. Just happened that one of the nurses was out on a medical leave so it was easy to cover her hours."

"I thought you were avoiding me," he admitted.

She lifted her shoulder in a half-shrug. "I was avoiding everyone, not just you."

He stared at her for several long seconds, the last few bites of his meal forgotten. "I feel so damned helpless," he said in a low, agonized tone. "Is there something I can do? Anything?"

She started to shake her head, but then stopped. She looked at Caleb, seated across the table from her, keeping his distance from the moment he'd discovered the truth, as if she were some sort of leper. They didn't have the same relationship they'd once had, but certainly over these past few days they'd re-established their friendship. Hadn't they?

"Actually, I could use a hug." The moment the words were out of her mouth, she wished she could call them back as they made her sound pathetic. Hadn't she just told him she didn't want his pity?

"Really?" The flare of cautious hope in his eyes caught her off guard. He quickly rose to his feet and crossed over to her, holding out his hand in a silent invitation.

Was she crazy? Maybe. Reaching out, she put her hand in his and allowed him to draw her to her feet. And then he slowly, carefully, as if she might break, drew her into his arms.

Enticed by his solid warmth and gentle strength, she wrapped her arms around his waist and buried her face against his chest, breathing deeply, as if she could never get enough of his heady, comforting scent. She'd missed this so much! More than she would have thought possible.

Maybe she'd made a mistake by not telling him. She'd avoided it because she'd known that the person he'd once been attracted to was gone for ever. She'd never be that free-spirited girl again. But she might have misjudged him. Caleb would have stood by her as a friend.

She tightened her grip, silently telling him how much she appreciated this. And when his mouth lightly brushed against the top of her head, she sucked in a quick breath, stunned by a flash of desire.

For a moment she closed her eyes, wishing desperately for the chance to go back, to make a better decision.

His broad hand lightly stroked her back, and she knew his intention was probably to offer comfort, but her skin tingled with awareness. She was tempted to reach up to kiss him. Ironically, she was happy to know she could still feel desire, this deep yearning for physical closeness. That what had happened to her, as awful as it was, hadn't stolen everything.

She still wanted Caleb. The attraction she'd felt for him the moment they'd met was still there.

But would he ever trust her with his whole heart?

She closed her eyes against the prick of tears. No, she didn't think Caleb was really capable of trusting her with his whole heart and soul. And crying wasn't going to change that. Enough of the poor-me syndrome. She had a lot to be thankful for. Negative energy wasn't productive.

Taking a deep breath, she let it out slowly. A tiny part of her wanted to stay in his arms like this for ever, but regretfully she pressed a quick kiss against the fabric of his shirt before loosening her grip on his waist. He immediately let go, and her moment of euphoria deflated when she realized the desire she'd experienced was clearly one-sided.

"Thanks," she murmured, determined not to show him how much she'd been affected by his embrace. "I needed that."

"Any time," he said, in a low husky tone.

Surprised, she glanced up at his dark gray eyes, realizing he sincerely meant it. Was it possible he may still have some desire for her? Even after what had happened? She was afraid to hope. "I…uh, should get going. I'm scheduled to work today."

She sensed he wanted to argue, but in the end he simply nodded. "Okay, give me a few minutes to clean up in here, I don't want to leave everything out with Grizzly around."

"I'll help." She stacked their plates and carried them over to the kitchen sink. And as they worked companionably side by side in the kitchen, she caught a glimpse of the future she might have had with Caleb.

If only she'd swallowed her pride and returned his calls instead of going to the bachelorette party in an effort to forget about him.

"Are you ready to go?" Caleb asked, glancing over at Raine. He wished he could come up with some valid or believable reason to encourage her to stay.

Rather than just the fact that he didn't want her to leave.

Holding her in his arms had been amazing. Humbling. He'd known she'd only wanted comfort from a friend and nothing more, so he'd garnered every ounce of willpower to keep his embrace non-sexual and non-threatening, despite his deeper desire for more.

One step at a time. He was still hurt that Raine hadn't come to him sooner, that she'd chosen to ignore his phone calls rather than to confide in him. But she was here now. Had spent the night on his sofa, with Grizz. Which meant she trusted him at least a little.

Didn't she?

"Sure. I'm ready if you are."

He wasn't ready at all, but he searched the kitchen counter until he found his keys. When he turned back to face Raine, he found she'd dropped to her knees to give Grizz a big hug. The dampness around her eyes wrenched his heart.

He couldn't stand the thought that she'd endured all this alone.

The atmosphere in the car during the ride back to the hospital was quietly subdued. He wanted to offer to give her another hug, but worried about coming on too strong. Logically, he knew it was best to let Raine set the pace for what she wanted or was comfortable with. He could only imagine what she'd gone through.

So he didn't reach for her, even though he desperately wanted to.

"Thanks for the ride," she said softly, when he'd pulled up to her car in the parking lot. "And thanks for letting me borrow Grizzly last night. It's the first night I've slept peacefully since…" Her voice trailed off as she fumbled for the doorhandle.

Oh, man, now he didn't really want her to leave, if

last night was the first night she'd slept well since the assault. But she seemed intent on getting out of the car quickly, so he jumped out and came around to open the door for her, trying to think of a polite way to convince her to stay. "I'm sure Grizz would be thrilled if you'd come spend another night on my sofa."

Her lopsided smile tugged on his heart, but she gave a small shake of her head, declining his offer. "Thanks again." She lifted up on tiptoe and brushed a light kiss on his cheek, surprising him speechless. He wanted badly to crush her close, but kept his arms at his sides so he wouldn't scare her. "Bye, Caleb."

He could barely force the words from his throat. "Bye, Raine. I'll be at work tonight too, so I'll see you later."

He stood, staring after her as she climbed into her car and started the engine. And when she backed out and drove away, it was all he could do not to follow her home.

She'd kissed him. Asked for a hug.

Was he a complete fool for thinking her actions were a sign she was willing to give him another chance?

Raine drove home, feeling better than she had in a long time. The cramping nausea that had plagued her endlessly seemed to have vanished.

Maybe her life was finally getting back on track. Telling Caleb, as difficult as it had been, had helped. At least around him she didn't have to pretend any more.

When she passed a drugstore, her previous doubts resurfaced. Quickly making a U-turn, she headed back to the store to purchase a home pregnancy test. Enough procrastinating.

It was time to know the truth, one way or the other.

Despite her extreme self-consciousness, no one looked at her with blatant curiosity when she purchased a two-in-one home pregnancy kit. The company had been smart enough to provide two tests in one box, providing a back-up in case she did something wrong the first time.

Clutching the bag tightly to her chest, she walked up to her second-story apartment and greeted Spice, who sniffed the remnants of Grizzly's scent on her scrubs with feline disdain.

"Don't worry," she said, scratching the cat behind the ears. "You're still my favorite."

Spice walked away, with her tail high in the air, seemingly looking at her with reproach.

Raine took the pregnancy test with her into the bathroom. She took a shower and then sat down to read the directions on the test kit. The process was easy enough and didn't require that she wait until the morning. Without giving herself a chance to change her mind, she carefully followed the instructions. The brief period of waiting seemed to take three hours instead of three minutes.

Gathering her strength and mentally preparing for the worst, she took a deep breath and went over to look at the test strip.

The words *Not Pregnant* practically jumped out at her. She blinked and leaned closer, looking again to make sure she wasn't simply imagining things.

Not Pregnant.

She wasn't pregnant. Her knees went weak and she

dropped onto the seat of the commode, her mind grappling with the news. This was good. She should be relieved she wasn't pregnant.

So why the strange sense of emptiness underlying the relief?

She'd always hoped to have children one day, but not yet. And not like this. But, still, she couldn't quite push aside the feeling.

She shook off her conflicting thoughts. Now she knew. Whatever was bothering her wasn't a baby. She put a hand over her stomach, which still didn't feel totally normal, but certainly not as upset as it had been earlier. Was it possible she'd tested herself too early? She turned back to pick up the box, reading the instructions again. Sure enough, the company did recommend taking the test again after a week, just to be sure.

Another week? She wasn't sure she could stand to wait that long. Hopefully she'd get her period before then.

She put the pregnancy kit up in the medicine cabinet. She could test herself again, but stress was the likely culprit making her feel sick. The fact that most of her nausea had faded after talking to Caleb only reinforced the possibility.

Her counselor had been right. Keeping everything that had happened to her bottled up inside wasn't healthy.

Caleb had sounded surprised that she hadn't told her three older brothers. She loved her brothers dearly, but they'd been completely against her moving to the big city from their small town of Cedar Bluff. They loved her, but if she told them what happened, she feared they would have gone straight into over-protection mode. They would have insisted on moving her back home and never letting her out of their sight again. And she also knew they might have been tempted to confront every rugby fan themselves—taking the law into their own hands.

She shivered, a cold trail of dread seeping down her spine. No, she couldn't tell them. Not yet.

Not until the police had caught the guy.

Maybe not ever.

For a moment she glanced helplessly around her apartment. Was she crazy to just sit back, waiting for the police to get a lead? Sure, they had Helen's case loosely linked to hers, but that news alone didn't mean they had a suspect. Should she be taking some sort of action? Would seeing a face trigger some latent memory?

She was scheduled to work tonight, unless she could find someone to cover for her. Caleb was scheduled to work, too. A part of her wanted nothing more than to take him up on his offer to spend the night again on his sofa.

But she couldn't lean on him too much. She needed to be strong. And maybe that meant taking action, rather than sitting around, doing nothing.

Caleb went to work early, to visit his dad and in hope of seeing Raine.

He'd been tempted to call her several times that day. Only the memories of how he'd over-reacted before when they'd been dating held him back.

She didn't need him constantly hovering. But doing nothing, and not seeing her at all, was killing him.

When he went up to his father's room on the regular

floor, he was disappointed to find Raine wasn't there. But at least his father looked much better.

"Hi, Dad. How are you?"

"Doc says I'm hanging in there. They made me get up and walk in the hallway." His father grimaced as he rearranged the photographs of the animals at the shelter on his bedside table. Caleb had to admit Raine's simple gift was genius.

"I'm glad to hear that. You need to move around if you want to go home." He glanced at the glossy pictures, realizing how in some ways Raine had known his father better than he had. "Tell me about the animals at the shelter."

That was all the encouragement his father needed. He went into great detail on the dogs he'd recently cared for, ending with a particularly engaging Irish setter. "This is Rusty, he's Raine's favorite."

Raine's favorite? She'd seemed quite taken with Grizz last night. Caleb leaned forward to get a better look. "He's cute."

"The color of his coat matches her hair," his father explained with a smile. "Her apartment doesn't allow dogs, or I know she would have already adopted him."

The idea of Raine longing for the companionship of a dog made his gut tighten. She deserved to have a dog as a pet. Look how quickly she'd bonded with Grizzly. He almost said as much to his father, but then realized that if his dad knew how Raine had spent the night, he'd only have more questions. Questions he didn't have the right to answer.

It was Raine's story to tell, not his. And the fact that

she hadn't told anyone but him was enough for him to keep quiet.

"Seems like you and Raine are pretty close," Caleb said.

His father shrugged. "Not really. We don't talk about our personal lives very much. But, yeah, I enjoy working with her."

"She, uh, hasn't stopped in to visit at all today, has she?" Caleb asked casually.

His father's gaze sharpened. "No. why? Is there something going on between the two of you?"

"Not in the way you're thinking," Caleb said wryly. "We work together in the ED, and I was curious, that's all."

"Hrmph." His father scowled at him. "What's wrong with you, son? Are you blind? Can't you see what a great catch Raine is?"

It was on the tip of Caleb's tongue to remind his father he didn't jump into relationships the way he did, but he bit back the retort. Because, truthfully, he had jumped into a relationship with Raine. Faster than he had with anyone else.

And the moment he'd seen her with Jake he'd assumed the worst.

"I'm not blind," he assured his father dryly. "Raine is beautiful and kind. She's also a great nurse."

His father rolled his eyes. "Now you're going to tell me you're just friends."

"We are. Don't push," he warned, when his father looked as if he might argue. "Besides, I have to go. It's almost time for my shift."

"Go on, then. Save lives." His father waved him off.

Caleb walked toward the door, but then turned back. "Dad?" He waited for his father to meet his gaze. "I love you. Take care of yourself, understand?"

His father looked surprised, but then he nodded. "Thanks, Caleb," he said in a gruff tone. "I will. And I love you, too."

Caleb headed down to the emergency eepartment, glancing around for Raine and frowning when he didn't find her. Had she decided to go back into the minor care area, the small exam rooms that were literally located just outside the main emergency department? After several minutes of looking, he sought help from the charge nurse on duty.

"Which area is Raine Hart working in tonight?" he asked.

"She's not here," the charge nurse informed him. "She called and asked Diane to work for her. Diane is assigned to the trauma bay."

For a moment he could only stare at her in shock, his breath lodged painfully in his chest. Raine wasn't working tonight? Why? Because she was avoiding him? Or because she was too upset?

Dammit, he never should have left her alone.

CHAPTER NINE

CONCENTRATING on patient care helped distract him for a while, but every time there was a lull between patients, his mind would turn to Raine. He tried to call her cellphone on his break, but she didn't answer, which only made things worse. By the time he'd reached the end of his shift, he was crazy with fear and worry.

Caleb went home to take care of Grizz and then paced the kitchen, inwardly debating what to do. He glanced at the clock, realizing it was past eleven-thirty at night, but at the moment he didn't care. He let Grizzly back in and then drove straight over to Raine's apartment complex.

She lived in an eight-unit building, on the second floor, in the upper right hand corner. He frowned when he saw the windows of her apartment were dark.

Because she was sleeping? Or because she wasn't home?

He pulled up to the curb, parked his car and got out. There was a long surface parking lot behind the building, and he ambled back to look for her car.

It wasn't there.

So she wasn't home. The knot in his gut tightened painfully, and the old familiar doubts came flooding to the surface. Where was she? Who was she with? What was she doing?

He knew that Raine wouldn't be with another man, not now. Not so soon after the assault. She'd had to gather her courage to ask him for a hug, for heaven's sake. But the edgy panic plagued him anyway. He thrust his fingers through his hair, wishing he could tune out his wayward thoughts.

He'd avoided serious relationships during medical school, concentrating on his studies. After watching the parade of women come and go in his father's life, he hadn't thought he'd been missing much. Until he'd become a resident and met fellow resident Tabitha Nash.

He remembered all too clearly how betrayed he'd felt when he'd walked into their bedroom to see his naked fiancée in the arms of another man. In their bed.

He'd immediately moved out, and had guarded his heart much more fiercely from that point on. Which was why he'd been so willing to believe the worst about Raine when he'd seen her with Jake.

He walked back to his car, climbed behind the wheel and tried to convince himself to go home. Raine was an adult and if she needed him, she knew how to get in touch with him.

But he couldn't make himself turn the key in the ignition.

When he'd met Raine, he'd told himself to go slow. She was four years younger and more naïve than some of the women he'd dated, probably because she hadn't been used to life in the big city. Regardless, her bubbly enthusiasm for life along with the strong pull of sexual attraction had been difficult to resist.

All too soon he'd found himself falling for her. And when they hadn't been together, he'd constantly questioned where she was and who she was with. Even though he'd known he'd been coming on too strong, he hadn't seemed able to stop.

After he'd realized she hadn't cheated on him with Jake, he'd wanted a second chance. Kept thinking that maybe, after some time had passed, they'd be able to get over their issues. But now he wasn't so sure that was even an option. Even after knowing what had happened, as much as he knew Raine's attack hadn't been her fault, he still didn't like to think about how she'd flirted with a stranger, however innocently. Her laughter had always drawn male attention…

He ground the palms of his hands into his eye sockets. He needed to get a grip. None of this was Raine's fault. None of it! He should go home. Sitting out here in front of Raine's building was making him feel like a stalker. Especially when, for all he knew, Raine could have driven home to see her brothers. Maybe she'd finally decided to tell them what happened.

Go home, Stewart. Stop being an idiot.

Bright headlights approached, momentarily blinding him as he was about to put the car into gear. When the oncoming car slowed and the blinker came on, his pulse kicked up.

Raine. Sure enough, the blue car turning into the parking lot was Raine's. She was home.

Relieved, he shut off the car and climbed out, loping around to the parking lot behind the building.

"Raine?" he called, catching her as she was about to go inside.

She whirled around, putting her hand over her heart. "Caleb?" she said, when she realized who he was. "What are you doing here? You scared me to death."

"I'm sorry." He stood, feeling awkward. "I was worried when you didn't come in for your shift. I wanted to come over to make sure you were okay."

She hitched her purse strap higher on her shoulder. "I'm fine."

He frowned when she realized she was dressed in a sleek pair of black slacks and a bright purple blouse. They weren't suggestive in the least, considering she had the blouse buttoned to her chin, but he couldn't imagine she'd dressed up to go and see her brothers. "Where were you?" the question came out harsher than he'd intended.

She arched a brow and let out a disgusted sigh. "You haven't changed much, have you?"

He'd tried not to sound accusatory. Obviously he hadn't tried hard enough. "I'm sorry, I know what you do in your free time isn't any of my business. I swear I'm only asking because I'm concerned about you."

She stared at him for several long seconds, toying with the strap on her purse. "If you must know, I went to the After Dark nightclub."

He sucked in a harsh breath. "What? Alone? Why for God's sake?"

"Shh," she hissed, glancing around. "You'll wake up

the entire neighborhood. And you can relax, it's not as bad as it sounds. I didn't go inside."

Calming down wasn't an option, but he tried to lower his voice even though his tone was still tense. "What do you mean, you didn't go inside?"

Her expression turned grim. "I'm so tired of feeling like a victim, so I decided to take control. To see if I could help find the guy. I went to the nightclub but stayed in my car, watching the various people coming and going, trying to see if any of the faces jogged my memory. But it didn't work." Her face reflected her disgust. "Unfortunately, I didn't recognize a single soul."

Caleb bit his tongue so hard he tasted blood. He would not yell at Raine. Would not chastise her for going to the nightclub alone. Even if she had stayed in her car, there was a chance that the guy who'd assaulted her might recognize her and either try for round two or silence her for ever.

He bit down harder, until pain pierced his anger. Finally, he took a deep breath. Everything was fine. Getting her upset wouldn't help matters. He lowered his voice, trying to reassure her. "Raine, I wish you'd told me. I'd have been happy to go with you."

"You were working, but I'll remember that if I decide to go again, which I sincerely doubt, since the entire attempt was pretty useless." She shook out her keys, choosing one from the ring to unlock the door. "Do you want to come in for a few minutes or not?"

Her half-hearted invitation caught him off guard but there was no way in the world he was going to turn her down. "Ah…sure."

She unlocked the door and held it open so he could follow her inside. He'd only been to her apartment a few times as they'd spent more time at his house while they'd been dating. When she opened the apartment door and flipped on the lights, his gaze landed on the sofa, half-buried beneath a blanket and pillow.

She slept on the couch in her own home? Because the bastard had brought her back here? He stumbled, useless anger radiating down his spine. He blocked off the anger, knowing it wouldn't help.

"Uh, make yourself comfortable," she said, her cheeks flushed as she swept away the bedding to make room on the sofa. "Do you want something to drink?"

Whiskey. Straight up. He tried to smile. "Whatever you're having is fine with me."

Her flush deepened. "I don't have beer or wine or anything. I drink a lot of bottled water these days." Her tone was apologetic.

"Water is fine." A soft mewling sound surprised him and he glanced down. "Is that a cat?"

Raine smiled, the first real smile since she'd come home. "Yes. This is Spice." She bent down to pick up the cat who'd strolled into the room, snuggling the feline for a moment. "I've had her about a month now, since I started volunteering at the shelter. But I have to warn you, I think she's jealous of Grizzly."

He crossed over, trying to be friendly with the calico cat, but she hissed at him, raising her hackles, so he backed off. "My dad mentioned you had a soft spot for Rusty, the Irish setter, at the shelter, but that your lease here didn't allow dogs. I'm glad you were able to get a cat."

Raine put the cat on the floor and shooed her away. "Yes, Rusty is adorable. He was brought in as a stray, severely malnourished." Her blue eyes clouded with anger. "We suspect he was abused by a man, since he's wary of the male workers at the shelter. He bonded with me right away, though, as I happened to be there when he was brought in. He's a wonderful dog. I have to say it took me a while to get him calmed down enough to let your father examine him."

His heart squeezed in his chest. Rusty was abused? No wonder Raine had bonded with the dog. The two had been kindred souls, needing each other. Once again, a feeling of helplessness nearly overwhelmed him. There was really nothing he could do to help her. Nothing.

Except to ignore his own issues to be there for her if she needed him.

"I'm glad he has you, then."

She nodded and went into the small kitchenette to get two bottles of water out of the fridge. She came back into the living room and took a seat on the sofa next to him. He was surprised and glad she'd chosen to sit next to him, rather than taking the chair halfway across the room.

Glancing around the apartment, he was struck once again by the fact that she'd taken to sleeping on the sofa. "Would you consider moving?" he asked, thinking she might be able to put the event behind her more easily if she wasn't here in this apartment with the constant reminders. Plus, if she was open to moving, maybe they could find a place that would allow dogs.

"Not right now. Unfortunately my lease goes through

to the end of the year." She twisted the cap off her water and took a long drink.

He could hear the regret in her tone and wanted to offer to pay off her lease just so she could move out. But the Raine he knew valued her independence. He decided it wouldn't hurt to ask around, see if anyone was interested in moving closer to the hospital and potentially taking over her lease. She couldn't fault him for that, could she?

"How is your father doing?" Raine asked, changing the subject.

"He's fine. I went up to see him before my shift. He misses you and the work at the shelter a lot, I think." Caleb stared at his water bottle for a moment. "I didn't appreciate just how much his volunteer work means to him."

Raine's smile was wistful. "Your father loves animals, but he's also pretty social with the other volunteers. I get the sense being alone is hard for him."

"Yeah. He definitely doesn't want to be alone." He dragged his gaze up to meet hers. "I probably should have explained to you a long time ago about how my mom took off when I was five years old, rather than springing that news on you when my dad was heading off to the cath lab."

"I'm sorry, Caleb. That must have been horrible for you."

He shrugged off her sympathy. "We survived, but my dad started dating again shortly afterwards, bringing home a series of stepmother candidates to meet me."

She winced. "I'm sure that didn't go over very well."

"Maybe it would have been all right if my dad had found someone great, but instead he seemed to make one mistake after another." He downed half his water and set it aside. "My dad went through four marriages and four divorces. Hell, you'd think he'd learn but. no, he keeps finding new women and jumping right back into the next relationship. I've finally convinced him to stop marrying them at least."

"I see," Raine said slowly. She didn't look as if she completely agreed with him. "But, Caleb, surely you realize that your father's mistakes aren't your own."

"I made a similar error in judgment," he said slowly. "Remember I told you that my fiancée cheated on me? We were both residents, working a lot of shifts, often on opposite schedules, but I trusted her. Until I came home early one night to find her in bed with another guy." He tried to soften the bitterness in his tone. "Good thing I found out before I married her."

Her frown deepened. "Not all women cheat, Caleb."

He nodded. "I know. Logically, I know that I can't assume the worst. But my gut doesn't listen to my head."

"So you've been overcompensating ever since," she said softly.

"Yes." He let out a heavy sigh. "I'm sorry I didn't believe you. I tried to call you to apologize but you wouldn't take my calls."

She glanced away. "I know. I wish I had. But we can't go back. Even if we had tried again, I doubt our relationship would have survived. Especially not after what I did."

"Raine, please. Don't say that. You didn't *do* anything. The assault was not your fault." He wished he could reach out and pull her into his arms, but he was afraid of scaring her.

"My counselor says the same thing, but saying that doesn't change how I feel." She finally brought her gaze up to meet his.

"I figured you didn't take my calls because you were still angry with me."

She stared at him for a few seconds. "I was angry with you, Caleb," she said finally. "I went to the bachelorette party in the first place to get over you. But afterwards, you need to understand, the real reason I didn't take your calls was because I'd changed. I'm not the same person I was when you first asked me out. I'll never be that person ever again."

Raine finished her water as a heavy silence fell between them. She wished, more than anything, she could ask Caleb to hold her. Despite how they'd broken off their relationship a month ago, she missed him. Missed being with him. When he'd hugged her that morning, she'd felt normal. The way she'd been before the night that had changed her for ever. As if maybe she really was healing.

"Does the attack still give you nightmares?" he asked in a low voice.

"Not exactly." She picked at the label around her empty bottle and then set it aside. "I don't remember anything from that night. Unfortunately, my imagination keeps trying to fill in the blanks."

Caleb's jaw tightened. "I hope to hell they find the bastard."

"Me too." She tried to think of a way to change the subject. Understanding Caleb's past helped clarify his actions. She could clearly see why he'd questioned her all the time about where she was going and who she was going to be with. But even if she had known all this back then, she didn't think she would have done anything differently. She still would have taken a break from their relationship. She still would have attended the bachelorette party with the rest of the girls.

And the outcome would have been the same.

They'd both made mistakes. Unfortunately, hers were insurmountable.

"Raine, you'll get through this," Caleb said finally, breaking the silence. "Maybe it will take time, but you're strong and I know you'll get through this."

He was completely missing the point. "I know I'll get through it, Caleb. It's already been over a month. I've done a pretty good job so far of moving on with my life. I volunteer at the animal shelter and I've returned to work. I know I'll get through this."

"So where does that leave us?" he asked with a frown.

Her heart tripped in her chest. If only it were that easy to salvage what they'd once had. "What do you want me to say?" she asked helplessly. "I just told you I'm not the same person I was before. I'm not the person you were attracted to. And even if I were, what's changed, Caleb? You didn't trust me before. Didn't believe me when I told you Jake had too much to drink that night. What's changed now?"

"I don't know," he said bluntly, and she had to give him points for being honest. "I can promise to try to work through my trust issues. But you won't know if I have or not unless you give me a second chance."

A second chance? Did she dare? "I'm a different person now," she reminded him.

"Maybe you are, but that doesn't mean I've stopped caring about you."

He cared about her? Her heart squeezed in her chest. Was she crazy to even think of trying to renew a relationship with Caleb? Was she even capable of such a thing? She'd enjoyed being held by him, but that was a long way away from actually dating. And there was a part of her that couldn't believe he'd be able to put aside his trust issues that easily. Would it bother him that she'd been with another man, however involuntarily?

She feared that innate distrust would eventually rip them apart.

Yet she trusted Caleb physically. Being with him felt a little like coming home. "I care about you too, Caleb." She took a deep breath and tried to smile. "If you're serious about wanting a second chance, then I'm willing to try, too."

His eyes widened, as if he hadn't expected her to agree. "Really? I promise I won't rush you. We'll take things slow and easy."

She hesitated, wondering if he was going to have more trouble with this than she was. Caleb's imagination could easily run amuck, just like hers had. "I won't break, Caleb. I was the one who asked you for a hug this morning, remember?"

"I remember."

She set her empty water bottle aside and inched closer. "And you told me I could ask for a hug any time, right?"

His expression turned wary. "Yes. But I don't want

to rush you, Raine. Don't feel like you have to do anything you're not ready for."

"I won't," she assured him, reaching out to take his hand in hers, feeling reassured when his fingers curled protectively around hers. "I'm ready for another hug, Caleb. Would you hold me?"

CHAPTER TEN

"OF COURSE. I aim to please," he said lightly, but there was the slightest hesitation before his strong arms wrapped around her, drawing her close.

Raine sighed and burrowed her face into the hollow of his shoulder. She took a deep breath, filling her senses with his warm, familiar, musky scent.

She closed her eyes against the sting of unexpected tears. This was what she'd wanted ever since leaving his house earlier that morning. This was what she'd been missing.

Caleb lightly stroked a hand down her back, and even though she knew he only meant to soothe her, a flicker of awareness rippled along her nerves. He paused when she trembled, and then slowly repeated the caress. This time she bit back a moan as a wave of desire stabbed deep.

"Are you all right?" Caleb asked, his voice a deep rumble in her ear.

"I'm fine," she whispered, trying to hide how much he was affecting her. "This is nice."

There was another moment of silence and she inwardly winced, knowing nice was the least appropriate word to describe how she was feeling. She'd asked for a hug because she cared about Caleb. But responding to him with awareness and desire only confirmed her feelings for him hadn't lessened during the time they'd spent apart.

But did Caleb feel the same way? Somehow she doubted it. Because deep down she knew that if Caleb had ever really loved her, he would have believed in her.

And despite how he'd asked for a second chance, he was treating her like a victim. Someone to protect. Not a partner. If their relationship had stumbled before, she couldn't imagine how they'd manage to overcome everything that had happened.

Were they crazy to even try? Could they really find a way to overcome their problems?

"I'm glad you're not afraid," Caleb murmured. "It's nice to know you can relax around me."

Relax? With her body shimmering with awareness? Was he kidding? She couldn't help but smile. She lifted her head and met his gaze. "I'm not afraid of being close to you like this."

His gaze locked on hers, and his eyes darkened with the first inkling of desire. She went still, afraid to move. Slowly, ever so slowly, he bent his head until his mouth lightly brushed against hers.

Caleb's kiss was whisper soft and so brief she almost cried out in protest when he pulled away. But then he repeated the caress, gently molding his mouth to hers, giving her plenty of time to push him off.

She didn't.

When his arms tightened around her and he shifted

his position slightly to pull her closer against him, she experienced a secret thrill. He kissed her again and again, but didn't deepen the kiss until she opened her mouth and tasted him.

With a low groan, he invaded her mouth, kissing her deeply, the way she remembered.

But after a few minutes of heaven he pulled away, tucking her head back into the hollow of his shoulder, his chest rising and falling rapidly beneath her ear. "Sorry," he muttered.

Sorry? She frowned. "For what?"

"I promised we'd go slow," he said in a low rough voice full of self-disgust. "A few more minutes of kissing you like that and I would have forgotten my promise."

She frowned. "I'm a woman, not a victim," she said, her tone sharp.

He pressed a chaste kiss to the top of her head. "I know, but there's no rush, Raine. Just holding you in my arms is more than enough for now."

She closed her eyes on a wave of helpless frustration. This wouldn't be enough for her. Maybe Caleb needed more time to grapple with what had happened.

He continued his soft caress, stroking his hand down her back and soon her irritation faded. She snuggled against him, relishing the closeness.

Maybe this was Caleb's way of starting over. Like from the very beginning. And if so, he was right.

There was no rush.

Raine realized she must have fallen asleep because her world tilted as Caleb lifted her off the sofa and carried her into the bedroom. She hadn't been in her bed since that night, but she didn't protest—unwilling to ruin the moment with bad memories.

When he slid in beside her, she relaxed, unable to deny the wide bed was much more comfortable than the cramped sofa, despite their bulky clothes. Using his chest as a pillow, she closed her eyes and tried to relax, regretting more than ever that they hadn't made love during the two months they'd been together. If they had, maybe she'd have that memory to sustain her now.

Hours later, she woke up again when Caleb shifted beneath her. This time she felt the mattress give, and she blinked the sleep from her eyes, watching as he sat on the edge of the bed running his fingers through his tousled hair. Her stomach tightened with anxiety. "Are you leaving?"

He twisted toward her, as if surprised to find her awake. He flashed a crooked smile and leaned over to brush a kiss over her mouth. "I don't want to go, but I almost forgot about Grizz. I let him out after work, but that was hours ago. I need to get home to take care of him."

She'd forgotten about Grizz too, but maybe he was just using the dog as an excuse. Sleeping in Caleb's arms had been wonderful, but suddenly it seemed as if the passionate kiss they'd shared had never happened. She tried to smile. "Too bad you can't bring him over here."

He must have sensed the wistfulness of her voice, because he rolled back toward her, stretching out beside her. "Raine, I wouldn't leave at all if it wasn't for the dog. I promised my dad I'd take care of him. I don't think Grizz has ever been alone all night before."

"I know. I'm sorry. Of course you have to go." She was ashamed of her selfishness. Hadn't they agreed there was no rush? Why was she clinging to him, afraid to let him go? "Thanks for staying, Caleb. I appreciate it more than you know."

"Raine," he murmured on a low groan as he gathered her close. "I don't want to leave. But I have to." He kissed her, deeply, his muscles tense, his need evident.

She drowned in the sensation as he gave her a glimpse of what their renewed relationship might hold. But then, all too soon, he broke away, moving as if to get up out of her bed. "You're making this difficult for me. I really have to go," he said in a gravel-rough tone.

She forced herself to let him go. "Give Grizzly a hug for me, okay?"

He stopped, and then turned back to her, propping his hand beneath his head so he could look down at her. "You could come with me. If you don't have other, more pressing plans, we could spend the day together."

She didn't have any plans, much less pressing ones. And spending the day with Caleb held definite appeal. But she didn't want to sound too pathetically eager. "You're not scheduled to work?"

"No. Are you?"

She shook her head. She wasn't needed at the animal shelter today either. What better way to start over than to spend a Sunday together? "All right, if you're sure."

For an answer, he kissed her again. She couldn't help pulling him close to deepen the kiss. "I'm sure," he said, breaking off from the kiss. "And we'd better leave soon, because I'm very close to not caring if Grizz relieves his bladder in my house."

She laughed, feeling light-hearted for the first time in weeks. She gave him a playful push. "All right, let's go."

Caleb scrubbed the exhaustion from his face as he waited for Raine to finish in the bathroom.

Holding Raine in his arms had been worth sacrificing his sleep. He didn't regret a moment of their night together. Kissing her, holding her, had been a test of his willpower.

Maybe his body was hard and achy this morning, but he didn't care. Somehow he'd managed to ignore his needs and give Raine the security she deserved. Her peace of mind was far more important than his discomfort.

Long into the night, he'd been unable to keep his imagination from dwelling on what she'd been through. He'd only brought her into the bedroom after she'd almost fallen right off the sofa. He'd hoped he could help her get over her aversion to sleeping in her bed.

Unfortunately he'd been tortured by images of how the bastard had brought her here, taking Raine against her will. He was surprised his suppressed anger and tense muscles hadn't woken her up.

Grimly, he told himself that focusing on what had happened wasn't going to help rekindle their relationship. He needed to get over it. And soon.

The way Raine had responded to his kiss proved she was on the road to recovery. He refused to hamper her healing in any way. If she could get past what had happened, surely he could do the same.

"Okay, I'm ready," she said, hurrying back into the

living room where he waited. She poured fresh water into a bowl for Spice and then gave the cat a gentle pat. "See you later, sweetie."

"We could bring Spice if you want. Maybe Grizzly will grow on her," he said, eyeing the cat doubtfully.

Raine brightened, but then reconsidered with a shake of her head. "That's a good idea, but maybe some other time."

He hid his relief. Considering the way the cat had hissed at him, he couldn't imagine Spice would be all too thrilled to meet Grizz, but he'd wanted the decision to be hers.

When they got to his house, he couldn't help feeling guilty when he found Grizz stretched out in front of the door, obviously waiting for him. The dog jumped excitedly, his tail wagging furiously when Raine came in behind him.

"Come on, Grizz, go outside first," he muttered, shooing the dog out back.

The dog took care of business and then came back to the door, looking eager to come back in. Raine opened the door for Grizz as he put out food and water for him.

"I need to call the hospital, see how my dad is doing," Caleb said, glancing at the clock. "And I'd planned to visit today, too, if you don't mind."

"Of course I don't mind," Raine said, looking affronted.

He flipped open his cellphone to call Cardiology. It took a few minutes before he was connected with his father's nurse.

After Caleb explained who he was, the nurse sounded relieved to hear from him. "Your father is not having a good day. He's refusing to get out of bed and has been crabby with the nurses. His surgeon has been in to see him, though, and medically he's doing fine. Emotionally, not so well."

He didn't like the sound of that. "Okay, let him know I'm coming to visit. And tell him I'm bringing company. Hopefully that will cheer him up."

"I will."

He closed his phone and glanced at Raine. "Dad's crabby today, refusing to get up and overall being a pain to the staff. I hope it's not a sign he's taking a turn for the worse."

Raine frowned at the news. "I hope not, too." She glanced down at Grizzly, who'd finished inhaling his food and had come over to nudge her hand with his head, seeking some attention. "Hey, I have an idea. Maybe we can take Grizzly in to visit."

Caleb stared at her. Had she lost her mind? "Since when are dogs allowed to visit patients? Especially on a surgical floor? And I think he's a little too big to sneak in."

"No, really, this could work." Raine took out her own cellphone and dialed a number. He soon realized she was talking to someone in the safety and security department. "Hi, Bryan? This is Raine Hart. How are you? It's nice to talk to you, too. Hey, I'd like to invoke the pet visitation policy. There's a patient, Frank Stewart, on the third-floor cardiac surgery unit who's depressed today. He's a veterinarian, volunteering his time at the animal shelter, and I'd like to schedule a visit with his black Lab, Grizzly."

Caleb listened in astonishment. A pet visitation

policy? He'd never heard of such a thing. But apparently Raine knew all about it and, more, she knew how to arrange the visit.

"Great. We'll be there in two hours, then. Thanks very much." Raine's expression was full of triumph as she snapped her phone shut. "It's all set. We need to stop by Security and the nurses will arrange for your dad to be brought down in a wheelchair to the family center. There's a private conference room we can use."

"Amazing," Caleb murmured. And he wasn't just talking about how she'd picked exactly the right way to cheer up his dad. Raine was a truly amazing woman in all the ways that mattered. "All right. Hopefully this will help to cheer him up." Because if this didn't work, he was afraid nothing would.

Caleb couldn't believe no one stopped them as he and Raine walked into the front door of the hospital, holding Grizzly's leash. Following the rules, they crossed over to the security offices, located down the hall from the main lobby.

"Hi, Bryan," Raine greeted the tall, rather young-looking security guard with a hug. For a moment he wondered if there had once been more between Raine and the handsome officer. A sharp pang of jealousy stabbed him in the region of his heart. "Good to see you. How's Melissa? And the baby?"

"They're great," Bryan said.

Belatedly, Caleb noticed the security officer's wedding ring. Cursing himself for being an idiot, he reached down to pat Grizz. Damn, he'd done it again.

Jumped to a stupid conclusion without giving her the benefit of the doubt.

"I think your patient is already down here, waiting for you." Bryan led the way down toward the family center conference room.

Sure enough, the door of the conference room stood ajar and he could see his father, slumped in a wheelchair with his eyes closed, looking almost as bad as he had that first night in the ICU. Alarmed, he pushed the door open and rushed in. "Dad? Are you all right?"

"Huh?" His father straightened in his seat, prising his eyes open. And then his entire face lit up, brighter than a Christmas tree, when he saw the dog. "Grizzly! Come here, boy."

Caleb let go of the leash, relaxing when his father bent over to pet the dog, who immediately tried to crawl up into his father's lap, not that the ninety-pound dog would fit.

"Grizz, it's so good to see you," his father crooned, lavishing the dog with attention. "Did you miss me? Huh? Do you miss me, boy?"

Caleb was very glad Raine had arranged the visit. When she came up to slip her arm around his waist, leaning lightly against him, he realized why his father kept trying to find someone to share his life with. Because it was nice to share everything, good times and bad, with someone.

He'd only been in kindergarten when his mother had taken off, but he was ashamed to realize he hadn't really looked at the situation from his father's point of view in the years since. His father had been abandoned by his wife. And he'd had a small son to care for while trying to run a veterinary practice. Could he blame his dad for wanting someone to share his daily life with? For wanting help in raising a son?

Was it his father's fault he'd picked the wrong women? His father deserved better. He suddenly he couldn't stand the thought of his father being alone.

"Have you thought about patching things up with Shirley?" he asked abruptly.

"Shirley?" His father's face went blank for a moment, and then the corner of his father's mouth quirked upward. "You mean Sharon?"

Oops. Damn. "Yeah, that's it. Sharon."

Raine scowled. "Wait a minute—Sharon? What about Marlene Fitzgerald? From the shelter?"

"Marlene?" His father's cheeks turned a dull shade of red and suddenly every iota of his father's attention was focused on Grizz. "We're just friends," he muttered.

"Just friends?" Raine's brows hiked upward. "Really? Because she looked devastated when she heard you'd had emergency open heart surgery."

She had? Caleb was exasperated to discover Raine knew more about his father's recent love life than he did.

"She came to visit, but I sent her away." His father frowned. "A woman wants a man who'll take care of her, not an invalid like me."

Caleb hid a wince, because he could certainly understand. Starting a relationship so soon after open heart surgery probably wasn't a good plan.

"That's not true," Raine protested, going over to kneel beside his father's wheelchair. Grizz licked her cheek, but she didn't take her imploring gaze off his father. "A woman wants a man to be her partner. And the whole point of a partnership is taking turns helping each other."

Caleb stared at her as the full impact of her words slowly sank into his brain.

He'd been an idiot. Like his father, Raine didn't want to be an invalid. She'd said as much, hadn't she? She didn't want him to take care of her, the way he'd been trying to do since he'd discovered she'd been assaulted.

His gut clenched in warning. He'd asked for a second chance, but he knew that a big part of his reasoning had been because he'd wanted to help Raine through her ordeal. To support her.

But obviously that wasn't at all what she wanted from him.

CHAPTER ELEVEN

A COLD chill trickled down his spine. Could he be a true partner for Raine? Could he put aside his doubts for good? God knew, he wanted to.

Just minutes earlier he'd watched her hug Bryan, the young security guard, and instantly the old familiar doubts had crept in.

He wanted a second chance with her—but if he blew it this time, he knew there wouldn't be another.

"Maybe you're right," his father said, giving Raine a half hopeful, half uncertain look. "But I can barely get around. I'll wait to talk to Marlene until after I get back on my feet."

"I think you should talk to her sooner rather than later," Raine mildly disagreed, scratching Grizzly behind the ears. "Unless you think for some reason she won't get along with Grizz?"

"The dogs at the shelter seem to like her well enough, and she's not afraid of them. I'm sure Grizz will like her, too."

"Well, that's good, because you certainly wouldn't

want to call on a woman who doesn't get along with your dog," Raine lightly teased.

"Sharon was afraid of Grizz," his father said. "I should have known that was a bad sign. I think Grizz could tell, too because he growled at her. And he never growls at anyone."

Raine laughed, a light-hearted sound that reminded Caleb of the wonderful times they'd spent together. She'd told him she wasn't the same woman she'd been before, but he didn't agree. The old Raine was still there, and given enough time and healing she'd return. "Definitely not a good sign. Spice hissed at Caleb, too," she confided.

He put a lid on his troublesome thoughts. "Guess that means I don't have much of a chance, huh?" he asked in a light tone.

Raine glanced over her shoulder at him and raised a brow. "I don't know. I'll think about it."

His father glanced between them with a knowing smile, looking a hundred times better than when they'd first arrived. "What plans do the two of you have for today?"

"Nothing special," Raine said with a shrug.

"Why not go to the state fair?" his father persisted. "It opened on Friday and goes all week."

"The fair? I haven't been on the Ferris wheel in ages," Raine murmured. But her eyes brightened with interest, and Caleb knew his father had presented the perfect solution.

"I haven't been to the fair lately either, but I'm up for it if you are," he said, hoping she'd agree.

Her smile widened. "I'd love to."

"Have fun," his father said, shifting in his seat. He glanced longingly at the dog. "Do you think the nurses would notice if Grizz stayed with me in my room?"

"I think they might become a tad suspicious, especially when he needs to go outside," he said wryly. "How much longer will you need to stay in the hospital?"

"They're talking about sending me home in a day or two, depending on how well I can walk," his father admitted.

"Well, I guess you'd better get walking, then." He made a mental note to talk to Steven Summers for himself. "I'll be happy to move in for a while to help once you're home."

"Thanks." The older man leaned over to give the dog one last hug. "See you soon, Grizzly," he murmured.

Caleb felt bad leaving his father at the hospital, but they needed to take Grizzly home. "Good idea, bringing Grizz in for a visit," he said to Raine as they walked with Grizzly outside.

"He really perked up, didn't he? And I bet Marlene would be willing to help your father, too, if he'd only give her a chance."

"Maybe he will." Caleb didn't want his father to be alone, but he also didn't want his father to rush into anything.

He wanted his father to take his time, to find the right woman to partner with.

And as he glanced at Raine he knew it was time to take his own advice. Raine wasn't Tabitha. She was a hundred times better than Tabitha. If he couldn't trust Raine, he couldn't trust anyone.

* * *

Thrilled with the idea of going to the state fair, Raine could hardly maintain her patience as Caleb took care of Grizz. She hadn't been to the fair since going with her older brothers, years ago.

When Caleb was finally ready to go, she nearly skipped with anticipation. The sounds and scents of the fair reminded her of happier times.

"There's the Ferris wheel," she said, clutching Caleb's arm with excitement.

"Do you want something to eat first? Or after the ride?" he asked.

"Eat first, but I don't want any of that weird fried food on a stick," she said, grimacing at the people in front of them who were eating deep-fried Oreo cookies on a stick. "I'm sorry, but that looks disgusting."

"Okay, nothing on a stick," he agreed good-naturedly.

They settled on burgers, and then wandered down the midway. She remembered the Ferris wheel as being huge, but now that she was an adult the ride wasn't nearly as impressive.

But Caleb had already bought their tickets, so she stood in line beside him. When it was their turn, she felt like a giddy teenager, sliding into the seat next to him.

Caleb put his arm around her and she leaned against him contentedly as they began their slow ascent. When they reached the top, she gazed down at the fairgrounds, amazed at how far she could see.

"Look at all the people," she said in a low whisper, suddenly struck by how much more crowded everything looked from up here.

"Check out the lines of people streaming in through the entrances," Caleb pointed out. "We must have arrived well before the rush."

She leaned a little closer to Caleb, abruptly glad to be up in the Ferris wheel, far away from the crowd. She'd never been enochlophobic before, but she was feeling apprehensive about going back down amidst the masses of people.

"You're not afraid of heights, are you?" Caleb asked, as if sensing her fear.

"No, not at all." And she wasn't afraid of crowds either. She was determined not to let anything ruin her day.

"Good." He leaned down and pressed a soft kiss against her mouth.

The ride was over too soon. When their car came to the bottom of the Ferris wheel and stopped, she stepped off with reluctance.

She led the way back down the midway, but people were pressing against her, and she must have muttered "Excuse me" a dozen times in her attempt to get past.

When a particularly large man shoved her backward, a rush of panic exploded. *"Let me through!"*

"Raine?" She could hear Caleb calling her name, but couldn't see him. And suddenly she wasn't standing in the midway of the state fairgrounds any more.

The music of the After Dark nightclub was deafening. Her feet ached from dancing, but suddenly she just wanted to go home. But where was Jamie? And the rest of her friends?

Sandwiched between two guys, she tried to brush

past, but their large frames held her captive. Yet despite the close contact, she wasn't alarmed.

"Hey, you're not leaving already, are you?" the one guy asked, taking hold of her arm. "I thought we were celebrating? I just bought you a drink."

She'd recognized two of the rugby followers they'd danced with earlier. The one guy talked a lot, but the other one just looked at her. "Just a soft drink, right?" she'd clarified, before accepting the glass.

"Yeah, just a soft drink."

The brief memory faded away. That had been the last thing she remembered before waking up the next day, feeling extremely hungover. Her body had ached in places it shouldn't have but it hadn't been until she'd found the white stain on her sheets that the sick realization had dawned.

She'd been drugged and raped.

"Raine!" Caleb's worried face filled her field of vision, his hands lightly clutching her shoulders. "What happened? Are you all right?"

She tried to nod but realized her face was wet with tears so she shook her head. "I need to get out of here," she whispered. "Can we leave now? Please?"

Caleb's expression turned grim and he nodded, tucking her close. "Excuse us," he said loudly, using his arm as a battering ram as he barreled through the crowd. "Move aside, please."

It seemed like an eternity but they eventually broke free of the worst of the mass of people. "What happened?" he asked in a low, urgent tone. "Did you see someone who looked familiar?"

She shook her head, unable to speak. He worried that she'd seen someone from that night, and she had, but only in her repressed memories. Caleb must have understood, because he didn't push for anything more but simply tucked her under his arm and led the way out of the fairgrounds to the street where they'd parked their car.

Safe in the passenger seat, she slowly relaxed. "Thanks," she murmured.

His gaze was full of concern. "I'm sorry. I didn't realize the crowds would get to you."

"Neither did I," she admitted. "And it wasn't just the crowd, it was being in that crush that brought back memories of that night."

Caleb started the car and pulled into traffic. "Do you think you could recognize him?" Caleb asked.

"Maybe." But she wasn't completely certain. For one thing, there had been two guys and she was sure only one of them had taken her home. But which one she had no idea. They'd claimed to be friends of one of the rugby players, but which player? "The nightclub was really crowded, and it was hard to move, just like it was on the midway. Two guys bought me a soda, but unfortunately, that's the last thing I remember."

"It's okay. They'll catch him," Caleb said with a confidence she was far from feeling. When he reached out to take her hand, she grasped it gratefully. She was relieved when he let the topic go without pressing for more details.

"Sorry we didn't get to see much of the fair," she said, feeling slightly foolish now that the initial panic had faded.

"It doesn't matter, Raine. I was only interested in

spending the day with you." His sincere tone made her believe he truly didn't mind. "I'm sure Grizz is lonely. I'll cook you dinner at my place instead."

"Really?" she couldn't remember him ever offering to cook for her when they'd dated before. She had to admit she was impressed with his willingness to start over. "Are you sure you don't mind?"

"Of course I don't mind. We'll have to stop at the grocery store, though, to pick up a few things."

"Okay." When they stopped at the grocery store, located not far from Caleb's house, they bought more than just a *few things*. Caleb started with thick ribeye steaks and fresh mixings for a salad, but somehow their entire cart was soon full of other goodies before they made their way to the checkout.

She'd never grocery shopped with a man before, other than with her brothers, but in her experience with the men in her family she knew the food they'd purchased today would be lucky to last a half a week. Less, if she stayed with him.

Not that he'd invited her to stay, she reminded herself. This was their second chance, and there was no rush.

Pushing the longing aside, she focused on spending the rest of the day with Caleb, without being affected by the shadows of the past.

Caleb tried to remain nonchalant after Raine's meltdown at the state fair, but he couldn't help sending her worried glances when she wasn't looking.

The frank fear etched on her face would remain seared into his memory for a long time.

He was stunned she'd remembered something from the attack. He'd wanted to press for more information about that night, but had forced himself to back off, grimly realizing the details he'd wanted to hear would only hurt her.

And he didn't want to hurt Raine, ever again.

He watched her play fetch with Grizzly out in the back yard; the dog had been ecstatic to see them when they'd returned home. Being with Raine seemed so right. As if she belonged here. Although in his scenario she'd be playing with her own dog, Rusty, instead of Grizz. Not that he wouldn't have minded keeping Grizz either. But clearly his dad needed Grizzly more than he did.

As he put the groceries away, he wondered how to broach the subject of her staying here with him overnight. The thought of letting her go home to face the night alone made him feel sick to his stomach. No matter how he tried, he couldn't get over feeling protective of her.

But he'd do his best to be a partner, like she wanted.

He made a quick call to his father's surgeon, verifying that indeed his father would likely be discharged on either Monday or Tuesday. He then made arrangements to be off work for a few days so that he'd have time to help his father make the transition home.

After that, he made two salads, cutting up the ingredients and putting everything in the fridge for later. He went outside, to find that Raine had dropped into one of his wide-backed Adirondack chairs, exhausted after her romp with Grizzly.

"Let me know when you're hungry, and I'll throw the steaks on the grill," he said, taking a seat in the chair next to hers.

"I'm ready whenever. I'm glad we came back, I think poor Grizz has been lonely."

"Yeah, I'm sure he'll be much happier when my father is finally discharged from the hospital." He reached over to scratch Grizz behind the ears. "I talked to Dr. Summers and he told me to plan on my father coming home tomorrow or Tuesday."

"That's wonderful news. I'm sure it will take a while, but your father will feel much better now that he's had the surgery."

"I hope so." He stood and walked over to light the charcoal sitting in the bottom of the grill. "Guess dad won't be eating steaks for a while," he mused.

She let out a quick laugh. "Nope, guess not. Good thing we're having them tonight, then, isn't it?"

He tried to make sure the atmosphere between them stayed relaxed and companionable as he grilled the steaks, sautéing some fresh mushrooms on the side. He brought out the salads and two TV trays so they could eat outside. He thought about offering to open a bottle of Merlot but, remembering Raine's preference for water, decided against it.

Certainly he didn't need any alcohol. Raine's presence was intoxicating enough.

As dusk began to fall, the mosquitoes came out, so reluctantly they carried everything inside.

Together, they cleaned up the mess Caleb had left in the kitchen. Working as a team, the chore didn't take long.

"Caleb, do you mind if I ask you a question?" Raine asked, after they'd finished.

"Of course not." He draped the damp dishtowel over the counter to dry.

"Do you want me? Intimately? The way you did before?" she asked, her cheeks stained bright red. "Or are you turned off because I was raped?"

What? He wanted to kick himself for making her doubt his feelings. Instantly he crossed over to her, clasping her shoulders and trying to encourage her to meet his gaze. "No, Raine, I'm not turned off by what happened. Why would you think that?"

"Because each time you kissed me last night, you were the one to pull away."

He couldn't deny it. But when he'd pulled back, it had been because he'd been close to forgetting what she'd been through. "Only because I promised I wouldn't rush you into doing anything you weren't ready for."

She bit her lower lip. "And what if I can't know what I'm ready for if we don't try?"

He stared at her. Was she really saying what he thought she was saying? "Raine, just a few hours ago you freaked out at the fair. I think that shows you still have a way to go before fully recovering from the assault." And he'd never forgive himself if he frightened her.

She must have read his mind. "You won't frighten me, Caleb. I freaked out at the fair because of the strangers surrounding me. But I didn't feel the least bit frightened last night. In fact, I felt safe and normal for the first time in weeks. You helped me realize that I've gotten over the worst of what happened." She frowned. "But I know that just because I'm getting over what happened, it doesn't mean you have."

Her insight struck a chord, because she was right. How long had he known about her assault? Three days? Not nearly enough time to come to grips with what she'd been through. But that was his problem to wrestle with, not hers. And he did want her, too much for his peace of mind. "Raine, please don't worry about me."

"I won't worry about you if you agree to stop worrying about me. Deal?"

"Deal," he said, his voice clogging in his throat when she stepped closer, wrapping her arms around his waist.

"Kiss me," she whispered.

He couldn't have denied her request to save his soul. He kissed her, lightly at first, but when she responded by melting against him, he deepened the kiss, sweeping his tongue into her mouth.

Last night he'd made the mistake of treating Raine like a victim, and he vowed not to make that same mistake again. He loosened his iron-clad grip on his control, showing her how much he wanted her.

Grizz barked, interrupting their kiss. Caleb struggled to calm his racing heart as he glared at the dog. "What is your problem? Get your own girl."

The dog looked at him, perplexed. Raine giggled. "Maybe he needs to go outside."

Muttering something not very complimentary about the dog, he peeled himself away from Raine long enough to let the dog out. Grizz did his business and then bounded back inside.

He turned back toward Raine. "I'd like you to stay with me tonight. No pressure, we can just sleep if that's all you want."

She tilted her head, regarding him solemnly. "And what if I want more than just to sleep?"

His groin tightened, betraying the depth of his need. Forgetting what she'd been through was easier if he concentrated on her. "Your decision, Raine. Always your decision. We can stop any time."

"Then I decide yes." Her simple words stole his breath. Her faith in him was humbling.

He was damned if he'd let her down.

He barely remembered leading her to his bedroom. One moment they were standing in the kitchen, the next she was in his arms, kissing him like she'd never stop.

He'd planned to take this slowly, to give her plenty of time to change her mind, but when she tugged at his clothes, he could barely suppress a low groan.

Taking control of the situation the best he could, he shucked off his jeans and shirt, keeping his boxers on, and then helped her strip down to her bra and panties. From there he lifted her up and set her gently on the bed.

She gazed up at him as he stretched out beside her. "Slow and easy, Raine," he murmured. "There's no rush, remember?"

"I want you, Caleb," she whispered, stroking her hand down his chest, dangerously close to the waistband of his boxers.

He swallowed hard, and bent to press a trail of kisses down the side of her neck to the enticing V between her breasts, as he stroked his hand down over the curve of her belly, and then lower to the moist juncture of her thighs. "I want you, too. Let me show you how much."

She gasped and arched when he pressed against her mound. "Make love to me," she begged.

"Absolutely," he promised huskily, determined to make this experience a night she'd never forget.

One that would forever replace the dark shadows of the past.

CHAPTER TWELVE

RAINE clung to Caleb's shoulders, her senses reeling from his sweetly arousing touch. They weren't even naked and her body hummed with tension. She knew Caleb was going slow, worried about scaring her—but right now nothing existed but this moment. The two of them together, at last.

His caresses grew more intimate, sending shivers of pleasure rippling down her back. He peeled away her bra and underwear. She lightly raked her nails down his back and the way his muscles tensed and the low groan that rumbled in his throat gave her a secret thrill of satisfaction.

Caleb wanted her. Truly wanted her. And knowing he wanted her was the best aphrodisiac in the world.

When he continued to caress her, driving her to the edge, she sensed what he intended and pulled away. "No, Caleb. Not just me. Both of us together."

He stared at her, his eyes glittering with desire. "Are you sure?"

"Yes, I'm sure." She reached out to stroke his hard length beneath his boxers and he let out a low groan. "You're overdressed," she chided.

He drew back and fumbled for a condom. After stripping off his boxers, he sheathed himself and then rose above her. For a split second she froze, but then he kissed her and she relaxed, knowing this was exactly what she wanted.

As if sensing her moment of unease, he flipped onto his back, tugging her over so that she straddled him. His smoky gray eyes were nearly black with need. "Your choice, Raine," he huskily reminded her.

She stroked his chest and lifted up, until he was right where she wanted him to be. And when she gingerly pressed against him, he let out another low groan.

Beads of sweat popped out on his forehead but he didn't move, refusing to take control. She wasn't very experienced, had only one lover in college, but she lifted her hips and slid down, until he filled her. Even then he didn't move so she repeated the movement, lifting up and down, finding the rhythm and enjoying being the one in control.

He grasped her hips, deepening his thrusts, and she gave a murmur of encouragement. The tension built to the point where she didn't think she could hold back another moment.

And then abruptly, she peaked, spasming with pleasure so intense she cried out at the same moment she felt Caleb pulsating inside her.

Together, at last.

She was asleep when Grizzly nudged her hand. She opened one eye and peered at the clock, noting the sun had just barely begun to peek over the horizon. It was early. Too early. She closed her eyes, trying to ignore him.

Grizz nudged her again, insistently, and she let out a tired sigh, knowing the poor dog probably needed to go outside. Carefully, so as not to wake Caleb, who was sprawled across the center of the bed, she slid out from beneath his arm. Grabbing her jeans and one of his sweatshirts, she hastily dressed before tiptoeing from his bedroom.

She softly closed the door behind her, so he could sleep a little longer, and then met Grizzly at the back door, where he waited rather impatiently.

"Go on, you big oaf," she said fondly, opening the door.

She made herself a pot of coffee, figuring Caleb wouldn't mind. When the coffee finished brewing, she added her favorite vanilla-flavored creamer, and then carried the mug outside.

Curled up in Caleb's Adirondack chair, she watched Grizz sniff the grass and basked in the glorious night they'd shared.

Being intimate with Caleb had been amazing. He had been tender and kind, treating her as a precious treasure yet making it clear how much he wanted her.

Maybe they could make this work. Surely he'd trust her now.

She sipped her coffee and forced herself to face the truth.

She was falling in love with Caleb.

Love. There was a part of her that was amazed, considering everything she'd been through, at how she could actually fall in love with Caleb. Somehow it was easier now to relinquish her heart.

Yet on the heels of her happiness came a warning

chill. What if Caleb didn't feel the same way? Sure, he cared about her, he'd told her that much, but love? In order to love someone you had to trust them completely. Implicitly.

Was Caleb capable of loving her the way she loved him?

Curling her fingers around the steaming mug, she tried to suppress her dire thoughts. He'd promised to work on his trust issues. She wasn't foolish enough to believe it would happen overnight. As long as he was making the effort, she could be patient.

Grizzly sniffed his way around the yard, happily marking every bush and tree with his scent, making her smile. From the very beginning she'd always felt at home with Caleb. There'd been this sense of rightness in being with him.

"Raine?" he bellowed so loudly she started, sloshing coffee onto the front of his sweatshirt. She uncurled herself from the chair, even as Grizzly bounded toward the door.

"I'm out here," she called.

He threw open the door, his gaze landing on her with something akin to wary disbelief. "I couldn't find you."

"Grizzly needed to go out and I didn't want to wake you." She tried to make light of the situation, but his brief yet very real panic couldn't be ignored.

He'd thought she'd left. Like his mother had abandoned him all those years ago. No wonder he found it so difficult to trust.

And in that moment she realized he'd never really

gotten over that feeling of being abandoned. Not really. And though she believed he'd try, she honestly didn't know if he ever would.

Raine began the process of cooking eggs and bacon for breakfast, sensing Caleb was annoyed with himself.

Determined to remain positive, she chatted as if nothing had happened. Caleb needed time and there was no rush. So she put forth her best effort, telling Caleb about some of the other animals at the shelter.

"Which reminds me, I probably need to get home soon," she said lightly. "Spice is going to be very unhappy with me."

"No, Spice is going to be unhappy with me," Caleb corrected. "Especially when you go home smelling like Grizz."

She shrugged. "I love my cat, but someday Spice is going to have to learn to co-exist with a dog, because I really want a dog of my own, too."

Caleb's smile was fleeting, but then he stared broodingly at his plate. "I hope you're not leaving because I acted like an idiot," he said finally.

"No, but tell me, how did you think I'd gotten home without a car? The distance between your place and mine is a pretty long walk."

He shrugged, his expression tense. "I wasn't thinking, it was a knee-jerk reaction."

Like the night he'd come in and found a semi-intoxicated Jake draped all over her, trying to kiss her.

She pushed her plate away. "Caleb, I could tell you I'd never betray you like that, but I'm pretty sure that nothing I can say will convince you. This is something you have to figure out on your own."

He gave a terse nod and rose to his feet. He stacked their dirty plates and then carried them into the kitchen. "I want to change, so maybe I'll take lessons from you."

"Not me," she protested. Her cellphone chirped and she frowned, pulling the instrument from the pocket of her jeans. She recognized her youngest brother's number on the screen. "Hello?"

"Raine?" Michael's familiar voice boomed in her ear. "Is that you?"

"Mikey! It's good to hear from you," she said, sincerely pleased to hear from the youngest of her three brothers. "What's up?"

"Where are you?" he demanded. "I'm at your apartment, and your car is here, but you're not answering the door."

Oh, boy. Her eyes widened in alarm. He was at her apartment? What on earth for? She ignored his overprotective tone. "Yes, Mikey, you're right. I'm not there. I can be there in a few minutes—though, if you need me. Is something wrong?"

"Nothing's wrong, but I'm in town for two days of training and figured I could bunk with my baby sister. I left you a message on your answering machine— didn't you get it?"

He had? She hadn't listened to her messages lately. "Er, no, I didn't."

"So I came to your apartment, and found your car was here, but you're not. You told me you worked second shift, right? I figured I needed to get here before you headed off to work."

She sighed and glanced at Caleb, who was listening to her one-sided conversation with a frown. "I don't work today, and it's fine if you want to stay with me for a few days."

"Where are you?" he demanded.

She refused to respond to her brother's Neanderthal tactics. "I'll be home in about fifteen to twenty minutes. You can either wait for me or go find something to do for a while."

"I'll wait," he said, and she could just imagine the scowl on her handsome brother's face.

"Fine. See you in a bit." She snapped her phone shut.

"Let me guess, one of your brothers?" Caleb asked wryly.

"Yes." She supposed it was a good sign that he didn't assume it was some former boyfriend. "He's at my apartment, waiting for me."

"Then I guess we'd better get going." Caleb let Grizzly outside and then led the way out to his car. "Are you going to tell him?"

"About us? I think he's going to figure it out when you bring me home," she said with a weary sigh. She wasn't in the mood for her brother's macho protectiveness, she really wasn't.

"No, not about us. About the assault."

She couldn't temper the flash of annoyance. "No. Why would I do that?"

"Because he's family, and he obviously cares about you. He should know," Caleb persisted.

After they'd spent the night making love, he went right back to the assault? Disappointment stabbed deep. Hadn't they moved beyond that? "No, he doesn't need to know. And if I were you, I'd worry about yourself, because Michael is not going to be pleased to meet you." At the moment she wasn't so pleased with Caleb either.

He sent her an exasperated glance. "It'll be fine."

"If you say so," she muttered darkly, crossing her arms over her chest.

When Caleb pulled up in front of her eight-unit apartment building, she saw her brother pacing on the sidewalk, talking and gesturing wildly into his phone. Great. No doubt he was telling Ian and Slade all about her spending the night with a man.

Good grief, she didn't need this.

She pasted a smile on her face when she climbed out of Caleb's car. Caleb came round to stand beside her and when Michael saw them, he abruptly ended his conversation and came striding toward her. "Hi, Raine. Who's this?"

"Caleb, this is my brother, Michael. Mikey, this is my friend Caleb Stewart. He's one of the ED physicians on staff at Trinity Medical Center."

"So what? Am I supposed to be impressed he's some sort of doctor?" Michael demanded, glaring at Caleb. "After he's spent the night sleeping with my baby sister?"

She rolled her eyes. "Knock it off. I'm twenty-six years old and you're acting like an idiot. What I do with my personal time is none of your business."

Her brother's gaze narrowed in warning. She'd known he'd react like this, as if she were some sixteen-year-old who couldn't make her own decisions.

"Michael, it's nice to meet you." Caleb stepped forward to offer his hand and she had to give him credit for trying to make peace. Her brother reluctantly shook it. "Raine talks about her three older brothers all the time. I know she cares about you very much."

Her brother's gaze softened a little. "I'm glad to hear that, because you need to know that if you hurt her, the three of us will hold you responsible."

She quickly interrupted to prevent the conversation from going anywhere close to the assault. "I can take care of myself, Mikey. And even if I can't, the mistakes I make are my own. Now, play nice with Caleb, or I won't introduce you to my boyfriends ever again."

"Sure, no problem." Michael rocked back on his heels and gave her a cheeky grin. "But just so you know, I already spilled the beans to Ian and Slade."

She knew it! She scowled at him. "Great. Thanks a lot. I should make you sleep in a hotel." She turned toward Caleb. "See what I mean? I tried to explain what it was like living with them, but you thought I was exaggerating."

The corner of Caleb's mouth quirked upward. "Nah, I knew you weren't exaggerating. I don't have a sister, but if I did, I think I'd probably feel the same way they do." He lifted one shoulder in an apologetic shrug.

"That's right, you would." Michael clapped him on the back, as they finally saw eye to eye on something.

She suppressed another sigh. "Well, grab your gear, then, and come on up. What time does your training start?"

"Noon." Michael glanced at Caleb in surprise when he fell into step beside them. "I hope you don't mind if I bunk here for the next two nights," he said, as if realizing three was, indeed, a crowd. "I haven't seen you in a while and figured this would be a good chance to catch up."

Which was his way of telling her that she'd better not plan on having Caleb stay over while he was there. As if she would.

"It's fine," she assured him. "Caleb's dad is actually scheduled to come home from the hospital either later today or tomorrow anyway."

"The hospital?" Michael's eyebrows rose. "I'm sorry to hear that. I hope he's okay?"

"He had triple bypass surgery and a valve replacement a few days ago, but he's doing much better," Caleb told him.

"I'm glad," Michael said.

"Mikey's a volunteer firefighter and a paramedic back home in Cedar Bluff," she explained for Caleb's benefit.

"I'm impressed. Fighting fires is a tough job."

"Well, I do more paramedic work than anything else," her brother said modestly. "Thankfully there aren't a lot of fires in Cedar Bluff. We have to do a lot more training, though, since we don't get as many chances to work in real fire situations. Which is why I'm here in Milwaukee."

Raine led the way inside her apartment, greeting Spice who lightly ran over to meet the newcomers. Spice veered away from Caleb, but meowed softly and brushed up against Michael's leg.

"She's a cutie. Probably smells Leo, the male tomcat we have down at the station," Michael said, bending down to stroke the cat. "Leo is quite the Romeo."

"Just like you, huh?" Raine said dryly. For all his protectiveness of her, her youngest brother was legendary with women. "Does anyone want coffee?" she called out, heading into the kitchen.

"I do," her brother announced. "Give me a minute to borrow your bathroom."

When her brother disappeared behind the bathroom door, she glanced at Caleb. "Are you all right?" she asked, considering he hadn't said much since meeting her brother.

He threw her an exasperated look. "Raine, your brother doesn't scare me. None of your brothers scare me. Don't worry about it. Although I do see what you mean about what it must have been like living with them. They don't recognize any personal boundaries, do they?"

"Not really." She filled the coffee-maker with water and started the pot brewing. "My parents died when I was just a sophomore in high school. The three of them were really pretty wonderful, moving back home to raise me."

Caleb's gaze was full of sympathy. "That must have been hard on you."

"It was hard on all of us. Mikey was a senior in high school himself, but Ian and Slade put their own college plans on hold to come home to help keep the family together. Truly, I owe them a lot. Which is why I pretty much got used to them sticking their nose into my personal business." She tried to lighten the sudden seriousness of the conversation. "Can you believe they went so far as to read my diary? Nothing was sacred. Absolutely nothing."

Caleb's lips twitched. "Will you let me read it?"

"No." She glowered at him. "Don't even think about it."

"Raine!" her brother bellowed from the bathroom.

She ground her teeth together, tempted once again to tell Michael to go find a hotel. "Now what's the problem?" she asked.

"My problem?" Her brother stomped out of her bathroom, a deep scowl creasing his forehead, and it took her a moment to realize he had her pregnancy test kit clutched in his hand. "Here's my problem. Are you pregnant?"

CHAPTER THIRTEEN

RAINE'S eyes widened in horror as her brother, the human bulldozer, revealed her most painful, shameful secret. She glanced frantically at Caleb in time to watch all the color drain from his face as he stared with utter disbelief at the pregnancy test kit.

And in that one awful, terrible moment she knew. No matter what he'd said earlier, he didn't trust her. Would likely never trust her.

Which meant he'd never love her the way she loved him.

There was a moment of dead silence before she moved, snatching the kit out of her brother's hand, wishing she dared to smack him with it. "No, I'm not pregnant." The stomach cramps she'd experienced earlier that morning convinced her that her period wasn't far off. "Keep your nose out of my business."

"Raine, you having a baby is my business. Our business. The child would be our niece or nephew. Of course, we'd help you raise the baby if some jerk took off and abandoned you." Michael glared at Caleb.

Caleb opened his mouth to speak and she sent him a

dark look, warning him not to say a word, either in his own defense about the child not being his or about the assault. "Leave Caleb alone, Mikey. I mean it. You're my brother and I love you, but that does not give you the right to intrude into my personal life."

Her brother raised his hands innocently, as if realizing he might have pushed too far. "Hey, I'm just saying—we'll stand by you."

She let out a sigh, knowing that at least that much was right. Her brother had always been there for her. And if she had gotten pregnant, her brothers would support her.

Unlike Caleb, whose face was suddenly completely devoid of all expression.

Obviously, she and Caleb needed to talk. Yet at the same time she couldn't help feeling irritated at his reaction. Why did she always have to explain herself? Couldn't he ever just once give her the benefit of doubt? What good would any explanation be if he refused to believe in her?

She'd known earlier that Caleb's lack of trust wasn't something she could help him overcome.

This was only irrefutable proof that he'd need to fix his problems on his own.

An awkward silence fell and she dreaded the conversation she and Caleb needed to have. "Mikey, give us a few minutes alone, would you?" she asked softly.

"Uh, yeah. Sure." Michael glanced between the two of them, with a shrug. "Actually, I was looking for a razor so I could shave." He scrubbed a hand over his jaw. "Can I borrow one of yours?"

"Help yourself," she said, knowing he would anyway.

After her brother left them alone, she turned to Caleb. "I'm sorry. I tried to tell you my brothers were over-protective."

"You thought you were pregnant?" His tone was accusing.

She lifted her chin. "I guess attempting a second chance wasn't a good idea after all."

A flash of disbelief glittered in his eyes. "What sort of second chance did we have if you weren't honest with me? You never said a word about possibly being pregnant."

She stared at him, wondering if he was using this as an excuse to quit on the relationship before it even started. "I told you about the sexual assault. Didn't it occur to you that pregnancy might be a consequence? Besides, what difference does it make now? I used the test, I'm not pregnant."

He blew out a breath and turned away, avoiding her gaze. "Why didn't you say anything to me about it? You told me everything else, didn't you?"

She shook her head, tears stinging her eyes. This was his issue, not hers. "And if I say yes, I've told you everything else, will you believe me?"

When he didn't immediately answer, she swallowed hard. "I'm sorry, Caleb, but this isn't going to work." Trying to ignore the way her heart was aching, she walked over to her apartment door and opened it. "Thanks for driving me home. I'm sure I'll see you around at work."

Caleb stared at her for a long moment, and then walked past her. "Yeah. See you around," he muttered as he left the apartment.

Fighting tears, she slowly closed the apartment door

behind him and then leaned heavily against it. Her stomach clenched and the familiar nausea that she now knew was a result of stress returned with a vengeance.

Caleb hadn't believed in her before the assault and he clearly didn't now. Even after the closeness they'd shared.

This time she knew their relationship was over.

Caleb left Raine's apartment and walked outside, reeling from their argument.

He couldn't believe she'd never told him her fears about being pregnant as a result of the assault. Of course he'd considered the possibility but hadn't pushed for the details. When she hadn't mentioned it, he'd assumed it wasn't a problem.

What else hadn't she told him?

Earlier that morning, he'd been angry when he'd thought she'd taken off without a word. He could readily admit that he'd overreacted, automatically thinking the worst.

When he'd found her outside, sitting on the deck with Grizzly, he'd felt like a fool. Especially when she'd given him a look full of reproach. He'd known then he needed to stop reading the worst into everything she said or did.

But this was different. They'd grown closer together over these past few days. They'd spent the night making love. Why would she keep secrets from him at this point in their relationship?

It was clear that if her brother hadn't found the test kit and bluntly confronted her with it, she wouldn't have mentioned the possibility at all.

He was so lost in thought he didn't realize he'd walked several blocks past his car until he came upon a stop sign for a major road. Muttering a curse, he spun on his heel and stalked back to where he'd left his car.

As he opened the door, about to slide in, he couldn't help glancing up at Raine's apartment window. Of course she wasn't standing there, watching him. He climbed in behind the wheel and slammed the door behind him.

He hoped, for her sake, she did tell her brother what had happened. Raine had been through a terrible ordeal. She needed all the support she could get.

His cellphone rang, interrupting his thoughts. He glanced at the number, surprised to realize it was the hospital. His dad? His heart rate spiked in alarm as he quickly answered. "Hello?"

"Caleb? Can you pick me up?" After yesterday's visit, his father sounded surprisingly upbeat. "Doc says I'm ready to be discharged."

"Really? Sure, of course I'll pick you up. I can be there in a few minutes."

"Are you bringing Raine with you?"

His father's innocent question sent a shaft of pain through his heart. Raine would have loved to come with him to pick up his father. For a moment the reality of what had just happened upstairs in her apartment hit hard.

Their relationship was over. For good.

But this wasn't the time to tell his father the news. Not yet. "No, her brother is in town right now, visiting with her." He tried not to let his father hear the desolation in his tone. "But I'll let her know you're coming home. She'll be thrilled."

"Okay." His father readily accepted the excuse. "And don't forget we have to pick up Grizz on the way home."

"I won't forget. See you soon, Dad."

Caleb started the car and headed straight over to the hospital, grateful for something else to think about rather than the mess he'd made of his personal life.

Because there was no denying how lonely his house would feel now that both Raine and Grizzly were gone.

Caleb had been fully prepared to stay with his father during the first week after his hospitalization to help care for him at home. But surprisingly his father seemed to have taken Raine's advice to heart.

"Caleb, this is Marlene Fitzgerald, one of the volunteers at the animal shelter," his father said, introducing him to a spry, silver-haired woman standing next to him. She looked to be similar in age to his father, which by itself was unusual, since his father's women in the past had all been much younger. "Marlene, this is my son, Caleb. He's a doctor on staff here in the emergency department at Trinity Medical Center. He chose the path of taking care of people rather than animals."

Caleb stepped forward to take the older woman's hand. "Hi, Marlene. It's nice to meet you."

"Same here, Caleb." Marlene smiled, blushing a bit. "I hope you don't mind if I temporarily move in to help care for your father for a few days."

Temporarily move in? He arched a brow at his father. "Uh, no. Of course not. But I can help too, Dad. You've had major surgery, and I've arranged to take some time off work."

"There's no need for you to take off work for me," his father said gruffly. "I appreciate your efforts, but Marlene offered to help and I think together we'll be able to manage just fine."

"If you're sure…" Caleb gave in, as it appeared his father had planned everything out. "I'd still like to stop by each day to see how things are going."

"I'll take you up on that offer. Can't pass up the opportunity to get a house call," his father joked.

Caleb carried his father's belongings as Marlene pushed his wheelchair down to the hospital lobby. He went round to bring up the car and, as promised, stopped by his house on the way home to pick up Grizzly.

Marlene didn't seem to mind the dog, greeting Grizz with enthusiasm. She clearly loved animals as much as his father did.

He wanted to believe Marlene and his father were meant to be together, but the old suspicions wouldn't go away. Marlene seemed perfect now, but his father's relationships never seemed to last.

After dropping Marlene and his father off at home, taking time to ensure his dad was settled comfortably in his favorite recliner, with Grizz at his feet, Caleb headed home.

Greeted by nothing more than the echo of his own voice, he called the hospital to notify them he was available to work if needed after all. They promised to call if something opened up or if someone called in sick. Dejected, he stared out at his back yard, wondering what to do with the extra time on his hands.

If Raine was here, he would have been thrilled to

have more time off work. But now he would rather have something to do to keep his mind off her.

Raine had been right about one thing. His trust issues were his own problem to fix. Keeping secrets wasn't the way to inspire trust, yet even before that he'd known he'd made mistakes.

Mistakes he wasn't sure how to fix.

Was he doomed to the same fate as his father? To have nothing but one failed relationship after another?

As much as he didn't want to go down that same path, he was at a loss as to how to break the pattern.

Raine sank down onto her sofa, overwhelmingly relieved when Mikey finally took off to attend his training session. She wanted, needed time alone to pull her battered emotions together.

She couldn't help replaying that moment her brother had asked if she was pregnant over and over in her mind. Her stomach clenched painfully. Even though she knew that Caleb hadn't fully trusted her before then, the shattered expression in his eyes still haunted her.

Did Caleb have a right to be upset? Should she have told him her fears?

Maybe.

She and Caleb had been doomed, right from the beginning. She'd been right to break things off before the assault.

The past would always stand between them.

Spice jumped up on the sofa beside her and she drew the cat into her arms, cuddling her soft fur. If only people were more like animals, full of unconditional love.

Her brothers loved her unconditionally. Was it unfair to expect the same from Caleb?

She didn't think so. Her parents had died too young, but she'd always known how much they'd loved and cared for each other. She wanted and deserved the same sort of love.

Since sitting around and wallowing in self-pity wasn't an option, she decided to spend the rest of her afternoon at the animal shelter. With Dr. Frank gone, they were probably short-handed. And she'd rather be busy to keep her mind off of Caleb.

She took a quick shower, shocked to discover her instincts were right. She'd gotten her period.

She'd begun blowdrying her hair when her phone rang. For one heart-stopping moment she wondered if the caller was Caleb. Was he calling to apologize and beg her to come back?

And why was she even tempted by the possibility when nothing had changed?

She dashed over to the phone, slowing down with a sharp stab of disappointment when the number displayed an unknown caller on her caller ID.

Letting the call go to her answering-machine, she headed back towards the bathroom to finish up. But stopped dead in her tracks when a familiar voice came over the speaker.

"Raine, this is Detective Carol Blanchard with the Milwaukee Police Department. Please call me as soon as you get this message. We need your help in identifying a suspect we have in custody. We believe he could possibly be the man who raped you."

They had a suspect? Raine dropped the brush she was holding, unable to believe it. Her fingers trembled so badly she had difficulty dialing Detective Blanchard's phone number. She told herself not to get her hopes up too high, but she held her breath, waiting for the detective to answer.

"Detective Blanchard."

"Detective, this is Raine Hart returning your phone call."

"Raine, I'm so glad you called me back so quickly. I know you don't remember the man who assaulted you, but we wanted to have you come down to the station to look at a line-up anyway. Our hope is that you can maybe pick out the guy who was at the nightclub the night of your assault."

"A line-up?" Her mouth went desert dry and her heart thudded painfully in her chest. "Uh, sure. If you think it might help."

"We do think this would help," Detective Blanchard assured her. "The DNA testing is going to take time, and we'd like to at least place this suspect at the scene of the crime. Could you be here in an hour?"

An hour? So soon? She swallowed a momentary flash of panic. "Of course. No problem."

"Great, we'll see you in an hour, then."

Raine hung up the phone, feeling jittery. She hurried to finish in the bathroom, wishing more than anything that Caleb was here with her. If they hadn't argued, he would have gone with her for moral support.

She pushed away the useless thoughts. But as she used the hairdryer, she couldn't help worrying.

What if she couldn't pick this guy out as one of the men who were at the After Dark nightclub that night? And if she couldn't identify him, would he go free?

CHAPTER FOURTEEN

As Raine walked up the concrete steps leading into the police station she saw a familiar figure walking down the stairs in the opposite direction. The woman walked with her shoulders hunched and her head down to avoid direct eye contact with anyone.

But Raine still recognized her. Helen Shore. Her sexual assault patient from the ED.

The knot in her stomach tightened. Had Helen successfully picked the suspect out of the line-up? Or was the fate of this man going to rest solely on her shoulders?

Her footsteps slowed as a tidal wave of doubt swept in. What if she picked the wrong man? Or, worse, what if she picked the suspect they had, but he was actually innocent?

The DNA evidence would eventually exonerate him if that were the case, but not for several weeks yet.

She took a deep breath, and walked into the police station. Detective Blanchard was waiting for her.

"Hi, Raine. How are you doing?" The detective's expression radiated true concern.

The tenseness in her stomach eased a bit. "Pretty good, all things considered."

Detective Blanchard's gaze was sharply assessing. "You look good," she said slowly. "Like you've really recovered. I'm glad. Well, are you ready?"

No, she wasn't ready. But she nodded. "Yes, but what happens if I can't pick this guy out of the line-up? Does he walk away?"

"Come with me, and I'll explain how this works." The detective led the way into a small room, with a one-way mirror lining the wall. "This suspect isn't going to walk away, no matter what happens here today. I don't want you to feel pressure to make the so-called right identification. We have enough evidence to hold this guy for a while. So don't worry about him being back on the street, because that's not going to happen. Just relax and do your best."

"Okay." She placed a hand over her heart, willing her pulse to slow down, and swallowed hard. "I'm ready."

Detective Blanchard hit a button on the intercom. "We're ready—bring the suspects in."

Raine watched as six men walked into the brightly lit anteroom in single file, each going to their assigned numbers. They all stood staring straight ahead, their hands down at their sides. A tingle of apprehension slithered down her spine, even though she knew they couldn't see her. She clasped her arms over her chest, wishing more than anything that Caleb was here to hold her.

She took her time, looking at each of the men. When she reached suspect number five, the tingle turned into a full-fledged shiver.

He was the silent one who'd been there that night. She was sure of it. But, still, she forced herself to look at suspect number six, too. And then Detective Blanchard gave the order for the men to turn to the right and then to the left, so she could get a thorough look at their profiles.

Her gaze went back to suspect number five. She was absolutely certain he was one of the two guys who'd been next to her that night. She remembered the way he'd watched her so intently without saying much, letting his buddy do all the talking for him.

"Number five," she said, looking at Detective Blanchard. "I recognize suspect number five as being in the nightclub that night. He and another man bought me a drink, and I don't remember anything after that."

"Are you sure?" Detective Blanchard asked, her gaze impassive.

For a moment her heart sank. Had she picked the wrong man? She turned back and looked at them again, but she knew number five was the man who'd been there. "Yes, I'm sure." Her voice rang out with confidence. "Number five."

A smile broke out on Detective Blanchard's face. She reached over to touch the intercom button. "Thanks, we're finished here." The men filed out of the room.

The detective turned toward her. "Good job, Raine. Number five is the suspect we arrested. His name is Colin Ward and your positive ID will help us when we present our case to the grand jury."

Overwhelming relief washed over her. Colin Ward? Sounded like such an average name. "What happened?" she asked curiously. "How did you end up arresting him?"

"We set up a sting operation at the After Dark night-club with one of our young, very attractive female officers. We also had a cop working undercover behind the bar and we caught him spiking her drink with Rohypnol. The bartender quickly swapped it out but she played along, as if she was drunk. Colin Ward insisted on helping her out to her car, and once he'd stashed her in the passenger seat and slid behind the wheel with her keys, we nailed him."

"I can't believe he did it again," she whispered.

"He's a predator, no question about it. And when the DNA match is confirmed, and we're very sure it will be, this guy will go to jail for a long time."

She was glad, fiercely glad, that he'd been caught. How many others had he raped? She knew only too often that many women didn't come forward after something like that. Especially when they couldn't remember what had really happened.

She wanted to ask if Helen Shore had been able to identify him, too, but she held back, unwilling to break her patient's confidentiality. Helen's ability to ID him wouldn't matter as she herself had been able to pick him out without a problem.

Detective Blanchard walked her back outside, telling her she'd be in touch when and if the case went to trial. The detective thought that if the DNA evidence was positive, Colin Ward would cop a plea.

Raine nodded, hardly listening. No matter what happened from here, her nightmare was over. She'd thought she'd feel better once the guy was caught, and she did, except there was a part of her that still felt empty.

Because she didn't have Caleb.

She walked to her car and slid behind the wheel. She was tempted, very tempted, to call Caleb. He was the only one who'd understand how she felt. And in spite of their most recent break-up, she knew he'd want to know. She went so far as to pull out her cellphone, bringing up his number, but then hesitated.

No. She flipped her phone closed. She needed to figure out how to move forward with her life without him. Because even if she called him now, and they managed to mend their rift from this morning, how long would the peace last?

Only until the next time she did something stupid. Or until the next time she grew tired of his inability to trust her.

She loved him, but they didn't have a chance at a future. Better to figure out a way to get over him, once and for all.

Caleb's father called two days after he'd been discharged, asking if Caleb could come over for a while because Marlene had to go and help her daughter, who needed an urgent babysitter for her sick child. He readily agreed, heading over right away.

Grizzly met him at the door, waving his tail excitedly. "Hi, Grizz, how are you? Taking good care of Dad, hmm?"

"Caleb? Is that you?" his father called from the kitchen.

"Yes, I'm here." Caleb made his way through the house into the kitchen. "Has Marlene left already?" he asked.

"Yeah, her daughter had to be at work by nine, so she went over first thing."

"I hope she doesn't bring germs back to you," Caleb said, pulling up a chair and sitting down beside his dad. "You need to stay as healthy as possible."

"Marlene said the same thing. She's just as worried as you are. I'm sure I'll be fine," his father said. "I'm surprised you didn't bring Raine with you. How is she?"

Caleb had dodged questions about Raine in the past few days, but he couldn't keep lying to his dad. He blew out a heavy breath. "She's fine, as far as I know. But we're not seeing each other any more."

"What?" His father glared at him. "Why not? What happened? Raine was perfect for you, Caleb. A keeper!"

He couldn't suppress a flash of annoyance. "And how would you know a keeper, Dad? You're hardly the expert. None of the women you picked stuck around long enough to be a keeper. What's the longest relationship you had since Mom left? Three years?"

His father's eyes widened and his frankly wounded expression hit Caleb like a punch to the gut.

His breath hissed out between his teeth. What was wrong with him? This wasn't his father's fault. "I'm sorry. I shouldn't have said that."

His father stared at him for a moment. "No, don't apologize. I never realized you felt that way."

Caleb winced. "I should have just kept my mouth shut," he muttered.

"No, I think you need to understand, Caleb. The reason I had trouble holding relationships together after your mother left was largely my own fault."

Caleb couldn't help but agree to a certain extent, because his father had obviously picked some losers.

"No, it wasn't your fault, Dad. The women you were with made lousy choices."

"Listen, Caleb. I didn't love them. I couldn't love them, because I was still in love with your mother."

Caleb stared at his father in shock. "You loved her? Even after she left us?"

His father's smile was sad. "Son, you don't always control who you love. Your mother got pregnant with you and we tried to make a marriage work. But she was young and a very talented dancer. She talked constantly about pursuing a dancing career. When she told me she was moving to New York, alone, I wasn't entirely surprised."

He'd heard the story of his mother getting a part in the Broadway play so the fact that she'd left them to dance wasn't a surprise. But his father's easy acceptance of her leaving was. "She left us both for her own selfish reasons and that's okay?"

"She was young," his father defended. "And I knew she wasn't ready to settle down. But I loved her. Even after she left, I didn't stop loving her."

"So why the string of women?" he asked.

His father flushed. "I felt bad for you, Caleb. I wanted you to have a mother. And I can't deny I was looking for some companionship, too."

Caleb scrubbed a hand over his face. "I understand. I can't blame you."

"You're missing the point. I couldn't give the women in my life the love they deserved. And they obviously knew that. So that's why those relationships ended. Carmen put up with me the longest, until she realized I wouldn't return her love. I think there was a part of me that kept holding back, hoping your mother would return once she'd gotten her dancing out of her system."

Caleb frowned. "She's married to someone else now. Heck, she has a new family of her own." He couldn't quite hide his bitterness. He'd reached out to his mother once, after high school, but she hadn't been very interested in the family she'd left behind.

"I know." His father didn't look surprised. "But it still took my heart a long time to give up hope. But don't blame the women who've come and gone over the years, Caleb. The blame is mine."

Caleb sat there, dumbfounded by the turn in the conversation. He sensed his father was telling the truth. For so long he had blamed the women in his father's life for not being trustworthy. And he'd blamed his father for his poor choices.

But it had never occurred to him how his father had ended up sabotaging his own relationships because he'd still loved his son's mother.

Had he let his own bitterness after the incident with Tabitha do the same? Ruin his chance at a decent relationship?

"If you love Raine with your whole heart and soul, you need to fight for her," his father urged in a low voice. "Don't let her go, Caleb."

Was it really that easy? He loved Raine. With his whole heart and soul. And he knew, honestly knew, she wouldn't intentionally hurt him.

His dad was right. Raine was a keeper.

He jumped to his feet. "Dad, I have to go." Then he realized he couldn't leave and abruptly sat back down.

"Sorry, I almost forgot. I can't go right now. I'll wait for Marlene to come back."

"Tell you what. Throw something together for me to eat for lunch, and then you can go." His father idly rubbed his chest. "I promise I'll do my physical therapy exercises."

"Really?" Caleb glanced at his father doubtfully, desire warring with duty. "Are you sure?"

"I'm sure." His father put a hand on Grizzly's head. "Grizz and I will be just fine. I'll call you if I need something."

"Okay." Caleb grinned, clapping his dad on the back. "Thanks. For everything."

He was going to win Raine back, although he knew it wouldn't be an easy task.

He needed help. And he wasn't afraid to use every possible resource at his disposal.

Raine glanced up in surprise when her doorbell buzzer went off. Mikey? If so, her brother was early.

"Yes?"

"Raine? It's Caleb. I'd like to talk to you if you have a minute."

Caleb? Her heart squeezed in her chest and hope, ever foolish, surged. "Uh, sure. Come on up."

"Actually, I need you to come down."

She frowned. Why did she need to come down?

Admittedly curious, she grabbed her keys and headed out of the apartment, taking the stairs down to the lobby level. When she went outside, she was surprised to see Caleb standing there with Rusty, the sweet Irish setter from the animal shelter.

"Rusty!" she exclaimed, going down into a crouch to greet the dog. He waved his tail excitedly, lavishing her with doggie kisses that she laughingly avoided as much as possible. "It's so good to see him. I'm surprised he's letting you near him without growling," she said. "He's normally afraid of men."

"I know. It took me a few days to win him over, but I did. He's not afraid of me. I'm taking that as a sign we were meant to be together."

"You adopted him?" She was glad Rusty was going to a good home, but she couldn't hide the wistfulness in her tone.

"I'd like to. But that depends on you."

She frowned, slowly rising to her feet. "What do you mean?"

"Rusty has learned to trust me, and I'm hoping you will, too, when I ask for you to give me another chance."

Hope lunged in her heart, but she held back. "I don't know if that's a good idea," she began.

"Wait, please hear me out," he interrupted. "You were right, my problems weren't about you. They were about me. I needed to learn to trust myself. To let myself love you. It's a long story, but my dad made me realize what an idiot I've been."

His dad? The kernel of hope grew bigger.

"I love you, Raine. More than I can say. Every time I pushed you away, it was because I was holding back, protecting myself from being hurt. But I've been hurting since I walked away from you. And even if you send me away right now, I'm still going to love you."

She wanted to believe him, she really did. "I love you,

too, Caleb. But sometimes love isn't enough. I don't think I can live with a man who constantly doubts me."

Contrary to her words, his face brightened. "But that's just it. I trust both of us. All I'm asking right now is for a chance to prove it to you."

Rusty nudged her hand, asking for attention. "You're not fighting fair," she murmured, glancing between the dog and the man she loved, who managed to gang up on her.

"I'm fighting for my life, Raine," he said, taking her comment seriously. "But I understand I've hurt you, even though I didn't mean to. So if you need time, that's fine, you can take all the time you need. But know that no matter what happens, I'll be waiting for you."

His willingness to back off surprised her. And she realized she couldn't let him take all the blame. "Not everything was your fault, Caleb. I didn't always confide in you. Living with three older brothers taught me that I couldn't talk about everything that bothered me because they would make such a big deal out of every little thing. So I learned to suppress a lot of what I was thinking and feeling. I'm sure my tendency to hide my deepest feelings didn't help your ability to trust me."

"Sweet of you to try to take the blame, Raine, but it's not your fault by a long shot. But if you're willing to give me a second chance, I won't argue."

Wasn't this the third chance? Maybe, but who was counting? Not her. Not any more. She was lucky enough to have people in her life who loved her unconditionally. Wasn't it time she did the same? Didn't Caleb deserve her unconditional love?

"I am willing," she said softly.

"You are?" He looked afraid to hope.

"Yes. Because I love you, too. I've been miserable without you. If you really think we can make this work, I'm more than willing to try again."

"Thank God," he murmured, reaching over to pull her into a warm embrace. "Things will be different this time, Raine. You'll see."

"I know." She lifted her eyes to his and he bent to capture her mouth in a searing kiss. Instantly she melted against him, longing for more.

"Wanna come to my place?" Caleb asked huskily, when she finally came up for air. "You could help Rusty get acquainted in his new home."

"Sure, I'll come over for a bit. But don't worry, he's going to love his new home," she assured him, giving the dog's silky ears a good rub.

"I don't want to rush you, Raine," Caleb said in a low voice. "But my home can be your home too. Rusty and I will be waiting for you whenever you're ready."

She went still. "Really? Just like that?"

He nodded, no sign of hesitation. "Just like that."

Wow. She wasn't sure what to say. "I should probably tell you that the police caught the guy who assaulted me."

"They did?" Caleb looked surprised. "That's good news, Raine. I'm happy for you."

"I had to pick him out of a line-up," she confessed. "I wanted you with me so badly, but it all worked out. He's going to stay in jail without bail until the DNA results are in."

"I'm sorry I wasn't there for you," Caleb said, pulling

her close for another hug. "I hope one day you'll be able to put all this behind you."

"I will," she said confidently. She couldn't help wondering if her relationship with Caleb hadn't somehow grown stronger through everything that had happened. If she hadn't changed, would the two of them be standing there right now? She doubted it. "I can face anything with you beside me."

Caleb gave her another one-armed hug, the other hand firmly on Rusty's leash. "I feel the same way, Raine. As if I can conquer anything with you at my side. I love you so much."

"I love you, too." Her smile shimmered straight from her heart as she tugged Rusty's leash from his hand. "Take us home, Caleb."

His eyes lit up with hope and promise. "Yes. Let's go home."

THE LAST
TEMPTATION OF
DR DALTON

ROBIN GIANNA

Mom, you always told me how important
writers are to the world.
This one's for you.

CHAPTER ONE

IT WAS ALL she could do not to throw her stupid phone out of the car window.

Why wasn't he answering? Charlotte Edwards huffed out a breath and focused on driving as fast as she possibly could—not an easy task on the potholed dirt road that was just muddy enough to send her sliding into a tree if she wasn't careful.

Thank goodness it was only May in Liberia, West Africa, and just the beginning of the rainy season. Her battered four-by-four handled the terrible roads pretty well, but once they were inches deep with mud and water all bets were off.

Adrenaline surging, Charlie cautiously pressed harder on the gas pedal. No matter how uncomfortable it would make her feel, she absolutely had to catch Trent Dalton at the airport before he left—then tell him off for not answering his phone. If he had, she'd have paid for a taxi to bring him back stat to her little hospital, instead of wasting time making this trek both ways.

The sudden ringing of her phone made her jump and she snatched it up, hoping it was Trent, seeing she'd called a dozen times. "So you finally decided to look at your phone?"

"It's Thomas."

The hospital technician sounded surprised and no wonder. Her stomach twisted with dread, hoping he wasn't delivering bad news. "Sorry. You calling with an update?"

"The boy is still holding his own. I pray he'll be okay until Dr. Dalton gets back here. But I wanted to tell you that Dr. Smith has offered to do the appendectomy."

"What? Tell him no way. I'm not having a liar and a hack working on any of our patients—unless Trent's already gone, in which case we'll have no choice but to reconsider. I'll let you know as soon as I get to the airport."

"Yes, Ma."

She hung up and shook her head, managing a little smile. The word "Ma" was used as a sign of respect in Liberia, and no matter how many times she'd asked Thomas just to call her Charlie, or Charlotte, he never did.

Dr. Smith had been sent by the Global Physicians Coalition to work at the Henry and Louisa Edwards Mission Hospital for a one-year commission. But when his arrival had been delayed they'd asked Trent to fill in for the five days until Smith could get there. Though he'd just finished a stint in India, Trent had thankfully not minded his vacation being delayed until Smith showed up.

Not long after Trent had left to start his vacation, though, the GPC called to tell her they had discovered that Smith had falsified his credentials. No way would she have him work here now.

And, because problems came in multiples, they had a very sick little boy whose life just might depend on getting surgery pronto. If only John Adams, her right-hand man for everything to do with the hospital and school, hadn't been off getting supplies today. Charlie would've sent him to drag Trent back to take care of the little boy, saving her from enduring an hour's drive in close quarters with the man. That was, if he hadn't flown off to wherever he was going next.

Anxiety ratcheting up another notch, Charlie almost called Trent again, knowing there was little point. Then she spotted the airport in the distance. Shoving down the gas pedal, hands sweating, she slithered and bumped her way down the road, parked nearly sideways and ran inside.

Relief at seeing him still sitting there nearly made her knees weak. And, of course, that weakness had nothing to do with again seeing the gorgeous man she'd enjoyed a one-night stand with just hours ago. Memories of what they'd spent the night doing filled her cheeks with hot embarrassment, and she wished with all her being she'd known their last kiss this morning wouldn't really be good-bye. She wished she had known before she'd fallen into bed with him. If she had, she most definitely would have resisted the delicious taste of his mouth and the all too seductive smile.

He was slouched in a hard chair, his long legs stretched out in front of him, a Panama hat pulled over his face with just his sensuous lips visible. Lips that had touched every inch of her body, mortified heat rushed back to her face. Even sitting, his height made him stand out among the passengers sprawled everywhere in the airport. A battered leather bag sat next to his feet. His arms were folded across his chest and he looked sound asleep.

Dang it, this was all too awkward. She squirmed with discomfort at the very same time her nerve-endings tingled at the pleasure of seeing him again. Disgusted with herself, she took a deep breath, stepped closer and kicked his shoe. "Wake up. We need to talk."

She saw him stiffen, but other than that he didn't move, obviously pretending he hadn't heard her. What—he thought she'd come all this way just to kiss him goodbye again? Been there, done that and now it was over between them. This was about business, not pleasure. But with that thought instantly came other thoughts. Thoughts of all the pleasure she'd enjoyed with him last night, which made her even more annoyed with herself.

"I know you're not asleep, Trent Dalton. Look at me."

She kicked him in the ankle this time, figuring that was sure to get his attention.

"Ow, damn it." He yanked back his leg and his finger inched up the brim of his hat until she could see the nearly black hair waving across his forehead. His light blue eyes looked at her, cautious and wary. "What are you doing here, Charlotte?"

"I'm here because you wouldn't answer your stupid cell phone."

"I turned it off. I'm on vacation."

"If you'd left it on, I wouldn't have had to spend an hour driving here, worried I wouldn't catch you before you left. We have to talk."

"Listen." His expression became pained. "It was great being with you, and moving on can be hard, you know? But going through a long-drawn-out goodbye will just make it all tougher."

"We can't say goodbye just yet."

"I'm sorry, Charlotte. I have to leave. I promise you'll be fine."

Of all the arrogant... Did he really think women had a hard time getting over him after one night of fun? Fabulous fun, admittedly, but still. She felt like conking him on the head. "Sorry, but you have to come back."

"I can't," he said in a soft and gentle voice, his blue eyes now full of pity and remorse. "We both knew we only had one night together. Tomorrow will be better. It will. In a few weeks, you'll forget all about me."

"You are so incredibly full of yourself." She couldn't control a laugh that ended in a little snort. The man was unbelievable. "Our fling was over the second you kissed me goodbye, tipped your hat and left with one of your adorable smiles and the "maybe see ya again sometime, babe" parting remark. What would make you think I had a problem with that? That's not why I'm here."

He stared at her, and she concentrated on keeping her

expression nonchalant, even amused. She wasn't about to give him even a hint that she would think about him after he was gone.

"So why are you here, then?"

"I'm throwing out the new surgeon."

"Throwing him out?" Trent sat up straight. "What do you mean?"

"The GPC contacted me to tell me they found he'd falsified his credentials. That he'd had his license suspended in the U.S. for alcohol and drug use—over-prescribing of narcotics."

"Damn, so he's a loose cannon." He frowned. "But that doesn't mean he's not a good surgeon."

"Just because we're in the middle of West Africa doesn't mean our docs shouldn't be top notch. The GPC left it up to me whether I wanted him to work for us or not. And I refuse to have someone that unethical, maybe even doped up, working on our patients."

"So when is the GPC sending a new surgeon?"

"As soon as possible. They think they can get someone temporary like you were in a few days, no more than a week. Then they'll round up a doc who can be here for the year. All you have to do is come back until the temp gets here, or a day or two before."

"I can't. I just spent a solid year in India and I need a break before I start my new job in the Philippines. I have vacation plans I can't change."

She had to wonder what woman those plans might be with. "I don't believe your vacation is more important to you than your job."

"Hey, the only reason I worked twelve straight months was to pay for my vacation."

"Yeah, right." She made a rude sound in her throat. "Like you couldn't make tons more money as a surgeon in the U.S., paying for vacations and country club memberships and fancy cars. Nobody works in a mission hospital for the money."

"Maybe I couldn't get a job in the U.S." His normally laughing eyes were oddly serious.

"Mmm-hmm." She placed her hands on the arms of his seat and leaned forward, her nose nearly touching his. The clean, manly scent of him surrounded her, making her heart go into a stupid, accelerated pit-pat. But she wasn't about to back down. "So, I never did ask—why *do* you work exclusively in tiny hospitals all over the world, pulling up stakes every year? Most docs work for the GPC part-time."

"Running from the law." His lips were so close, his breath touching her skin, and more than anything she wanted to close that small gap and kiss him one more time. "Murdered my last girlfriend after she followed me to the airport."

She had to chuckle even as she watched his eyes darken, showing he still felt the same crazy attraction she felt. That she'd felt the first second she'd met him. "I always knew you were a dangerous man, Trent Dalton. I just didn't realize quite how dangerous."

Just as she felt herself leaning in, about to kiss his sexy mouth against her will, she managed to mentally smack herself. Straightening, she stepped back.

"So. We have an immediate problem that can't wait for you to think about whether playing golf or chasing skirts, or whatever you do on vacation, is more important than my little hospital."

"What problem?"

"We've got a seven-year-old boy who's got a hot appendix. Thomas is afraid it will rupture and says he doesn't have the skill to handle it."

"Why does he think it's his appendix? Even if it is, Thomas is a well-trained tech. I was impressed as hell at the great job he does on hernias."

"Hernias aren't the same thing as an appendix, which I think you know, Dr. Dalton. Thomas says he's sure that's what it is—that you're the only one who can do it. And to tell you that the last thing the kid needs is to get septic."

His brow lowered in thought before he spoke. "What are his symptoms?"

"His mother says he hasn't eaten for two days. He's been feverish—temp of one-hundred-point-four—and vomiting."

"Belly ache and vomiting? Maybe it's just the flu."

"The abdominal pain came first, then the vomiting."

"Has the pain moved?"

"From his umbilicus to right lower quadrant." She slapped her hands back onto the chair arms. Was the man going to ask questions all day in the hope of still getting away from here? "Listen, Trent. It's been thirty-six hours. If the appendix doesn't come out, it's going to rupture. I don't need to tell you the survival rates of peritonitis in this part of the world."

A slow smile spread across Trent's face before he laughed. "Maybe *you* should do the surgery. Why the hell didn't you become a doctor?"

"I can get doctors. I can't get somebody to run that hospital. So are you coming?"

He just looked at her, silent, his amusement now gone. The worry on his face touched her heart, because she was pretty sure it was on her behalf—that he didn't want to come back because she might get hurt, which she'd bet had happened often enough in his life as a vagabond doctor.

As though it had a mind of its own, her palm lifted to touch his cheek. "I've only known you a few days, but that's enough time to realize you're a man of honor. I'm sure you'll come take care of this little boy and stick it out until we can get someone else. A one-night fling was all it was meant to be for either of us—anything more would be pointless and messy. From now on, our relationship is strictly professional. So let's go before the boy gets sicker."

His hand pressed against the back of hers, held it a moment against his cheek then lowered it to gently set her away from him. "You're good, I'll give you that." He unfolded from the chair and stood, looking down at her. "But I can only stay a few more days, so don't be trying to guilt me into more than that. I mean it."

"Agreed." She stuck out her hand to seal the deal, and he wrapped his long, warm fingers around hers. She gave his hand a quick, brisk shake then yanked her own loose but didn't manage to erase the imprint of it.

It was going to be a long couple of days.

As the car bounced in and out of ruts on the way back to the hospital, Trent glanced at the fascinating woman next to him while she concentrated on her driving. The shock of seeing Charlotte's beautiful face at the airport had nearly knocked the wind out of him. The face he'd seen all morning as he'd waited to get away from it.

He stared at her strong, silky eyebrows, lowered in concentration over eyes as green as a Brazilian rainforest. Her thick brown hair touched with streaks of bronze flowed over her shoulders, which were exposed by the sleeveless shirts she liked to wear. He nearly reached to slide his fingers over that pretty skin, and to hell with distracting her from driving.

He sucked in a breath and turned his attention back to the road. How could one night of great sex have seemed like something more than the simple, pleasant diversion it was supposed to have been?

"The road is worst these last couple miles, so hang on to your hat," she said, a smile on the pink lips whose imprint he'd still been feeling against his own as he'd sat in that damned airport for hours.

"You want me to drive?"

"Uh, no. We'd probably end up around a tree. You stick with doctoring and let me handle everything else."

He chuckled. The woman sure took her role as hospital director seriously, and to his surprise he enjoyed it. How had he never known he liked bossy women?

"So, where were you headed?" Charlotte asked.

"Florence." But for once he hadn't known what the hell he was going to do with himself for the three weeks the GPC gave doctors off between jobs. Getting in touch with one of his old girlfriends and spending time with her, whoever it might be, in London, Thailand or Rio until his next job began was how he always spent his vacation.

"Alone? Never mind. Pretend I didn't ask."

"Yeah, alone." She probably wouldn't believe it, but it was true. He hadn't called anyone. He couldn't conjure the interest, which was damned annoying. So he'd be spending three weeks in Italy all by his lonesome, with too much time to think about the fiery woman sitting next to him. The woman with the sweet, feminine name who preferred going by the name of a man.

Charlotte. Charlie. If only he could have three weeks of warms days and nights filled with her in Florence, Rome and the Italian Riviera—with her sharp mind, sense of humor and gorgeous, touchable body. Last night had been… He huffed out a breath and stared out of the window. Not a good idea to let his thoughts go any further about *that* right now.

At least there hadn't been a big, dramatic goodbye. Seeing tears in those amazing green eyes of hers and a tremble on her kissable lips would have made him feel like crap. He had to make sure that during the next few days he kept his distance so there would be no chance of that happening. Which wouldn't be easy, since he'd like nothing more than to get her into bed again.

He looked out over the landscape of lush green hills and trees that led to the hospital compound and realized he hadn't got round to asking Charlotte how she'd ended up here. "You never did tell me how your family came to be missionaries in Liberia. To build all this."

"My great-grandparents were from North Carolina. My great-grandfather came from a family of schoolteachers and missionaries, and I'm told that when he and his new wife were barely twenty they decided to head to Africa to open a school. They came to Liberia because English is the primary language. Three generations later, we're still here."

"They built the whole compound at once?" The hard work and commitment so many missionaries had put into their projects around the world amazed him.

"The hospital came about twenty years after they built the house and school in 1932. I've always loved the design of that house." She gave him a smile. "Since Liberia was founded by freed slaves, my great-grandparents brought the Southern antebellum style with them. Did you know that antebellum isn't really an architectural style, though? That in Latin it means 'before war'? It refers to homes built before the U.S. Civil War. Sadly ironic, isn't it? That the same could be said for here in Liberia too." She was talking fast, then blushed cutely. "And you probably didn't want or need a history lesson."

"Ironic's the word," he said, shaking his head. "I've never worked here before. What the civil wars have done to this country is… Heck, you can't begin to measure it."

"I know. Unbelievable how many people died. What the rest have had to live with—the chaos and terror, the shambles left behind. The horrible, disfiguring injuries." Her voice shook with anger, her lips pressed in a tight line. "Anyway, nothing can fix the past. All we can do is try to make a difference now."

"So, your great-grandparents moved here?" he prompted.

A smile banished her obvious outrage. "Apparently my great-grandmother said she'd only move here if she could make it a little like home. They built the house, filled it with beautiful furniture and even got the piano that's still in the parlor."

"And Edwardses have been here since then? What about the wars?"

"The wars forced my parents to leave when I was little and go back to the U.S. Eventually we moved to Togo to start a new mission. The hospital and school here were badly damaged by gunfire and shrapnel, but the house was just in bad disrepair, stripped of things like the windows and sinks. John Adams and I have been fixing it up, but it's third on the list of priorities."

He couldn't imagine how much work—and money— it was taking to make that happen. "So what made you want to resurrect all this? It's not like you really remember living here."

"Just because I haven't lived here until now doesn't mean my roots aren't here, and John Adams's roots. They are. They're dug in deep through our ancestors, and I intend to keep them here. My plan is to grow them, expand them, no matter what it takes."

"No matter what it takes? That's a pretty strong statement." He'd met plenty of people committed to making things better for the underprivileged, but her attitude was damned impressive.

"These people deserve whatever it takes to get them the help they need." Her grim tone lightened as they pulled in front of the one-story, painted cement hospital. "Let's get the boy fixed up. And, Trent…" Her green eyes turned all soft and sweet and he nearly reached for her. "Thanks for coming back. I promise you won't be sorry."

CHAPTER TWO

THOMAS HOVERED IN the clinic outside the door to the OR, looking anxious. "Where is the patient?" Trent asked. "Is he prepped and ready, or do you want me to examine him first?"

"I thought he should be examined again, to confirm my diagnosis. But he's in the OR. With Dr. Smith."

"Dr. Smith?" Charlie asked. What the heck was he doing in there? Hadn't she asked him to stay out of the hospital and away from patients? "Why? Did you tell him Dr. Dalton was coming back?"

"Said since he was here and the boy needs surgery fast he'd take care of it."

Anger welled up in Charlie's chest at the same time she fought it down. She supposed she should give Smith kudos for stepping up despite the circumstances, instead of being mad at her refusal to let him work there. "Well, that's…nice of him, but I'll tell him our other surgeon is here now."

"Give me a minute to scrub," Trent said as he grabbed a gown and mask and headed to the sink.

Charlie hurried into the OR to find Don Smith standing over the patient who was being attended to by the nurse anesthetist but not yet asleep. She stopped short and stared at the anxious-looking little boy. Could there be some confusion, and this wasn't the child with the hot appendix?

His eyelid and eyebrow had a red, disfiguring, golf ball-sized lump that nearly concealed his eye completely. How in the world could he even see?

Her chest tightened and her stomach balled in a familiar pain that nearly made her sick. The poor child looked freakish and she knew all too well how horribly he must be teased about it. How terrible that must make him feel.

She lifted a hand to her ear, now nearly normal-looking after so many years of disfigurement. Her hand dropped to her side, balled into a fist. How wrong that he'd lived with this, when a kid in the States never would have. More proof that the project so dear to her heart was desperately needed here.

"Is this the child with appendicitis?" At Dr. Smith's nodded response, she continued. "I appreciate you being willing to take care of this emergency, but my other surgeon is here now. Help yourself to breakfast in the kitchen, if you haven't already."

"I'm here. Might as well let me operate. You'll see that I'm a capable and trustworthy surgeon. I want you to change your mind."

"I won't change my mind. Losing your license and falsifying your credentials is a serious matter, which frankly shows me you're *not* trustworthy."

"Damn it, I need this job." Smith turned to her, his face reddening with anger. "I told everyone I'd left to do humanitarian work. If I don't stay here, they'll know."

"So the only reason you want to work here is to save your reputation?" Charlie stared at him. "Hate to break it to you, but your drug addiction and loss of license is already public record in the States."

"For those who've looked. A lot of people I know haven't."

"I'm sorry, Dr. Smith, but you'll have to leave. Now."

"I'm doing this surgery and that's all there is to it. Nurse, get the anesthesia going." He turned to the patient and, without another word, began to swab the site while the child stared at him, his lip trembling.

Anger surged through her veins. Who did this guy think he was? The jerk wouldn't have spoken to her like this if she'd been a man. "Janice, don't listen to him. Stop this instant, Dr. Smith. I insist—"

Trent stepped between Charlie and Smith, grasping the man's wrist and yanking the cotton from his hand. "Maybe you didn't hear the director of this hospital. You're not doing surgery here."

"Who the hell are you?" Smith yanked his arm from Trent's grasp. "You can't tell me what to do."

"No, but she can. And I work for her." Trent had a good three inches on the man, and his posture was aggressive, his usually warm and laughing eyes a cold, steely blue. "I know your instincts as a doctor want what's best for this boy, which is immediate attention to his problem. Your being in here impedes that. So leave."

Smith began to sputter until his gaze met Trent's. He stepped back and looked away, ripping off his gown and mask and throwing them to the floor. "I can't believe a crappy little hospital in the middle of nowhere is too stupid to know how good I am. Your loss."

He stalked out and Charlie drew in a deep, slightly shaky breath of relief. She'd thought for a minute that Trent would have to physically take the guy out, and realized she'd completely trusted him to do exactly that. Then she pulled up short at the thought. She was in charge of this place and she couldn't rely on anyone else to deal with tough situations.

"Thanks, but you didn't need to do that. I had it handled."

Trent looked down at her with raised brows. "Did you, boss lady?"

"Yeah, I did."

He reached out, his long-fingered hand swiping across

her shoulder, and she jerked, quickly looking down. "What, is there a bug on me?"

"No—a real big chip. I was wondering what put it there." His lips tipped up as his eyes met hers.

What? Ridiculous. "I don't have a chip on my shoulder. I'm just doing my job."

"Accepting help is part of being head honcho, you know." Those infuriatingly amused eyes lingered on her before he turned to the nurse. "Have you administered any anesthesia yet?"

"No, doctor."

"Good." He rolled a stool to the gurney and sat, that full smile now charmingly back on his face as he drew the sheet further down the child's hips. "So, buddy, where's it hurt?"

He pointed, and Trent gently pressed the top of the boy's stomach, slowly moving his hand downward to the right lower quadrant.

"Ow." The boy grimaced and Trent quit pressing his flesh to give the child's skinny chest a gentle pat.

"Okay. We're going to fix you up so it doesn't hurt any more. What's your name?"

"Lionel." The child, looking more relaxed than when Charlie had first come into the room, studied Trent. With his small index finger, Lionel pushed his bulging, droopy eyelid upward so he could see. "My belly will be all better? For true?"

"For true." Trent's smile deepened, his eyes crinkled at the corners as his gaze touched Charlie's for a moment before turning back to the child. "Inside your body, your appendix is about the size of your pinky finger. It's got a little sick and swollen, and that's what's making your belly hurt. I'm going to fix it all up while you sleep, and when you wake up it won't hurt any more. Okay?"

"Okay." Lionel nodded and smiled, showing a missing front tooth.

"But, before we take care of your sore belly, I want to talk about your eye." Trent gently moved the boy's hand before his own fingers carefully touched all around the protrusion on and above the eyelid. "Can you tell me how long it's been like this?"

Lionel shrugged. "I'nt know."

"I bet it's hard to see, huh?"

"Uh-huh. I can't see the football very well when we're kicking around. Sometimes Mommy has tape, though, and when she sticks it on there to hold it up that helps some."

"I'm sure you look tough that way. Scare your opponents." Trent grinned, and Lionel grinned back. "But I bet you could show how tough a player you are even more if you could see better."

Charlie marveled at the trusting expression on the child's face, how unquestioning he seemed as he nodded and smiled. She shifted her attention to Trent and saw that his demeanor wasn't just good bedside manner. The man truly liked kids, and that realization ratcheted the man's appeal even higher. And Lord knew he didn't need that appeal ratcheted up even a millimeter.

"Is your mother around? Or someone I can talk to about fixing it at the same time we fix your belly?"

"My mommy brought me. But I don't know where she is right now."

As his expression began to get anxious again, Trent leaned in close with a smile that would have reassured even the most nervous child. "Hey, we'll find her. Don't worry."

He stood and took a few steps away with a nod to Charlie. When they were out of hearing distance, he spoke in an undertone. "I want to take care of his hemangioma and we might as well do it while he's under for the appendix. There'll be a lot of bleeding to control, and I'll get him started on antibiotics first. After I remove the tumor, I'll decide if it's necessary to graft skin from his thigh to make it look good. In the States, you wouldn't do a clean surgery and an appendix at the same time, but I can do it with no problems."

"If it wouldn't be done in the States, we're not doing it here." Didn't he get that this was why she'd thrown Smith out?

"If you think mission doctors don't do things we wouldn't do in the U.S., you have a lot to learn." No longer amused, a hint of steel lurked within the blue of his eyes. "Here, I can follow my gut and do what's best for the patient, and only what's best for the patient. I don't have to worry about what an insurance company wants, or cover my ass with stupid protocol. You can either trust me to know I'm doing what's best for Lionel, or not. Your call."

Charlie glanced at the boy and knew better than anyone that they were talking about a tremendously skilled procedure, one that would require the kind of detailed work and suturing a general surgeon wouldn't be capable of. "I'm in the process of getting a plastic surgery center together. That's what the new wing of the hospital is for. How about we suggest to his mommy that she bring him back when it's operational?"

He shook his head. "First, there's a good chance they live far away and it won't be easy to get back here. Second, he's probably had this a long time. The longer we wait, the more likely the possibility of permanent blindness. Even if it is fixed later, if his brain gets used to not receiving signals from the eye that part of his brain will die, and that'll be it for his vision. Not to mention that in West Africa a person is more susceptible to getting river blindness or some other parasitic infection in the eye. What if that happened and he ended up blind in both eyes? Not worth the risk."

"But can you do it? Without him still looking…bad? The plastic surgery center will be open soon. And a plastic surgeon would know how to do stuff like this better than you would."

"You don't know who you're dealing with here." His eyes held a mocking laugh. "He'll look great, I promise."

She stared at him, at his ultra-confident expression, the lazy smile. Would she be making a mistake to let him fix the hemangioma when in just a few weeks she was supposed to have a plastics specialist on board?

She looked back at Lionel, his finger still poked into the disfiguring vascular tumor so he could see out of that eye as he watched them talk. She looked at the trusting and hopeful expression on his small face. A face marred by a horrible problem Trent promised he could fix.

"Okay. You've convinced me. Do it."

CHAPTER THREE

HOURS PASSED WHILE Trent worked on Lionel. Worry over whether or not she'd made the right decision made it difficult for Charlie to sit in her office and do paperwork, but she had to try. With creditors demanding a big payment in three weeks, getting that funding check in her pocket for the new wing from the Gilchrist Foundation was critical.

She made herself shuffle through everything one more time. It seemed the only things that had to happen to get the money were a final inspection from a Gilchrist Foundation representative and proof she had a plastic surgeon on board. Both of which would happen any day now, thank heavens.

So how, in the midst of this important stuff, could she let her attention wander? She was thinking instead about the moment five days ago when Trent had strolled into this office. Thinking about how she'd stared, open-mouthed, like a schoolgirl.

Tall and lean, with slightly long, nearly black hair starkly contrasting with the color of his eyes, he was the kind of man who made a woman stop and take a second look. And a third. Normally, eyes like his would be called ice-blue, but they'd been anything but cold; warm and intelligent, they'd glinted with a constant touch of amusement. A charming, lopsided smile had hovered on his lips.

When she'd shaken his hand, he'd surprised her by tugging her against him in a warm embrace. Disarmed, she'd found herself wanting to stay there longer than the brief moment he'd held her close. She'd found her brain short-circuiting at the feel of his big hands pressed to her back; his lean, muscled body against hers; his distinctive masculine scent.

That same friendly embrace had been freely given to every woman working in the hospital, young and old, which had left all of them grinning, blushing and nearly swooning.

No doubt, the man was dynamite in human form, ready to blast any woman's heart to smithereens.

But not Charlie's. She'd known the second he'd greeted her with that genial hug that she would have to throw armor over that central organ. She'd cordially invited him to join her and John Adams for dinners, enjoying his intelligence, his amusing stories and, yes, his good looks and sophistication. She'd been sure she had everything under control.

But the night before he was to leave, when that embrace had grown longer and more intimate, when he'd finally touched his lips to hers, she hadn't resisted the desire to be with him, to enjoy a light and fun evening. An oh-so-brief diversion amidst the work that was her life. And, now that circumstances required they be in close contact for a little longer, there was no way she'd let him know that simply looking at him made her fantasize about just one more night. That was not going to happen—period.

Yes, their moment together was *so* last week. She smirked at the thought, even though a ridiculous part of her felt slightly ego-crushed that he, too, wanted to steer clear of any possible entanglement.

But that was a good thing. The man clearly loved women, all women. She'd known she was just one more notch in his travel bag, and he'd been just another notch in the fabric of her life too. Except that there hadn't been too many opportunities for "notching" since she'd finished grad school and come back to Africa.

She had to grin as she grabbed the info she wanted to share with the teachers at the school. Notching: now there was a funny euphemism for great sex if ever there was one.

She was so deep in thought about the great sex she'd enjoyed last night that she stepped into the hall without looking and nearly plowed her head into Trent's strong biceps.

"Whoa." His hands grasped her shoulders as she stumbled. "You late for lunch or something?"

Her heart sped up annoyingly as he held her just inches from his chest. "Is that a crack about how much I like to eat?"

"Not a crack. I've just observed that when you're hungry you don't let anything get between you and that plate."

She looked up into his twinkling blue eyes. "Hasn't anyone ever told you that women don't like people implying they're gluttons?"

"No negative implications from me. I like a woman who eats." His voice dropped lower. "I like the perfect and beautiful curves on your perfect and beautiful body."

As she stared up at him, the light in his eyes changed, amusement fading into something darker, more dangerous.

Desire. It hung between them, electric and heavy in the air, and Trent slowly tipped his head towards hers.

He was going to kiss her. The realization sent her heart into an accelerated tempo. A hot tingle slipped across her skin as his warm breath touched her mouth, and she lifted her hands to his chest, knowing she should push him away, but instead keeping her palms pressed to his hard pecs.

She couldn't let it happen, only to say goodbye again in a few more days. He'd made it clear he felt the same way. But, as she was thinking all that, she licked her lips in silent invitation.

His hands tightened on her arms as though he couldn't decide whether to pull her close or push her away, then he released her. "Sorry. I shouldn't have said that. I forgot we're just casual acquaintances now." He shoved his hands in his pockets, his expression now impassive, all business. "I wanted to let you know it went well with Lionel."

She sucked in a breath, trying to be equally business-like, unaffected by his potent nearness and the need to feel his lips on hers one more time. "He's okay? You fixed the hemangioma? And he looks good?"

"You probably wouldn't think he looks good."

Her stomach dropped. "Why...? What, is it messed up?"

He laughed. "No. But right now it's sutured and swollen and would only look good to a zombie. Or a surgeon who knows what he's doing. We'll take the bandage off in a few days."

"Okay. Great." She pressed her hand to her chest, hoping to goodness it really had turned out all right. Hoping the hard beat of her heart was just from the scare, and not a lingering effect of the almost-kiss of a moment ago.

"Can you unlock your car for me? I need to get my stuff out and take it to my room."

"Of course. But I didn't tell you—even though I'm not happy with our Dr. Smith, I couldn't exactly throw him out on the streets until his flight leaves tomorrow. So he's going to be staying in the room you were in for just tonight."

"What? I'm not staying at your house again."

It was hard not to be insulted at the horror on his face. 'Goodbye, Charlie' took on a whole new meaning with Trent. "Sorry, but you're sleeping on a rollaway here in my office. I don't want you staying in my house, either."

"You do too." His lips quirked, obliterating his frown.

"Uh, no, I don't. Like I said before, you're an egomaniac. Somebody needs to bring you down a peg or two, and I guess it's going to be me."

"Thanks for your help. I appreciate it more than you know." That irritating little smile gave way to seriousness.

"And it's good we're on the same page. Second goodbyes can get…sticky."

"Agreed. And you're welcome. I'll get my keys now before I head to the school." She turned, so glad she hadn't fallen into an embrace with the conceited guy. His long fingers grasped her elbow and the resulting tingle that sped up her arm had her jerking it away.

"Wait a second. You're going up to the school?"

"Yes. I have some things I want to go over with the teachers. I'm having lunch with them and the kids."

He was silent, just looking at her with a slight frown over those blue eyes, as though he couldn't decide something. He finally spoke. "Mind if I come along? I'd like to see it, and I'm not needed in the clinic right now."

"Sure. If you want." She shrugged casually. Did the man have to ponder whether seeing the school was worth being with her for a few hours? Or was she being hypersensitive?

She led the way down the short hall into the soupy, humid air, making sure to stand on Trent's left so her good ear would be closest to him. "The kids love visitors. But we'll be walking, so don't be surprised if you get a little muddy."

"Glad I'm not wearing my designer shoes today. Then again, I could've taken them off. Nothing like a little mud between the toes."

The thought of cool, squishy mud on bare feet, then playing a little footsie together, sounded strangely appealing, and she rolled her eyes at herself as they trudged up the road to the schoolhouse. Maybe she needed to try and find a local boyfriend to take off this edge she kept feeling around Trent. He reached for the binder of papers she was carrying and tucked it under his arm.

"So you were the boy who earned points by carrying a girl's books to school? Why doesn't that surprise me?"

"Hey, I looked for any way to earn points. Carrying books was just one of them."

"I can just imagine. So what other ways did you earn points?" And why couldn't she just keep her mouth shut? "You know, never mind. I don't think I want to know."

"You already know some of them." He leaned closer as they walked, the scent of him teasing her nose. "But a few things got me more points than others. For example, my famous shoulder-rubs always scored big."

The memory of that shoulder rub came in a rush of clarity—them naked in her bed, sated and relaxed, the ceiling fan sending cool whispers of air across their skin. Her breathing got a little shallow and she walked faster.

"One of the ground rules is to stop with the references to last night. Got it?"

"I wasn't referring to anything but the shoulder rub I gave you at your office desk. Can I help it if your mind wants to go other places?"

She scowled at the bland innocence on his face. The man was about as far from innocent as he could be. "Mmm-hmm. So, when you mention back rubs, you don't picture me naked?"

His slow smile, his blue eyes dancing as he leaned closer, made her feel a little weak at the knees. "Charlotte, you can bet I frequently picture you naked." His gaze held hers, then slid away to the road. "Again, I'm sorry. That was inappropriate. Let's talk about the school. Did you open it at the same time as the hospital?"

Phew; she had to stop just blurting out what she was thinking, though he seemed to have the same problem. Good thing he changed the subject, or she just might have melted down into the mud.

"John Adams concentrated on getting the school open while I focused on the hospital. His daughter, Patience—I think you met her?—will be going to school next year, so he's been pretty excited about the project. They live in a small apartment attached to the school, so she'll probably be there today. She loves to hang out in the classrooms and pretend she can read and write."

"Patience is a cutie. She and I bonded over ice-cream." His eyes always turned such a warm blue when he talked about children; it filled her chest with some kind of feeling she didn't want to analyze. "So, is John from here?"

"Just so you know, he's always gone by both his first and last name. I'm not sure why." She smiled. "John Adams's parents both worked with my parents here. They left too when the war broke out. Their family and mine met up again in Togo and, since he's just a few years older than I am, he's kind of like a brother. And I love Patience like I would a niece."

"Where's her mother?"

"She died suddenly of meningitis. It was a terrible shock." She sighed. "Moving here with me to open this place has been a fresh start for John Adams and Patience, and hugely helpful to me. I couldn't have done it alone."

"I've been wondering where your funding is coming from. The GPC's been cutting back, so I know they can't be floating cash for the whole hospital."

"We've shaken down every possible donor, believe me. The school was as big a shambles as the hospital, and usually donor groups focus on one or the other. But we managed to get the building reasonably repaired and the basics in—desks and supplies and stuff. We opened with thirty primary-school-aged kids enrolled and have almost a hundred now." She shook her head. "It's not nearly enough, though, with half a million Liberian kids not attending school at all. And sixty percent of girls and women over fifteen can't read or write."

He frowned. "Is it as hard to raise cash for a school as it is for a hospital?"

"It's all hard. But I'm working on getting a donation from a church group in the States that'll help us hire a new teacher and have enough food for the kids' lunches. I'm excited. It looks like it's going to come through." Charlie smiled at Trent, but his expression stayed uncharacteristically serious. "We hate turning families away, but can't just endlessly accept kids into the program, you know? It's not fair to the teachers or the students to have classrooms so big nobody gets the attention they need. So I'm sure hoping it works out."

"How soon will you know?"

"In the next day or two, I think."

His expression was oddly inscrutable. "Be sure to tell me if the donation comes through or not, okay?"

"Okay." She had to wonder why he wanted to know, but appreciated his interest. "As for the hospital, I'm supposed to get a giant check from the Gilchrist Foundation as soon as the new wing is ready to go, thank heavens."

He stopped dead and stared at her. "The Gilchrist Foundation?"

"Yes. You've heard of them?"

"Yeah. You could say that."

CHAPTER FOUR

"Has the Gilchrist Foundation donated to hospitals you've worked at before?" Charlotte asked. "Did they come through with their support? I'm a little worried, because we're scraping the bottom of the barrel just to get the wing finished."

Trent looked into her sweet, earnest face before turning his attention to the verdant landscape—not nearly as vivid and riveting as the color of her eyes. "They're a reputable organization."

"That's good to hear." She sounded slightly breathless, her footsteps squishing quickly in the mud, and he slowed his stride. He resisted the urge to grasp her arm to make sure she didn't slip and fall. "I heard they were, but they're making us jump through some hoops to get it."

He almost asked *what hoops?*, but decided to keep out of it. The last thing he wanted was to get involved with anything to do with the Gilchrist Foundation. Or for Charlotte to find out his connection to it. "It'll be fine, I'm sure. So, this is it." He looked up at the one-storey cement building painted a golden yellow, the windows and door trimmed in a brick color. "Looks like you've done a nice job restoring it."

"It took a lot of money and manpower. It was basically a shell, with nothing left inside. The windows were gone and there were bullet holes everywhere. John Adams and I are pretty proud of how it turned out."

As they reached the wooden door of the school he saw Charlotte glance up at the sky, now filling with dark-gray clouds. "Looks like rain's coming, and I wasn't smart enough to bring an umbrella. Sorry. We won't stay too long."

"I'm not made of sugar, you know. I won't melt," he teased. Then the thought of sugar made him think of her sweet lips and the taste of her skin. It took a serious effort to turn away, not to pull her close to take a taste.

They left their muddy shoes outside before she led the way in. Children dressed in white shirts with navy-blue pants or skirts streamed from classrooms, laughing and chattering.

"Mr. Trent!" Cute little Patience ran across the room, the only one in a sleeveless dress instead of a uniform. "Mr. Trent, you bring me candy?"

"Sorry, Miss Impatience, I don't have any left." She wrapped her arms around his leg and the crestfallen expression on her face made him wish he'd brought a whole lot more. Too bad he hadn't known he'd be here longer than a few days.

"How about gum?"

He laughed and swung her up into his arms. "Don't have any of that left either." He lowered his voice. "But, next time you're at the hospital, I'll sneak some pudding out of the pantry for you, okay?"

"I heard that." Charlotte's brows lifted. "Since when are you two best friends? Dr Trent just got here a few days ago."

"Mr. Trent and me are good friends, yes." The girl's arms tightened around his neck, which felt nice. Kids didn't want or expect anything from you but love. And maybe candy too, he thought with a smile. There weren't too many adults he could say that about.

"Patience and I share a fondness for that chocolate pudding."

"Hmm." A mock frown creased Charlotte's face as she leaned close to them. "I didn't know you were stealing supplies, Dr Dalton. I'm going to have to keep an eye on you."

"What's the punishment for stealing?" His gaze dropped from her amused eyes to her pink lips. Maybe if he stole a kiss he'd find out.

"I don't think you want to know." Her eyes were still smiling and he found himself riveted by the glow of gold and brown flecks deep within that beautiful green.

"Miss Edwards!" Several kids ran their way. "You coming to see our play this Wednesday? Please come, Miss Edwards!"

Charlotte wrapped her arms around their shoulders in hugs, one after another, talking and smiling, making it obvious she wasn't a distant director around here; that she put in a lot of face time, truly cared about these kids. That impressed the hell out of him. He'd seen a lot of hospital directors in his day, even some in mission hospitals, who were more focused on the bottom line and making donors happy than they were about helping the patients they existed for.

Trent set Patience back on her feet. "Have you been doing any more drawing? You know I like to see your art." Nodding enthusiastically, her short legs took off running back down a hall.

He watched Charlotte with the kids. He'd never worked at a mission hospital that included a school in its compound. He hadn't been able to resist a chance to peek at it and see what they were accomplishing, even when he knew it wasn't the best idea to spend much time with Charlotte.

The whole reason he'd come was to see the school children, but he found it impossible to pull his attention from the smiling woman talking to them. He'd teased her about picturing her naked, but the truth was he couldn't get the vision of her out of his mind at all: clothed or unclothed, smiling and happy or ready to kick someone's ass.

Damn it.

Time to get his mind on the whole reason he was here— to find out what the kids were learning and how the school helped them. Charlotte patted a few of the children and turned her attention to him.

"Is this where we're going to eat?" he asked. The room was filled with folding tables that had seats attached, and some of the children were already sitting down.

"What, are you hungry? And you were making fun of me wanting lunch."

He grinned at her teasing expression. Man, she was something. A fascinating mix of energy, passion and determination all mixed in with a sweet, soft femininity. "I haven't eaten since five a.m. But I still wouldn't knock someone over in a hallway in search of a meal."

"As if I could knock you over, anyway." She took the binder from him and gestured to the tables. "Find a seat. I'll be right back."

Standing here, looking at all the bright-eyed and happy kids, he was annoyed with himself. Why hadn't it hadn't ever occurred to him to donate some of his fortune to this kind of school? He'd focused on giving most of his anonymous donations to the kind of hospitals he worked in. To those that medically served the neediest of humans in the world.

But that was going to change to include helping with education—a whole other kind of poverty. Not having access to learning was every bit as bad as having no access to health care.

"Here's my picture, Mr. Trent!" Patience ran up with a piece of construction paper crayoned with smiling children sitting at desks, one of them a lot bigger than the others.

"Who's this student?" he asked, pointing at the large

figure he suspected just might be a self-portrait of the artist.

"That's me." Patience gave him a huge smile. "I sit in class sometimes now. Miss Jones said I could."

"I bet you're really smart. You'll be reading and writing in no time." And to make that happen for a lot more kids, he'd be calling his financial manager pronto.

"Yes." She nodded vigorously. "I go to read right now."

She took off again and he chuckled at how cute she was, with her little dress and pigtails flying as she ran. He sat at one of the tables and saw the kids eyeing him, some shyly, others curious, a few bold enough to come close. Time for the tried and tested icebreaker. He pulled a pack of cards from his pocket and began to shuffle. "Anybody want to see a card trick?"

Faces lit, giggles began and a few children headed over, then more shoved their way in, until the table was full and the rest stood three-deep behind them.

"Okay." He fanned the cards face down and held them out to a grinning little girl with braids all over her head. "Pick a card. Any card." When she began to pull one out, he yanked the deck away. "Not that one!"

Startled, her grin faded and she stared at him.

"Just kidding." He gave her a teasing smile to let her know it was all in fun, and she giggled in relief as the other children hooted and laughed. He held out the fanned deck again. "Pick a card. I won't pull it away again, honest. Look at it, show it to a friend, but don't let me see it. Then stick it back in the deck."

The girl dutifully followed his directions. He did his sleight-of-hand shuffling before holding up a card. "Is this it?" He had to grin at how crestfallen they looked as they shook their heads. "Hmm. This it?"

"No, that's not it." She looked worried, like it would somehow be her fault if the trick didn't work.

"Well, you know third time's a charm, right? *This* is the

one you picked." He held up what he knew would be the card she'd chosen, and everyone shrieked and whooped like he'd pulled a rabbit from a hat or held up a pot of gold.

"How you do that, mister?" a boy asked, craning his neck at the card deck as though the answer was written there.

"Magic." One of the best parts about doing the trick was showing the kids how to do it themselves. "How about we do it a few more times? Then I'll teach you exactly how it's done."

Before Charlie and the teachers even got back to the common room, the sound of loud talking and laughter swept through the school's hall. Mariam, the headmistress, pursed her lips and frowned. "I'm sorry, Miss Charlotte. I don't know why they're being so rowdy. I'll take care of it."

"It's fine. They're at lunch, after all." Though she was pretty sure it hadn't been served yet. Curious as to what was causing all the excitement, she walked into the room, only to stop in utter surprise at the scene.

Looking ridiculously large for it, Trent sat at a table completely surrounded by excited children, like some handsome Pied Piper. He was holding up cards, shuffling and flicking them, then handing them to kids who did the same, all the while talking and grinning. As she came farther into the room, she could hear the students bombarding him with questions that he patiently answered more than once.

She hadn't seen this side of Trent before. Yes, she'd seen his gentle bedside manner with Lionel, his obvious caring for the boy. Still, she couldn't help but be amazed at the connection she was witnessing. So many of the children in this school had been traumatized in one way or another and a number of them were orphaned. Yet, to watch this moment, you'd think none of them had a care in the world other than having a fun time with whatever Trent was sharing with them.

She moved closer to the table. "What's going on here?"

One of the older boys waved some cards. "Mr. Trent is showing us card tricks, Miss Edwards! See me do one!"

"I'd love to." Her eyes met Trent's and her heart fluttered a little at the grin and wink he gave her. "But you should call him Dr Trent. He's a physician working at the hospital for a few days."

"Dr Trent?" Anna, a girl in the highest grade they could currently offer, looked from Charlie to Trent, her expression instantly serious. "You a doctor? My baby brother is very sick with the malaria. Mama Grand has been treating him, but we're worried. Would you care if I go get him and bring him here for you to see?

"Can your mommy or grandmother bring him to the hospital?" Charlie asked.

Anna shook her head. "Mommy is away working in the rice fields. But I can get him and carry him there if that is better."

"How old is he?" Charlie asked.

"Six years old, Ma."

Charlie knew many of these kids walked miles to get to school, and didn't want Anna hauling an ill six-year-old that kind of distance. Not to mention that she could hear rain now drumming hard on the roof of the school. "How about if I drive and get him? You can show me where you live."

Trent stood. "It's pouring outside. I'll go back and get the car and pick you two up, then we'll just see him at your home."

Charlie pulled her keys from her pocket and headed for the door. "It's okay, I'll just…"

In two strides, Trent intercepted her and snagged the keys from her hand. "Will you just let someone else help once in a while? Please? I'll be right back."

Charlie watched as he ducked out of the doorway into the heavy rain, all too aware of the silly surge of pleasure she felt at the way he insisted on taking on this problem, never mind that she could handle it herself. Well, not the medical part; she was thankful he'd be able to contribute his expertise as well as the nurses and techs at the hospital.

Her car pulled up in no time and, before she and Anna could come out, Trent had jogged to the door with an open umbrella and ushered Anna into the backseat. Water slid down his temples and dripped from his black hair as he opened the passenger door for Charlie. "You're riding shot-gun this time, boss lady."

"It's my car. I know how to drive in this kind of weather."

He made an impatient sound. "Please just get in and stop arguing."

She opened her mouth to insist, but saw his set jaw and his intent blue eyes and found herself sliding into the seat, though why she let him tell her what to do she wasn't sure. It must have something to do with the man's over-whelming mojo.

She wasn't surprised that he proved more than compe-tent at the wheel, despite the deepening mud and low vis-ibility through the torrential rain. Even in good weather, this thinning road was barely more than a track through the bush. It couldn't really be called a road at all at the moment.

A group of crooked, heartbreakingly dilapidated zinc shacks appeared through the misty sheets of rain, and the distinctive smell of coal fires used for cooking touched Charlie's nose.

"It's up here. That one," Anna said, pointing.

The car slid to a stop. "Sit tight for a sec," Trent said. He again grabbed the umbrella and brought it to their side of the car before opening Charlie's door.

"I'm not made of sugar, you know. I won't melt," Charlie said, repeating what he'd said to her earlier as she climbed out to stand next to him.

"You sure about that? I remember you tasting pretty sweet." Beneath the umbrella, he was so close she could feel his warmth radiating against her skin. The smell of the rain, mud, coal fires and Trent's own distinctive and appealing scent swirled around her in a sensory overload. His head dipped and those blue eyes of his met hers and held. She realized she was holding her breath, struck by a feeling of the two of them being completely alone in the world as the rain pounded a timpani concerto on the fabric above their heads.

Her heart did a little dance as his warm breath touched her face. Blue eyes darker now, his head dipped closer still until his lips slipped across hers, whisper-soft, clinging for a moment. "Yeah. Like sugar and honey."

His lids lowered in a slow blink before he straightened, turning to open Anna's door.

The child led the way as they trudged up to a group of metal shacks, giving Charlie's heart rate a chance to slow. Why had he kissed her when they'd agreed not to go there? Probably for the same reason she'd wanted him to—that overwhelming chemistry between them that had caught fire the first day they'd met.

They approached a shack that looked as though it must be Anna's home. A cooking pot sat over a coal fire with what smelled like cassava simmering inside. The shack's crooked door was partially open, and Anna shoved it hard, scraping it along the muddy ground until they could step inside the dark interior.

A young child lay sleeping on a mat on the dirt floor and another was covered with a blanket, exposing only his or her outline. An older woman with a brightly patterned scarf on her head sat on a plastic chair, stitching some fabric.

"Mama Grand, I bring a doctor to see Prince."

The woman looked at them suspiciously. "No need, Anna. I use more healing herbs today and Prince will be fine soon."

Anna twisted her fingers and looked imploringly at her. "Please. The doctor is here, so let him see if Prince is getting better."

Trent stepped forward and gave one of his irresistibly charming smiles to the woman. "I'm sure you're doing a fine job taking care of Prince. But the boss lady, Miss Edwards here, will be mad at me if I don't have work to do today. She might not even pay me. Can I please just take a look at your fine little one while I'm here?"

The woman's stern expression softened slightly, and after a moment she inclined her head. Charlie had a hard time suppressing a smile. Trust Trent to turn it around to make Charlie look like the bad guy, and to know exactly how to twist it so his being there was no reflection on the older woman's treatments.

Trent crouched down and looked back at the woman. "Is this Prince hiding under the blanket? May I look at him?"

She nodded again, and Trent reached to pull the blanket from the small, huddled shape. He quickly jerked back when he saw the exposed child.

"What the…?" Trent's face swung towards Charlie, his eyebrows practically reaching his hair.

CHAPTER FIVE

THE LITTLE BOY looked like a ghost. Literally. He'd been covered head to toe in white paint. In all Trent's years of seeing crazy and unusual things around the world, he'd never seen this.

Charlotte covered a small smile with her fingertips, and he could tell she wanted to laugh at whatever the hell his expression was. Could he help it if it startled him to see the little guy looking like that?

"It's a common home remedy here for malaria. The sick person is painted white as part of the cure."

"Ah." Trent schooled his features into normal professionalism and turned back to the boy. He touched his knuckles to the sleeping child's cheeks, then pressed the child's throat, both of which were hot and sweaty. The boy barely opened his eyes to stare at him before becoming wracked by a prolonged, dry cough. When the cough finally died down, Trent leaned close to him with a smile he hoped would reassure him. "Hi, Prince. I'm Dr Dalton. How do you feel? Anything hurting?"

Prince didn't answer, just slid his gaze towards his sister. She knelt down next to him and touched her hand to the boy's thin shoulder. "It's okay, Prince. Dr Dalton is here to help you get better."

"Have you had belly pain or diarrhea?" The boy still just stared at him, looking scared, as though Trent was the one who looked like a ghost. Maybe the child was delirious. "Anna, do you know about any belly pain? Has he been confused or acting strange?"

She nodded. "He did complain about his tummy hurting. And he has been saying silly things. I think he seems the same as when I had the malaria—shaking and feeling very hot and cold."

"Trent, how about I drive back to the compound and get the malaria medicine?" Even through the low light, he could see the green of Charlotte's eyes focused intently on his. "I'll bring it back here; maybe we won't have to scare him by taking him to the hospital."

He shook his head, not at all sure this was malaria. "If he has belly pain, it might be typhoid, which requires a different kind of antibiotic. Hard to tell with a child who's sick and obtunded like he is. The only way to know for sure is if we take him back to the hospital and get a blood test—see if it shows the parasites or not."

"No hospital." The older woman's lips thinned. "If de boy go, he will never come back."

Obviously, the poor woman had lost someone she loved. "I'll watch over him myself," Trent said. "I promise to keep him safe."

"Mama Grand, no boys are kidnapped any more. For true. The war is over a long time now."

Damn, so that was what she was worried about. He could barely fathom that boys this young had been kidnapped to be soldiers, but knew it had happened so often that some parents sent their children out of the country to be safe, never to see them again.

He stood and reached for the woman's rough and gnarled hand. "I understand your worries. But it's important that Prince have a test done that we can only do at the hospital. I promise you that I will care for Prince and look after him like I would if he were my own child, and return him to you when he's well. Will you trust me to do that?"

The suspicious look didn't completely leave the woman's face, but she finally nodded. Trent didn't want to give her a chance to change her mind and quickly gathered Prince in his arms, wrapping the blanket around him as best he could.

"You want to come with us, Anna? You don't have to, but it might make Prince feel more comfortable," Charlotte said.

"Yes. I will come."

"Are you going to hold Prince so I can drive, or do you want to take the wheel?" he asked Charlotte as they approached the car.

"You know the answer to that." Her gorgeous eyes glinted at him. "You're in the passenger seat, Dr. Dalton."

He had to grin. "You really should address this little controlling streak of yours, Ms. Edwards. Find out why relinquishing power scares you so much."

"It doesn't scare me. I just trust my own driving over anyone else's."

"Mm-hm. One of these days, trying to control the direction the world spins is going to weigh heavy on those pretty shoulders of yours. Drive on, boss lady."

Tests proved that Prince did indeed have typhoid, and after a couple days he'd recovered enough to return home. Charlie was glad that Trent's expertise had led him to insist the child be tested, instead of just assuming it was malaria, as she had.

She was also glad that, in the days that had passed since Trent had come back, she'd managed to stop thinking about him for hours at a time. Well, maybe not *hours*. Occasionally, the man sneaked into her thoughts. Not her fault, since she wasn't deaf and blind—okay, a little hard of hearing in that one ear of hers she was grateful to have it at all.

His voice, teasing and joking with the nurses and techs,

sometimes drifted down the hall to her office. His distinctively tall form would occasionally stride in front of her office on his way from the clinic to the hospital ward until she decided just to shut the darn door.

She'd made a conscious effort to stay away from the hospital ward where she might run into him. She got dinner alone at home, or ate lunch at her desk so she wouldn't end up sitting with him in the kitchen. She spent time at the school instead of here, where thoughts of him kept invading her brain, knowing he was somewhere nearby.

It helped that Trent had kept their few interactions since the brief kiss in the rain short and professional. When the man said goodbye, he sure meant it, never mind that she felt the same way. Thank heavens he'd be leaving again in the next few days so she wouldn't have to suffer the embarrassment of thinking about all they'd done in their single night together.

Her door opened and her heart gave an irritating little kick of anticipation that it just might be his blue eyes she'd see when she looked up.

But it was John Adams standing there. "Any word yet on the funding for another teacher?"

She smiled and waved a paper. "Got the green light. I'm sending the final forms today, and they said we should get a check in about a month. Is the woman you've been training going to work out?"

"Yes, most definitely." He dramatically slapped a hand to his barrel chest. "She is smart and beautiful and I am in love with her. Thanks to God I can officially offer her a job."

"You're starting to remind me of ladies' man Dr Dalton. No mixing business with pleasure." A flush filled her cheeks as soon as the words were out of her mouth, since she'd done exactly that, and the pleasure had been all too spectacular.

"Yes, ma'am." He grinned. "Anyway, I also stopped to tell you to come look at our little patient this morning."

"What little patient?"

"Lionel. The one with appendicitis and the hemangioma—or who used to have a hemangioma. You won't believe what Trent's done with it."

Alarm made Charlie's heart jerk in her chest. She'd worried from the moment she'd agreed to let Trent take care of such a delicate procedure. Had he messed it up? She'd checked on the child a couple of times, but a patch had still covered his eye. "What do you mean? Is it going to have to be redone when we get a plastic surgeon in here?"

"Just come and see."

She rose and followed him to the hospital ward, her fears eased a bit by John Adams's relaxed and smiling expression. Still, she couldn't shake the feeling that she might have made a big mistake.

Lionel's head was turned towards his mother, who sat by his bedside, and Charlie found herself holding her breath as they came to stand beside him.

"Show Miss Charlotte how well you're seeing today, Lionel," John Adams said.

The boy turned his head and she stared in disbelief.

The patch had been removed and, considering he'd had surgery only days before, he looked shockingly, amazingly normal.

The angry red bulge that had been the vascular tumor was gone. His eyebrow and eyelid, other than still being bruised and slightly swollen from surgery, looked like any other child's. His big, brown eye, wide and lit with joy, was now completely visible, just like his other one.

"Oh, my. Lionel, you look wonderful!" She pressed her hands to her chest. "Can you see out of that eye?"

"I can see! Yes, I can! And Mommy show me in the mirror how handsome I look!"

"You even more handsome than your brothers now,

boyo, and I told them so," his mother said with a wide smile.

Tears stung Charlie's eyes as she lifted her gaze to the child's mother and saw so many emotions on the woman's face: happiness; profound relief; deep gratitude.

All because of Trent.

Where was the man? Had he seen the amazing result of his work? She turned to a smiling John Adams. "Has Dr Dalton seen him since the patch was removed?"

"Oh, yes. He took it off himself this morning."

"Dr. Dalton told me he gave me special powers, too, like Superman." The child's face radiated excitement. "Said I have x-ray vision now."

His mother laughed. "Yes, but Dr. Dalton was just joking and you know it. Don't be going and telling everyone that, or they'll expect you to see through walls."

"I can see so good, I bet I can see through walls. I bet I can."

"Maybe you'll become a doctor, Superman, who can see people's bones before you operate." Trent's voice vibrated into the room from behind Charlie's back. "That would be pretty cool."

"I want to be a doctor like you. I want to fix people like you do, Dr. Trent."

Trent's smile deepened as he came to stand next to Charlie. "That's a good goal, Lionel. If you study hard in school, I bet you can do anything you set your mind to."

Charlie stared at Trent, looking so relaxed, like all this was no big deal. Maybe it wasn't to him, but it was to her, and to Lionel and to his mother. A very, very big deal.

"I can't believe the wonderful job you did," she said, resting her hand on his forearm. "You told me I didn't know who I was dealing with and you were sure right."

"Now she learns this, just before I'm ready to leave."

The twinkle in his eyes, and his beautifully shaped lips curved into that smile, were practically irresistible. She again was thankful that he would be heading out of her life very soon before she made a complete fool of herself. "Good thing you don't have x-ray vision too. Hate to think what you'd use it for."

"Checking for broken bones, of course." His smile widened. "What else?"

She wasn't going where her mind immediately went. "Probably to decipher a bank-vault combination, so you could go on vacation without working a solid year. Speaking of which, the GPC says a general surgeon should be here in a matter of days, so you can have them schedule your flight out of here soon."

"Great."

The relief on his face was obvious and she hated that it hurt a tiny bit to see it. "I can't help but wonder, though, why are you working as a general surgeon when you can do things like this?"

His smile faded. "You think plastic surgery has more value? More than saving someone's life? I don't."

"It's a different kind of value: changing lives; changing the way someone is viewed, the way they view themselves. You have an obvious gift for this, a skill many would envy." Did he not see how important all that was? "Your focus should be on plastic surgery. On helping people that way."

"The way other people view a person, what they expect them to be and who they expect them to be, shouldn't have anything to do with how they view themselves." He took a step back and pulled his arm away from her touch. She hadn't known those eyes of his were capable of becoming the chilly blue that stared back at her. "Excuse me, I have a few other patients to check on."

She frowned as she watched him walk through the hospital ward. What had she said to make him mad?

"I have things to do too," John Adams said. But, like

her, his gaze followed Trent, his expression thoughtful. "Bye, Lionel. See you later, Charlie."

"Okay. Listen, can you come have dinner tonight at my house? I'd like to talk to you about some things."

He nodded and headed off. Charlie watched Trent examining another patient and could only hope John Adams came up with a good idea for how she could accomplish her newest goal—which was to encourage Trent to perform surgery on a few patients in the day or two he'd still be here, patients who'd needed reconstructive surgery long before the plastic surgery wing had even been conceived.

She knew how desperately some of these people needed to have their lives changed in that way. Not to mention that it wouldn't hurt for her to have a few "before and after" photos that would impress the Gilchrist Foundation with what they were already accomplishing. And, really, how could Trent object?

As she headed back to her office, her cell phone rang and she pulled it from her pocket. "Charlotte Edwards."

"Hey, Charlie! It's Colleen. How're things going with Trent Dalton?"

"With Trent?" What the heck? Did the gossip vine go all the way to GPC headquarters? Besides, nobody here knew she and Trent had briefly hooked up...did they? "What do you mean?"

"Is it working out that he came back until the new temp gets there?"

Phew. Thank heavens she really didn't have to answer the first question, though their moment together was history anyway. "He's doing a good job, but I know he wants to move on. Do you have a final arrival date for the new doc?"

"Perry Cantwell has agreed to come and we're finalizing his travel plans. Should be any day now." Her voice got lower, conspiratorial. "Just tell me. I've seen photos of Trent that make me salivate, but is he really as hunky as everyone says? Whenever I talk to him on the phone his voice makes me feel all tingly."

If just his voice made Colleen feel tingly, Charlie hated to think what would happen if she saw him in person. She wasn't about to confess to Colleen that, despite his reputation, she'd fallen into bed with him for one more than memorable night. While she felt embarrassed about that now, she still couldn't regret it, despite unexpectedly having to work with him again. "He's all right. If you like tall, good-looking surgeons who flirt with every woman in sight and think everything's amusing."

"Mmm. Sounds good to me if the surgeon in question has beautiful black hair and gorgeous eyes." The sound of a long sigh came through the phone and Charlie shook her head. She supposed she should feel smug that über-attractive Trent had wanted to spend a night with her. But, since he likely had a woman in every port, that didn't necessarily say much about her personal sex appeal. "I actually have his new release papers on my desk to send out today. Are you going to hit on him before he leaves?" Colleen asked. "Might be a fun diversion for a couple days."

Been there, done that. And, yes, it had been—very fun. Keeping it strictly professional now, though, was the agreed goal. "I've got tons to do with the new wing opening any time now. And my dad called to say he's coming some time soon to see how things are going with that."

"Actually, I have some bad news about the new wing, I'm afraid." Colleen's voice went from light to serious in an instant.

Her heart jerked. "What bad news?"

"You know David Devor, the plastic surgeon we had lined up to work there?" Colleen asked. "He has a family emergency and can't come until it's resolved, which could be quite a while."

"Are you kidding me? You know I have to have someone here next week, Colleen! The Gilchrist Foundation made it clear we won't get the funding we need until I have at least one plastic surgeon on site."

"I know. I'm doing the best I can. But I'm having a hard time finding a plastic surgeon who wants to work in the field. I'm turning over every rock I can, but I can't promise anybody will be there until Dr. Devor is available. Sorry."

Lord, this was a disaster! Charlie swiped her hand across her forehead. The hospital was scarily deep in the red from getting the new wing built. It had to be opened pronto.

"Okay." She sucked in a calming breath. "But I have to have a plastic surgeon, like *now*."

"I know, but I just told you—"

"Listen. I need you to hold off a day or two before you send Trent's release papers. Give me time to talk to him about maybe staying on here. If he agrees, you can send Perry Cantwell somewhere else."

There was a long silence on the phone before Colleen spoke. "Why? Cantwell's expecting to come soon. And I can't just hold Trent's paperwork. He's already filled in for you twice and is way overdue for his vacation. I don't get it."

"I found out Trent's a plastic surgeon, not just a general surgeon." She gulped and forged on. "If Devor can't be here, I have to keep Trent here at least long enough to get the wing open and the funding in my hand. Otherwise I won't be able to pay the bank, and who knows what'll happen?"

"Maybe he'll agree to stay."

"Maybe. Hopefully." But she doubted he would. Hadn't he made it more than clear that he wanted to head out ASAP? The only reason he'd come back for a few days was because of how sick Lionel had been. "All I'm asking is for you to hang onto his release papers until I can talk to him."

"Charlie." Colleen's voice was strained. "You're one

of my best friends. Heck, you got me this job! But you're asking me to do something unethical here."

"Of course I don't want you to do anything you feel is unethical." This was her problem, not Colleen's, and it wouldn't be right to put her friend in the middle of it. "Just send them out tomorrow instead of today, address them to me and I'll make sure he gets them. That will give me time to contact the Gilchrist Foundation and see if they'll make an exception on their requirements before the donation check is sent. If they won't, I'll try to get their representative to come right now while Trent's still here. I'm pretty sure the guy is close—somewhere in West Africa. I'll go from there."

Colleen's resigned sigh was very different from the one when she'd been swooning over Trent earlier. "All right. I'll wait until tomorrow to send the release papers and finalize Perry's travel plans to give you time to talk to Trent. But that's it."

"Thanks, Colleen. You're the best." Charlie tried to feel relieved but the enormity of the problem twisted her gut. "Hopefully they'll send the funding check even if we don't have a plastic surgeon here yet and we'll be out of the woods. I'll keep you posted."

The second she hung up, she searched for the Gilchrist Foundation's number. What would she do if they flat out said the conditions of the contract had to be met, which would probably be their response? Or if they couldn't send their representative here immediately? If the GPC couldn't find a plastic surgeon to come in any reasonable period of time, the whole hospital could fold. Every dollar of the GPC's funding, and all the other donations she'd managed to round up, had been spent renovating the nearly destroyed building, buying expensive equipment and hiring all the nurses, techs and other employees needed to run the place. And the money she'd borrowed to build the new wing was already racking up interest charges.

Adrenaline rushed through her veins as she straightened in her seat. The end justified the means. The hospital absolutely could not close and the plastic surgery wing had to open. It had to be there to help all the people who had horrible, disfiguring injuries left from the war. It had to help all the kids living with congenital deformities, like cleft palates, which they'd never have had to live with if they'd been born somewhere else. Somewhere with the kind of healthcare access she was determined to offer.

If the Gilchrist Foundation insisted on sticking with the contract stipulations, she had no choice but somehow to make sure Trent stayed on until the money was in her hand.

CHAPTER SIX

TRENT HAD BEEN relieved that Charlotte wasn't in the hospital commons for dinner. He hadn't wanted to make small talk with her while pretending he didn't feel insulted by her words.

The book he tried to read didn't hold his attention, and he paced in the sparse little bedroom until he couldn't take the confinement anymore. He headed into the humid, oppressive air and strode down the edges of the road, avoiding the muddy ruts as best he could.

When he'd first met Charlotte, he'd been impressed with her enthusiastic commitment to this place, to her vision of what she wanted it to become. And, as they'd spent time together, she'd seemed interested in his life. She'd asked smart and genuine questions, and he'd found himself opening up, just a little—sharing a few stories he usually kept to himself, nearly talking to her about things he just plain didn't talk about.

But, when it came right down to it, she was like anyone else: a woman who questioned who he was and why he did what he did. Who didn't particularly care what he wanted from his own life. Had she asked him *why* he didn't do plastic surgery exclusively? Expressed any interest in his reasons?

No. She'd just made the same snap judgment others had made. She'd told him what he should do, convinced she knew. Exactly like the woman in his life he'd trusted completely to have his back, to know him, to care.

A trust he'd never give again.

It was disappointing as hell. Then again, maybe this was a good thing. Maybe it would help him feel less drawn to her.

He needed to see this as a positive, not a negative. And, when he left in just a day or two, maybe the peculiar closeness he felt to her would be gone. He'd leave and hope to hell his world would be back to normal.

He kept walking, not having any particular destination in mind, just feeling like he didn't want to go back to that room and smother, but not wanting to chit-chat with people in the hospital either. Maybe he should call up a buddy on the phone, one of the fraternity of mission doctors who understood his life and why he did what he did. They always made him laugh and put any personal troubles in perspective.

As he pulled his cell from his pocket, he noticed a light up ahead. Had he somehow got turned around? He peered through the darkness and realized he was practically at Charlotte's doorstep. Had his damned stupid feet unconsciously brought him here because he'd been thinking of her so intently?

About to turn off on a different path, he was surprised to see little Patience bound out the door, holding a rope with a tiny puppy attached, bringing it down the porch steps. It sniffed around before doing its business, and Trent wanted to laugh at the look of distaste on the little girl's face as she picked up a trowel from the steps.

He didn't want to scare her by appearing out of nowhere in the darkness. "You have a new dog, Patience? When did you get it?"

She looked up at him and smiled. "Hi, Mr. Trent! Yes, Daddy got me another doggie. After my poor Rex was killed by that ugly, wild dog, I been asking and asking.

He finally said yes, and my friends at the school like having her to play with too."

"What's its name?"

"Lucky—cos I'm lucky to have her. Except for this part." The look of distaste returned, replacing the excitement as she gripped the trowel. "I promised Daddy I would do everything to take care of her."

He scratched the cute little pup behind the ears, chuckling at the way its entire hind end wagged in happiness before he reached for the trowel. A little doggie doo-doo was nothing compared to many of the things he'd dealt with. "Here. I'll do it for you this time." With a grateful smile, Patience let him dig a hole to bury the stuff. "What are you and your new pup doing here at Charlotte's house?"

"Miss Charlie fixed dinner for me and Daddy. They talking about work."

The door opened and the shadow of John Adams's big body came onto the porch. "Somebody out here with you, Patience?"

"Mr. Trent, Daddy. He's meeting Lucky."

"Trent. Come on inside. Charlie and I were just talking about you."

Damn. He didn't want to know what they were talking about and didn't particularly want to see Charlotte. But his feet headed up the steps, with Patience and the puppy trailing behind.

The warm glow of the quaint room, full of an odd mix of furniture styles and colorful rugs, embraced him as he stepped inside and he wondered what it was about this old house that gave it so much charm and appeal. An old upright piano against a wall had open sheet music leaning against the stand. Charlotte, dressed in sweatpants and a T-shirt, was curled on a sofa, and she looked up, her lips slightly parted.

The surprise in her green eyes gave way to a peculiar mix of wariness and warmth. As their gazes collided, as he took in the whole of her silken hair and lovely face, he was instantly taken back to earlier today. To their physical closeness beneath that umbrella. To the moment it had felt like it was just the two of them, alone and intimate. Despite all his promises to himself and to her, he'd found himself for that brief second leaning in to taste her mouth, to enjoy the sweetness of her lips.

Being in her house again sent his thoughts to the moment they'd sat on that sofa and kissed until both of them were breathless, ending up making love on the floor. Why did this woman make him feel this way every time he looked at her?

"Trent. I'm…surprised to see you."

Could she be thinking about their time together here too? "I was taking a walk. Then saw Patience and her new pup."

Patience ran to the piano and tapped on the keys, bobbing back and forth as the dog pranced around yapping. "Lucky likes to sing and dance, Mr. Trent, see?"

"She has a beautiful voice." As he smiled at the child, he was struck by a longing to go to the piano himself. To finger the keys as he'd done from the time he was six, until he'd left the U.S. for good. He hadn't realized until he'd first walked into this room with Charlotte a few days ago how much he'd missed playing.

"Miss Charlie has a very pretty voice," Patience enthused. "Please play for us, Miss Charlie. Play and sing something!"

Charlotte shook her head. "Not tonight. I'm sure Mr. Trent doesn't want a concert."

Her cheeks were filled with color. Surely the ultra-confident Charlotte Edwards wasn't feeling shy about performing for him? "Of course I'd like to hear you. What's your favorite thing she plays, Patience?" Surprised at how much he wanted to hear Charlotte sing, he settled himself into a chair, figuring there was no way she could say no to the cute kid.

"That song from church I like: *How Great Thou Art*. Please, Miss Charlie?" The child's hands were clasped together and for once she stood still, her eyes bright and excited.

As Trent had predicted, Charlotte gave a resigned sigh. "All right. But just the one song."

She moved to the piano, and his gaze slid from her thick hair to the curve of her rear, sexy even in sweatpants. Her fingers touched the keyboard, the beginning measures a short prelude to the simple arrangement before she began to sing. Trent forgot about listening to the resonance of the piano's sounding board and heard only the sweet, clear tones of Charlotte's voice, so moving and lovely his chest ached with the pleasure of it.

When the last piano note faded and the room became quiet, he was filled with a powerful desire for the moment to continue. To never end. Without thought, he found himself getting up from the chair to sit next to Charlotte, his hip nudging hers to scoot over on the bench.

"Let's sing a Beatles tune Patience might like," he said, his hands poised over the keys, his eyes fixed on the beautiful green of hers. He began to play *Lean On Me* and, when she didn't sing along, bumped his shoulder into hers. "Come on. I know you know it."

"Yes, Miss Charlie! Please sing!" Patience said, pressing her little body against Charlotte's leg.

John Adams began to sing in a slightly off-key baritone before Charlotte's voice joined in, the dulcet sound so pure it took Trent's breath away. When his hands dropped from the keyboard, he looked down into Charlotte's face, seeing Patience next to her, and he was struck with a bizarre and overwhelming vision of a life he hadn't even considered having: a special woman by his side, a family to love; the ultimate utopia.

"That was wonderful," she said, her eyes soft. "I didn't know you could play. Without music, even."

He drew in a breath to banish his disturbing thoughts. "I was shoved onto a piano bench from the time I was little, and had a very intimidating teacher who made sure I was classically trained." He grinned. "I complained like heck sometimes when I had to practice instead of throwing a football around with my friends, but I do enjoy it." He hadn't realized how much until just now, shoulder to shoulder with her, sharing this intimate moment.

"Play something classical. Simple modern songs are about it for my repertoire."

He thought about what he'd still have memorized from long ago and realized it shouldn't be Bach or Haydn. That it should be something romantic, for her. "All right, but don't be surprised if I'm a little rusty. I bet you know this one: Debussy's *Clair de Lune*."

When the last notes of the piece died away, the softness on her face only inches from his had him nearly leaning in for a kiss, forgetting everything but how much he wanted to, and the only thing that stopped him was Patience's little face staring up at him from next to the keyboard.

"I liked that, Mr. Trent!"

"Yes." Charlotte's voice was a near-whisper as she rested her palm on his arm. "That was…beautiful."

As he looked at the little girl, and stared into Charlotte's eyes filled with a deep admiration, the whole scene suddenly morphed from intimate and perfect to scary as hell. Why was he sitting here having fantasies about, almost a longing for, a life he absolutely did not want?

Abruptly, he stood. He needed to get out of there before he said or did something stupid.

Hadn't he, just earlier this evening, been annoyed and disappointed in her? Then one more hour with her and, bam, he was back to square one with all those uncomfortable and mixed feelings churning around inside. What the hell was wrong with him, he didn't want to try to figure out.

"You know, I need to head back to my quarters. I'm going to get most of my things packed up. I'm sure the GPC let you know the new temp is coming in just a day or two?"

"We need to talk about that." The softness that had been in her eyes was replaced by a cool and professional expression. He was damned if it didn't irritate him when he should be glad. "We have an issue."

"What issue?"

She glanced at John Adams before returning her attention to Trent. "Come sit down and we'll talk."

"I'm happy standing, thanks." Her words sounded ominous and he folded his arms across his chest, the disconcerting serenity he'd been feeling just a moment ago fading away like a mirage in the desert. He had a feeling this conversation had something to do with him staying longer, and that wasn't happening.

"The new temp is delayed. I'm not sure when he's going to get here." She licked those tempting lips of hers and, while her expression was neutral, her eyes looked strained and worried. As they should have.

"I told you not to try to guilt me into staying. I can't be here indefinitely." Except, damn it, as he said the words the memory of the comfort he'd felt a moment ago, that sense of belonging, made it sound scarily appealing.

"I'm not trying to guilt you into anything. I'm simply telling you the facts. Which are that, if you leave, there won't be another surgeon here for a while."

"The GPC does a good job finding docs to fill in when there's a gap. Especially when a place has nobody. Besides, you have Thomas here, and he does a great job on the hernias and other simple procedures."

"But what if we get another appendicitis case? Ectopic pregnancy? Something serious he can't handle?"

He shoved his hands into his pockets and turned to pace across the room, staring out the window at the heavy blackness of the night sky. Looking anywhere but into her pleading eyes.

"If there's one thing I've learned over the years, it's that one person can't save everybody who needs help, Charlotte. I'd be dead if I tried to be that person. Think about the ramifications of this for others, too: the longer I'm here, the more the snowball effect of docs having to fill in where I'm supposed to be next, which is the Philippines." He turned to her, hoping to see she understood what he was saying—not that the idea of staying here longer was both appealing and terrifying. "If the GPC hospital in the Philippines doesn't have anyone because I'm not there, is that okay? Better for patients there to die, instead of patients here?"

Her hands were clasped together so tightly her knuckles were white. "Just a couple of weeks, Trent. Maybe less, if it works out."

He shook his head. "I'm sorry, Charlotte. As soon as my release paperwork comes through from the GPC, I have to head out."

"Trent, all I'm asking is…"

The room that had felt so warm and welcoming now felt claustrophobic. He turned his attention to John Adams so he wouldn't have to look at her wide and worried eyes. "I have a few patients scheduled for surgery early, so I'm going to get to bed. If either of you know of patients needing surgery, you should schedule them in the next couple days before I leave." He scratched the dog behind the ears before he walked out the door, finding it impossible to completely stuff down the conflicting emotions that whirled within him.

As he walked through the darkness, a possible solution

struck him that would assuage his guilt. Maybe a phone call to an old friend would solve all his problems and let him move on.

CHAPTER SEVEN

"How the hell are you, Trent?"

Trent smiled to hear Chase Bowen's voice on the phone. He'd worked with Chase for a number of years in different parts of the world, and the man had been the steadiest, most committed mission doctor he'd ever met. Until a certain wonderful woman had swept into the man's life, their little one in tow, and had changed him into a committed dad rooted in the States.

"I'm good. Decided to try to get hold of you during my lunch break before I see some patients in the clinic this afternoon. How's Drew doing?" When he'd heard the shocking news that Chase and Dani's little boy had cancer, it had scared the crap out of him. Thank goodness they'd caught it in time and the prognosis was excellent.

"He's doing great." The warmth and pride in Chase's voice came through loud and clear. "Completely healthy now, swimming like a fish and growing like crazy. So where are you working?"

"I'm filling in as a temp here in Liberia, hoping to head off on vacation soon, but there are some issues getting a new doc here." A problem he knew Chase was more than familiar with.

"So who's the lucky woman vacationing with you this time? Where are you going?"

"Still figuring all that out." No reason to tell Chase

about his weird feelings, that he hadn't been able to find an interest in calling anyone. The man would laugh his butt off, then suggest he see a shrink. "How's Dani?"

"Wonderful. I haven't told you that Drew's going to have a baby brother or sister."

"That's great news. Congratulations." Of all the people he knew, Chase was the last one he'd ever have expected mostly to leave mission work to have a family. But he had to admit, the man seemed happy as hell. "You doing any mission stints at all?"

"Dani and I have gone twice to Honduras together, then I stayed for another week after she headed home. It's worked out well."

"You have any interest in coming to Liberia for just a week or so to fill in for me until the new doc gets here? The GPC needs me to head to the Philippines as soon as possible." Which wasn't exactly true, but he was going with it anyway, damn it.

"I don't know." Chase was silent on the line for a moment. "I'd really like to, but I'm not sure now's a good time. Dani's been a little under the weather, and I wouldn't want to leave her alone with Drew if she's not up to it. Let me talk to her and I'll call you back."

"Great. Give her a hug for me, and tell her I'm happy for both of you. And Drew too."

"Will do. Talk to you soon."

Trent shoved the phone in his pocket and headed back into the hospital. He'd known it was a long shot to think Chase might be able to fill in for him, but with any luck maybe it could still be a win-win. Chase could enjoy a short stint in Africa and Trent could shake the clinging dust of this place off his feet and forget all about Charlotte and her work ethic, spunkiness and warmth.

He thought about Dani, Chase and Drew and their little family that was about to grow. A peculiar sensation filled his chest and he took a moment to wonder what exactly it was. Then he realized with a shock that it was envy.

Envy? Impossible. He'd never wanted that kind of life: a wife who would have expectations of who you should be and how you should live. Kids you were responsible for. A life rooted in one place.

But there was no mistaking that emotion for anything else, and he didn't understand where the hell it had come from. Though Chase had never wanted that kind of life either—until he'd met a woman who had changed how he viewed himself.

The thought set an alarm clanging in his brain. He didn't want to change how he viewed himself. He'd worked hard to be happy with who he was and what he wanted from his life, leaving behind those who hadn't agreed with that view. Now wasn't the time to second-guess all that.

Resolutely shaking off all those disturbing feelings, he continued down the hospital corridor, hoping Charlotte's office door was closed, as it often was, since he had to walk by to get to the clinic. Unfortunately, the door was wide open and her melodic voice drifted into the hallway as she talked with John Adams.

"I'll be fine. I know how to use a gun, remember?"

"I'm not okay with that, Charlie. Patience and I'll pack a bag and move in for a few days until we're sure it was a one-time thing."

A gun? What was a one-time thing? He stopped in the doorway and looked in to see John Adams standing with his arms folded across his chest, a deep frown creasing his brow, and Charlotte staring back with her mulish expression in place.

"Except somebody needs to be at the school too, you know. After all the work and money we've put into the place, we can't risk it being wrecked up and having things stolen."

"What are you talking about?" Trent asked.

"This is not your concern, Trent. John Adams, please close the door so we can talk."

Trent stretched his arm across the door to hold it open. "Uh-uh. You want me to be stuck here for a while longer, you need to include me. What's going on?"

"Somebody broke into her house early this morning after she came to work. When she went there at lunch to get something, she found the door jimmied open and some things gone."

Trent stared at John Adams then swung his gaze to Charlotte. She frowned at him, her lips pressed together, but couldn't hide the tinge of worry in the green depths of her eyes. "What the hell? What was stolen?"

"A radio. The folding chairs I keep in a closet. Weird stuff. Thankfully, I had my laptop with me at work. It's not a big deal."

"It is a big deal." The protectiveness for her that surged in his veins was sudden and intense. "You can't stay there alone, period. The obvious solution is for John Adams to stay in their quarters at the school, and for me to stay with you until I leave."

Had those words really come out of his mouth? It would be torture to stay in her house with her, knowing she was close by at night in her bed. Bringing back hot memories of their night together. Making him think of the unsettling closeness and connection he'd felt while they'd sat at the piano together singing.

But there was no other option. Keeping her safe was more important than protecting himself from the damned annoying feelings that kept resurfacing.

"That's ridiculous, Trent." Her eyes still looked alarmed, but he was pretty sure it wasn't just about the break-in. "I'll be fine. Whoever it was probably just hit the place once and isn't likely to come back."

"You have no idea if that's true or not." He stepped to her desk and pressed his palms on it, leaning across until his face was as close to hers as hers had been to his at the airport. She smelled so damned good, and the scent of her and the lip gloss she was wearing made him want to find out what flavor gloss it was. "So, you never did tell me," he said, mimicking what she'd said to him at the airport. "What makes you so damned stubborn and resistant to accepting help when you need it? Except when it comes to the hospital, that is?"

"I'm not stubborn. I just don't think this is worth getting all crazy about."

"Maybe not. But it's not a hardship for me to stay at your house so you're not alone until we see if this is a one-time thing or not." So, yeah, that wasn't true. It would be a hardship to be so close to her without taking advantage of it, but no way was he leaving her at risk.

"Good." John Adams spoke from behind him. "Thanks, Trent. I appreciate it. I'm going back to the school now. See you both later."

He straightened. "I've got patients to see in the clinic then I'll get my things. See you back here at six."

"Seriously, Trent—"

"Six."

As he headed to the clinic, he was aware of a ridiculous spring in his step, while at the same time his chest felt a little tight. Obviously, his attraction to Charlotte was keeping the smarter side of his brain from remembering why he needed to keep his distance. And how the hell he was going to keep that firmly in mind while sharing her roof was a question to which he had to find an answer.

"So, Colleen, I'm all set!" Charlie forced a cheerful and upbeat tone to her voice. "Trent has agreed to stay on until the Gilchrist rep does his evaluation. So you can wait to schedule Perry Cantwell until then."

"That's great news for you, Charlie! So all your worries were for nothing."

The warmth in her friend's voice twisted her stomach into a knot. Lying to her felt every bit as bad as lying to Trent, but what choice did she have? "Yes, no worries." Oh, if only that were true.

"I'll let Perry know so he can plan his schedule. After the Gilchrist rep comes, give me a call to tell me how it goes."

"Will do. Thanks, Colleen." Charlie hung up and dropped her head into her hands.

How had her life become a disaster?

As if it wasn't enough to have the bank breathing down her neck, the plastic surgeon indefinitely delayed, Gilchrist insisting on the original stipulations of their agreement and having to skulk around lying to Trent and Colleen, she had a burglar who might come back and a gorgeous man she couldn't stop thinking about spending the night in her bed.

No. Not in her bed. In her spare bedroom. But that was almost as bad. Knowing his long, lean, sexy body was just a few walls away would be tempting, to say the least. But now there was an even better reason to steer clear of getting it on with him again for the days he was here.

She was pretty sure that if he knew she was delaying Perry Cantwell's arrival and had shoved his release papers beneath a pile on her desk he wouldn't take it lightly. In fact, she was more than sure that his easygoing smile would disappear and a side she hadn't seen yet would emerge—a very angry side— and she wouldn't even be able to blame him for it.

Her throat tight, Charlie took inventory of the new supply delivery, trying not to look at the big invoice that came with it. This whole deception thing felt awful, even more than she'd expected. But she just couldn't see another solution. Thank heavens the Gilchrist Foundation had said their representative should be here within the week. After they gave their approval and she got the check, Trent could be on his way. No harm, no foul, right?

The end justifies the means, she reminded herself again.

With a box of syringes in her arms, she stepped on a stool, struggling to shove the box onto a supply shelf, when a tall body appeared next to her. Long-fingered hands took the box and tucked it in front of another.

"Why don't you just ask for help from someone who's not as vertically challenged as you are?" Trent asked, his eyes amused, grasping her hand as she stepped off the stool.

Looking at his handsome, smiling face so close to hers, a nasty squeeze of guilt made it a little hard to breathe. She didn't even want to think about how that affable expression would change if he knew about her machinations.

"Just because I'm not tall doesn't mean I'm handicapped. And I'm perfectly capable of getting off a stool by myself."

"I know. I only helped you to see those green eyes of yours flash in annoyance. Amuses me, for some reason."

"Everything amuses you." Except, probably, liars.

"Not true. Burglars don't amuse me. So are we eating here, or at your house to crack heads if anybody shows up?"

His low voice made her stomach feel squishy, even though he was talking about cracking heads. "Nobody's going to show up. And I still don't think you need to come. I have a gun, and I doubt you're very good at cracking heads anyway."

"Don't count on that." The curve of his lips flattened and his eyes looked a little hard. "Anybody tries breaking into your house, you'll find out exactly how good I am."

The thought of exactly how good she knew he was at a number of things left her a little breathless. "I just want to be clear about the ground rules—"

"Dr. Trent." Thomas appeared in the doorway and Charlie put a little distance between her and Trent, not wanting to give the gossip machine any more ammo than they might already have. "There's a boy in the clinic whose mother brought him in because he's not eating. I did a routine exam, but I don't see anything other than a slightly elevated temperature. He is acting a little odd, though, and his mother's sure something's wrong, so I thought you should come take a look."

"Not eating?" Trent's brows lowered. "That's not a very significant complaint. Did you look to see if he has strep or maybe tonsillitis?"

"His throat looks normal to me."

"Hmm. All right." He turned his baby blues to Charlie. "Don't be going home until I come back. I mean it."

"How about if I come along? I haven't had time to visit the clinic for a while." She might not be in medicine, but the way doctors and nurses figured out a diagnosis always fascinated her. And she had to admit she couldn't resist the chance to watch Trent in action again.

"Of course, Ma," Thomas said, turning to lead the way.

CHAPTER EIGHT

THE BOY, WHO looked to be about ten years old, was sitting on the exam table with a peculiar expression on his face, as though he was in pain. "Hey, buddy," Trent said, giving him a reassuring smile. "Your mommy tells us you're having trouble eating. Does your stomach hurt?"

The child shook his head without speaking. Checking his pulse, Trent noted that he was sweaty, then got a tiny whiff of an unpleasant odor. It could be just that the child smelled bad, or it could be a symptom of some infection.

"Let's take a look in your throat." Using a tongue depressor, he studied the boy's mouth, but didn't see any sign of an abscess or a bad tooth. No tonsil problem or strep. Once Trent was satisfied that none of those were the problem, the boy suddenly bit down on the stick and kept it clamped between his teeth. "Okay, I'm done looking in your mouth. Let go of the stick, please."

The boy didn't budge, then started to cry without opening his mouth. Trent gently pressed his thumb and fingers to the boy's jaw to encourage him to relax and unclamp his jaw. "Let me take the stick out now and we'll check some other things." The boy kept crying and it was all Trent could do to get him to open his mouth barely wide enough to remove the stick.

Damn. Trent thought of one of his professors long ago talking about giving the spatula test, and that sure seemed to be what had just happened with the stick. "Did you hurt yourself any time the past week or two? Did something poke into your skin?"

"I'nt know." The words were a mumble, the boy barely moving his lips, and Trent was now pretty sure he knew what was wrong.

"Thomas, can you get me a cup of water?"

"Yes, doctor."

When he returned with the cup, Trent held it to the boy's lips. "Take a sip of this for me, will you?" As he expected, the poor kid gagged on the water, unable to swallow.

"All right. I want you to lie down so I can check a few things." Trent tried to help him lie on the exam table, but it was difficult with the child's body so rigid. The simple movement sent the boy into severe muscle spasms. When the spasms eventually faded and Trent finally was able to get him prone, the child's arms flung up to hug his chest tightly while his legs stayed stiff and straight. He began crying again, his expression formed into a grimace.

Trent was aware of both Thomas and Charlotte standing by the table, staring with surprise and concern. He grasped the boy's wrist and tried to move his elbow. The arm resisted, pushing against his hand.

"What do you think is wrong, Trent?" Charlotte said, obviously alarmed.

He couldn't blame her for being unnerved, since this wasn't something you saw every day. It was damned disturbing how a patient was affected by this condition.

"Tetanus. I'm willing to bet he's had a puncture wound, probably in the foot, that maybe he didn't even notice happened. The infection, wherever it is, is causing his jaw to lock, as well as all the other symptoms we're seeing."

He released the child's arm and lifted his foot, noting it was slightly swollen. Bingo! There it was: a tiny wound oozing a small amount of smelly pus.

The poor kid was still crying, the sound pretty horrible

through his clenched teeth. He placed the boy's foot back down and refocused his attention on calming him down. "You're going to be all right, I promise. I know this is scary and you feel very uncomfortable and strange. But I'm going to get rid of the infection in your foot and give you medicine to make you feel better. Okay?"

The brown eyes that stared back at him were terrified, and who could blame the poor little guy? With tetanus, painful spasms could be so severe they actually pulled ligaments apart or broke bones.

"What do you do for tetanus?" Charlotte asked. "Is it…?" She didn't finish the sentence, but he knew what she was asking.

"He'll recover fine, now that we've got him here. Thomas, can you get what we need for an IV drip of penicillin? And some valium, please."

"Penicillin?" Charlotte frowned and leaned up to speak softly in his ear. "Since he's so sick, shouldn't you give him something—I don't know—stronger?"

"Maybe it's a good thing you're not a doctor after all." He couldn't resist teasing her a little. "In the U.S., they'd probably use an antibiotic that costs four hundred dollars a day and kills practically every bacteria in your body instead of just the one causing the disease—kind of like killing an ant with a sledgehammer. But, believe me, penicillin is perfect for this. You can't kill bacteria deader than dead."

Her pretty lips and eyes smiled at him. "Okay. I believe you. So that's it? Penicillin? Do you need a test to confirm that's what it is?"

"No, his symptoms are clear. That's what it is." He found himself feeling pleased that she trusted him to make the right decision. Since when had he ever needed other people to appreciate what he did and what he'd learned over the years?

He reached to pat the child's stiffly folded arms. "Hang

in there. I'll be right back." Grasping Charlotte's elbow, he walked far enough away that the boy couldn't hear them.

"Penicillin is just part of the treatment. We'll need to do complete support care. I have to get rid of the clostridium tetani, which is the bacteria in his foot that's giving off the toxin to the rest of his body. It's one of the most lethal toxins on earth, which is why it's a damned good thing his mother brought him in. He wouldn't have made it if it was left untreated."

She shuddered. "How do you get rid of the…whatever it was called…tetani toxin?"

"I'll have to open his foot to remove it and clean out the dead and devitalized tissue so it can heal. It'll give the penicillin a chance to work. I'll give him fluids and valium to keep him comfortable so he can rest. He'll have to stay here several days, kept very quiet, to give his body time to process the toxin."

She nodded and her eyes smiled at him again, her soft hand wrapping around his forearm. "Thank you again for coming back, Trent. I bet our lying Dr. Smith would never have been able to figure out what was wrong with this boy. You're…amazing."

He didn't know about all that. What he did know was that *she* was amazing. In here, looking at this boy, concerned and worried but not at all freaked out by the bizarre presentation of tetanus, despite not being in medicine herself. He'd bet a whole lot of his fortune that the women he'd dated back in the days of his old, privileged life in the States would have run hysterically from the room. Or, even more likely, would never been in there to begin with.

"I have to take care of his foot right now, which is going to take a little time. Promise you'll stay here in the hospital until I'm done?" He found himself reaching to touch her face, to stroke his knuckles against her cheek. "I know you think you're all tough and can handle any big, bad burglar that might be ransacking your house as you walk in the door. But, for my peace of mind, will you please wait for me?"

"I'll wait for you." The beautiful green of her eyes, her small smile, her words, all seemed to settle inside his chest and expand it. "Since it'll be past time for dinner to be served here, I'll fix something for us when we get there."

"Sounds great." He wanted to lean down and kiss her, the way he had in the rain the other day. And the reasons for not doing that began to seem less and less important. Charlotte definitely didn't act like she'd be doing much pining after he was gone.

That was good news he hoped was really true, and the smart part of him knew it was best to keep it that way, to keep their relationship "strictly professional," and never mind that he'd be spending the night back in her house. The house in which, when the two of them *weren't* just colleagues, they hadn't gotten much sleep at all.

Despite the comfort of the double bed, with its wrought-iron headboard and soft, handmade quilt, Trent turned restlessly, finally flopping onto his back with his hands behind his head. The room was girly, with lace curtains, a pastel hooked rug and an odd mix of furniture. The femininity of it made him even more acutely aware that Charlotte was sleeping very close by.

Every time he closed his eyes, he saw her face: the woman who had fascinated him from the first second he'd walked into her office. That long, silky brown hair cascading down her back, her body with curves in all the right places on her petite frame and her full lips begging to be kissed were as ultra-feminine as the bedroom.

But her willful, no-nonsense personality proved that a woman who oozed sexiness and femininity sure didn't have to be quiet and docile.

He'd guessed being here would be a challenge. How the hell was he going to get through the night keeping his word that their relationship would stay strictly professional? Get through the next few days?

Focusing on work seemed like a good plan. He'd tell her he wanted to head into the field to do immunizations, or whatever else patients might need, keeping close proximity to Charlotte at a minimum. The last thing he wanted to do was hurt her, and so far it seemed their brief time together hadn't negatively affected her at all. No point in risking it—not to mention that he didn't want to stir up that strange discomfort he'd felt at the airport when he'd tried to get out of there the first time.

A loud creak sent Trent sitting upright in bed, on high alert. Had someone broken in? Surely, lying there wide awake, he would have heard other sounds if that was the case?

Probably Charlotte wasn't sleeping well, either. He stared at the bedroom door, his pulse kicking up a notch at another creak that sounded like it was coming from the hall. Could she possibly be planning to come into his room?

He swung his legs to the floor and sat there for a few minutes, his ears straining to hear if it was her, or if he should get up to see if what he'd heard was an intruder. While it seemed unlikely someone could break in without making a lot of noise, he threw on his khaki shorts and decided he had to check the place out just to be sure.

He opened the bedroom door as quietly as possible and crept out in his bare feet, staring through the darkness of the hallway, looking for any movement. The scent of coffee touched his nose and he relaxed, since he was pretty sure no intruder would be taking a coffee break.

Charlotte was up; he should just go back to bed. But, before he knew what he was doing, he found himself padding down the narrow staircase to the kitchen.

"Did you have to make so much racket in here? I was sound asleep," he lied as he stepped into the cozy room.

Seeing Charlotte standing at the counter in a thin, pink robe, her hair messy, her lips parted in surprise, almost obliterated his resolve to keep his distance. Nearly had him striding across the room to pull her into his arms, and to hell with all his resolutions to the contrary. But he forced himself to lean against the doorjamb and shove his hands in his pockets.

"I was quiet as a mouse. Your guilty conscience must be keeping you awake."

"Except for that 'murdering my old girlfriend' thing, my conscience is clean. I abandoned my vacation plans, didn't I? Came back here to work for you?"

She nodded and the way her gaze hovered on his bare chest for a moment reminded him why he hadn't been able to sleep, damn it.

"You did," she said, turning back to the percolator. "I'm grateful, and I know Lionel's family is grateful too. And the other patients you've taken care of since then." She reached into the cupboard to grab mugs. "Coffee?"

He should go back upstairs. Try to sleep. "Sure."

He settled into a chair at the table and she joined him, sliding his cup across the worn wood. His gaze slipped to the open vee of her robe. He looked at her smooth skin and hint of the lush breasts he knew were hidden there, pictured what kind of silky nightgown she might be wearing and quickly grabbed up his cup to take a swig, the burn of it on his tongue a welcome distraction.

Time for mundane conversation. "So, tell me about what you studied in school. Didn't you say you got an MBA?"

"Yes. I got a hospital administration degree, then went to Georgetown for my masters. I knew I'd be coming here to get the hospital open and running again, so all that was good." She leaned closer, her eyes alight with enthusiasm. "I met a lot of people who shared their experiences with me—about how they'd improved existing facilities or started from scratch in various countries. I learned so much, hearing the things they felt they did right or would do differently."

He, too, leaned closer, wanting to study her, wanting to know what made this fascinating and complex woman tick. "I've been surprised more than once how much you know about medicine. Tell me again, why didn't you become a doctor?"

"Somebody needs to run this place. Create new ways to help people, to make a difference. Like I said before, I can get doctors and nurses and trained techs. I focused my training on how to do the rest of it. My parents encouraged that; they've trusted me and John Adams with the job of bringing this place back."

A surge of old and buried pain rose within him and he firmly shoved it back down. It must be nice to have someone in your life who believed in you, who cared what you wanted. It must be nice to have someone in your life who didn't say one thing, all the while betraying you, betraying your blind trust, with a deep stab in your back.

"I've worked at a lot of hospitals in the world. That experience might come in handy if you have any questions."

"Thanks. I might take you up on that."

Her beautiful eyes shone, her mouth curved in a pleased smile, and the urge to grab her up and kiss her breathless was nearly irresistible. Abruptly, he stood and downed the last of his coffee, knowing that between the caffeine and her close proximity there'd be no sleep for him tonight.

"I'm going to hit the hay. Try not to make a bunch of noise again and wake me up. I don't want to fall asleep in the middle of a surgery tomorrow."

She stood too and the twist of her lips told him she knew exactly why he was awake. "Don't worry. The last thing I want to do is disturb your sleep."

"Liar." He had to smile, enjoying the pink that stained her cheeks at the word. "Anyway, you've already done that, so you owe me. Maybe you should disturb my sleep for a few more hours; help me relax."

Why did his mouth say one thing, when his brain told him to shut up and walk out? Until the slow blink of her eyes, the tip of her tongue licking her lips, the rise and fall of that tantalizing vee of skin beneath her robe, obliterated all regrets.

"I don't think your sleep is my responsibility," she said. "You're on your own."

She swayed closer, lids low, her lips parted, practically willing him to kiss her. What was the reason he'd been trying not to? Right now, he couldn't quite remember. Didn't want to.

"Seems to me we agreed you were in charge of my life while I'm here." Almost of their own accord, his feet brought him nearly flush with her body. Close enough to feel her warmth touch his bare chest; to feel her breath feather across his skin. "Got any ideas on a cure for insomnia?"

"Less coffee in the middle of the night? Maybe a hammer to the head? I've got one in the toolbox in the closet."

He reached for her and put his hands on her waist. "I know you said you couldn't promise not to hurt me, but that seems a little drastic." His head lowered because he had to feel her skin against his lips. He touched them softly to her cheek, beneath her ear. "Any other ideas?"

Her warm hands flattened against his chest. When they didn't push, he drew her close, her curves perfectly fitted to his body. Much as he knew he should back off right now, there was no way he could do it. He wanted her even more than the night they'd fallen into her bed together. And that night had knocked him flat in a way he couldn't remember ever having experienced before.

Her head tipped back as he moved his mouth to the hollow of her throat and could feel her pulse hammering beneath his lips. "We have morphine in the drug cupboard at the hospital," she said, her voice breathy, sexy. "A big dose of that might help."

"You're a much more powerful drug than morphine, much more addictive, and you know it." Her green eyes filled his vision before he lowered his mouth to hers and kissed her. He drew her warm tongue into his mouth, and the taste of her robbed him of any thoughts of taking it slow. Of kissing her then backing off.

Her hands roamed over his chest, sending heat racing across his flesh, and he sank deeper into the kiss, tasting the hint of coffee, cream and sweet sugar on his tongue. Her fingers continued on a shivery path down his ribs, to his sides and back, and he wrapped his arms around her and pulled her close, the swell of her breasts rising and falling against him.

His thigh nudged between her legs and, as she rocked against him, he let one hand drift to her rear, increasing the pressure, loving the gasp that left her mouth and swirled into his.

The rattling sound of a doorknob cut through the sensual fog in his brain and Trent pulled his mouth from Charlotte's. They stared at one another, little panting breaths between them, before her gaze cut toward the living room.

"What the hell? Are you expecting someone?"

Her eyes widened and she pulled away from him. "No," she whispered. "Darn, I left my gun upstairs. I'll have to go through the living room to get it. Should I run up there? If he—or they—get in you could punch them or something till I get back down with it. Or maybe you shouldn't. Maybe *they* have a gun."

Metal scratched against metal then a creaking sound indicated the door had been opened, and Charlotte's hands flung to her chest as she stared out of the kitchen then swung her gaze back to Trent.

"The door was locked, wasn't it? Does someone have a key?" It hadn't sounded like forced entry to him. Maybe it was somebody she knew. And the thought that it could be a boyfriend twisted his gut in a way it shouldn't twist for a sweet but short interlude.

"No. The only other key is in my office at the hospital."

Her whisper grew louder, likely because she was afraid. He touched his finger to her lips and lowered his mouth to her ear. "Is there really a hammer in the closet?"

She nodded and silently padded to it in her bare feet, wincing as the door shuddered open creakily. She grabbed the head of a hammer and handed it to him, then pulled out a heavy wrench and lifted it in the air, ready to follow him.

What would she have done if he hadn't been here with her tonight? The thought brought a surge of the same protective anger he'd felt when he'd heard about the first break-in, which had made him more than ready to bust somebody's head.

"Stay here," he whispered. He slipped to the doorway and could see a shadowy figure with a bag standing near the base of the stairs.

CHAPTER NINE

HEART POUNDING, CHARLIE stepped close behind Trent, peeking around him as he stood poised to strike the intruder. Never would she have thought that the burglars would come back, especially at night when she was home. Thank goodness Trent was here. Much as she said she could look after herself—and she could; she was sure she could—having a big, strong man in the house definitely made her glad she wasn't alone as someone was breaking in.

She looked up to see Trent's jaw was taut, his eyes narrowed, his biceps flexed as he raised the hammer. He looked down at her, gave a quick nod, then burst across the room with a speed sure to surprise and overwhelm whoever had broken in.

The man was shorter than Trent, who slammed his shoulder into the intruder's chest like he was an American football linebacker. The intruder landed hard, flat on his back, and Trent stepped over him, one leg on either side of the man's prone figure. With one hand curled in a menacing fist, Trent's other held the hammer high.

"Who the hell are you? And you better answer fast before you can't answer at all," Trent growled.

"What the heck? Who are *you*? Charlie?" Her father's voice sounded scared and trembly and she tore across the room in a rush.

"Oh, heavens! Stop, Trent! It's okay. It's my dad." The wrench in her hand suddenly seemed to weigh twenty pounds and she nearly dropped it as she shook all over in shock and relief. She fell to her knees next to her father, placing the wrench on the floor so she could touch his chest and arms. "Dad, are you all right? Are you hurt?"

"I…I'm not sure." He stared up at Trent, who stepped off him to one side and lowered the hammer. "Next time I'll know to knock, seeing as you have a bodyguard."

"Sorry, sir." Trent crouched down and slipped his arm beneath her dad's shoulders, helping him to a sitting position. "You okay?"

"I think so. Except for the hell of a bruise I'm going to have in the morning." He stood with the help of Trent and Charlie and rubbed his hand across his chest, then offered it to Trent. "I'm Joseph Edwards. Thanks for looking out for my daughter."

"Uh, you're welcome. I guess. Though I think this is the first time I've been thanked for beating somebody up. I'm Trent Dalton."

Charlie glanced at Trent to see that charming, lopsided smile of his as he shook her dad's hand. The shock of it all, and the worry of whether her dad was okay or not, had worn off and left her with a hot annoyance throbbing in her head. "What are you doing here, Dad? I thought you weren't coming for a couple more nights. Why didn't you call? You're lucky you don't have a big lump on your head. Or a gunshot through your chest."

"I tried to call but couldn't get any cell service. After I met with Bob in Monrovia, I decided not to stay at his house like I'd planned, because his wife's not feeling well. Then I got the key from the hospital so I wouldn't wake you—though that obviously wasn't a problem." He raised his eyebrows. "I won't ask what you're doing up in the middle of the night."

"That wouldn't be any of your business," Charlie said,

glaring at Trent as his smile grew wider. His grin definitely implied something it shouldn't, and it sure didn't help that the man had no shirt on. Though, as she thought back to what exactly they were doing when her dad had arrived, it wasn't too far off. It had, in fact, been quickly heading in the direction of hot and sweaty sex and she felt her cheeks warm. "But if you must know, Trent is doing surgeries at the hospital for a few days and, um, needed a place to stay. We were just talking about the hospital and stuff."

"She obviously doesn't want you to know, but that's not entirely the truth," Trent said.

She stared at him. Surely the man wasn't going to share the details of their relationship—or whatever you'd call their memorable night together—to her *father?*

"What is the truth?" her dad asked.

"The reason I'm spending the night here is because someone broke into the house yesterday. I didn't think she should be alone until it seemed unlikely the guy was coming back. Which is why I knocked you down first and asked questions later."

"Ah." Her father frowned. "I have to say, it's concerned me from the start that you were living here by yourself. Maybe we should rethink that—have a few hospital employees live here with you."

"I've been here two years, Dad, and nothing like this has happened before. I'm sure it's an isolated incident. I like living alone and don't want that to change."

"Maybe you should get a dog, then—one with a big, loud bark that would scare somebody off."

A dog? Hmm. It might be nice to have a dog around and she had to admit she might feel a touch safer. "If it will ease your mind, I'll consider it."

"We'll talk more about this later." Her dad lowered himself into a chair and rubbed his chest again, poor man. Though she felt he'd brought it on himself by sneaking in. "I'm looking forward to hearing about how the new wing is coming along. Must be about finished, isn't it? When is the first plastic surgeon supposed to get here?"

"Um, soon." She glanced at Trent and saw his brows twitch together. This was her chance to ask him to stay until the Gilchrist rep got here, to do a few plastic surgery procedures, since the subject had come up. Maybe, with her dad there, he wouldn't be so quick to say no. She pulled the ties of her robe closer together, trying not to give off any vibes that said, *I'm desperate here.*

"Trent. Ever since I saw what a wonderful job you did on Lionel's eye, I've been meaning to ask." She licked her lips and forged on. "There are a few patients who've been waiting a long time to have a plastic surgery procedure done. Would you consider doing one or two before you leave?"

"You know, I'm not actually a board-certified plastic surgeon." His eyes were unusually flat and emotionless. "Better for you to wait until you have your whole setup ready and a permanent surgeon in place."

"You do plastic surgery?" Her father's eyebrows lifted in surprise. "I assumed you were a general surgeon, like the ones who usually rotate through the GPC-staffed hospitals."

"I am."

"Come on, Trent." Charlie tried for a cajoling tone that might soften him up. "I saw what you did for Lionel's eye. You told me, when you wanted to do it, that I didn't know who I was dealing with, remember? And you were right."

He looked at her silently for a moment before he spoke. "I'm leaving here any day now, Charlotte. It wouldn't make sense for me to perform any complex plastics procedures on patients, then take off before I could follow up with them."

"Please, Trent." Her hands grew cold. "Maybe you could even stay a few extra days, to help these patients who so desperately need it. When you see some of them, I think you'll want to."

"I can't stay longer. And it's not good medical practice for me to do a surgery like that, then leave. I'm sorry." He turned to her dad, the conversation clearly over by the tone of his voice. "Since you're here tonight, sir, I'm going to grab my things and head back to my quarters."

Charlie watched him disappear up the steps and listened to his footsteps fade away down the hall. Why was he so adamant about this? And what could she possibly do to convince him?

Trent managed to avoid Charlotte the entire following day. He took dinner to his room, and if she noticed she didn't say anything. When his phone rang and he saw it was Chase, a strange feeling came over him before he answered. A feeling that told him he'd miss this place when he left, whether it was tomorrow or days from now.

"So, I'm sorry, man, but it's just not going to work out," Chase said in his ear. "Wish I could sub for you. I'd love to head back to Africa for a week or so. But I'm pretty busy at work here and, like I said, Dani's not feeling great this month. Says she didn't have morning sickness with Drew, but she sure does now."

"Maybe it's you that's making her sick this time, and not her pregnancy," Trent said. "Which I could fully appreciate."

"Yeah, that could well be true." Chase chuckled. "Any chance you'll be coming to the States some time? Dani and I go to the occasional conference here. It would be great to catch up."

"No plans for that right now. I'll let you know if I do." He wouldn't mind a visit back to the States, so long as it wasn't New York City. It would be nice to see Chase and Dani, and maybe even cute little Drew and his new baby sibling. He hadn't been back for quite a while. "Who

knows, maybe we can temp at the same time in Honduras when I'm between jobs. Let's see if we can make that
happen."

"That would be great. Stay in touch, will you?

"Will do. Take care, and give your family a hug for me."

Well, damn. He shoved his phone in his pocket. So
much for that great idea. But he'd known it was a long shot
that Chase would be able to fill in for him here in Liberia
until the new doctor arrived.

The uneasy feelings he had about being stuck here were
peculiar and annoying. It wasn't like it was a big deal if
he went on his vacation all by his lonesome tomorrow or
a couple weeks from now. The GPC was used to delays
like this, so they probably had a temp lined up for him in
the Philippines until he got there.

But this tug and push he kept feeling around Charlotte
was damned uncomfortable. One minute all he wanted
was to kiss her breathless, knowing that was a bad idea
for all kinds of reasons; the next, she was bugging him
about doing plastic surgery that he plain didn't want to do,
which put the distance between them he knew they should
keep in place. That he knew he should welcome.

There had been a number of times his plastics skills had
come in handy over the years, doing surgeries on a cleft
palate, or a hemangioma like Lionel's, that were important to how the patient could function every day. But actually working in a plastic surgery hospital? One dedicated
to procedures that mostly improve someone's looks? No,
thank you. He'd rather keep people alive than just make
them look better to the world.

He sat at the tiny desk in his room and went through the
mail that had arrived this week. One was from the GPC
and he tore it open, wondering if it was finally his release
papers, or if they'd had to relocate his next job to somewhere other than the Philippines because of this delay.

Perplexed, he read through the letter twice. Clearly,

there was some mess-up here. How come the director, Mike Hardy, thought the new doctor was already at the Edwards Hospital? Mike's letter advised him that, because of the imminent arrival of this doctor in Liberia, a temp filling in at his new job wouldn't be necessary and he could still take his full three weeks off. His revised arrival date in the Philippines was exactly three weeks from today.

He picked up his phone to call Mike, but figured it would make sense to talk to Charlotte first. Maybe she knew something he didn't.

He left his room and strode down the long hallway from the residence quarters into the hospital. Dinner had been over an hour ago, so she very well might be back at home. And he wasn't about to follow her over there. If she'd already left, he'd forget about talking to her and just call Mike.

A glance in her office showed she wasn't there, so he went to the dining hall. Her round, sexy rear was the only part of her he could see. With her head and torso inside a cupboard as she kneeled on the floor, he stopped to enjoy the view and had to resist the urge to shock her by going over and giving that sexy bottom of hers a playful spank.

"Does anyone know if the rest of Charlotte Edwards is in here?" he asked instead.

Her body unfolded and she straightened to look at him, still on her knees. "Very funny. I'm just trying to organize this kitchen equipment. Too many cooks in here are making it hard to find anything when you want it."

"When you have a minute, I need to talk to you about the new doc coming."

He had to wonder why her expression was instantly alarmed. Was she worried there'd been an even longer delay? Thank goodness her dad was here now, so Trent wouldn't be spending any more tempting nights in her house.

She shoved to her feet and walked over. "What about the new doc?"

"I got a letter from Mike Hardy telling me all systems are go for my vacation. I'm wondering what the mix-up is. Or if someone is coming tomorrow and they somehow forgot to send my release papers."

She snatched the letter from his hand and looked it over, her fingers gripping it until they were practically white. "Um, I don't know. This is weird. Last I heard, there was nobody in place yet. Let me see what I can find out and I'll let you know. Believe me, I'm as anxious to get you out of here as you are to leave."

"Never mind." He tried to tug the paper from her hand, but she held on tight. It pissed him off that she wanted him out of there so badly, which was absolutely absurd, since he wanted the same thing. "I'll call Mike in the morning. Give me my letter back."

"I'm the director of this hospital and staffing is my responsibility."

Her green eyes were flashing irritation at him, as well as something else he couldn't figure out. The woman was like a pit bull sometimes. "Why are you so controlling? Technically, the GPC employs me, you know. And this is my job, my vacation and my life. Give me my letter."

"Fine. Take the letter." She let it go and spun on her heel toward the doorway. "But I'm going home, then calling Mike. I'm asking you to let me handle this; I'll let you know what he says. Hopefully this means you're on your way very soon."

His hand crumpled the letter slightly as he watched her disappear into the hall. Why he wanted to storm after her and kiss her until she begged him to stay was something he wasn't going to try to understand.

CHAPTER TEN

CHARLIE HELD TRENT'S release papers in slightly shaky hands then shoved them deeper under the pile on her desk. She tried to draw a calming breath and remind herself that Colleen believed Trent had agreed to stay, so the new doctor wouldn't just show up on the doorstep and give Trent the green light to leave. But if Trent called Mike Hardy, who knew what would happen?

She prayed the Gilchrist representative would show up fast. Surely they'd be impressed with what a great job the hospital's plastic surgeon had done on Lionel's eye; they would never know the talented man would be out of there as soon as the rep left. Trent would charm them, even if he didn't know he was supposed to, because the man oozed charm just by breathing. And all would be well. It would.

Paying bills wasn't exactly the way to forget about the problem, but it had to be done. Charlie tore open the mail and grimly dropped every invoice into the box she kept for them. One thing she could do to relieve the stress of it all was work harder on other sources of funding besides Gilchrist. Her dad had always told her to never put all her eggs in one basket, so she tried to have multiple fundraising efforts going. Time to make some more calls and send more letters to previous donors. There was no way any of them would come close to what the Gilchrist Foundation had committed, but something was a whole lot better than nothing.

A letter with a postmark from New York City and the name of some financial organization caught her eye and made her heart accelerate. The Gilchrist Foundation was based in NYC. Could they possibly just have decided to send a check without worrying about the final approval?

She quickly ripped it open then sighed when she read the letterhead: not from the foundation. But her brief disappointment faded as she read the check that was enclosed with the letter. She stared, not quite believing what she was seeing.

Fifty thousand dollars, written to The Louisa Edwards Education Project. With slightly shaky hands, she scanned the letter that came with the check.

> *Please find enclosed an anonymous donation to provide supplemental funding for the Louisa Edwards School.*

It was signed by someone who apparently worked at the financial firm it came from.

She stared at the bold numerals and the cursive below them. Fifty thousand dollars. Fifty thousand! Oh, heavens!

She leaped up and tore out the door of her office, about to run all the way to the school to show John Adams and her dad, who was there with him. To have John Adams plan to hire another new teacher. To think of all the supplies on their wish-list they'd decided not to buy for now.

And she ran, *kapow*, right into Trent Dalton's hard shoulder, just as she had before when he'd asked if she was late to lunch.

He grabbed her arms to steady her. "Wow, you must be extra-hungry today. Something special on the menu?"

"Funny." She clutched the check to her chest and smiled

up at him. "But even you can't annoy me today. You won't believe what just came in the mail!"

"A new designer handbag? Some four-inch heels?" he asked, little creases at the corners of his eyes as he smiled.

"Way, way better. Guess again."

"A brand-new SUV?"

She held the check up in front of his face. "Look." She was so thrilled she had to gulp in air to keep from hyperventilating. "Somebody sent a check—a huge check—to the school. I have no idea who it's from, or how they even heard about us. We can serve so many more kids now. Get stuff we've been wanting, but couldn't afford. Can you believe it?"

"No. Can't believe it."

There was a funny expression on his face, a little amused smile along with something else she couldn't quite figure out. "You're laughing at me, aren't you? I can't help being excited. More than excited! Oh my gosh, this is so amazing and wonderful. Just like a gift from the heavens."

Beyond jubilant, she flung her arms around Trent's neck and gave him a big, smacking kiss on the lips, because she just plain couldn't help herself. She drew back slightly against his arms, which had slipped across her back, and could see his eyes had grown a tad more serious. The warm kiss he gently pressed to her forehead felt soft and sweet.

"I'm happy for you. You and John Adams deserve it for the work you're accomplishing in that school, and obviously your donor knows that. You're literally changing those kids' lives, giving them a fighting chance in the tough world they live in."

"Thank you. But you change lives too, you know." She stepped out of his hold, instantly missing the warm feel of his arms around her. "Gotta go. I need to tell John Adams and Dad about this."

"I'll come, too. I'm not busy right now and I'd like to see the kids again."

It hadn't rained in a few days, so the earth wasn't nearly as muddy as the last time they'd trekked over to the school. Her brain was spinning with possibilities, until a thought made her excitement drop a notch.

Maybe she shouldn't be so quick to hire another teacher or two and immediately spend some of it on teaching supplies and another couple sewing machines for the students to learn that skill on. Maybe she needed to hold onto it just in case she couldn't pay the hospital bills when they came in if the Gilchrist funding didn't come through.

No. They'd always run the hospital and the school separately: different sponsors and donors, different bookkeeping, different projects. Whoever had donated this money wanted it to go to the school and she had to honor that. It was the only fair and right thing to do for both the donor and the students.

"Did you get hold of Mike about my letter? Or am I allowed to call him now, Miss 'I'm The Director Of The Hospital And The Whole World'?" His lips were curved in a teasing smile, but his eyes weren't smiling quite as much.

"I'm…sorry if I was being bossy and…and acted like I want you to leave. I don't, really. I've just got a lot on my mind." And, boy, wasn't that the truth. "I spoke with Colleen, and apparently she does have someone lined up to come soon, but not today or tomorrow. I'm sorry about that also. I would greatly appreciate it, though, if you would stay just another few days." And all that was the truth, too, which made her feel a tad better. She wasn't being quite as deceitful as she felt.

"All right. Thanks for checking. I guess I can hang around for just a little while longer."

She drew a deep breath of relief, then glanced up at Trent's profile, at his prominent nose, black hair and sensual lips. It didn't feel like just over a week since he'd returned from the airport. As he walked next to her, not touching but close enough to feel his warmth, it seemed much longer. Oddly natural, like she should just reach over to hold his hand.

Which was not good. Not only would he be leaving in a matter of days, she didn't want to think about how shocked and angry he'd be if he ever found out about her little fibs. Okay, big fibs; the thought of it made her stomach knot.

Three figures, two taller and one small, along with a little dog, appeared up ahead on the road—obviously, her dad, John Adams, Patience and Lucky. Seeing them obliterated all other thoughts as Charlie ran the distance between them, waving the check.

"You're going to faint when you see this!"

Trent followed slowly behind Charlotte, not wanting to intrude on her moment, sharing her excitement with the two men and Patience. Though he'd been itching to leave, to move on with his life, he felt glad—blessed, really—that he'd still been here when she got the check. He'd never been around when someone received one of his donations, and it felt great to see how happy it made her. To know it would help them achieve their important goals.

He watched her fling her arms around both men, first her dad, then John Adams, just as she'd done with him. Well, not exactly the same. Her arms wrapped around their middles in a quick hug. That was different from the way she'd thrown her arms around his own neck, drawing his head close, giving him that kiss; her breasts pressing softly against his chest, staying there a long moment, her fingers tucked into his hair, sending a shiver along his scalp and a desire to kiss more than just her forehead.

"You don't know who the donor is?" her father asked.

She shook her head, the sun touching her shining hair as it slipped across her shoulders. "No. I wish I did. I wish

I could thank them. That *we* could thank them. Think there's any way to find out?"

"Not likely. But you could always contact the company it came from and ask."

"I'll do that," Charlotte said as they turned and headed back toward the hospital. "Maybe even ask if there's anything specific they want the money used for."

Trent knew his finance man was discreet and they'd get no information that could trace it back to him. "Whoever donated it stayed anonymous because they wanted to. I say just spend the money as you see fit and know they trusted you to do that," he said.

"Good point, Trent," John Adams said. "We do get the occasional anonymous donation, though nothing like this, of course. I think we should respect that's how they wanted to keep it."

"Okay." Charlotte's chest rose and fell in a deep breath, and Trent found his attention gravitating to her beautiful curves. "I'm feeling less freaked out. Just plain happy now. Why are you three leaving the school?"

"Daddy promised he would take me to the beach," Patience said. "He's been promising and promising, but kept saying it was s'posed to rain. But today the sun is shiny so we can go!" The little girl danced from one foot to the other, the colorful cloth bag on her shoulder dancing along with her.

"Mind if I come?" Trent asked. "I'll build a sandcastle with you." The kid was so cute, and he hadn't seen an inch of Liberia other than the airport and the road to and from the hospital and school. One of the things he enjoyed about his job was exploring new places, discovering new things. He turned to Charlotte. "Would that be okay? Thomas is taking care of a man needing hernia surgery, and I've already seen the patients in the clinic. The nurses are finishing up with all of them. I can check on everyone when I get back."

"Of course, that's fine. I'll see what's in the kitchen for you all to take for a beach lunch."

"Why don't you go along, Charlie?" her dad suggested. "You never take much time off to do something fun. I've been wanting to go through the information you gave me, anyway, so I can keep an eye on things while you're gone."

"Well…" Her green eyes held some expression he couldn't figure out. Wariness? Anxiety? "I'm not really a beach person, you know. And I don't want you stuck here doing my work, Dad."

"You may be the director, but I'm still a part of this hospital too, remember." Joseph smiled. "You need to get over this fear of yours. Go get your things together. John Adams and I will scrounge up some food for you all to take."

"What fear of yours?" Trent asked. From being around Charlotte just the past week or so, he couldn't imagine her being afraid of much of anything.

"Nothing. Dad's exaggerating."

"Exaggerating? The last time we were at the beach, I thought you were going to hyperventilate just going into the water up to your knees." Joseph turned to Trent. "When Charlie was a teenager back in the States, we didn't realize we were swimming where there was a strong rip current, like quite a few beaches here in Liberia have. She got pulled farther and farther out and I couldn't get to her. Her mom and I kept yelling at her to relax and not fight the current, to just let it take her. Then swim horizontal to the shore until she came to a place without a rip so she could swim back in."

"Rip tides can be dangerous." Trent looked at Charlotte and saw her cheeks were flushed. Surely she wasn't embarrassed by something that happened when she was a kid? "Scary for anybody. But obviously you lived through it."

"Yes. I admit I thought for sure that was it, though. That I was going to end up in the middle of the ocean and either drown or be devoured by a shark. So I just don't like going in the water."

"In the water? You don't even like getting in a small boat. Which has been a problem a few times," Joseph said. "You need to move past it and get your feet wet."

"Can we just drop this subject, please? I have a lot of work to do, anyway."

"Come to the beach, Charlotte," Trent said, wishing he could pull her into his arms and give her soothing kisses that would ease her embarrassment and the bad memory. "We'll work on getting you to move past your fear. You don't have to get in the water if you're not comfortable. But, you know, I did do a whole rotation in psychiatry at school. I'm sure I'm a highly qualified therapist." He gave her a teasing smile, hoping she'd relax and decide to come. Living with any kind of debilitating fear was no fun.

"Just go, Charlie," Joseph said. "It'll make me feel less guilty that I let you swim in that rip to begin with."

Charlotte gave an exaggerated sigh. "So this is about you now? Fine. I'll go. But I'm not promising to swim. I mean it."

"No promises needed," Trent said. "We can always just build a sandcastle so big that Princess Patience can walk inside."

"I like big sandcastles!" Patience beamed. "And In't care if we don't swim, Miss Charlie. Swimming isn't my favorite, anyway. We'll have fun on the beach."

"All right, then, that's settled," Joseph said. "John Adams and I will pack lunch while you get your things."

Trent grabbed swim trunks, a towel and his medical bag, which he'd learned always to have along on any excursion. Heading to the car, he had an instant vision of how Charlotte would look in a swimsuit: her sexy curves and smooth skin. Oh, yeah, he would more than enjoy a day at the beach with a beautiful woman; at the same time, he'd be glad to have chaperones to keep him from breaking his deal with her.

The thought of chaperones, though, didn't stop more compelling thoughts of swimming with Charlotte. How she'd feel in his arms when he held her close, trying to relieve her mind and soothe her fears, their wet bodies sliding together. How much he wished that, afterwards, they could lie on the hot sand and make love in the shade of a palm tree with the warm breeze tickling their skin.

Damn. His pulse kicked up and made him a little short of breath.

Chaperones were a very good thing.

CHAPTER ELEVEN

THE DRIVE THROUGH farms of papaya, mangoes and acres of rubber trees brought them to the soaring Grand Cape Mount, then eventually to the shoreline. Though John Adams had offered, Charlotte insisted on driving, of course. Trent had to wonder what made the woman feel a need to be in charge all the time. Didn't she ever want just to relax and go along for the ride?

Patience kept up a steady chatter until her father told her he'd give her a quarter if she could stay silent for five minutes. After she failed to manage that, Trent entertained her with a few simple card tricks he let her "win" that earned her the quarter after all.

They parked at the edge of the road and, as they unpacked their things from the car, Charlotte shook her head at Trent. "Is there a soul on the planet you can't charm to death?"

"To death? Doesn't exactly sound like you mean that in a nice way." Trent hooked a few beach chairs over his arm and they followed John Adams and Patience, who carried their lunches and a few plastic pails and shovels.

"Okay, charm, period. Everyone in the hospital thinks you're Mr. Wonderful."

"Does that include the director of the hospital?"

"Of course. I'm very grateful you filled in here—twice—until we can get another doctor."

Her voice had become polite, her smile a little stiff. Was she regretting that her rare time off had to be spent with him? Or could she be having the same problem he was having—wanting to take up where they'd left off at her house, knowing it was a hell of a bad idea?

As they approached the beach, Trent stopped to soak in the visual spectacle before him. A wide and inviting expanse of beige sand stretched as far as he could see, palm trees swaying in the ocean wind. A few houses sat off the shore, looking for all the world as though they were from the Civil War era of the deep south in the United States.

"How old do you think those houses are?" he asked Charlotte.

"Robertsport was one of the first colonies founded here by freed slaves. I think it goes back to 1829, so some of the houses here are over a hundred and fifty years old."

"That's incredible." He looked back down the beach and enjoyed the picturesque lines of fishermen with their seining nets stretched from the beach down into the water, about ten of them standing three feet apart, holding the nets in their hands. Several canoes sat on the shore, obviously made from a single hand-carved tree. One was plain, but the other was splashed with multiple colors of paint in an interesting hodgepodge design.

He was surprised to see a few surfers in the water farther down the beach, not too far from a cluster of black rocks in the distance. The waves were big and powerful, but were breaking fairly far out.

"I didn't know the people here surfed. I know Senegal is popular for surfing, but didn't know the sport had made its way here."

"I'm told an aid worker was here surfing maybe six or seven years ago. A local was fascinated and gave it a try. It's starting to take off, I guess, with locals competing and some tourists coming now."

"You know, we could always borrow a board from

them. Want to give it a try?" he teased. The waves were pretty rough, so he knew there was no way she'd even consider it. The water closer to shore, though, was comparatively calm. Hopefully, he could get her into the lapping waves without it being too scary for her.

"Um, no. I think I'm going to be happy just beaching it, thanks anyway."

He'd have to see what he could do about changing her mind. They stopped in the middle of the wide beach and Charlotte laid some blankets on the soft sand. Patience tossed her toys and plopped down next to them. "Daddy, come help me build the castle!"

"How about we eat first, li'l girl?" John Adams said. "Miss Charlie and I brought some jollof rice, which I know you like. I don't know about everybody else, but I'm starving."

"You always starving, Daddy." The child grinned up at her father and Trent saw again what a strong bond there was between the two. The same kind of bond he'd seen grow so quickly between Chase and his son, even though he hadn't met them until the child was a toddler.

That surprising emotion tugged at Trent again, just as it had when Chase had told him about having a new little one on the way. A pinch of melancholy, knowing he'd likely never experience that kind of bond—though he knew only too well that not every family was as close as it seemed. That sometimes the chasm grew too large ever to be crossed.

After lunch and some sandcastle building, complete with a moat, Trent decided it was time to push Charlotte a little, to encourage her to face her fear. She was on her knees smoothing the last turret of the castle, and he pushed to his feet to stand behind her, smacking the sand from his hands. "Come on, Miss Edwards. Time for your psychotherapy session."

Immediately, her back stiffened. "I'm not done with the castle yet. Maybe later."

"Come on. It's hot as heck out here. Think how cool and refreshing the water will be."

"I'm going to watch Patience swim first." She turned to the little girl. "Remember you told me you wanted to learn to float in the lagoon? I want to see you."

And, if that wasn't an excuse, he'd never heard one. Obviously, it was going to be tough going getting her in the water.

John Adams grasped the child's hand and pulled her to her feet. "Good idea. Come on, let's get in the lagoon and cool off."

The child's expression became even more worried than Charlotte's. "No, Daddy. I don't want to."

"Why not?"

She pointed at the lagoon water, separated from the ocean by about fifty feet of sand. "There's neegees in there. I don't want to get taken by the neegees."

"There's no neegees in there, I promise."

"For true, Daddy, there are. They talk about it at school." She stared up at her father with wide eyes. "The neegees are under the water and they grab people who swim. They suck people right out of the lagoon, and nobody knows where they go, and then they're never, ever seen again. Ever."

John Adams chuckled and pulled her close against his leg. "Sugar, I promise you. There's no such thing as neegees. Just like there's no witchcraft where someone can put a curse on you. All those are just stories. So let's get in the water and I'll help you learn to float."

Patience shook her head, pressing her face to her dad's leg. "No, Daddy. I'm afraid of the neegees."

Inspiration struck and Trent figured this was a good time to put those psych classes he'd teased Charlotte about to good use and solve two problems at once. "Patience, you know how Miss Charlie is afraid of the rip currents in the ocean? How she's afraid to go in the water too?"

The little girl peeked at him with one eye, the other still pressed against her father's leg. "Yes."

"How about if Miss Charlie decides she's going to get in the water even though she's afraid? Then, when you see how brave she is, and how she does just fine and has fun, you can get in the lagoon with your dad and have fun too. What do you say?"

Patience turned to look at Charlotte, whose expression morphed from dismay to serious irritation as she glared at Trent. He almost laughed, except he knew she was genuinely scared.

"I guess if Miss Charlie gets in the water and doesn't get bit by a shark then I can be brave too."

"Thanks for that encouragement, Patience. Now I really can't wait to swim," Charlotte said. She narrowed her eyes at Trent, green sparks flying. "And thank *you* for leaving me no choice here. I'll be back after I get my swimsuit on."

"I'll check out the rip situation before we go in." Trent jogged into the water and leaped over the smaller waves before diving into a larger one. The water felt great and the inside of his chest felt about as buoyant as the outside. Charlotte was trusting him to help her feel safe in the water and he was going to do whatever he could to be sure she did.

Swimming parallel to the beach for a little in both directions, he didn't feel or see any major rips in the sand, though he'd still have to pay attention. Satisfied, he bodysurfed an awesome wave into shore, standing just in time to see Charlotte emerge from the path that led to the car.

Her beautiful body wore a pink bikini that wasn't super-skimpy but still showed plenty of her smooth skin and delectable curves. His pulse quickened and he reminded himself this little swim was supposed to make her feel safer and get past her fear. It was not an excuse to touch her all over.

Yeah, right. It was a damned great excuse, and not taking advantage of it was going to be nearly impossible.

"Ready?" He walked to her and stroked the pads of his fingers across the furrows in her brow, letting them trail softly down her cheek.

"Not really," she said under her breath. "But, since I'm now responsible for Patience not being afraid of the water for the rest of her life, I guess I have to be."

"I hope you're not mad at me. It's a good thing you're doing for her. And yourself." He grasped her hand and gave it a reassuring squeeze. "Don't worry. I'll be with you the whole time, and if you get really freaked out we'll head back in."

She nodded and gripped his hand tightly as they waded into the water, up to their knees, then her waist. In just another minute, the water was lapping at her breasts, which was so distracting he almost forgot to look for too-big waves that might be bearing down on them. He forced himself to look back at the ocean, making sure they weren't ending up in a dangerous spot, before returning his gaze to Charlotte's face. Her eyes were wide, the fear etched there clear, and he released her hand to put his arm around her waist, holding her close.

"I'm going to hold you now, so you feel more comfortable. Don't worry, I'm not getting creepy." He grinned and she gave him a weak smile in return. "In fact, why don't you get on my back and we'll just swim a little together that way until you feel more relaxed?"

"I admit I feel...uncomfortable. But I'm not a little kid, you know. Riding on your back seems ridiculous."

With that body of hers, there was no way she could be mistaken for a little kid. "Not if it makes you feel less nervous. Come on." He crouched down in the water up to his neck. "Get on, and wrap your arms around my throat.

Just don't choke me if you get scared or we'll both drown," he teased.

To his surprise, she actually did, and he swam through the water with her clinging to him like a remora attached to a shark, enjoying the feel of the waves sluicing over his body. Enjoying the feel of her weight on him and of her skin sensuously sliding across his, just the way he'd fantasized.

"Okay?" he asked as a slightly bigger wave slapped into them, splashing water into their faces.

"Okay. I admit the water feels…nice."

"It does, doesn't it?" He grinned, relieved that this seemed to be working. "Ready to try a little on your own, with me holding your hand?"

"Um, I guess."

She slid from his back and, as she floated a foot or so away, her grim expression told him she wasn't anywhere near feeling relaxed. He took her hands and wrapped her arms behind his head, then placed his arms around her. Her face was so close, her mouth wet and parted as she breathed, her dripping hair glistening in streaks of bronze. He wanted, more than anything, to kiss her.

And, now that they were facing one another, pressed together, the sensuous feel of her soft breasts against his chest, of her legs sliding against his, was impossible to ignore. The sensation pummeled him far more than any wave could, and he battled back the raw need consuming him. He could only hope she couldn't feel his body's response to the overwhelming one-two punch that was delectable Charlotte Edwards.

"I…I'm not too freaked out, so that's good, isn't it?" Her voice was a bit breathless, but of course they were swimming a little, and treading water—though his own breath was short for a different reason.

"Yes. It's good." Holding her close was good. The feel of her body, soft and slick against his, was way better than good. He wanted to touch her soft satiny skin all over. Wanted to slide his hand inside her swimsuit top to cup her breast, to thumb the taut nipple he could feel poking against his chest. To slip his fingers inside her bikini bottom and caress her there, to see if she could possibly be as aroused as he was.

The world had shrunk to just the two of them floating in the water. Intensely focused on all those thoughts, Trent forgot to pay attention to the waves. A large whitecap broke just before it reached them, crashing into their bodies and engulfing them.

Charlotte shrieked and her wide, scared eyes met his just before the wave drove them toward shore. He held on to her, crushing her against him so she wouldn't get flung loose, and her arms squeezed around him in return, tightening behind his neck. "Hold on!" he said as the surf took them on a long, rapid, undulating ride to shore.

Pressed tightly together, they rode the wave, and as it flattened Trent rolled to be sure it was his back and not hers that scraped along the sandy bottom. They slid to a stop in about five inches of water, just a short distance from the dry shore. With Charlotte still clutched in his arms, Trent rolled again so she was beneath him, shielding her from the surf. The last thing he wanted was for a wave to hit her from behind and startle her before she could see it coming. He looked into her eyes as water dripped from his face and hair onto hers. "Are you all right?"

"Yes. I'm all right." She dragged in some air. "Though I think I know how a surfboard feels now. Or a piece of seaweed."

He chuckled, then glanced up to see that John Adams and Patience were in the lagoon, the child's little body lying flat with his hands supporting her as she practiced her floating.

With a grin, he looked back down at Charlotte. "Looks

like it worked. You being brave helped Patience be brave. You even rode a wave into shore!"

"Only because I was attached to you." A little laugh left her lips and she smiled at him. One thick strand of hair lay across one eye and clung to her face and lips. "I'm glad Patience got in the lagoon. Funny; I kind of forgot to be scared, too. Because of you."

"You're just a lot braver than you give yourself credit for. Hell, you're the bravest woman I know, living in that house alone, doing what you're doing here. Being afraid of a rip tide after nearly drowning in one is normal. Just a tiny, human nick in that feisty spirit of yours." He lifted the strand away from her face as he looked at the little golden flecks in her eyes, her lashes stuck together with salt water. "I'm proud of you for facing that fear. For getting in the water even though you didn't want to." Tucking her hair behind her ear to join the rest that lay flat against her scalp, he suddenly saw something he'd never noticed before.

Her ear was oddly shaped—not just different, slightly abnormal. Nearly invisible scarring appeared on and around it. Probably no one without plastic surgery experience would be able to see it at all, but he could. He pressed his mouth to it, touching the contours of it with his lips and tongue.

"What happened to your ear?"

Her fingers dug into his shoulder blades. "My…ear? What do you mean?"

He let his mouth travel down her damp throat and back up to her jaw, because he just couldn't resist any longer; across her chin then up, slipping softly across her wet, salty lips before he lifted his gaze back to hers. "Your ear. Were you in an accident? Or was it something congenital?"

She was silent for a moment, just looking back at him, her eyes somber until she sighed. "Congenital. I was born with microtia."

"What grade of microtia? Was your ear just mis-shapen?"

"No, it was grade three. I only had this weird little skin flap that didn't look like an ear at all. We were told that's often accompanied by atresia, but I was blessed to have an ear canal, so I can hear pretty well out of it now."

"When did you have it reconstructed? Were you living in the States?"

She nodded. "I think doctors sometimes do the procedure younger now. But mine wanted to wait until I was nine, since that's when the ear grows to about ninety percent of its adult size." A small smile touched her mouth. "I still remember, when I was about five, why he told me I should be a little older before it was fixed—that it would look strange for a little girl to have a big, grown-up-sized ear, which at the time I thought was a pretty funny visual."

He gave her a soft kiss. "So you remember living with your ear looking abnormal?"

"Remember?" She gave a little laugh that had no humor in the sound at all. "Kids thought it was so hilarious to tease me about it. Called me 'earless Edwards.' One time a kid brought a CD to class for everyone to listen to, then said to me, 'Oh, right, you can't because you don't have an ear!' I wanted to crawl under my desk and hide."

He shook his head, hating that she'd had to go through that. "Kids can be nasty little things, that's for sure; convinced they're just being funny. Now I know where you got that chip on your shoulder from."

He was glad to see the shadows leave her eyes as she narrowed them at him, green sparks flying. "I do not have a chip on my shoulder. I just believe it's more efficient for me to drive and do whatever I need to do than take ten minutes talking about it just to dance around a man's ego."

"Good thing I'm so full of myself, which you've enjoyed telling me several times. Otherwise you would have crushed my feelings by now."

"As though I could possibly hurt your feelings."

"You might be surprised." And she probably would be, if she knew how rattled he'd felt for days. How much he wanted to leave while somehow, at the very same time, wanting to stay a little longer.

Her palms swept over his shoulder blades, wrapped more fully around his back, and he took that as an invitation for another soft kiss. Her mouth tasted so good, salty-sweet and irresistible.

"Tell me more about your surgery." He lifted his finger to stroke the shell of it. "Did they harvest cartilage from your ribs to build the framework for the new ear?"

"Yes. I have a small scar near my sternum, but you can barely see it now. They finished it in three procedures."

"Well, it looks great. Whoever performed the surgery was very good at it. I bet you were happy."

"Happy?" Her smile grew wider. "I felt normal for the first time in my life. No longer the freak without an ear. It was…amazing."

Now it was all clear as glass. He pressed another kiss to her now smiling mouth. "I finally get why you built the plastic surgery wing, and why it's so important to you. You know first-hand how it feels to be scarred or look different from everyone else."

She nodded, her eyes now the passionately intense green he'd seen so often the past week; the passion that was such an integral part of who she was. "I know saving lives is important—more important than helping people view themselves differently, as you said. But I can tell you that feeling good about the way you look, not feeling like a freak, is so important to a person's psyche. And, even though I had to live for a while feeling like that, I know how blessed I was to have access to doctors who could make it better. You know as well as anyone that so many people around the world don't. And I want to give the people here, at least, that same opportunity to look and feel normal. Can you understand that?"

His answer was to stroke her hair from her forehead, cup her cheek in his palm and kiss her. From the minute he'd met her, she'd impressed him with her determination, and now he was even more impressed. She'd used a negative experience from her own life to try to make life better for others and worked damn hard to make it happen.

His tongue delved into her mouth, licking, tasting the ocean water and the flavor that was uniquely, delectably her. Tasting the passion that was so much a part of her. He was swept along by her to another place, deeper and farther and more powerfully than any wave could ever take him.

CHAPTER TWELVE

As the surf lapped over their bodies, Charlie let herself drown in the kiss, in the taste of his cool, salty lips, his warm tongue deliciously exploring her mouth. Her hands stroked down his shoulder blades and back, reveling in the feel of the hard muscle beneath his smooth skin.

She tunneled her fingers into his thick, wet hair, wild and sexy and black as Liberian coal. His muscled thigh nudged between hers, sending waves of pleasure through every nerve. The taste of his mouth, the touch of his hands, the feel of his arousal against her took her breathlessly back to their incredible night of lovemaking.

"Charlotte," he whispered, his lips leaving hers to trail down her throat, to lick the water pooled there, then continuing their journey lower until his mouth covered her nipple, gently sucking on it through her wet nylon swimsuit.

She gasped. "Trent. That's so good. I—"

The sound of Patience laughing made her eyes pop open as he lifted his head from her breast. His eyes— no longer the light, laughing blue she was used to seeing, but instead a glittering near-black—met hers. Everything about him seemed hard—his chest rising and falling against hers, his arms taut around her, his hips and what was between them.

"Charlotte," he said through clenched teeth. "More than anything, I want to make love to you right now. Right here. To wrap your legs around me and swim back into the waves; nobody would know I'm diving deep inside of you." His mouth covered hers in a steaming kiss. "But I guess that will have to wait until later."

If it hadn't already been difficult to breathe, his words nearly would have made her faint from the lack of oxygen in her brain. Even though she knew Patience and John Adams were fairly close by, she couldn't bring herself to move. The undulating water that wrapped around them was the most intimate cocoon she'd ever experienced in her life and she didn't want it to end. Couldn't find the will to detangle herself from his arms. "So I guess our deal is off."

"Our deal?"

"Not to start anything up again."

"Our deal has obviously been a challenge for me." His mouth lifted in a slow smile, his eyes gleaming. "Maybe we can come up with a slightly modified deal."

"Such as?"

His mouth traveled across her cheek, lowered to her ear. "We make love one more time. Cool down this heat between us and get it out of our systems. Then back to just colleagues for the last days I'm here so we won't have that second goodbye we both want to avoid."

The thought of one, just one more time with him, sent her heart into a crazy rhythm. "I agree to your terms. Just once."

"Just once. So—"

The sound of distant shouting interrupted him. They both turned their heads at the same time and saw a few of the surfers down the beach pulling what looked like an unconscious young man, or a body, from the water.

Trent sprinted down the beach with Charlotte on his heels.

Blood poured through the fingers of a young man sitting on the sand, holding his hand to his forehead. The group of surfers gathered around him looked concerned, and one shouted to another who was running to a mound of things they'd apparently brought with them. He returned with a shirt that he handed to the injured surfer, who pressed it to his head.

"Looks like you need a hand here," Trent said as he approached the injured boy. "I'm a doctor. Will you let me take a look?"

"You a doctor?" The young man looked utterly surprised, and no wonder. There weren't too many doctors around there, period, and it was just damned good luck he happened to be on the beach when the kid was hurt.

"Yes. I work at the Edwards Mission Hospital. This lady is the director." He smiled at Charlotte, now standing next to him, before crouching down. "What's your name? Will you show me what we're dealing with here?"

"Murvee Browne," he replied, lowering his hand with the now-bloody shirt balled up in it. "I was surfing and, when the board flipped, I think the fin got me."

"Looks like it." Trent leaned closer to study the wound. It was one damned deep gash, probably five centimeters, stretching from the hairline diagonally across his forehead to his eyebrow. The injury appeared to slice all the way to the skull, but it was a little hard to tell while it was still bleeding so much. He'd let the kid know it was serious, but reassure him so he wouldn't freak out at what he was going to have to do to repair it. "You've got a pretty good one there. But at least it's just your forehead. I took care of one nasty surf accident victim where the guy's eyelid was slit open too."

Murvee grimaced while his friends gathered even closer to stare at the gash.

"You did it good, oh!" one friend said. "You so lucky the doctor is here today."

Murvee looked worried as he stared at Trent. "What you charge for fixing me up, doc? I don't make much. My mother makes money at the market, but she needs what I have to help take care of my brothers and sisters."

"Why don't you press that cloth against your forehead real firmly again and keep it there to stop the bleeding, okay, Murvee?" Chase said. "You don't have to worry about paying me. Miss Charlotte here pays me a lot, and she gets mad if I don't do any work to earn it."

He shot a teasing glance at her and she rolled her eyes in return, but there was a smile in them too. "We're going to have to have a little talk about your spreading rumors of what a tyrant I am," she said.

He chuckled and turned his attention back to Murvee. "Are you feeling okay? Not real dizzy or anything?"

"No. I feel all right."

"I'd like to take you back to the hospital to get you stitched up."

"No hospital." Murvee frowned, looking mulish. "I have to be home soon and I have to go to work. I can just have my mom fix it."

"Murvee…"

"How about stitching him in the jeep?" Charlotte suggested, giving him a look that said he was going to have to be flexible here. "I know you brought your bag with you. I'll help any way I can."

Trent sighed. He knew taking Murvee to the hospital and getting his wound taken care of there would take hours, and likely be tough on his family—if he could get the kid to go at all. "Fine. Since you seem okay other than the gash, I won't insist. Let's go to the car."

Murvee's friends helped him stand and the three of them headed down the beach. Trent kept an eye on the young man as they trudged to the car, and he thankfully did seem to be feeling all right, not shocked or woozy. Charlotte opened the back of her banged-up SUV and they worked together to get the kid situated inside and lying on a blanket with his feet propped up on the side beneath the window before Trent grabbed his medical bag.

"What do you need me to do first?" Charlotte asked.

"Did you bring any fresh water I can wash it out with? And are all the towels sandy, or do we have a clean one?" he asked.

"I brought extra towels. And I have water."

"Good." He turned to Murvee. "Let me see if the bleeding has stopped." The young man lifted away the shirt; the bleeding had, thankfully, lessened. Trent got everything set up as best he could in the cramped space, putting his flashlight, gauze, Betadine, local anesthetic and suture kit next to the young man. Squeezing out some of the sanitizer he always kept in his bag, he thoroughly rubbed it over his hands and between his fingers then snapped on gloves.

"Here's the water and towels." Charlotte came to stand next to him, knees resting against the bumper of the car. "What else can I do?"

He looked at her, standing there completely calm, and marveled again that she took on any task thrown at her calmly and efficiently. Including dealing with a bleeding gash that would look so awful to most non-medical professionals, it might make them feel a little faint, or at least turn away so they wouldn't have to look at it.

"You want to wash out the wound to make sure it's good and clean before I suture it? Put the folded towel under his head. After I inject the lidocaine, I want you to pour a steady stream of the water through the wound." He drew the anesthetic into the syringe. "You still doing all right, Murvee? I'm going to give you some numbing medicine. I have to use a needle, and it'll burn a little, but you won't feel the stitches."

Murvee held his breath and winced a few times as he injected it. "Sorry. I know this hurts, but pretty soon it will feel numb."

"I don't care, doc. I'm very grateful to you for help-ing me."

"I'm glad we were here today." He'd felt that way on many occasions in his life, since this kind of thing seemed to happen fairly often when he was working in the field, or even like today when he was touring and relaxing. Which was why he'd become convinced that whatever higher power was out there truly had a hand in the work-ings of the universe.

"Am I doing this right?" Charlotte asked as she contin-ued washing out the wound.

"Perfect." He studied it, satisfied that it looked pretty clean now. "I think we're good to go. Thanks." He squeezed a stream of antiseptic on gauze then brushed it along the wound's edges.

Trent saw Charlotte reach for the young man's hand and give it a squeeze. "Tell me about surfing, Murvee. How long have you been doing it?"

"Me and my friends surf for a year now. A guy from the UK was surfing here a while ago and he was really good. He showed some people how to surf, and now many of us do. I want to get good enough to compete in the Liberian Surfing Championships, which has been around about five years now, I think."

Trent glanced at Charlotte again as he got the suture materials together, smiling at the warm and interested expression on her face. He loved the many facets to her personality: the feisty fireball, the take-charge director, the soft and sexy woman whose love-making he knew would stay in his memory a long, long time and the per-son he was seeing now. She was nurturing and caring for this young man, distracting him with casual chit-chat so Murvee wouldn't think too hard about the time-consum-ing procedure Trent was about to do on him.

He nodded at his small but powerful flashlight and looked at Charlotte. "Will you shine that on the wound so

I can see better?" They were parked within the trees and, while it was far from optimal conditions for suturing, the flashlight illuminated well enough.

She pointed the light at the wound. "Does that help?"

"Yes, great," he said as he began suturing. It was deep and would require a three-layer closure. The boy was lucky a medic was here today. While the injury would likely have healed eventually on its own, his scars would have been bold and obvious, not to mention there was a good chance the wound would have become infected, maybe seriously.

"You should see the way your head looks, Murvee. You want to check it out in a mirror, so you can watch what Dr. Trent has to do to repair that nasty gash?"

"I don't know about that, Charlotte." Trent frowned at her in surprise. Trust a non-medical assistant to come up with a wacky idea like that, though it was probably because, if she'd had a wound that required suturing, Ms. Toughness would have wanted to watch.

"I would like to see," Murvee said. "I want to tell my friends what you had to do, what it looked like."

"So long as you don't faint on me." He smiled at the young man, who gave him a nice smile in return that seemed pretty normal and not particularly anxious.

Charlotte held up a small mirror in a powder compact and Murvee took it from her, moving his head around so he could see himself.

"Please hold still, Murvee." When this was over, he was going to give Charlotte a few pointers on doctor-assisting. She'd done a great job helping the boy relax, but this wasn't helping *him*, though he had to appreciate the ingenuity in her distraction techniques. If the boy didn't get queasy, that was.

"What exactly you doing?" Murvee asked as he looked at Trent suturing his wound in the mirror, seeming fascinated, thankfully, instead of disturbed.

Since the kid asked, he figured he might as well give

him the full details. "Your wound was so deep I could see some of your skull bone."

Murvee's eyes widened. "No kidding?"

"No kidding. I repaired the galea first—that's the layer that covers the bone. Now I'm sewing up the layer under the skin—we call it the subcutaneous tissue, or 'sub-Q.' You've got some very healthy sub-Q."

"Yeah, man. Fine sub-Q." He grinned, obviously proud, and Trent and Charlotte both laughed. "That's crazy-looking," Murvee said, staring into the mirror.

"The whole human body is kind of crazy-looking. One of the cool things about being a doctor is learning about how crazy it really is. And amazing."

Murvee looked at him then and Trent was glad the boy finally lowered the mirror. "Is my head going to look like this always, doc?"

"Not always." He gave Charlotte a look that she interpreted correctly, thank goodness, since she took the mirror from Murvee and tucked it into her purse. "After I finish, you'll look a little like Frankenstein, and your friends will be jealous of how cool and tough you look." He smiled, knowing from experience that boys and young men related to that and were usually amused. "But by sewing it in three steps using very tiny stitches it will heal well and, over time, the scar will become a thin line. You'll be as handsome as ever and all the girls will think you're great."

Murvee grinned at Trent's commentary, as he'd expected. "Girls think I'm great already."

The sound of Charlotte's little laugh brought their attention back to her. "I bet they do," she said. "And now you can talk to them about how you were hit by your board while you were surfing, which not many guys around here do, and ended up getting stitched up on the beach by a world-class surgeon."

"World-class?" Trent smiled, wondering if she'd really meant that, or if she was just talking to keep Murvee relaxed as he worked. Wondering why it felt nice for her to say it, when he'd always been sure he didn't need anyone's admiration or accolades.

"Are you kidding me?" Her green eyes met his and held, a brief moment of connection that warmed him in a totally different way than she'd warmed him in the water. "You're amazing. With technique like yours, you could be working as a plastic surgeon in Beverly Hills."

"Which would be your idea of having really made it, right?" Concentrating on suturing Murvee, disappointment jabbed at him that she apparently felt that way. He'd been there and done the Beverly Hills-type vanity plastic surgery and rejected it for a reason. A reason nobody understood or cared about.

"Is that a real question?" Charlotte asked, her expression one of annoyed disbelief. "If my idea of 'making it' was a Beverly Hills lifestyle, I'd have set my sights on a big hospital in the States after I got my degrees or gone to work on Wall Street. Not come to Liberia."

He looked back up at her. He should have realized her comment had just been intended as a light-hearted compliment. She was as far from a New York City or Beverly Hills socialite as a woman could be. "I know you haven't exactly chosen glamour over substance here. Except those pretty, polished toenails of yours could be considered pretty glamorous."

"Does that mean you like them? I changed the color last night." She smiled as their eyes met again and lingered.

"Yeah. I like them." He looked back down and continued the detailed suturing of Murvee's wound, trying to focus on only his work and not her lethal combo of femininity and toughness.

"Do you mind if I take a photograph of your injury, Murvee?" Charlotte asked.

When he agreed, she snapped a number of pictures and Trent wondered what she planned to use them for. Probably to put in a portfolio of the plastic surgery wing. Except it wasn't open yet.

Trent gave the young man some antibiotic tablets and instructions on how to take care of the wound.

"I know the hospital's a long way off. Any way you can get there in a week? I probably won't be there anymore, but there are several great techs who can remove your stitches. I'd also like you to have a tetanus shot."

"My family has a scooter, so I can come. Thank you again for everything." He pumped Trent's hand then reached for Charlotte's too, a smile so wide on his face you'd never have known the injury he'd just suffered if you hadn't seen the bandage on his head.

"You're very welcome. Like I said, I'm glad we were here today."

The young man headed back down the beach. Charlotte looked at Trent and the expression in her eyes made his breath hitch. He reached for her hand. "Ready, Miss Edwards?"

"Yes. I'm ready to head back."

He was pretty sure she knew that heading back to the compound wasn't what he'd been asking.

CHAPTER THIRTEEN

DARKNESS HAD NEARLY enfolded the hospital compound as Charlie pulled the car up to her house. When she'd dropped Trent off at his quarters, the look he'd given her before he'd walked away was sizzling enough practically to set her hair on fire.

Both excited and nervous, her insides felt all twisted around, thinking about her subterfuge with his release papers, the new doctor and all the things she was trying to manipulate. But all that worry wasn't quite enough to douse cold water on her plans. To keep her from wanting to relive, one more time, the passionate thrill of the night they'd spent locked in one another's arms the previous week.

Still sitting in her car with the engine off, she stared at a small impediment to that plan, all too clearly apparent in the lights that were currently burning in her house. Her dad was staying with her and wasn't leaving for another day or two.

Which meant that her house as a rendezvous for Trent and her to make love all night was out. Her mind spun with ideas of where else they might meet, though it couldn't be from now into the morning. The various possibilities, and the memories of their past love-making, had her ready to leap out of the car to run and pound on the man's door, despite the fact that she'd dropped him off only minutes ago.

Had she suddenly become a sex maniac? The thought made her laugh at herself, at the same time her anticipation ratcheted higher. For whatever reason, the secretiveness added a certain allure; why that was, she didn't know. But she wasn't going to fight the excitement she felt, because she knew she'd only get to enjoy it one more time.

The real question was, should she go inside and have dinner with her dad, take a shower to wash off the beach then find an excuse to leave again? Or just not come back until later? Her dad had encouraged her to take time off today, after all. Maybe he'd just assume they'd made a long day of it in Robertsport.

Except he'd know that wasn't true, because Patience had been with them and would be ready for bed very soon.

She shook her head at her ambivalence, reminding herself that she was twenty-seven years old and a grown woman. Her father wasn't naive or judgmental. Shoving open the car door, she decided she'd just go in and say hello, then tell him she had dinner plans with Trent; never mind that there couldn't be a candlelit dinner in a restaurant, just leftovers in the hospital kitchen.

The sound of her father's favorite jazz music met her as she opened the front door. He sat in one of the upholstered chairs she'd bought when she'd moved here, since little of the original furniture had survived the pillaging during the wars. The hospital files were open on his lap and he looked up with a smile as she entered the room.

"Did my girl get in the water today?"

"I did. I even rode a wave all the way in to shore. How about that?"

He clapped his hands. "Bravo! I'm proud of you. And not just for swimming today. For all you've done here." He gestured to the files. "I'm so impressed with what you've accomplished with the funding you have. You're making huge headway, especially considering the shambles you were left to work with."

"Thanks, Dad. That means a lot to me." When her parents had trusted her to bring the hospital and school back to life, it had been scary and admittedly daunting. But, with John Adams's help, they'd done a lot. And she had to admit she felt pretty proud of what they'd accomplished too.

"I know the plastic surgery wing is important to you, and of course I understand why." His expression was filled with both sympathy and pain. "You had to deal with a lot as a little girl."

"Things happen for a reason, Dad. You know that as well as anyone. I hope that experiencing what it feels like to look abnormal will end up helping people who have to deal with things a whole lot worse than my childhood embarrassment."

"I do know. And I'm excited about your project. But I have to ask some hard questions now, not as a father, but as a businessman. And this has to be treated like a business."

Uh-oh. She gulped, afraid she knew what was coming next. "What are your hard questions?"

"What happens if, by some stroke of bad luck, the Gilchrist Foundation money doesn't come through? Do you have a backup plan?"

She closed her eyes for a moment, wondering how she should answer. Should she tell him she'd known all along that it was a risk? That maybe it was a risk she shouldn't have taken? She forced herself to open her eyes and tell him the truth. "Honestly? No. I don't. If the foundation money doesn't come through, we're in serious trouble. I'm trying to solicit other sources of income, but none of it is for sure until we have it in our hands."

He nodded. "All right. So when will you know about the foundation money?"

"Soon. They're sending their rep here in the next few days to see if we meet their requirements."

"And I see that you've met all those requirements except for one: a plastic surgeon on site."

"I *do* have a plastic surgeon on site—Trent. I just need for him to stay until their representative gives us the green light. Then we'll have the Gilchrist check and it'll all be good."

He looked at her steadily. "Except that something tells me Trent doesn't know about all this."

For once, she wished her dad wasn't so darned intuitive. "No. He doesn't. I don't see any reason for him to know."

"Why not? Seems to me he's an important part of the equation."

"Only for a short time. He performed a brilliant plastic surgery on a boy here in the hospital and another today on the beach that I can show pictures of." She sucked in a fortifying breath so she could continue. "He doesn't want to be involved, Dad. For some reason, he doesn't want to perform plastic surgeries. But I'm still hoping he'll agree to help a few patients with serious problems before he leaves."

"He seems like a good man. You should tell him the truth."

The truth? Her dad didn't know about the lies she'd told and her stomach twisted around when she thought about what his reaction would be if he did. If he'd still be as proud of her as he said he was. "I'm handling it, Dad. It will turn out okay; we'll get the funding." And she prayed that would really happen and every problem would be solved.

"I hope you're right. Now, there's something else we need to talk about, Charlie." Her father threaded his fingers together in his lap and looked at her. "Your goals are worthy goals. Your hard work is to be commended. But have you ever asked yourself if there's more you need to consider?"

"Such as?"

"Your own life." He stood and placed his hands on her shoulders. "Have you thought about exploring a relationship with a man who lives here? Or one of the single doctors coming through? Trent has impressed me, and I've met Perry Cantwell—who's coming soon, I think you said. He's nice enough, and good-looking to boot. I know it's damned difficult to meet someone when you live and work where there aren't too many folks around. I don't want to see you give everything of yourself for this place until there's nothing left of you to share with anyone else. I've seen it happen and I don't want it to happen to you."

"It won't. I promise. I just need to get that wing open and the place running smoothly then I'll think of other things besides work. I will."

And that was the truth. Even in the midst of this serious conversation with her dad, and all the stress over the hospital's finances, thoughts of Trent were foremost in her mind, thoughts of meeting with him and finishing what they'd started this afternoon. All those thoughts sent her breathing haywire and her pulse skipping and she just wanted to end this conversation and be with him.

"In fact, Dad, Trent and I are going to have a late dinner over in the hospital. Are you okay here eating leftovers on your own?"

His serious and worried expression gave way to a big smile. "Of course. Leftovers are my favorite."

"Good." She kissed his cheek then gave him a fierce hug. She wouldn't tell her dad that the thought of giving up her freedom forever, her ability to live as she wanted and do as she wanted and run the hospital as she wanted, sent a cold chill down her spine. Or that one more wonderful night with Trent just might be enough to satisfy her relationship needs for a long, long time. "Thanks for the advice, Dad."

"Okay." He hugged her back just as fiercely. "Go on, now."

* * *

The night air embraced Charlie with a close, sultry warmth as she walked toward the hospital quarters. A huge gibbous moon hung in the sky, casting a glow of white light across the earth. Her feet moved in slow, measured steps, her dad's words echoing in her head.

Could there possibly ever be anything between her and Trent other than physical pleasure and friendship, a friendship based on both of their experiences working in developing nations and an appreciation of the tremendous need there?

No. She shook her head in fervent denial. What the two of them had experienced during their one night together was what anyone would feel after being focused on only work for months and months. What Trent no doubt felt for all the various women in his life, which if rumor was to be believed were many. He was famous in the GPC community for enjoying short and no doubt very sweet interludes until he moved on to his next job.

She could deal with that. After all, hadn't she known it from the start? Enjoying one more night of fantastic sex with a special man would be wonderful, just as it had been last week, without thoughts of tomorrows and futures and what any of it might mean.

The employee quarters loomed gray in the darkness, its roof lit by moonlight, and her steps faltered, along with her confidence. He'd said he wanted to be with her just one more time, hadn't he? She could only hope, now that they were on dry land and no longer only half-dressed, a knock on his door wouldn't bring the cool Trent who sometimes appeared. The one who had shown very clearly how little he wanted to be stuck with her in this little, forgotten place in Liberia.

A shadowy figure suddenly became visible in front of her and she nearly let out a small shriek at the apparition.

"Charlotte? Is that you?"

"Yes." She exhaled at the sound of Trent's low voice, blaming the surprise of his sudden appearance for her weak and breathy reply. "I was…coming to see if you wanted to find some dinner in the kitchen."

"Now there's a surprise—you being hungry again. Let's see what we can do about that." Through the darkness, she saw the gleam of his eyes for what seemed like barely a second before he moved fast and was there, right in front of her, his arms wrapping around her, pulling her close. Before she could barely blink, he was kissing her.

And kissing her. His mouth possessed hers in a thorough exploration that stole her breath. Not rushed, but intense and deep, giving and taking, completely different from his teasing, playful kisses of before. Every hard inch of him seemed to be touching her at once, his chest pressing against her breasts, his thighs to her hips, his taut arms against her back.

A small moan sounded in her throat as his mouth devoured hers. She wanted this: wanted this sensory explosion; wanted his kisses and touch and the heat that crawled and burned across her skin.

His mouth left hers, softly touching her eyelids, her nose, her lips, stealing her breath. "You taste so good to me, Charlotte. Way better than any food, though I have a feeling that the more I taste you, the hungrier I'm going to get."

"Me too. Food is overrated." He tasted so delicious, so wonderful, so right. His lips and tongue returned to her mouth with an expertise that dazzled, so mind-blowing that her skin tingled, her knees got wobbly and, if he hadn't been holding her so tightly, they might have simply crumpled beneath her.

She flattened her palms against the firm contours of his chest, up to his thick, dark hair that was getting a little long, and the feel of its softness within her fingers was as sensual as the feel of his body pressed to hers.

The little moan she heard this time came from him, and he pulled his mouth from hers, his heartbeat heavy against her breasts. "Charlotte." His hands roamed across her back and down to her bottom, pulling her so close that his erection pressing against her stomach nearly hurt. "Do you have any idea how hard it's been for me to keep my distance this week? Not to come into your office and lock the door and make love to you right on top of your desk?"

She might have had some idea, since the thought of knocking on the door of his quarters had crossed her mind more than once when she'd been sitting alone in her house, lying alone in her bed. "On top of my desk? It's a little small, don't you think?"

"Probably." She could see the adorable, perpetual gleam of humor behind the sexual glint in his eyes. "And the examination table is too narrow. My bed is small, too, and pretty squeaky at that. Which leaves us with finding a soft place on the ground beneath the stars tonight."

"I hope you're not thinking of making love in the mud. That sounds a little….messy."

He kissed her again, his hands moving to her waist, up her ribs, stopping for a breathless moment just beneath her breasts before moving up to cup them both. They tightened and swelled within his palms, and she wanted to be done with the talking and drag him to the ground.

"I have the place already picked out, with a thick blanket already unfolded on the ground. After I make love to you, we'll take a shower together." His lips moved to her ear, his voice a hot whisper that sent shivers skating across her flesh. "I want to taste the sea on you, lick the salt from your skin. Wash every inch of you and start all over again."

Her heart pounded so hard in her ears, she thought he just might be able to feel the vibration on his tongue as he traced it over the shell of her ear. Her breath was coming in short gasps, and she was burning up inside, wanting him more than she'd ever wanted anything in her life.

"What about dinner?" Goodness, she could barely talk. "You must be hungry."

"For you. Most definitely hungry for you." The expression in his eyes told her he wanted her every bit as much as she wanted him, and she loved that she could make him feel that way. "But I know about that stomach of yours. I have a picnic dinner all ready in my room. For later."

She managed a small laugh. "How did you find time to do all that?"

"I had powerful motivation to move fast." His lips touched one corner of her mouth, then the other, and she found herself chasing after them for a real kiss.

"So where is this blanket? If we don't go there soon, my knees will be too weak to walk."

"Not a problem." He released her and quickly swung her into his arms. A squeak of surprise left her lips and he pressed his mouth to hers as he strode through the darkness. "Quiet." His eyes, now dark, glittered with both passion and amusement. "You want somebody in the hospital quarters to investigate a possible murder? Or your dad?"

"No. Though you are about killing me here." She wrapped her arms around his neck and pressed her mouth to his throat. "How far do we have to go?"

"Are you talking about where the blanket is? It's close." His eyes, glinting, met hers. "But if you're talking about something else, the answer is, as far as we possibly can."

His words made her laugh at the same time as a wave of hot need enveloped her. A need to experience another unforgettable night as exhilarating as the one they'd shared before.

He carried her deeper into the palm forest then stopped. She glimpsed the blanket lying open on the ground before he released her, letting her body slowly slide down his until she stood teetering slightly on her own feet, her dress bunched up to her hips where he still held on to her.

The dress bunched higher, slipping up her torso as he tunneled his hands beneath it until it was up and off of her. Until she stood in only her white bra and panties, and the misty touch of the moonlight made them seem to glow in the darkness. He looked at her, and even through the low light she could see the heat in his gaze, the tautness of his jaw, and her body throbbed for him.

"Do you have any idea how beautiful you are?" His voice was low, rough, and he lifted one hand to trace his finger along the lacy edge of her bra. "The very first moment I saw you in your office, I wanted to know what you looked like naked. And when you gave me that gift, it was more amazing than I could ever have dreamed."

He lowered his mouth to hers, one hand closing over her breast. The other cupped her waist then deliciously stroked along her ribs and down over her bottom covered in only her thin panties. She gasped at the pleasure of it. How had she managed to keep him at arm's length for the past few days? And, as his touch caressed her, thrilled her, she wondered why she had.

She broke the kiss to fumble with the buttons on his shirt, wanting to feel his skin too. Wanting to run her fingers across the hardness of his muscles, the surprising silkiness of his skin, the soft, dark hair covering it. "You know what I thought was the sexiest thing about you when we first met?" she asked.

"My amazing intelligence?" The teasing look was back in his eyes, along with a sexual gleam that intensified the ache between her legs.

"Your hands. Those long surgeon's fingers of yours. I just had a feeling they were very, very talented. Little did I know exactly how talented, with your plastics skills and magic skills and piano skills."

"And other skills." His lips curved and with a quick, deft movement, he flicked open her bra and slid it from her arms. "I'm looking forward to showing you some you haven't seen yet."

She wished her fingers were as magical as his as she struggled to get the last of the annoying buttons undone. Finally, finally, she was able to shove his shirt from his shoulders to see his muscled chest. She flattened her hands against it, loving the feel of it, thrilling in the quick, hard beat of his heart against her palms. "Oh, yeah? Like what?"

"Showing is always better than telling." He shucked his pants and underwear until he stood fully naked, the moonlight illuminating the broadness of his shoulders, his lean hips, his strong thighs and the powerful arousal between them.

"Hmm. Is this what you wanted to show me?" Desire for him nearly buckled her knees and she decided to take matters into her own hands, so to speak. She reached for him as she kissed him, stroking him, teasing him, and she felt him respond with a deep shudder. A low groan sounded in his throat. His hands tightened on her back and his fingers dug into her bottom until it nearly hurt.

"Not exactly. Oh, Charlotte." There was a ragged hitch to the way he said her name, and in the next breath he practically pushed her down onto the blanket, kissing her, covering her body with his heavy warmth that felt impossibly familiar, considering how short their time had been together the week before.

His fingers teased her nipples, glided slowly down, over her ribs, her belly, then lower. They slipped slowly, gently in and around the moist and slick juncture between her thighs; the sensation was most definitely magical. She couldn't control the movement of her hips as they reached for his talented fingers, sought more of the erotic sensation he gave her.

She needed more. Needed all of him. "Now, please, Trent. I want you now."

"If I could say no, not yet, I would. But, damn it, I can't

wait any longer to be inside of you." Propped onto his elbows, he stared down at her. The intensity in his blue eyes held hers, mesmerized, as she opened for him, welcomed him. And, when he joined with her, it felt so wonderful, so familiar and yet so new all at the same time.

Rhythmically, they moved together, faster and deeper, until the earth seemed a part of them and the night stars seemed to burst into an explosion of light. And as she gave herself over to the pleasure of being in his arms, to the ecstasy of being at one with him, she cried out. He covered her mouth with his, swallowing the sounds of both of them falling.

For a long while, they lay there together as they caught their breath and their heart rates slowed. His face was buried in her neck. His weight felt wonderful pressing her into the soft earth, and she made a little sound of protest as he eventually rolled off her, keeping her hand entwined with his.

Still floating in other-worldly sensation, the sound of his laughter surprised her. She turned her head to look at him. "What's so funny?"

"Looks like we managed to lose the blanket." Despite the darkness, his eyes met hers, his teeth gleaming white as he grinned. "I guess we made love in the mud after all."

She looked down and realized that they were, indeed, squished down into the mud; how they hadn't noticed that, she couldn't imagine. Actually, she could. Her mind slipped back to how wonderful it had been to be with him again, and just thinking about it made her feel like rolling her muddy body on top of him.

So she did, and he laughed again as she smeared a handful of mud on his chest and stomach then wriggled and squished against him. "I think I like it. Don't people pay good money for mud baths?"

"They do. I'm pretty sure pigs like mud too."

"Are you calling me a pig?"

He gave her a lazy, relaxed smile as he stroked more cool mud over and across her bottom, which felt so absurdly, deliciously sensual she couldn't help wriggling against him a little more. "I've been around enough women in my life to never, ever say anything that stupid."

The thought of all the women he'd had in his life shouldn't have had the power to bring the pleasure of the moment down, but somehow it did. Which was silly, since she knew the score, didn't she?

Something of her thoughts must have shown in her expression, because he wiped his muddy hand on the blanket then stroked her hair back from her face, all traces of amusement gone. "I have been to a lot of places and known a lot of people." He tucked her hair behind the ear her plastic surgeon had created for her then traced it softly, tenderly, with his finger. "But you're special. I've never met anyone who is such an incredible combination of sexiness, compassion and take-no-prisoners toughness. You amaze me. Truly."

"Thank you." Her heart swelled at his sweet words and she used her one not-muddy hand to cup his cheek as she leaned down to give him a soft kiss. "You amaze me too. Truly."

"And I can tell you that, if I was going to fund a school or a hospital anywhere, I'd trust you to run it." Through the moonlit darkness, his eyes stared into hers with a deep sincerity. "I'd trust you with anything."

Damn. His words painfully clutched at her heart and twisted her stomach, making her feel slightly sick. He'd trust her with anything?

She could only hope and pray he never found out exactly how misplaced that trust really was.

CHAPTER FOURTEEN

THE DELICIOUS PICNIC Trent had put together for them, complete with a bottle of wine he said he'd tucked in his bag for the right moment, was the most intimate and lovely meal Charlie had experienced in her life. It didn't matter that they'd both been curled up on his skinny bed, towels wrapped around and beneath their muddy bodies, and that the wine "glasses" had been plastic cups.

After they'd eaten, the pleasure of the shower they'd shared—laughing as they'd washed the mud off their bodies, then no longer laughing as they enjoyed making love again within the erratic spray of water—wasn't quite enough to make Charlie completely forget his words. To forget his misplaced trust in her. To remember her conviction that the end was worth the means.

She'd hardly slept after she'd crept into her house and fallen into her bed, tired, wired and worried. And still she ended up back at her desk as the sun rose. She stayed closeted in her office much of the day, contacting every potential donor, digging everywhere she could to possibly find some cash commitments in case the Gilchrist donation fell through.

Thankfully, the hospital and clinic had been busy too so she and Trent hadn't seen one another except when he'd passed by her accidentally left-open door, giving her a sexy, knowing smile and a wink.

Deep in thought, a knock on the now closed door startled her. "Come in." She readied herself to see a tall, hunky doctor with amused blue eyes, but relaxed when her dad appeared.

"Hi, honey. Have a second?"

"Of course."

He settled himself in the only other chair in her tiny office. "I've decided to head on home tonight, instead of waiting until tomorrow. Your mom called to say a church group has sent a few members to study our school, and I'd like to be there to talk with them when they get there."

"I understand, Dad. I'm planning to come see you and Mom soon for a few days anyway, as soon as…things are settled here." No point in starting up another conversation about the hospital funding and potential problems there. She stood and rounded the desk, leaning down to kiss his cheek. "But you should wait until tomorrow morning. Why in the world would you drive at night on these roads if you don't have to?"

"I'm stopping on the way. Do you remember Emmanuel and Marie? I'm going to visit them and check out their school, which is just across the border in the Ivory Coast. I'm staying there a day, then heading home." He threaded his fingers together like he always did when he had something serious to say, and she braced herself. "Will you remember what I said about not giving everything to this place? About being open to the possibilities that may come along in your personal life? Think about giving Perry Cantwell a fair shot."

"Does Charlotte have a personal life with Perry Cantwell?"

She swung around and stared at Trent leaning casually against the doorjamb, a smile on his face. But his eyes were anything but amused. They looked slightly hard and deadly serious.

A nervous laugh bubbled from her throat. The man was

leaving in a matter of days. Surely he wasn't jealous of some possible future relationship with his replacement? "I've never even met Perry Cantwell. But seems to me you've been anxious for him to get here so you could leave. Maybe I'm anxious for him to get here, too."

It wasn't nice to goad him like that after what they'd shared together last night and she knew it. But her emotions were all over the place when it came to Trent: needing him to stay until the Gilchrist rep came; wanting him to stay because she'd grown closer to him than was wise, closer than she should have allowed. This looming goodbye was going to be so much harder than the first one, as she'd worried all along it would be. And added to that was the fear that he'd somehow find out about her machinations, destroying the trust, the faith, he said he had in her.

Which shouldn't really have mattered, since he'd be out of her life all too soon. But somehow it mattered anyway. A lot.

His posture against the doorjamb relaxed a little, as did the cool seriousness in his eyes. His lips curved as he shook his head, but that usual twinkle in his eyes was still missing. "Perry's a good surgeon, but I hear he cheats at golf. Talks down to nurses. Sometimes dates men. Not a good fit for you, Charlotte."

"I'm pretty sure you're making all that up." She stepped back to her desk and rested her rear end against it. "Dad's right that I need to keep all possibilities open—except maybe not men who date men."

Her dad chuckled, which reminded her he was there. "I've got to get going before it gets any later. Will you stay with Charlie tonight, Trent? I know we haven't had any sign of burglars since before I got here, but I'd feel better if we gave it a few more nights."

"Dad, I don't—"

"Of course I will. You didn't have to ask; I would've been there, anyway."

The smoldering look he gave her both aroused and embarrassed her, and she hoped her father didn't see it, along with the blush she could feel filling her cheeks. Though she had a feeling her dad wouldn't exactly be surprised to know that she and Trent were a little more than just acquaintances and colleagues.

Her father stood. The small smile on his face told her he'd seen Trent's look and was more than aware of the sizzle between them. She blushed all over again. "I need to grab my files before I go." He looked at the various piles on her desk and frowned, lifting up one or two. "I thought they were right here. Did you move them?"

"I put them—" Oh no; he had his hands on the pile she'd shoved Trent's release papers into, practically right in front of the man! Why, oh why hadn't she buried them deep in a drawer? She hastily reached to grab them. "Don't mess with that pile, Dad. Yours are—"

And because she was so nervous and moving too fast, and karma was probably getting back at her, the middle of the pile slid out and thunked on the floor, with some of the papers fluttering around Trent's feet.

He reached down to gather the mess and she feared she just might hyperventilate. Snatching them up and acting even stranger than she was already would just raise suspicion, so she forced herself to quickly but calming retrieve and stack the files. Until her heart ground to a stop when she saw Trent had a paper in his hand and was reading it with a frown. She couldn't think of anything else that would make him look so perplexed.

"When did this come?" His attention left the paper and focused on her. "This isn't my original release from the GPC. It's dated—" he looked down again "—three days ago. Why didn't you give me this? And why didn't they send it directly to me, like usual?"

She licked her dry lips. "Because Cantwell wasn't here yet, I guess. He was all scheduled to come, which is why they sent your papers, but then something went wrong, I don't know what." Except she did know. Colleen hadn't arranged for Cantwell's travel because a certain desperate, deceiving hospital director had lied and told her Trent had agreed to stay until the Gilchrist rep came.

The end justified the means, she tried to remind herself as she stared at the confusion on Trent's face. Except it was getting harder and harder to feel convinced of that.

"You still should have given them to me. Once the GPC releases me, my vacation is supposed to officially start. I need to find out when I'm expected in the Philippines now. That might have changed."

Her heart in her throat, she forced a smile. "I'm sorry if I messed this up. I'll call Colleen."

"Don't worry about it. I'll call."

His face relaxed into that charming smile of his, which somehow made the nervous twist in her stomach tighten even more painfully. The man really did like and trust her. Thank heavens the Gilchrist rep was due here any day, then this would all be over and he could be on his way.

And that thought made her stomach twist around and her chest ache in a whole different way.

"I've got my files here, Charlie. So I'm going to hit the road."

She turned to her dad, having nearly forgotten— again—that he was in the room. How was that possible since he stood only three feet from her? His expression was serious, speculative. Probably he, too, was wondering what was going on with her and why she'd buried Trent's papers deep within a pile.

"It's been nice to meet you, sir," Trent said, reaching to shake her dad's hand. "And don't worry. I'll take care of your daughter until I leave here."

"Thank you. I appreciate it."

"I'm standing right here, remember?" Relieved to be back to a joking mood, Charlie waved her hands. "How many times do I have to tell you two? I don't need to be taken care of."

"We know." Her dad smiled, but his eyes still held a peculiar expression as he looked at her. "We just like to look after you. Is that so bad?"

She looked at Trent, horrified at the thought that filled her head. That she couldn't think of anything better than for him to stay here a full year, living with her and looking after her, the two of them looking after each other.

She could only imagine how appalled he'd be if he somehow read those thoughts in her face and she looked down at her desk as she changed the subject. "Can I help you get your things together, Dad? I'm about to head to the house anyway."

"Already done. My car's outside, ready to go." He pulled her into his arms for a hug. "We'll see you when you come visit next month."

"Can't wait to see both of you. Bye, Dad."

With a smile and a squeeze of Trent's hand, he disappeared, leaving the two of them alone in a room that now seemed no larger than a broom closet. She felt the heat of Trent's gaze on her, felt the electric zing from the top of her head to her toes, and slowly turned to look at him.

His hand reached out and swung the door closed, and that gesture, along with the look in his eyes as they met hers, made her heart beat hard at the same time as her stomach plunged.

She was crazy about this man. There was no getting around it, and she wanted so much to enjoy every last day, every last hour, every last minute she had with him. Surely he wouldn't find out about her lies? Maybe, even, he'd decide to stay longer on his own. It could happen, couldn't it?

She stepped forward at the same moment he did, their arms coming around one another, their lips fusing in a burning kiss that held a promise of tonight, at least, being one she'd never forget.

His warm palms slid slowly over her back, down her hips and back up, her body vibrating at his touch. The kiss deepened, his fingers pressed more urgently into her flesh and, when he broke the kiss, a little sound of protest left her tingling lips.

"You sure your desk is a little too small?" His eyes gleamed hotly, but still held that touch of humor she loved.

"Yes. We already had files all over the floor once tonight." The thought of why exactly that had happened took the pleasure of the moment down a notch, but she shook it off. She wasn't going to let anything ruin what could be one of her last nights with him. Reluctantly, she untangled herself from the warmth of his arms. "I'm going to head home. Join me for dinner about seven?"

"I'll be there." He leaned in once more, touched his lips to hers and held them there in a sweet and intimate connection that pinched her heart. "Don't be surprised if I'm even a little early."

She watched him leave, gripping the edge of her desk to hold herself upright, refusing to think about how, for the first time since she'd moved here, she would feel very lonely when he was gone.

The lowering sun cast shadows through the trees as Charlie approached her house, surprised to see Patience in front of the porch with little Lucky jumping around her feet.

"What are you doing here, Patience? Where's your dad?"

The little girl's smile faded into guilt. "Daddy was in a long, long meeting with Miss Mariam and I got tired of waiting. I came to show you the new trick I taught Lucky."

Oh, dear. John Adams was not going to be happy about this. "You know you're not allowed to leave the school and come all the way down here by yourself."

"I know. But it's just for a little bit. So I can show you. Then will you take me home?"

Charlie sighed. The child had the art of cajoling and wheedling down to a science. So much for getting showered and primped up before Trent came for their big datenight. "Okay. But promise me you won't do this again. You're not big enough to be running around all by yourself."

"I promise." The words came out grudgingly, but when Lucky yapped her eyes brightened again. "So, look! Sit, Lucky. Sit!"

The little pup actually did and Patience gave her some morsel as a reward, beaming with triumph as the dog began yapping and dancing again. "See Miss Charlie? She's really smart!"

"She is." She clapped her hands in applause, smiling at how cute and excited the child was. "And you being a good dog trainer helps her be smart."

"I know. I—"

A long, low growl behind her made Charlotte freeze, every hair on her scalp standing up in an instinctive reaction to the terrifying sound. She swung around and, to her horror, a large, feral and very angry dog stood there, its own hackles rising high on its back.

CHAPTER FIFTEEN

"PATIENCE." THE HARD hammering of her heart in her chest and her breath coming in short gasps made it difficult to sound calm. But the last thing she needed was for Patience to panic and make the situation worse. "Move very, very slowly and pick up Lucky, then quietly go up the porch steps and into the house. Don't make any sudden movements."

The child didn't say a word, probably as terrified as Charlie felt. The dog's lips were curled back in a snarl, showing every sharp tooth in its foamy mouth, and its jaws snapped together as it stared right at her. She couldn't risk turning around to see if Patience had done as she'd asked, because if it attacked she had to be ready. And it looked like it was about to do exactly that.

She glanced around for some weapon she could use to bash the dog if she had to. A sturdy stick was lying about five feet away and she slowly, carefully, inch by inch, sidled in that direction, her heart leaping into her throat as the dog growled louder, drool dripping as it snapped its jaws at her again.

Damn, this was bad. The animal had to be rabid; there was no other explanation for its aggression. That thought brought a horrified realization that this was probably the animal that had attacked and killed Patience's other dog. It was unusual enough to see feral dogs here and she knew the likely reason this one was still around was because it was very, very sick.

The sound of her screen door closing was a relief, and she prayed that meant Patience was out of harm's way. Should she try to talk soothingly to the dog? Or yell and try to scare it? She didn't know, and the last thing she wanted to do was something that would trigger it to attack her.

Sweat prickled at every pore, and her breath came fast and shallow as she kept her slow progress toward the stick, never taking her eyes off the animal. She was close. So close now. But how to pick it up when she got there? A fast movement to grab it and swing hard if the dog lunged? Keep her actions slow and steady, so she could get the stick in her hand and maybe not have to use it at all if she could just get back to the porch and in the house?

With her heart beating so hard it was practically a roar in her ears, she leaned down slowly, slowly, keeping her movements tight and controlled as she closed her fingers around the stick.

In an instant, the dog leaped toward her, mouth open, fangs dripping, knocking her to the ground, its teeth sinking deep into the flesh of her arm as she held it up in futile defense.

A scream of panic, of primal terror, tore from her throat. She tried to swing the stick at the dog, screaming again, but her position on the ground left her without much power behind the blow, and she realized the animal's teeth were sinking even deeper.

Some instinct told her to freeze and not to try to pull her arm from the dog's mouth, that it would just hold on tighter, shake her and injure her even worse. Its eyes were less than a foot from hers, wild eyes filled with fury above the jaws clamped onto her arm. It was so strong, so vicious, and a terrible helplessness came over her as she frantically tried to think how she could get away without getting hurt even worse, or maybe even being killed.

A loud, piercing gunshot echoed in the air and a split-second later the dog's jaws released her, its body falling limply on top of hers. Unable to process exactly what had happened, she grabbed her bleeding arm and tried to squirm out from under the beast.

"Charlotte." Trent was there, right there, his foot heaving the lifeless dog off her, crouching down beside her. "Damn it, Charlotte. Let me see."

"Trent." Her voice came out as a croak. It was Trent. Trent carefully holding her arm within his cool hands, looking down at it. Trent who had saved her life.

Her head dropped to the ground and she closed her eyes, saying a deep prayer of thanks as she began to absorb everything. Began to realize that the danger was past.

"Charlotte. Look at me." His gentle hand stroked her hair from her forehead and cupped her jaw, his thumb rubbing across her cheekbone. "Let me see." He tugged at her wrist and she realized she was still clutching her arm. She loosened her grip, feeling the sticky wetness of her blood on her hand as she dropped it to the ground. "You feel faint?"

"Y…yes." Stars sparkled in front of her eyes as she stared at the jagged gashes. At the oozing blood.

"Hang in there with me, sweetheart." He looked only briefly at her wounds before he yanked his shirt open—a nice, white button-down shirt, she processed vaguely—and quickly took it off. He wrapped it around her arm and applied a gentle pressure then lifted her hand up and placed it where his had been. "Squeeze to help stop the bleeding. I'm getting you to the clinic."

She could barely do as he asked but she tried. The screen door slammed behind them and Charlie became aware of the sound of Patience crying.

"Mr. Trent! Is Miss Charlie okay?"

"She's okay, but I need to take care of her. You stay in the house and I'll call your dad to come get you."

"O…okay."

The door slammed again as Trent lifted Charlie into his arms and strode in the direction of the hospital. She let her head loll against his muscled, bare shoulder, at the same time thinking she shouldn't let him haul her all the way there. She might not be big, but she wasn't a featherweight either.

"It's too far for you to carry me. I can walk."

"Like hell. For once, will you let someone take care of you? Let yourself off the hook for being in charge of the world?"

"I don't…I don't think I do that. But I admit I'm feeling a little shaky."

He looked down at her, his blue eyes somehow blazingly angry and tender at the same time. "A little shaky? You were just mauled by a rabid dog. You've lost a lot of blood. It's okay for you to lean on me a little, just once."

"Yes, doctor."

He gave her a glimmer of a smile. "Now that's what I like to hear. Keep pressing on your arm," he said as they finally got to the hospital and he laid her on an exam table. He placed a pillow beneath her head then made a quick call to John Adams. She watched him pull the pistol from his waistband and place it on the counter, wash his hands, then move efficiently to various cupboards, stacking things on the metal table next to her.

"Thank you. I…don't want to think about what might have happened if you hadn't come when you did."

"I don't want to think about it either." His lips were pressed together in a grim line, his eyes stark as they met hers. "When I heard you scream, my heart about stopped."

"Why did you have a gun with you?"

"I work in plenty of unsafe places in the world, and always pack my thirty-eight. I had it with me because you left yours upstairs last time when you were supposed to be ready for a burglar, remember?"

She thought of how the dog had been right on top of her and shuddered. "How did you learn to shoot like that? Weren't you afraid you'd hit me instead?"

"No. Even though I was scared to death, I knew I'd hit the dog and not you." A tiny smile touched his lips as he placed items on the table. "I was on the trap and skeet shooting team at Yale. Rich boys get to have fun hobbies, and this one paid off."

Rich boys? She was about to ask, but he handed her a cup of water and several tablets. "What is this?"

"Penicillin. And a narcotic and fever-reducing combo. It'll help with the pain. I have to wash out your wounds, which is not going to feel good."

He lifted up her arm, placed a square plastic bowl beneath it and began to unwrap his poor white shirt from it, now soaked in blood. Those little stars danced in front of her eyes again and she looked away. "Tell me the truth. How bad is it?"

"Bad enough. I'll know more in a few minutes." His expression was grim. "Because that dog was obviously rabid, I have to inject immunoglobulin. I'm also going to inject lidocaine because—"

"I know, I know. So I won't feel every stitch. Do it quick, please, and get it over with."

He gave a short laugh, shaking his head. "You're something else." He pressed a kiss to her forehead, before his eyes met hers, all traces of amusement gone. "Ready? This is going to hurt like hell. Hang in there for me."

She nodded and steeled herself, ashamed that she cried out at the first injection. "Sorry," she said, biting her lip hard. "I'm being a baby."

"No, you're not. I've seen big tough guys cry at this. You're awesome. Just a little longer."

When it was finally over, she could tell he felt as relieved as she did. "That's my girl." He pressed another lingering kiss to her head. "This next part is going to hurt, too, but not nearly as bad as that."

He poured what seemed like gallons of saline over her arm. He was right; it did not feel good. She thought he'd finally finished until he grabbed and opened another bottle. "Geez, enough already! What could possibly still be in there?"

"Is there some reason you have to keep questioning the doctor?" His blue eyes crinkled at the corners. "With all the technology and great drugs we have, thoroughly washing wounds like this—any animal bite, but especially when the dog is rabid—is the best treatment there is. But this is the last jug, I promise."

"Thank goodness. I was about to accuse you of making it hurt as much as you possibly can."

"And here I'd been giving you credit for being the bravest patient ever." His smile faded and he gave her a gentle kiss, his eyes tender. "I'm really sorry it hurts. Good news is, it looks like there's no arterial damage and the bites didn't go all the way to the bone. I'm going to throw some absorbable stitches into the deep muscle tears to control the bleeding then get everything closed up."

Instead of watching him work on her arm, she looked at his face. At the way his brows knit as he worked. At the way his dark lashes fanned over the deep focus of his eyes. At the way he sometimes pursed his lips as he stitched. Almost of its own accord, her hand lifted to cup his jaw and he paused to look at her, his blue eyes serious before he turned his face to her palm, pressing a lingering kiss there.

"Are you going to use a bunch of tiny stitches so I don't have awful scars?"

"I can't this round, sweetheart." He shook his head. "This kind of wound has a high risk for infection. We have to get the skin closed with as few stitches as possible, because the more I put in the more chance of infection. After it's healed completely, though, I can repair it so it looks better."

Except he wouldn't be here then. Their eyes met as the thought obviously came to both of them at the same time.

"I mean, one of your plastic surgeons can when the new wing is opened." His voice was suddenly brusque instead of sweet and tender.

She nodded and looked down, silently watching him work, her heart squeezing a little. How had she let herself feel this close to him? So close she would miss him far too much when he was gone.

When it was all over and her arm was wrapped in Kerlix, taped and put in a sling, he expelled a deep breath. "How about we head to your house and get you settled and comfortable? I'll carry you."

"I really am okay to walk." She didn't trust herself not to reveal her thoughts and feelings if he carried her, folded against his chest. "I need to."

He looked at her a moment then sighed. "All right. So long as you let me hold you in case you get dizzy."

Trent held her close as they walked slowly toward the front porch of her house and she let herself lean against his strength. The dog's body was gone, thank goodness, though there were bloodstains in the dirt. John Adams must've taken care of it. She was glad she didn't have to look at it and remember its wild eyes; see again those teeth that had ripped her flesh and held her tight in their grip.

"I feel kind of bad for the dog," she said.

"You feel sorry for the dog?" He stared down at her, eyebrows raised.

"Rabies is a pretty horrible way to die, isn't it? You shooting it was the best way for it to go."

"Yeah. It's one hundred percent fatal after it's been contracted. It's a good thing we have the vaccine to keep you safe from the virus." He looked away, his voice rough when he spoke again. "After you get settled inside, I'll come out and rake up the dirt. Don't think you want to be looking at your own blood every time you come in and out of your house."

"No. I don't." She looked up him and marveled at his consideration. "Who knew you were Mister Thoughtful and not the full-of-yourself guy I was convinced you were?"

"I'm both thoughtful *and* full of myself—multi-faceted that way."

His eyes held a touch of their usual amusement and as she laughed her chest filled with some emotion she refused to examine.

CHAPTER SIXTEEN

TRENT KNEW THE narcotics would have worn off and Charlotte would be in pain again this morning. He'd slipped from the bed and gone downstairs to make toast and coffee for her, wanting something in her stomach before he gave her more fever medication, and the narcotic, too, if she needed it.

When he came back to her room with a tray, he had to pause inside the doorway just to look at her. Her lush hair tumbled across the pillow, the sun streaking through the windows highlighting its bronze glow. Her lips were parted, her shoulder exposed as one thin strap of her pretty nightgown had slid down her bandaged arm, leaving the gown gaping so low, one pink nipple was partly visible on her round breast.

He deeply inhaled, a tumble of emotions pummeling his heart as he stared at her. To his shock, the foremost emotion wasn't sexual.

It was a deep sense of belonging. Of belonging with her.

He wanted to stay here with her. He wanted to wake up in her bed, in her arms, every morning. He wanted to see her, just like this, at the start of each and every day.

Her eyelids flickered and she opened her eyes and looked at him. She smiled, and that smile seemed to reach right inside of him, pull him farther into the room. Pull him closer to her.

He managed to speak past the tightness in his chest. "Good morning, Charlotte." He set the tray on her night-stand and perched himself on the side of the bed. He stroked her hair from her face, wrapped a thick strand around his finger. "How's the arm feeling?"

"Not so great." She rolled onto her back, her lips twist-ing.

He ran his finger down her cheek. "I figured that. I brought you some toast and coffee and more meds."

"Thank you." Her good arm lifted to him and her palm stroked his cheek. He wished he'd shaved already, so the bristles wouldn't abrade her delicate skin when he kissed her. "But all I want is the fever stuff. I can't spend the day all doped up. I want to know exactly what's happening."

He nodded. "If you decide you need it later, you can always take it then. Why don't you sit up and have a little bit to eat first." He started to stand, but her hand grabbed the front of his shirt and bunched it up as she tugged him toward her.

"I am hungry again. But not for food—for you."

"Charlotte." He wanted, more than anything, to make love with her. But she was in pain and the need to take care of her, to keep her arm still so she wouldn't be in worse pain, took precedence over everything. "You need to rest."

"I've been resting all night. I slept very well, thanks to the drugs you gave me." She smiled at him and pulled harder on his shirt, bringing him closer still, and he could feel his resolve weakening at the way she looked at him. It was as though she was eating him up with her eyes and he knew he wanted to eat her up for real. "I do need to feel better. And you're very, very good at making me feel better."

"Well, I am a doctor. Took the Hippocratic Oath that I'd do the best I could to help my patients heal." He smiled, too, and gave up resisting. He gave in to the desire spiraling through his body. "What can I do first to make you feel better?"

"Kiss me."

Her tongue flicked across her lips and he leaned forward to taste them, carefully keeping his body from resting against her arm. It took every ounce of self-control to keep himself in check, to touch her and kiss her slowly, carefully.

"Does it make you feel better if I do this?" He gently drew her nightgown down and over her bandages, then lifted her arm carefully above her head to rest it on her pillow. He traced the tops of her breasts with his fingertips, slowly, inching across the soft mounds, until he pulled the lacy nightgown down to fully expose her breasts.

The sunlight skimmed across the pink tips and his breath clogged in his throat as he enjoyed the incredible beauty of them. Of her. He lowered his mouth to one nipple then rolled it beneath his tongue, drew it into his mouth and lifted his hand to cup the other breast in his palm.

"Yes," she murmured. The hand on her good arm rested on the back of his head, her fingers tangling in his hair. "I'm feeling better already."

"How about this?" His mouth replaced his hand on her other breast, his fingertips stroking along her collarbone, her armpit, down her ribs, and he reveled in the way she shivered in response.

"Yes. Good."

He slowly tugged her nightgown farther down her body, gently touching every inch he could with his mouth, his tongue, his hands. He could feel her flesh quiver, felt the heat pumping from her skin, and marveled at how excruciatingly pleasurable it was to take it this slow. To think only of making her feel good, to feel wonderful, to feel loved.

The shocking thought made him freeze and raise his head.

Loved? He didn't do love.

But as he looked down at her eyes, at the softness, heat and desire in their green depths, his heart squeezed at the same time it expanded.

He did love her. He loved everything about her. He loved her sweetness, her toughness and her stubbornness and was shocked all over again. Shocked that the realization didn't scare the crap out of him. Shocked that, instead, it filled him with wonder.

He lowered his mouth to hers, drinking in the taste of her, and for a long, exquisite moment there was only that simple connection. His lips to hers, hers to his, and through the kiss he felt their hearts and souls connecting as well.

He drew back, and saw the reflection of what he was feeling in her eyes. Humbled and awed, he smiled. "Still feeling good? Or do you need a little more doctoring?"

"More please." She returned his smile, which changed to a gasp when he slipped his hand beneath her nightgown, found her moist core and caressed it.

"We need to lose this gown. I want to see all of you. Touch and kiss all of you." He dragged the gown to her navel, her hipbones, his mouth and tongue following the trail along her skin. He wanted nothing more than this. He wanted to help her forget her pain. For her to feel only pleasure.

She lifted her bottom to help him pull it all the way off, and he took advantage of the arch of her hips, kissing her there, touching and licking the velvety folds until she was writhing beneath his mouth.

"Trent," she gasped. "You've proven how good you are at making me feel better. But I want more. Why are you still dressed? I don't think I can strip you with only one hand."

He looked at her and had to grin at the desire and frustration on her face. "You want me to strip? I'm at your command, boss lady." He quickly shucked his clothes and took one more moment to take in the beauty of her nakedness, before carefully positioning himself on top of her as she welcomed him.

With her eyes locked on his, he moved within her. Slowly. Carefully. She met him, moved beneath him, urged him on. The sounds of pleasure she made nearly undid him and he couldn't control the ever-faster pace. There was nothing more important in the world than this moment, this rhythm that was unique to just the two of them, joining as one. And, when she cried out, he lost himself in her.

Curled up with Trent's body warming her back, his arms holding her close, Charlie felt sated, basking in the magic of being with him; wanting to know more about him.

"Tell me about being a rich boy. That's what you said you are, isn't it?"

He didn't respond for a moment then a soft sigh tickled her ear. "Yes. My family is wealthy and I have a trust fund that earns more money each year than most people make in ten."

"And yet you work in mission hospitals all over the world. Why?"

"For the same reason you live and work here—to give medical care to those who wouldn't have any if we didn't."

She turned her head to try to look at his face. "When did you decide to live your life that way instead of working in some hospital in the States? Or being a plastic surgeon for the rich and famous?"

The laugh he gave didn't sound like there was much humor in it. "Funny you say that. My dad and grandfather have exactly that kind of practice. I was expected to follow in their footsteps, but realized I didn't want to. When I was about two-thirds of the way through my plastics residency, I knew I wanted to do a surgical fellowship in pediatric neurosurgery instead."

Wow. She'd known he had amazing skills, but he did brain surgery too? "Did you?"

"No. I couldn't get into a program. Was rejected by every one I applied to. Then found out why."

She waited for him to continue but he didn't. "So, why?"

He didn't speak for a long time. She was just about to turn in his arms, to look in his eyes and see what was going on with him, when he answered. His voice was grim. "My mother was hell-bent on me joining the family practice. I didn't realize how hell-bent until I found out she'd used her family name, wealth and the power behind all of that to keep me out of any neurosurgery program. All the while pretending she supported my decision, when in fact she was manipulating the outcome. So I left. Left the country to do mission work, and I haven't been back since."

Charlie's breath backed up in her lungs and her heart about stopped. His mother had deceived him and lied? He'd obviously been horribly hurt by it. So hurt that he'd cut his family from his life. So hurt that he'd left the U.S. and hadn't returned.

It also sounded horrifyingly similar to what she'd been doing to him, too.

Her stomach felt like a ball of lead was weighing it down. "I'm…sorry you had such a difficult time and that you were hurt by all that."

"Don't be. It's ancient history, and it was good I learned what kind of person she really is."

The lead ball grew heavier at his words, making her feel a little sick, and she couldn't think of a thing to say. He kissed her cheek, his lips lingering there, and a lump formed in her throat at the sweetness of the touch.

"I'm going to fix you some brunch. Something better than the toast you didn't eat." He nipped lightly at her chin, her lips. "And, just for you, I'm going to perform a surgery today that I think will make you happy. But I'm not telling until after it's done."

She squeezed his hand and tried to smile. "Can't wait to hear about it." She drew in a breath and shook off her fears. He wouldn't find out. It would be okay. They'd get the donation check, the new wing would open and, when all that was behind them…then what?

She knew, and her heart swelled in anticipation. She'd ask him to stay, and not for the hospital. She'd tell him she was crazy about him, that she wanted to see where their relationship could go. The thought scared her and thrilled her; she was not sure how risky that would be. How it would feel to share her life and her world with someone. But she knew, without question, it was a risk she had to take.

By the way he'd made love to her, looked at her, taken care of her, maybe he'd actually say yes.

CHAPTER SEVENTEEN

TRENT LEFT THE OR, feeling damned pleased at the way the cleft palate surgery had gone for the child. He knew Charlotte would be happy too and couldn't wait to tell her.

The satisfaction he felt made him realize he'd been too hasty believing the skills he had were superfluous and not a good way to help people, and children in particular, as he wanted to. Working in his family's cosmetic surgery practice hadn't been what he wanted. But Charlotte had helped him see that those skills really were valuable in helping people have better lives.

While he'd done plastics procedures at many of his other jobs, it had taken her dogged persistence to make him see how important those techniques could be to those without hope of improving their lives that way except through a hospital like this one.

Striding down the hall, he couldn't believe his eyes, seeing the woman who was on his mind. There she stood, talking to John Adams, like it had been a week instead of a day since her ordeal. Hadn't he specifically told her to stay home and rest?

"What possible excuse do you have for being here, Charlotte?"

"I got bored. There's too much to do to just sit around."

"You're not just sitting around." He wanted to shake the damn stubborn woman. "Resting helps your body heal.

Gives it a chance to fight infection. Which, in case you don't remember, is particularly important after a nasty dog bite." He turned to John Adams. "Can you talk sense into her?"

"Last time she listened to me was about six months ago or so," he replied, shaking his head.

Trent turned back to her, more than ready to get tough if he had to. "Don't make me drag you back there and tie you down."

She scowled then, apparently seeing that he was completely serious, gave a big, dramatic sigh. "Fine. I'll go rest some more. Though every hour feels like five. Can I at least take a few files with me to go over while I'm being quiet?"

The woman was unbelievable. "If you absolutely have to. But no moving around unnecessarily. No cooking dinner. I'll take care of that."

"Yes, Dr. Dalton."

He ignored the sarcastic tone. "That's what I want to hear from my model patient." He noted the blue shadows beneath her eyes, the slight tightness around her mouth that doubtless was from pain she was determined not to show, and couldn't help himself. He leaned down to give her a gentle kiss, not caring that John Adams was standing right there. "I just finished the cleft palate surgery I promised you I'd do. Now I want you to give me a promise in return— that you'll take care of yourself. For me, if not for yourself."

Her eyes softened at the same time they glowed with excitement. "You fixed the boy's cleft palate today? That's wonderful! Did you take pictures like I asked you to? I need pictures to— Well, I just think we should keep a record."

"All taken care of. Now for your promise."

"I promise." She sent him a smile so wide, it lit the room. "I'll see you at home."

At home. That had a nice sound to it. He found himself admiring her shapely legs beneath her skirt, watching the slight sway of her hips all the way down the hall and out the door, and when he turned he saw John Adams eyeing him speculatively.

"So, is something going on between you and Charlie? I thought you were leaving in just a day or two. Speaking of which, did you go over everything Thomas needs to know about her stitches and the rabies vaccine course?"

He looked back at the door Charlotte had disappeared out of, and realized if he left it would be just like that— she'd disappear from his life and he'd likely never see her again.

With absolute conviction that it was the right decision, he knew he wasn't going to leave. He had to be here to take care of her, to improve the scarring on her arm after she was healed, to see exactly what a year with her would be like.

He turned back to John Adams. "I'm staying."

The man smiled and clapped him on the shoulder. "Good to hear. Welcome to the family."

Trent changed out of his scrubs, cleaned up and called Mike Hardy before going to Charlotte's so he could tell her his decision. He could only hope she'd be as happy about him staying as he felt about it. Thinking of the way they'd made love just that morning, the look on her face and in her beautiful eyes as they'd moved together, he had a pretty powerful feeling that she would be.

"Mike? Trent Dalton. How are you?"

"Good, Trent. Great to hear from you. Are you enjoying your vacation in Italy?"

"No." Had the man forgotten about all the delays? "I'm still at the Edwards Hospital in Liberia."

"You're still in Liberia?" The man sounded astonished.

"Why? Perry Cantwell went there last week, so you should be long gone by now."

"Perry was delayed, so I had to stay on until he could get here." How could Mike not know all this? "I've decided I want to stay here for the next year. I'd like you to find a replacement for me in the Philippines and draw up a new contract for me."

"Trent, we never have two doctors at the Edwards Hospital. We just can't afford it."

He frowned. Mike usually bent over backwards if he had a special request, which he rarely did. Trent was one of only a handful of GPC docs that worked for them full-time, year-round. "I don't need another doc here with me. I'm sure Perry wouldn't care if he's here or in the Philippines. Ask him."

There was a silence on the line, which made Trent start to feel a little fidgety, until Mike finally spoke again. "I just found your file to see what's going on. Your release papers were sent well over a week ago. And I know Perry was about on his way when I had Colleen send them, so I'm confused. This is all a real problem, messing up your pay and vacation time and next assignment. I need to talk to Colleen and find out how these mistakes happened before we have any more discussion about you staying there. I'll call you back."

"All right."

The conversation with Mike left him feeling vaguely disturbed, but he brushed it off. He couldn't imagine there would be a problem. It probably would just come down to shuffling paperwork.

Since he had no idea when Mike would call him back, he went on to Charlotte's house. If he didn't find her resting, he was going to threaten her with something—maybe refusing to kiss her or make love with her would be a strong enough incentive, he thought with a smile. He knew that if she threatened him with something similar he'd follow any and all instructions.

He let himself in the door. Seeing her curled up in the armchair, her hair falling in waves around her shoulders, her expression relaxed, filled his chest with a sense of belonging that he couldn't remember having felt since before he'd left the States. Since before the betrayal by his mother. A cozy, welcoming old home with a beautiful and more than special woman inside waiting for him was something he'd never thought he wanted until now.

He stood there a moment, knowing he was beyond blessed to have been sent to this place on what was supposed to have been a fill-in position for just a few days. Another example of the universe guiding his life in ways he could never have foreseen.

"Hey, beautiful." He leaned down to kiss the top of her head, his lips lingering in the softness of her hair. "Thank you for being good, sitting there reading. I'm proud of you."

Her hand cupped his cheek, her eyes smiled up at him, and that feeling in his chest grew bigger, fuller. "I decided I should do what you ask, since you did that cleft palate surgery today like you promised. Not to mention that whole saving my life thing." Her voice grew softer. "I'm so lucky to have you here."

He was the lucky one. "I want you to eat so you can take some more pain medicine before that arm starts to really hurt again. Let me see what's in the kitchen."

His cell rang while he was putting a quick dinner together and he was glad it was Mike Hardy. "What'd you find out?"

"You're not going to like it." Mike's voice was grim and a sliver of unease slid down Trent's back. "Colleen's over here wringing her hands."

"Why?"

"She sent your release papers to the director of the hospital, instead of to you, because Charlotte Edwards asked her to. Apparently she's a good friend of Colleen's, and said she'd pass them on to you. Ms. Edwards also told her not to schedule Perry's travel yet because she claimed you'd agreed to stay on another two weeks.

"According to Colleen, the hospital has to have a plastic surgeon on site when the Gilchrist Foundation rep comes there in another day or so. If it doesn't, she won't get the donation she needs and won't be able to pay the bills. I guess they're pretty deep in the hole over there, might even have to shut the whole thing down. Charlotte Edwards's solution was to keep you there—get you to do some plastic surgeries she could impress Gilchrist with and pass you off as her new plastic surgeon. After that, Colleen was going to get Perry there and you could be on your way. But it's obvious you didn't know about any of this."

With every word Mike spoke, Trent's hands grew colder until he was practically shaking from the inside out with shock and anger. Everything Charlotte had said to him spun through his mind: praising his plastic surgery skills, begging him to do those surgeries and take photos, telling him there were problems with his paperwork, delays in getting Perry there. Coming up with a fake excuse when he'd found his release papers in her office.

Flat-out lying to him all along. Manipulating his papers, his life. His heart.

It was like *déjà vu*, except this was so much worse. Because she'd obviously only been pretending to like him. She'd obviously only had sex with him to keep him there, to tangle him up with her so he wouldn't leave until after the Gilchrist rep came.

And what had Mike said? After that, Colleen had the green light to get him out of there. *Bye-bye, have a nice life, I don't need you anymore.*

How could he have been so stupid, so blind? It was

all so clear now, all the plastic surgery crap lines she'd fed him.

She hadn't cared when he'd left the first time and she sure as hell wouldn't care this time.

Balling his hands into fists, he sucked in a heavy breath, trying to control the bottomless anger and pain that filled his soul until it felt like it just might rip apart.

He had to get out of there. He'd already gone over with Thomas what had to happen with the rabies vaccine. She'd be all right. And the fact that the thought came with a brief worry on her behalf made him want to punch himself in the face.

Fool me once, shame on you. Fool me twice, and I'm obviously a pathetic moron.

"Thanks for telling me, Mike. I'm going to make my own arrangements to leave."

"All right. Perry's travel arrangements are being finalized this minute, so he'll be there soon."

Somehow, he managed to finish fixing Charlotte's dinner while he dialed the airline, relieved to find he could be out of there at the crack of dawn tomorrow.

He set her food on the table, placed two pain tablets next to it and forced himself to go into the parlor. The smile she sent him across the room felt like a stab wound deep into his heart. "Dinner's on the table. Come eat, then take your pills."

As she passed through the kitchen doorway, he stepped back, not wanting to touch her. Knowing a touch would hurt like a bad burn, and he'd been scorched enough.

"Where's yours?" She looked at him in surprise, her pretty, lying lips parted.

He'd play the part she'd once accused him of, so she wouldn't know he knew the truth. So she wouldn't know how much it hurt that she'd used him. That the pain went all the way to the core of his very essence, leaving a gaping hole inside.

It seemed like a long time since she'd told him he was full of himself and famous for kissing women goodbye with a smile and a wave. He'd do it now if it killed him.

"Colleen Mason just called to tell me I have a plane reservation in the morning, that I've been given the all-clear," he said, somehow managing a fake smile.

She sank onto the kitchen chair, staring. "What? I don't understand. I don't have… Perry Cantwell's not… I mean, that can't be right."

"It is. My vacation's been delayed long enough, and I'm meeting a…friend…in Florence." He leaned down to brush his lips across hers, and was damned if the contact wasn't excruciating. "It's been great being with you. But you know how I feel about long goodbyes, so I'll get out of here."

"But, Trent. Wait. I—"

"Take care of that arm." He turned and moved quickly to the door, unable to look at her face. To see the shock and despair and, damn it, the tears in her eyes. To know her dismay had nothing to do with him and everything to do with her precious hospital.

The thought came to him that he was running again. Running from pain, disillusionment and deep disappointment. And this time he knew he just might be running for the rest of his life.

CHAPTER EIGHTEEN

CHARLIE LAID HER head on her desk because she didn't think she could hold it upright for one more minute.

In barely forty-eight hours, her life had gone to ruin, and no amount of hard work and positive attitude was going to fix it.

She'd been a fool to think there had been any possibility of her relationship with Trent Dalton becoming anything bigger than a fling. It'd been foolish to allow her feelings to get out of control. To allow the connection she felt to him to grab hold of her—a connection that had bloomed and deepened until she could no longer deny the emotion.

She thought she'd seen that he felt it too. Had seen it in his eyes; seen it in the way he cared for her when she'd been hurt; seen it through his kisses and his touch.

Then he'd walked out. One minute he was sweetly there, the next he was kissing her goodbye with a smile and a wave, just like the first time. But, unlike the first time, he'd taken a big chunk of her heart with him.

How could she have been so stupid? She'd known all along it could never be more than a fling. Had known he was right, when he'd come back, that they should keep their relationship platonic—because, as he'd so eloquently said, second goodbyes tended to get messy.

Messy? Was that the way to describe how he'd left? It

seemed like their goodbye had been quite neat and tidy for him.

Anger burned in her stomach. Anger that she'd let herself fall for a man who'd never hidden that he didn't want or need roots. Anger that the pain of his leaving nagged at her far more than the physical pain of her torn and stitched-up arm.

And of course, practically the minute he'd moved on, the Gilchrist rep had shown up. He'd been impressed with the wing but, gosh, there was this little problem of there not being a doctor there. She'd hoped the photographs of Trent's work would help, but of course it hadn't. After all, the man was long gone, and they'd made their requirements very clear.

A quiet knock preceded the door opening and Charlie managed to lift her head to look at John Adams, swallowing the lump that kept forming in her throat.

"I'm guessing things didn't go well," he said as he sat in the chair across from her.

"No. The Gilchrist Foundation can't justify giving us the check without meeting all their requirements. Which I knew would happen."

"What are you going to do?"

Wasn't that a good question? What was she going to do to keep the hospital open? What was she going to do to mend her broken heart? What was she going to do to move past the bitterness and regret that was like a burning hole in her chest?

"I don't know. I have to crunch the numbers again, see what can be eliminated from the budget. Lay off a few employees. See if any of the other donors I've approached will come through with something." Though nothing could come close to what Gilchrist had offered. To what the hospital needed.

"There is the money the anonymous donor gave the school." John Adams looked at her steadily. "I can put off hiring another teacher, hold off on some of the purchases we made."

"No." She shook her head even as the suggestion was tempting. "Whoever donated that money gave it to the school. It wouldn't be right to use it for the hospital. I'll figure something out."

"All right." John Adams stood and gently patted her head, as though she were Patience. "I'm sorry about all this. And sorry about Trent leaving. I've got to tell you, that surprised me. Especially since it was right after he'd told me he was staying."

"He told you he was staying?"

"He did. After he was irritated with you being in the hospital when you were supposed to be resting."

And his caring for her through all that was part of what had made her fall harder for him. "Well, he obviously didn't mean it the way most people would. Staying the night is probably what that word means to him." She tried to banish the acrid and hurt tone from her voice. After all, she'd known the reality. Regret yet again balled up in her stomach that she'd allowed herself to forget it.

Trent walked beneath the trees in Central Park to his parents' Fifth Avenue apartment on Manhattan's Upper East Side. He breathed in the scents of the city, listened to children playing in the park and the constant flow of traffic crowding the street and looked at the old and elegant apartment buildings that lined the streets.

It didn't seem all that many years ago since he'd been a kid roaming these streets, not realizing at the time how different growing up here was from the average kid's childhood in suburbia. But it had been great too, in its own way, especially when your family had wealth and privilege enough to take advantage of everything the city offered and the ability to leave for a quieter place when the hustle got wearying.

His mother had been more hands-on than most of the crowd his parents were friends with, whose full-time nannies did most of the child-rearing. He'd appreciated it, and how close they'd been, believing that the bond she shared with her only child was special to her.

Until she'd lied and betrayed him. The memory of that blow still had the power to hurt.

He thought of how his mother had tried to reach out to him during the years since then. She'd kept tabs on wherever he was working, and each time he moved on to a new mission hospital a Gilchrist Foundation donation immediately plumped their coffers. She'd sent him a Christmas card every year, with updates on what she and his dad were doing, where they'd traveled, asking questions about his own life. Questions he hadn't answered. After all, what he wanted to do with his life hadn't interested her before, so he figured it didn't truly interest her now.

She'd been shocked and seemingly thrilled to get his phone call that morning and he wondered what it would be like to see her after all this time. A part of him dreaded it. The part of him that still carried good memories wanted, in spite of everything, to see how she was. Either way, the need at the Edwards hospital was what had driven him here. Not for Charlotte—for all the patients who would have nowhere to go if the place shut down.

"Mr. Trent! Is that you? I can't believe it!" Walter Johnson pumped his hand, a broad smile on the old doorman's face.

"Glad to see you're still here, Walter." Trent smiled, thinking of all the times the man had had his back when he'd been a kid. "It's been a long time since my friends and I were causing trouble for you."

"You just caused normal boy trouble. Kept my job interesting." Walter grinned. "Are your parents expecting you? Or shall I ring them?"

"My mother knows I'm coming. Thanks."

The ornate golden elevator took him to his family's fourteen-room apartment and he drew a bracing breath before he knocked on the door. Would she look the same as always? Or would time have changed her some?

The door opened and his question was answered. She looked lovely, like she always had. Virtually unchanged—which wasn't surprising, considering his dad was a plastic surgeon and there were all kinds of cosmeceuticals out there now to keep wrinkles at bay. Her ash-blonde hair was stylishly cut and she wore her usual casual-chic clothes that cost more than most of his patients made in a year.

"Trent!" She stepped forward and he thought she was going to throw her arms around him, but she hesitated, then grasped his arm and squeezed. "It's just…wonderful to see you. Come in. Tell me about yourself and your life and everything."

Sunlight pouring through the sheer curtains cast a warm glow upon the cream-colored, modern furnishings in the room as they sat in two chairs at right angles to one another. One of her housekeepers brought coffee and the kind of biscuits Trent had always liked, and he felt a little twist of something in his chest that she had remembered.

"My life is good." Okay, that was a lie, right off the bat. His life was absolute crap and had been ever since he'd found out Charlotte had lied to him, that their relationship had been, for her at least, a means to an end and nothing more.

For the first time in his life, he'd fallen hard for a woman. A woman who was like no one he'd ever met before. Had finally realized, admitted to himself, that what he felt for Charlotte went far beyond simple attraction, lust or friendship with benefits.

And, just as he'd been ready to find out exactly what all those feelings were and what they meant, he'd been knocked to the ground by the truth and had no idea how he was going to get back up again.

"We've…we've missed you horribly, Trent." His mother twisted her fingers and stared at him through blue eyes the same color as his own. "I know you were angry when you left and I understand why. I understand that I was wrong to do what I did and I want to explain."

"Frankly, Mom, I don't think any explanation could be good enough." He didn't want to hash it out all over again. It was history and he'd moved on. "I'm not here to talk about that. I'm here to ask you a favor."

"Anything." She placed her hand on his knee. "What is it?"

"I've been working at the Edwards hospital in Liberia. They'd applied to you, to the Gilchrist Foundation, for a large donation to build and open a plastic surgery wing."

She nodded. "Yes. I'm familiar with it. In fact, I just received word that we won't be providing the donation now because they didn't meet the criteria."

"They're doing good work, Mom, and use their money wisely. I performed some plastic surgeries there and saw how great the need is. I'd appreciate it if you would still give them the donation."

"You did plastic surgery there?" She looked surprised. "Last time I spoke with you, when you stormed out of here, you told me that wasn't what you wanted to do. What changed your mind?"

"I haven't changed my mind. I didn't want to join the family practice doing facelifts and breast implants. I wanted to use my surgical skills to help children. But I've realized that I can do both."

"Are you working at the Edwards hospital full-time now? Permanently?"

"No." He'd never go there again, see Charlotte Edwards again. "It was time to leave. But I know they're getting a surgeon as soon as they can. I'd appreciate you giving them the funding check, which will help the rest of the hospital too. The people there need it."

"All right, if it's important to you, I'll get it wired out tomorrow."

"Thank you. I'm happy that, this time, what's important to me matters to you." Damn it, why had that stupid comment come out of his mouth? She'd agreed to do as he asked. The last thing he wanted was for her to change her mind, or dredge up their past.

"Trent." He looked at her, and his gut clenched at the tears that swam in her eyes. "Anything that's important to you is important to me. I know you don't want to hear it, but I'm telling you anyway—why I did what I did." She grabbed one of the tiny napkins that had been served with the coffee and dabbed her eyes. "When I went to college, all I wanted was to be a doctor. To become a plastic surgeon like my father and join his practice. I studied hard in college, and when I applied to medical schools I got in. But my father said no. Women didn't make good doctors, he said, and especially not good surgeons. I couldn't be a wife and mother and a surgeon too and needed to understand my place in our social strata."

He stared at her, stunned. It didn't surprise him that his autocratic grandfather could be such a son-of-a-bitch. But his mother wanting to be a doctor? He couldn't wrap his brain around it. "I don't know what to say, Mom. I had no idea."

"So I married your dad and he joined the practice. Filled my life with my philanthropy, which has been rewarding. And with you. You were…are…the most important thing in my life. Until I messed everything up between us." The tears filled her eyes again and he was damned if they didn't send him reaching to squeeze her shoulder, pat her in comfort, in spite of everything.

"It's all right, Mom. It was a long time ago."

"I want you to understand why, even though there's no excuse, and I know that now." Her hand reached to grip his. "I just wanted you to have what I couldn't have. I wanted that for you, and couldn't see, because of my own disappointment from all those years ago, that it was for me and not for you. That I was being selfish, instead of caring. I'm so very, very sorry and I hope someday you can forgive me. All I ever wanted was for you to be happy. You may not believe that, but it's true."

He looked at her familiar face, so full of pain and sadness. The face of the person who had been the steadiest rock throughout his life, until the moment she wasn't.

He thought about the fun they'd had when he was growing up, their adventures together, her sense of humor. He thought about how she'd always been there for him, and for his friends too, when most of their parents weren't around much. And he thought about how much he'd loved her and realized that hadn't changed, despite the anger he'd felt and the physical distance between them for so long.

He thought of how many times she'd tried to reach out to him through the cards she sent and through giving to the places he worked, places that were important to him.

As he stared into her blue eyes, he knew it was time to reach back.

"I do believe it, Mom. I'm sorry too. Sorry I let so many years go by before I came home. I don't completely understand, but I do forgive you. Let's put it all behind us now." He leaned forward to hug her and she clung to him, tears now streaming down her face.

"Okay. Good." She pulled back, dabbing her face with the stupid little napkin, and smiled through her tears. "So I have a question for you."

"Ask away."

"Are you in love with the woman in charge of the Edwards hospital?"

He stared at her in shock. She had on her "mom" look he'd seen so many times in his life. The one that showed she knew something he didn't want her to know. He was damned if the woman hadn't always had a keen eye and a sixth sense when it came to her only child. "Why would you ask that?"

"Because you've been working in hospitals all over the world for years, and I know you donate money to them. There must be some reason you came here to see me and ask me to give the Edwards hospital the foundation money, and some reason you're not donating your own." She arched her brows. "If she hurt you, I'm taking back my agreement to give them the money."

He shook his head, nearly chuckling at her words, except the pain he felt over Charlotte's lies was too raw. "She worked hard to get the Gilchrist Foundation donation. I'd like it to come through for her and the hospital."

"And?"

He sighed. Sitting here with her as she prodded him for information felt like the years hadn't passed and he was a teenager again. "Yes, I'm in love with her. No, she doesn't return my feelings." Saying it brought to the surface the pain he was trying hard to shove down.

"How do you know? Did she tell you that?"

"She lied to me and used me. Tried to keep me there just to get your donation for her precious hospital. Not something someone does to someone they love."

"I don't know. I love you but I lied and made stupid mistakes. Have you told her how you feel?"

He stared at her, considering her words. Could Charlotte have done what she did and still cared about him at the same time? "No. And I'm not going to."

"But you still love her enough to make sure she gets the donation from my foundation."

"It's for the hospital, not her." But as he said the words he knew it was for Charlotte as well, and hated himself for it.

She regarded him steadily. "I think it's for both the hospital *and* her. I made a bad mistake. Maybe she did too. Don't compound it by making your own mistakes." She stood and smiled, holding out her hand like he was still a little kid. "Come on, prodigal son. Your dad will be home soon. Stay for dinner and we'll catch up."

"I'm sorry, Colleen. For everything. I hope Mike wasn't mad that you sent the release papers to me instead of Trent." Charlie studied her online bank statements as she talked to her friend, despairing that she'd find a way out of their financial problems. With everything else a total mess, getting Colleen in trouble would make the disaster complete.

"No, he's not. I wish you hadn't lied to me, though."

"I know. I'm so, so sorry. Everything I did was stupid and didn't even solve anything."

"I bet Trent was really angry about it." Her voice was somber. "I know he left there—I arranged his travel for when he heads to Europe from the U.S. What did he say?"

"He never found out, thank heavens." That would have been the worst thing of all. Despite the crappy way he'd left, she wouldn't have wanted him to know what she'd done.

"What do you mean? Of course he did. He was telling Mike he wanted to stay there in Liberia. Be assigned at your hospital for the year. And that's when Mike told him everything you'd done."

Charlie's heart lurched then seemed to grind to a halt. The world felt a little like it was tilting on its axis, and as she stared, unseeing, at her office wall, it suddenly became horribly, painfully clear.

Trent hadn't left because he was tired of her, ready for vacation, ready to move on. He'd left because he knew she'd lied and manipulated his paperwork. He'd left because of what she'd done to him.

"Oh my God, Colleen," she whispered. Trent had once told her that trying to control the direction the world spun would end up weighing heavily on her shoulders. Little had he known exactly how true that was. At this moment, that weight felt heavy indeed.

Numb, she absently noted a ping on her computer that showed a wire transfer from a bank. Mind reeling, she forced herself to focus on business. Any money would help pay a bill or two.

But when she pulled it up, her mind reeled even more dizzily. Air backed up in her lungs and she couldn't breathe. "Oh my God," she said again, but this time it was different. This time it was in stunned amazement. "It's the donation from the Gilchrist Foundation. All of it they'd committed to us. What…? Why…this is unbelievable!"

"Oh, Charlie, I'm so happy for you! This is awesome!"

"Yes. It is. Listen, I need to go. I'll call you later." Charlie hung up and stared at the wire transfer, unable to process that it had come through, beyond relieved that the hospital wouldn't have to shut down. Once the plastic surgeon showed, they'd be able to get the wing open and operating for a long time, helping all those who so needed it.

But knowing her project would now be complete didn't bring the utter satisfaction it should have. Didn't feel like the epitome of everything she'd wanted. And as she stared at her computer she knew why.

She'd ruined the sweet, wonderful, fledging romance that had blossomed between her and Trent. Through her adamant "the end justifies the means" selfish attitude, she'd no doubt hurt the most amazing, giving, incredible man she'd ever known.

He'd wanted to stay the year with her, which just might have turned into forever. But instead, she'd destroyed any chance of happiness, of a real relationship with him.

Her computer screen blurred as tears filled her eyes and spilled down her cheeks. How could she have been so stubbornly focused on the hospital's future that she couldn't see her own, staring her in the face through beautiful blue eyes?

She'd always prided herself on being a risk-taker. But when it came to the most important risk of all—risking her emotions, her life and her heart—she'd cowardly backed away in self-protection. Afraid to expose herself to potential pain, she'd tried to close a shell around her heart, hiding inside it like a clam. But somehow he'd broken through that shell anyway.

Why hadn't she seen she should have been honest with Trent, and with herself, about all of it? Maybe the outcome would have been different if she had, but now she'd never know. Trent doubtless hated her now, and she had only herself to blame.

Her phone rang, and she blinked at the tears stinging her eyes, swallowing down the lump in her throat to answer it. "Charlotte Edwards here."

"Ms. Edwards, this is Catherine Gilchrist Dalton. I'm founder and president of the Gilchrist Foundation. I wanted to make sure you received our donation via wire."

"Yes, I did, just now." The woman was calling her personally? "I'm honored to speak with you and more than honored to receive your donation. I appreciate it more than I can possibly say, and I promise to use it wisely."

"As you know, your hospital was originally denied because it didn't meet our requirements."

"Yes. I know." And she hoped the woman would tell her why they'd changed their minds, though she supposed it didn't really matter.

"My son, Trent Dalton—I think you know him?—he came to see me, asking me to still provide the donation. Convinced me your hospital is more than worthy of our funding."

Charlotte nearly dropped her phone. Trent? Trent was the woman's son? She tried to move her lips, but couldn't speak.

"Hello? Are you there?"

"Y…yes. I'm sorry. I'm just…surprised to hear that

Trent is your son." Surprised didn't begin to cover it. He'd called himself a rich boy? That was an understatement.

"Perhaps I'm being a busybody, but that's a mother's prerogative. Trent told me he'd wanted to spend the next year working at your hospital with you, but you made a mistake by lying to him which has made him change his mind."

"Yes, that's true." Her voice wobbled. "I was selfishly stupid and would give anything to be able to do it over again. To be honest with him about…everything."

"Would that 'everything' include caring for him in a personal way? Being his mother, I would have to assume you do."

The woman's amused tone reminded her so much of Trent, she nearly burst into tears right into the phone. "You're right, Mrs. Dalton. I do care for Trent in a personal way, because he's the most incredible man I've ever known. I'm terribly, crazy in love with him but, if he cared at all about me before, I don't think he does anymore. I don't think he'll ever forgive me."

"You won't know unless you try to find out, will you? I made a terrible mistake with him once, too, tried to manipulate his life and paid a harsh price for that. Our years of separation were very painful to me, and I should have tried harder to apologize, to ask him to forgive me. I suggest you make the effort, instead of wondering. And maybe regretting."

She was right. A surge of adrenaline pulsed through Charlie's blood. She'd find Trent and she'd make it right or die trying. "Thank you. Do you know where he is?"

"He's here in New York City, visiting with a few friends. He's leaving soon. I can try to find out his travel plans, if you like."

Colleen. Colleen had his itinerary. "Thanks, but I think I know how to get them."

CHAPTER NINETEEN

CHARLIE CAREENED DOWN the muddy road, hands sweating, heart pounding, as she desperately drove to the little airport, trying to catch the plane that would take her to Kennedy Airport in New York City, which Trent was scheduled to fly out of in about ten hours. And, of course, the rain had begun the moment she'd left, slowing her progress and making it nearly impossible to get there in time.

But she had to get there. A simple phone call wasn't enough. She had to find Trent and tell him she loved him and beg him to forgive her.

As she'd thrown a few necessities into her suitcase and tried to process the whole, astonishing thing about his mother being a Gilchrist, and the unbelievable donation and phone call, she'd realized something else.

The fifty-thousand-dollar donation for the school must have come from Trent. Who else would just, out of the blue, anonymously donate that kind of money to their little school? The incredible realization made her see again what she'd come to know: that he was beyond extraordinary. A man with so much money, he could choose not to work at all. Instead, he'd trained for years to become a doctor and a specialized surgeon. He helped the poor and needy around the world, both financially and hands-on. He was adorable, funny, sweet and loved children. And if she didn't get to the airport on time, and find a way to make him forgive her, she'd never, ever meet anyone like him again.

She loved him and she'd hurt him. She'd tell him, show him, how much she loved him and make right all her wrongs.

She jammed her foot onto the accelerator. She had to get there and get on that plane. And if she didn't, she'd follow him to Florence or wherever else he was going. If she had to, she'd follow him to the moon.

Trent stretched his legs out in front of him and pulled his Panama hat down over his eyes. His flight from Kennedy was delayed, so he might as well try to sleep.

Except every time he closed his eyes he saw Charlotte Grace Edwards. Never mind that there were five thousand miles between them, and that she'd lied and obviously didn't care about him the way he'd thought she did. Her face, her scent, her smile were all permanently etched in his brain and heart.

He'd broken his own damned rules and was paying the price for it. Knew he'd be paying the price for a long, long time.

He'd been happy with his life. He liked working in different places in the world, meeting new people, finding new medical challenges. Setting down roots in one place hadn't occurred to him until he'd gone to Liberia. Until he'd met Charlotte. Until she'd turned upside down everything he thought he knew about himself and what he wanted.

He hadn't gotten out fast enough. Their one-night fling had become something so much bigger, so much more important, so deeply painful. His vacation alone in Italy was going to be the worst weeks of his life, and his new job couldn't start soon enough.

A familiar, distinctive floral scent touched his nose, and to his disgust his heart slapped against his ribs and his breath shortened. Here he was, thinking about her so intently, so completely, he imagined she was near. Imagined he could touch her one last time.

Except the firm kick against his shoe wasn't his imagination.

He froze. Charlotte? Impossible.

"I know you're not asleep, Trent Dalton. Look at me."

Stunned, he slowly pushed his hat from his face and there she was. Or a mirage of her. He nearly extended his hand to see if she could possibly be real. He ran his gaze over every inch of her—her messy hair, her rumpled clothes, her bandaged arm.

She was real. The most real, the most beautiful woman he'd ever seen. His heart swelled and constricted at the same time, knowing what a damn fool he was to still feel that way.

"Why aren't you wearing the sling on your arm?"

She laughed, and the sound brought both joy and torment. "I nearly killed myself running off the road in a rainstorm to get to the airport, flew thousands of miles to find you, and the first thing you do is nag me?"

Yeah, she was something. He had to remind himself that single-minded ruthlessness was part of the persona he'd adored. "What are you doing here, Charlotte?"

She crouched down in front of him, her green eyes suddenly deeply serious as they met his. "I came to apologize. I came to tell you how very sorry I am that I lied to you. That I realize no hospital wing, no donation, no amount of need, could possibly justify it, no matter how much I convinced myself it did."

It struck him that she'd gotten the Gilchrist donation, and that his mother had probably meddled and spilled the beans about who he was. Charlotte must somehow feel she had to apologize, to make it right, because of the money, even though it was an awful big trek for her to catch him here. His chest ached, knowing that was all this was.

"No need to apologize. I know the hospital means everything to you."

She slowly shook her head as her hand reached for his and squeezed, and his own tightened on hers when he should have pulled it away. "No, Trent. The hospital doesn't mean everything to me. I know that now."

"Well, pardon me when I say that's a line of bull. Like so many others you fed me." She'd already proven he couldn't trust anything she said. "You've shown you'll do anything to make things go your way for the place. You've shown it's your number-one priority over everything."

"Maybe it was. Maybe I let it be. But it isn't anymore." She stood and leaned forward, pressing a kiss to his mouth, and for a surprised moment he let himself feel it all the way to his soul. He let it fill all the cracks in his heart before he pulled away.

"You're my number-one priority, Trent. You're what means everything to me. Only you. I hated myself for lying to you. After you left, I hated myself even more for letting myself fall for you, because I was sure you'd just moved on to be with some woman in Italy. That I didn't mean anything to you but a brief good time."

"What makes you think that's not the case?" Though it was impossible to imagine how she could have believed that. That she hadn't seen the way he felt about her; hadn't known what she'd come to mean to him. But, if she didn't know, he sure as hell didn't want her to find out.

"Because I know you told Mike you wanted to be assigned to my little hospital for your year assignment." Tears filled her green eyes and he steeled himself against them; wouldn't be moved by them. "When I realized you'd left because of my stupid, misguided mistakes, I knew I had to do whatever I could to find you."

Obviously, she'd come because she still needed a plastic surgeon to get the hospital wing running. "You've found me. But my plane leaves in an hour, and I really don't want to go through a third goodbye. So please just go." The weight in his chest and balling in his stomach told him another goodbye might be even more painful than the second one in her kitchen, which he'd never have dreamed could be possible.

"No. No more goodbyes. I love you. I love you more than anything, and all I want is to be with you."

She loved him? He stared at her, wishing he could believe her. But he'd learned through a very hard lesson that she lied as easily as she breathed. He wasn't about to go back to Liberia with the woman who "loved" him only as long as she needed him to do plastic surgery work, or whatever the hell else was on her agenda, then doubtless wouldn't "love" him anymore.

"Sorry, Charlie, but I'm sure you can understand why I just don't believe you."

Tears welled in her eyes again. "You just called me Charlie," she whispered. "You're the only person who always calls me Charlotte."

He shrugged casually to show her none of this was affecting him the way it really was. "Maybe because you're not the person I thought you were."

He had to look away from the hurt in her eyes. "I hope I am the person you thought I was. Or at least that I can become that person. And I do understand why you don't believe me. I deserve that disbelief. I understand you need proof that I mean every word." Beneath her tears, her eyes sparked with the determined intensity he'd seen so often. "You once asked me why I went to Liberia to rebuild the hospital and school. And I told you my roots were dug in deep there, and I wanted to grow those roots, and I'd do it no matter what it takes. But I've changed my thoughts about that."

"How?"

"I'm not willing to do whatever it takes for the hospital, because that attitude led to some terrible mistakes. But I am willing to do whatever it takes to convince you I love you. That I want to grow roots with you and only you—wherever you choose to grow them. I always told you I can find doctors to work at the Edwards hospital, but not someone to run it. But you know what? I'm sure I *can* find someone to run it, and I will if you'll let me travel with you, be with you, help you, wherever it is you're headed."

He stared at her, stunned. The woman would be willing to leave the Edwards Mission Hospital to be with him instead? As much as he wanted to believe it, he couldn't. Her lies and machinations had been coldly calculated, and he had to wonder what exactly it was she was trying to achieve this time around. "No, Charlotte. You belong in Liberia and I belong wherever I am at a given moment."

"I belong with you, and I believe that you belong with me. I'm going to work hard to convince you how sorry I am for what I did. To give you so much love, you have to forgive me." She swiped away the tears on her lashes as her eyes flashed green sparks of determination. "You said I'm sometimes like a pit bull? You haven't seen anything yet. I'll get on the plane with you. I'll follow you wherever you go and keep asking you to forgive me and keep telling you how much I love you. I'm going to quit trying to control the world, like you always teased me about, and beg you to run it with me, for us to run it together. I want that because I love you. I love you and my life isn't complete without you."

He stared into her face. Would it be completely stupid of him to believe her again?

His heart pounded hard and he stood and looked down into her eyes focused so intently on his. In their depths, he saw very clearly what he was looking for.

Love. For him. It wasn't a lie. It was the truth.

He cupped her face in his hands and had to swallow past the lump that formed in his throat as he lowered his mouth to hers for a long kiss, absorbing the taste of her lips that he never thought he'd get to taste again.

"I love you too, Charlotte. I wish you'd just been honest with me but, standing here looking at you, I realize what you did doesn't matter if you really do love me. What matters is that I love you and you love me back." As he said the words, he knew with every ounce of his being it truly was the only thing that mattered. "Maybe if you'd told me, I would have left, I don't know. I do know that the way I felt about you scared the crap out of me."

"The way I felt about you scared me too. I knew you'd be out of my life in a matter of days, and it would be beyond stupid to fall in love with you. But I did anyway. I couldn't help it."

"Yeah?" Her words made him smile, because he'd felt exactly the same way. "I kept telling myself to keep my distance. But I found it impossible to resist a certain beautiful woman who tries to run the world." He tunneled his hands into her soft hair and looked into her eyes. "I've been running for a long time, Charlotte. I didn't really see it, until being with you made me look. But being with you made me realize that maybe, in all that running, I was really searching. And then I knew: I'd been searching for you."

A little sob left her throat and she flung her good arm around his neck. "Do you want me to come with you? Or would you like to go back to Liberia together? Will you live with me and work with me? Share my life with me?"

"I'm thinking heading back to Liberia is a good plan." He wrapped his arms around her, pressed his cheek to hers and smiled at the same time emotion clogged his chest. "So, is that a marriage proposal? Trust you not to let me be the one to ask."

"I'm sorry." She paused. "If we go back, I'll let you drive whenever you want."

He laughed out loud. "I'll believe that when I see it.

And yes, Charlotte Grace Edwards, I'll marry you and live with you and work with you for the rest of our lives." He lowered his mouth to hers and whispered against her lips. "This is the last time you have to drag me back from an airport. This time, I'm staying for good."

* * * * *

LET'S TALK
Romance

For exclusive extracts, competitions
and special offers, find us online:

Get in touch on 01413 063232

For all the latest titles coming soon, visit

millsandboon.co.uk/nextmonth

MILLS & BOON

THE HEART OF ROMANCE

A ROMANCE FOR EVERY KIND OF READER

MODERN

Prepare to be swept off your feet by sophisticated, sexy and seductive heroes, in some of the world's most glamourous and romantic locations, where power and passion collide.
8 stories per month.

HISTORICAL

Escape with historical heroes from time gone by. Whether your passion is for wicked Regency Rakes, muscled Vikings or rugged Highlanders, awaken the romance of the past.
6 stories per month.

MEDICAL

Set your pulse racing with dedicated, delectable doctors in the high-pressure world of medicine, where emotions run high and passion, comfort and love are the best medicine.
6 stories per month.

True Love

Celebrate true love with tender stories of heartfelt romance, from the rush of falling in love to the joy a new baby can bring, and a focus on the emotional heart of a relationship.
8 stories per month.

Desire

Indulge in secrets and scandal, intense drama and plenty of sizzling hot action with powerful and passionate heroes who have it all: wealth, status, good looks…everything but the right woman.
6 stories per month.

HEROES

Experience all the excitement of a gripping thriller, with an intense romance at its heart. Resourceful, true-to-life women and strong, fearless men face danger and desire - a killer combination!
8 stories per month.

DARE

Sensual love stories featuring smart, sassy heroines you'd want as a best friend, and compelling intense heroes who are worthy of them.
4 stories per month.

To see which titles are coming soon, please visit

millsandboon.co.uk/nextmonth

JOIN US ON SOCIAL MEDIA!

Stay up to date with our latest releases, author news and gossip, special offers and discounts, and all the behind-the-scenes action from Mills & Boon...

 millsandboon

 millsandboonuk

 millsandboon

It might just be true love...

MILLS & BOON
Desire

Indulge in secrets and scandal, intense drama and plenty of sizzling hot action with powerful and passionate heroes who have it all: wealth, status, good looks… everything but the right woman.